Praise for *The Day He Left*

"Compelling and utterly original, both as a procedural and a novel of human frailty, Frederick Weisel's *The Day He Left* begins as a missing-persons investigation that blossoms into a much larger story touching all of the players, detectives and survivors alike: a novel written with remarkable compassion and understanding."

—J. P. Smith, author of *The Drowning*

"Second book in an excellent police procedural series that reminds me of Ed McBain's 87th Precinct mysteries. Weisel manages to make the minutiae of police work mesmerizing... Get in on the ground floor with this series. You won't be sorry."

—Dana Stabenow, author of the award-winning, bestselling Kate Shugak series

"Frederick Weisel expertly weaves together an intriguing cast of characters in *The Day He Left*, pulling us along for the ride at breakneck speed. Atmospheric, peppered with humor, [and] laced with suspense, this story kept me on my toes until the very last page."

—Gina LaManna, *USA Today* bestselling author

Praise for *The Silenced Women*

"In this propulsive debut, Weisel writes evocatively about a detective in crisis, a complex crime, and a city pushed to the edge by a killer's grip. With *The Silenced Women*, you're in for a smart and gritty ride."

—Zoë Ferraris, author of *Finding Nouf*

"The debut of a promising new series, *The Silenced Women* is a timely and compelling police procedural."

—Jeff Abbott, *New York Times* bestselling author of *Never Ask Me*

"Weisel's debut thriller is a crackling how-to-catch-'em, stacking equally intelligent and tenacious adversaries on both sides of the law, then setting them loose on each other."

—Joseph Schneider, author of the critically acclaimed LAPD Detective Tully Jarsdel mysteries

"This start of a cinematic new series is an intense police procedural. Readers will be immersed in the investigation by a talented team, while also privy to the actions of a brilliant killer."

—"Debut of the Month" Starred Review in the *Library Journal*

"An excellent procedural series debut with complex characters who carry the story."

—*Kirkus Reviews*

"In this very promising start to Weisel's Santa Rosa Violent Crimes Investigations [Team] series…Weisel delivers sensitive and well-developed portrayals of the beleaguered detectives, without skimping on the action. Readers will be reminded of

P. D. James's Adam Dalgliesh when Mahler describes the art of interrogation as being 'like a gentle hand at the suspect's back,' or when he reflects on the irony of homicide investigations, which often victimize already violated human beings."

—*Booklist*

"The discovery of a young woman's body in a public park in Santa Rosa, Calif., drives Weisel's strong debut and series launch... Bolstered by careful attention to detail and authentically drawn characters, this finely paced story builds to a satisfying finale. Police procedural fans will look forward to more."

—*Publishers Weekly*

"Frederick Weisel...delivers a satisfying procedural that touches all the bases: good writing, a compelling mystery, and equally compelling characters squaring off against worthy adversaries."

—*Mystery Scene Magazine*

"The first-class police procedural is a rare thing indeed today, in both meanings of the word. This debut effort by Frederick Weisel qualifies right across the board."

—Dana Stabenow, author of the
award-winning, bestselling Kate Shugak series

Also by Frederick Weisel

VIOLENT CRIME INVESTIGATIONS TEAM MYSTERIES
The Silenced Women

THE
DAY
HE
LEFT

A VIOLENT CRIME INVESTIGATIONS TEAM MYSTERY

FREDERICK
WEISEL

Poisoned Pen
PRESS

398 2297

Published by Poisoned Pen Press, an imprint of Sourcebooks
P.O. Box 4410, Naperville, Illinois 60567-4410
(630) 961-3900
sourcebooks.com

Library of Congress Cataloging-in-Publication Data

Names: Weisel, Frederick, author.
Title: The day he left : a violent crime investigations team mystery /
    Frederick Weisel.
Description: Naperville. Illinois : Poisoned Pen Press, [2022] | Series:
    Violent crime investigations team ; book 2
Identifiers: LCCN 2021014778 (print) | LCCN 2021014779
    (ebook) | (trade paperback) | (epub)
Subjects: GSAFD: Mystery fiction.
Classification: LCC PS3623.E432475 D39 2022 (print) | LCC PS3623.E432475
    (ebook) | DDC 813/.6--dc23
LC record available at https://lccn.loc.gov/2021014778
LC ebook record available at https://lccn.loc.gov/2021014779

Printed and bound in the United States of America.
SB 10 9 8 7 6 5 4 3 2 1

*For my parents, Lorraine and Jonas, and all
they taught me about a family's love*

PART I

PART I

Chapter One

(i)

Annie never saw Paul drive away, her husband getting smaller and smaller until he was a speck on the horizon. Instead, all of him, every unlucky molecule, suddenly vanished, like those characters on *Star Trek* dematerialized by the transporter.

The ingredients, the essence, of Paul Behrens departed— his sad face, that daily uniform of oxford shirt and khaki trousers, the sound of his Nikes on the kitchen floor, the stale paper smell he had carried around with him the last few years, which was like putting your nose close to the pages of an old book. Just like that, those things no longer existed where Annie was. Here, then there. Although it was not a there she could actually name.

The way he left shouldn't have mattered, at least not more than the fact of his leaving. But somehow it did. It seemed aimed at her, like something she wasn't smart enough to understand.

Annie could picture it: Paul full of his English-teacher thing, using a literary reference to explain his departure. It would take five minutes because there would be a book or play she'd never read, and he'd have to tell her about it—like she was a slow student. He'd start by saying something about the cat in *Alice*, and Lewis Carroll's writing style, and she'd stop listening after the first twenty seconds.

That, of course, became a problem later when the police had questions. For more than a year Annie had been in the habit of not listening to Paul. She was a kind of expert at it. Her superpower was envisioning him across the kitchen table or on the other side of the family room, hearing the sound of his voice with its puking sincerity, all of it locked in her head, without being able to tell you anything specific he said.

The first thing Annie did remember about the day Paul left was that moment when she was lying on the sofa in the family room and heard her phone ping. She was covered in an afghan, still wearing her nurse's scrubs from the previous day's three-to-eleven shift. With the blinds closed, it was impossible to tell the time. The house was quiet and dark. Paul had already left for his job. Jesse and Claire were off to school.

Annie's head was pounding, her mouth dry. *Had she drunk a whole bottle of zinfandel before she fell asleep?*

She found her purse on the floor and dug out her phone. 8:32 a.m. Her brain immediately did the math: six hours' sleep. On the home screen, she saw a text message from Jennifer Steeley, the principal at Brookwood Middle School: Paul didn't come in. Not answering cell. Called sub. He OK?

Oh, Christ. He's home after all.

Annie threw off the afghan and walked through the kitchen to go upstairs. On the table were the remains of the kids' breakfast—cereal boxes and dirty bowls—and beside them her empty bottle. That last bit was a classic passive-aggressive message from Paul: *I'm not going to hide it for you.*

Going up the stairs, she felt through her cotton scrubs that her panties were missing. Her fogged brain drew a blank. Then she remembered the night before, leaving them on the back seat of the car. *Shit. Had Paul seen them?*

At the top of the stairs, Annie noticed the open door to the master bedroom and braced for a confrontation with Paul. But the room was empty. The bed on his side was mussed, pajamas thrown on the bedspread.

Annie headed back downstairs and opened the door to the garage. Paul's silver Elantra was gone. On the rear seat of her own Camry, she found her panties and stuffed them in her pocket.

Back in the kitchen, Annie rooted through a cabinet for a bottle of Advil. She washed down two tablets with a full glass of sauvignon blanc, poured another half glass, and sat at the table.

The empty zinfandel bottle stared back at her across the table. The label was an artsy painting of a vineyard. Screw cap, $9.95. Annie remembered the clerk in the supermarket wine department. Thirtyish, kind of cute, with that unshaved, not-quite-a-beard thing guys were doing these days. She had smiled, found herself flirting, asking about the tannin-to-alcohol balance, or some shit she'd read online. He looked into her eyes and wasn't fooled. He reached to the lower shelves for one of the "value bottles."

Annie dialed Paul's cell. It rang three times before his voicemail clicked in. There was her husband's deep, earnest voice. "Hi. This is Paul. Sorry I missed your call. Leave me a message and—" She clicked off.

She found the number for Jennifer Steeley on her phone and tapped it. The time was 8:45 a.m. Busiest time of day for a principal.

Steeley picked up on the second ring, talking over the noise of a crowded hallway. "Hey, Annie. Thanks for calling back."

"Yeah. Got your message. Sorry about that."

"It's okay. We found a sub. Remember Penny Freese? Taught seventh-grade history before her first kid?"

"Good. Good. Glad it worked out."

"Part of the job. Is Paul okay?"

"I'm sure he's fine." Annie took a deep breath and tried to think how to start. "He's... The thing is, I'm working second shift these days and get home late. Sometimes we don't see each other for days. I didn't talk to him before he left this morning." As the words came out, Annie realized she was explaining it not to the principal but to herself.

"No problem, Annie. Really." Steeley's voice sounded impatient to end the call. "If he could just let me know how long he'll be gone and where he left his lesson book."

The buzz from the sauvignon blanc kicked in after she hung up. Annie refilled her glass and carried it to the living room. She opened the curtains to look out on the backyard.

If Paul isn't at work, where the fuck is he? She thought of her father-in-law, recovering from chemo and staying with Paul's sister.

She clicked on the number. "Hey, Beth. It's Annie. This too early?"

"Yeah, right. No, honey. We've been up since four."

"Sorry to bother you, but is Paul there? We missed each other this morning, and he didn't show up at school. Just trying to track him down."

"Nope, not here. My experience is—and you probably know this, too—the guy's driving somewhere. Mister Careful never picks up while he's driving, even on Bluetooth. Try again in a few minutes. Tell the jerk to come by tonight for dinner. Dad wants a word. I'm making burgers."

Annie hung up and tried Paul's number again. This time she heard the phone's ringtone coming across the room, from her husband's briefcase lying beside the recliner. She crouched next to it and clicked open the latches. Paul's phone lay atop a pile of student assignments. She turned it off and stared at it. He never went anywhere without his phone.

Beneath the student assignments lay her husband's lesson plan. *How could he teach the day's classes without his plan?* Under the lesson plan was a sealed manila envelope with no address. She felt something inside the envelope and tore it open. Out fell a thin, multicolored friendship bracelet—the kind teenage girls tie around their wrists. Attached to one end of the bracelet was a tiny red plastic heart. She shook the envelope, but it was empty. No note, no letter.

Annie dug deeper through the briefcase, not knowing what she was looking for. At the bottom, she found a photo. As she picked it up, she froze. She held it away from her body like an object arrived from another world. Without thinking, she crushed the photo, squeezing so hard her fingernails cut her palm. Then she shoved it into the pocket of the scrubs and pushed down until her fingers felt the silk of the panties crumpled at the bottom.

(ii)

(WEDNESDAY, 8:45 A.M.)

"No one's good at surveillance," retired homicide cop Tommy Woodhouse once told Frames. "It's like saying you're good at putting your pants on. You're there to see something. The tricky part comes when that something isn't what you thought it would be."

Frames sat alone in the front seat of an unmarked Malibu. He was on temporary part-time loan from Violent Crime to the Narcotic Investigations team. His car was parked in a residential section of Roseland, on the opposite side of the street and a few doors from a lime-green stucco rented by Lucia Cervantes. The Narcotics team wanted surveillance on Cervantes, known to be the girlfriend of a street dealer named Jorge Lopez. A week ago, Lopez had been identified as the supplier for a thirty-eight-year-old user who suffered a fatal overdose. After the OD, Lopez disappeared. One of the team's snitches said Lopez might show up to visit Cervantes.

In four days, Frames had seen Cervantes three times—twice when she emerged to drive to Safeway for groceries, and once when she watered the dying roses along the front fence. She was a small woman with straight, black hair who wore, on all three occasions, tight-fitting spandex workout suits. Watering the flowers, Cervantes stood in one spot for five minutes, smoking a cigarette and aiming the spray at the top of the plants. Halfway into it, Frames fought the urge to climb out of his car, walk down the street, and tell her what his grandmother had drummed into his head: water the plant base, not the blossoms.

On this latest shift, Frames passed the time by making a mental list of everything that hadn't changed since he arrived: no one in or out of the house, no lights on, window shades unmoved, no sound from inside the house, roses dead as the day before.

"What do you suppose she does all day?" a voice asked in his ear. Wiggins.

The other half of the surveillance team—Wiggins and Buckley—sat in a Ford parked across from Cervantes's driveway. Connected by wireless mikes, the three men had begun the surveillance observing a strict no-chatter policy. Wiggins ended the policy on the first day.

"TV," Buckley said. "Most people watch TV."

"All day? How do you watch TV all day?"

"Look on the roof. She's got the Dish. One hundred ninety channels. Other night, I turned mine on, and there was a soccer game from Albania."

"So you're saying she's inside there right now watching Albanian soccer?"

Buckley sighed. "No. That was an example. Are you familiar with normal conversation?"

"You know what I'd like right now?" Wiggins asked.

"Really? We're going to do this again?"

"One of those ham croissants from that place downtown. Don't tell me you couldn't eat one right now."

"Sure," Buckley said. "We'll have it delivered to the car. What could go wrong?"

"How about you, Steve-O? You hungry?"

"No," Frames said. "And remember how I asked you not to call me that?"

For Frames, the most frustrating part of working with Wiggins was not that he talked incessantly but that he had beaten Frames to it. Frames was known in Violent Crime as the talker. It was his signature. But here Wiggins had been first off the mark and grabbed the play. Now, with the earpiece, it was like Wiggins had gotten inside Frames's brain. Or had *become* his brain.

"Okay. De-tec-tive Frames, tell me this. What's the longest surveillance you've been on?"

"This one," Frames said. He wanted to say *Any surveillance with you would seem longer.*

"Really? I had one last year that was ten days. How about you, Buckminster?"

"A whole month. 2012."

"You're kidding. Department had the budget for that? Hey, Frames, somebody said you were a jarhead. Anything this boring in the Corps?"

Frames debated not answering, but he knew Wiggins wouldn't give up. A few weeks earlier, Frames had seen an anonymous list on Twitter. Five most irritating Santa Rosa Police Department officers. Wiggins was number three. Frames had never met numbers one and two, but he was impressed two officers were more irritating than Wiggins.

"Guard duty. Fallujah. Third Battalion, First Marines." Frames remembered the adrenalized mindset of Iraq. "Stood all night in a doorway of the house where guys in the platoon were sleeping. Had to be on your toes. Local paramilitary came out after dark."

"Nothing like guys coming to kill you to keep your eyes open, right?"

In an instant, Frames felt the M16 in his hands and smelled the decaying bodies in the desert night air. "That's just it," he said. "There were always lots of sounds—dogs barking, gunfire on the perimeter—but not much to see. From where I stood, the only light came from a window a block away." He saw the little square of light again at the end of a dark street.

"I couldn't look inside obviously, but I kept myself awake imagining the family living where that light was. Father, mother, couple kids. Going about their normal life in the middle of a war zone. Every day you had bodies in the street, helicopters just over the housetops, bombs going off. But this little family went on with life. I made up this whole thing. The father drove a taxi. He met his wife when they were teenagers. The boy was the oldest, just starting to read. The little girl was afraid of the gear the American soldiers wore.

"At night the father told a story before the kids fell asleep. The story was always about a beautiful flying woman. She was, the father said, as beautiful as their mother, and she flew through the air and rescued the people of the city. Every night was a new story of rescue."

When Frames finished, the mikes were silent. "That's what I imagined anyway," he said.

"That's what you thought of?" Wiggins said after a few seconds. "In fucking Iraq? You are one weird dude, Steve-O."

"Hey, Wiggins." Frames let his head fall back on the top of the seat. "Do you think if I came down there and pounded your ass, there's any chance you'd stop calling me that?"

"Wait a second, boys." Buckley suddenly serious. "We've got somebody on the move. One. Two of them. Running fast."

Frames sat up and peered down the street. He couldn't see anything. "Where?"

"Back of the driveway." Buckley spoke quickly. "It's Cervantes. And somebody else. Male. Six feet. See them?"

Frames stared ahead. A hedge blocked his view. "What're they doing?"

"Looks like Cervantes is trying to get away from the guy." Wiggins this time. "Wait. The guy's got something in his hands. Poles."

"Poles?"

"Or sticks. Let me get the scope."

Frames still couldn't see anyone. He heard Wiggins's scope bang against the window glass.

"Oh shit. They're swords."

"Wait. What?" Frames yelled. "Did you say swords?"

"Yeah. You know, like a pirate."

"You see them, Frames?" Buckley, breathless. "They're fucking behind us, on your side, turning into the street."

Frames leaned close to the windshield. He could see Cervantes now racing toward him down the sidewalk. Bathrobe open, hair flying, face wild with fear. Behind her was a man with a sword swinging in each hand.

Frames pulled the Glock from its holster. He let Cervantes run past. Then, opening the car door, he leveled the gun at the approaching figure. "STOP. Police."

The figure kept coming. He was close enough now Frames could see the guy's shaved head, bare chest, and heavily tattooed upper arms.

"STOP!" Frames shouted again.

With the man nearly in front of him, Frames fired a shot and saw it hit the man but not slow his approach.

"Frames! Frames!" Wiggins, yelling in his ear.

Buckley on the radio: "David 12. Shots fired. 418 Greenwood Drive. Code three medical."

The man lunged with the right-handed sword over the top of the car door. Frames shielded himself with the door and fell backward inside the car. Thrown across the driver's seat and console, Frames fired again and missed. The attacker thrust the sword through the doorway. The blade sliced into Frames's calf like a hot poker.

Suddenly Frames's senses heightened. He smelled the man's sour body odor. Half a block away, the Ford's engine roared. Time slowed.

The attacker ripped the blade out and came at Frames again—this time with the sword held in his left hand.

Frames steadied his gun and fired three times. The rounds hit the man in the chest.

The Ford screamed down the street, skidding to a stop.

The attacker fell, slamming onto the door frame and landing on Frames's legs. The man lay still. Frames saw his own arms extended, frozen in place, blood sprayed across his fingers, the tip of the Glock nearly touching the top of the man's head.

Outside, the flash of Wiggins sprinting after Cervantes. Then Buckley filled the car doorway, yanking the swords out of the dead man's hands. "Frames, you hurt? You need help? You okay?"

Frames looked at the other officers without really seeing them. He felt the dead man's weight and sweaty skin on his legs. The body was large and soft and seemed to be settling, as if the man had crawled inside the car to fall asleep.

"Yeah," Frames said. "Yeah. I'm okay."

Chapter Two

(i)

"Your name's really Eddie?" the woman asked.

Mahler smiled. "You find men on dating websites lie about their names?"

The woman, Sharon Weyrich, smiled back. "Not names. But just about everything else." She gave Mahler a you-know-what-I-mean smile.

Mahler was getting used to the conversational style of dates from the online service, which seemed to veer easily toward the sexually suggestive.

They sat in Café Liguria's only window seat, a valuable table for the small downtown restaurant. Mahler could see the owner, Carina, eyeing him. He'd need to order a second Americano soon to justify occupying the space.

"All I'm saying"—Weyrich leaned forward to make the point—"is you don't often meet a…mature man with that name. Usually it's Edward, or even Ed."

"Growing up, my mother called me Edward when she was angry."

"Does she still call you that?"

"Hard to tell. She died in 1987."

Weyrich winced, and Mahler regretted the sarcasm.

"Sorry," he said. "Maybe we can talk about something besides names."

"You're a cop, right?" Weyrich asked. "Your profile said Santa Rosa Police Department."

"Yeah. Seventeen years next month."

"You do anything exciting? Like the cop shows on TV?"

Mahler looked across the room at Carina, who was noisily flipping the steamed-milk spout. The restaurant's tables were covered with crisp white tablecloths. Framed photographs of Italian seaside villages lined the walls. "I'm in a group that investigates violent crimes—homicides, assaults."

"Wow. So you're an investigator, a detective. So tell me a story, detective."

Should he tell Sharon Weyrich that a year before he had suffered chronic migraines related to his work, that for a while he talked to a dead girl? It didn't seem right for a first date. "You know, it's mostly mundane stuff. Gang members shooting each other." He watched her. "But this isn't what we should be talking about, is it?"

"Isn't it? I'm sure those hazel eyes have seen things."

She was flirting again. Mahler wanted to end the date but knew it was too soon. He tried to recall what had attracted him in her online profile. It was a quote, something about hope. Mahler remembered admiring the optimism of it. He respected this woman's will to make the unlikeliness of online dating work, to overcome the inertia that can drag down any middle-aged romantic effort. He met her look and smiled.

"You must see people who've been killed. Shot. I've never seen someone who's been shot. What's that like?"

"About what you would think." Mahler remembered a victim, Caroline Rainey, lying in her kitchen. In a fit of rage over the announcement that she was leaving him, her husband had taken a gun from a bedroom safe, marched back to the kitchen, and shot her as she turned to face him. Now Mahler looked away from Sharon Weyrich's eyes, to the fringe of her brown bangs. There, in the center of her forehead, he saw what he'd seen on Caroline Rainey's forehead—a single dark hole, smaller than a penny.

"What was that?" Weyrich asked.

"What was what?"

"I lost you for a second. You go somewhere on me?"

"No. Just thought of something. What about you? Commercial loan officer, right?"

Weyrich held her coffee cup with her fingertips. "Yeah. How're we going to make that interesting, right?" She clicked her long nails on the side of the cup. Mahler saw the nails were painted blue to match her dress. He thought how women's grooming rituals require more commitment, energy—and hope—than men's. Was it any wonder men so often disappointed them?

"Oh, come on." Mahler straightened in his seat, trying for a fresh start. "Meeting young people starting new businesses. Lot of confidence, fresh ideas."

Weyrich sipped her coffee. "Mostly it's old guys in mall-store sports jackets. Arguing over terms, touching me whenever they get the chance."

"Well, there goes one fantasy about banking."

"You have fantasies about banking? Like what?"

"I don't know. You hand the keys for a retail space to a young couple."

Weyrich smiled. "Yeah. That never happens. Sorry... Ed-die." She spoke his name slowly. "Just trying to be honest here."

"So what do you do when you're not being touched by men in cheap sports jackets?"

"What're you hoping I'll say? Hang out at the firing range?"

What was he hoping she'd say? Was it something Kate would say—the woman he'd left and regretted afterward? Or, was it something—anything—that would not remind him of Kate? How was it he had come to just those two choices?

He saw the curls of Sharon Weyrich's hair and a sudden image of the woman checking herself in the mirror before leaving home that morning. He tried not to look at the spot on her forehead. "Is that what you think cops do?"

"Aren't detectives supposed to be intuitive? Suppose you were interrogating me. What would you imagine I do?"

Mahler hated this kind of role-playing. He tried again to remember the quote about hope on Weyrich's dating profile.

"Tell me something, Eddie Mahler," she said. "Why do you keep looking at my forehead? What's the deal with that?"

"I wasn't aware I was."

"Please. It's obvious. You look at me, and then you get this weird stare going on. Do I have something there?" She rubbed her forehead with the palm of her hand.

He couldn't help looking. Once her hand moved out of the way, the dark hole returned.

"That. Right there. You just did it again." She looked at nearby tables to find a witness.

"I'm sorry," Mahler said. "You asked what it's like to see someone who's been shot. When you said it, I remembered a victim a couple of years ago, who was shot...there." Mahler had the sense every word he spoke was making it worse.

"A woman?"

"Yes. In that case—"

"On her forehead? You were imagining it now on my forehead? In this restaurant?" Her voice rose. Diners at the nearest table paused in their breakfast to listen.

"Not intentionally." As he spoke, Mahler wondered if this was an important distinction. "It wasn't personal."

"Wasn't personal? You're picturing me shot in the head?" Weyrich stood and pulled her purse strap over one shoulder. "This is just so inappropriate. It's…creepy." Two men waiting at the counter turned to watch.

She stepped away, then came back, bowing close to Mahler. "You need therapy. You know that?"

"I'm sure you're right," he said.

Once she had gone, Carina appeared beside the table to pick up the empty cups. "Wow. *È molto drammatico*. Little morning soap opera?"

Mahler shrugged. "I blame your coffee."

"*Quante date questo mese?* How many dates this month, Eduardo?"

"Four. No. Five."

"*Per favore*. At least one woman could order a brioche?" Carina balanced the empty cups and wiped the table with her free hand.

Mahler pushed back his chair and stood. "You know the problem with your brioche, Carina? They're too beautiful. *Bellissima*. People are afraid to eat them."

"*Che cosa?*" Carina laughed. "Will you leave now, *Tenente*, or do I call the *polizia*? The cops?"

Mahler laid a large bill on the table. "What good would those guys do?"

(ii)

Annie parked in the vacant end of the high school parking lot, between the school and the athletic fields, where the smokers stood before and after classes. She texted Jesse: Need to talk. Behind school.

A few seconds later came a reply: Can't. In class.

She wrote: Now or I come in and threw the phone in the console.

She needed a buzz. Soon. But first she had to think about something else. Anything. She looked across the football field. Jesse had tried out for JV his freshman year. When had he stopped playing? Farther in the distance, along the horizon, lay a green, wooded hillside. She remembered a Sunday hike there years before with Paul and the kids when they were still little. Claire, just two, was having trouble pronouncing her *l*'s. After an hour, she said, "Can we go home, Mommy? My eggs are tired." The line became a family joke, repeated whenever one of them wanted to tease Claire. It seemed a long time since any of them had made the joke.

The back door to the school swung open, and Jesse came toward her. He walked in long, loping strides—head down, hands in his pockets. If Annie hadn't known he was coming, she wouldn't have recognized him. He wore a T-shirt, jeans, and a leather bomber jacket. His hair was longer than she remembered. He yanked open the passenger door and flopped beside her. From his jacket pocket, he took out a joint and a Bic. Lighting the stubby end, he sucked in air and blew a stream of smoke to the windshield.

"Do you have to do that?" Annie tried to find something familiar in the tall, angry boy beside her.

Jesse studied the burning end of the joint. "What do you care? You're wasted."

Annie straightened. "What do you mean?"

"I'm not a kid, okay? I know what wine smells like. I smelled you when I got in the car. Jesus." He inhaled and blew out. The car filled with marijuana smoke.

Chastened, she crossed her arms. She wished sometimes she could press rewind on her life. Go back to those moments where her world turned—the first time a faint shadow crossed over her desire for Paul, the first time her little boy felt the strength of withholding love, the first time the afterglow of a glass of wine showed the promise of intoxication. If she had a chance to replay those moments, she'd take another path, and while the wish was founded on a fantasy, it seemed more possible now than anything else in her life. "At least crack a window."

Jesse opened his window and trimmed his ash against the top edge. "What do you want? I've got five minutes before they notice I'm not there."

"Your father's gone somewhere. He's not at work."

"So what? What difference does it make?"

"He didn't call the school or leave a note for me. He never does that. He left his phone and briefcase."

Jesse looked back at her and smiled. His you-don't-get-it look.

"What's that mean?" She heard her own voice suddenly loud in the car. "Tell me! Tell me what you fucking know."

"I don't know anything."

"For chrissakes, Jesse." She was screaming now. "I'm—not—fucking—kidding. I need to find out where he is."

She saw fear in her son's eyes. He recoiled against the car

door. She found her right hand, where it had grabbed the front of Jesse's jacket in an angry fist. She let go and settled back in her seat. "I'm sorry. I'm a little... freaked out."

Jesse turned away without speaking.

"Where'd you get that jacket? It's new, isn't it?" She was surprised she could speak in a way that sounded normal.

"I bought it," Jesse said.

"Those things are expensive. I don't remember giving you money."

"You didn't. I bought it. Look, I really have to go back in there."

His face stared ahead, determined not to look at her. His cheeks were covered with black stubble, like Paul's. She noticed for the first time how much he looked like her husband, back when Paul was young. "Just tell me what you know. Did you see your father this morning?"

"Why're you asking about him? You two aren't... Whatever. You're doing your own thing."

Annie decided not to probe what her son knew about her and Paul doing their own thing. Looking out the windshield, she watched three girls in gym clothes stretching out before a run, propping one leg at a time against the school wall. "I just want to find out if you saw him this morning before you went to school." Her voice softened. "Did he say where he was going?"

Jesse took another drag from his joint and blew the smoke out the window. He glanced across the car and then turned away. "I don't know."

"You don't know if you saw him, or you don't know if he said where he was going?"

"I saw him. It was early—six, six fifteen. He was at the sink in the upstairs bathroom, and the door was open."

"What'd he say?"

"Nothing. I don't think he saw me."

"How'd he seem?"

"How'd he seem? I don't know. He was dressed up—in a jacket and tie."

"Why would he be dressed up?"

"How should I know? He didn't come home last night 'til late, like ten or something."

"Did you talk to him then?"

"I don't remember."

"Come on. I need you to remember." Annie reached out to touch her son's shoulder. "I think something's happened. I don't know where your father is. He's never done something like this. So tell me what you know."

"I just did." He shrugged off her hand.

"Does Claire know anything? Did she talk to him?"

"Claire?" Jesse snorted. "You're kidding, right? Jesus. I really have to get back in there."

"You know something, don't you? You always know something."

He flipped the joint out the window and watched it burn on the tarmac. Then he rubbed his palms on his thighs. "When I saw him this morning at the bathroom sink, he was standing there, and I saw his face in the mirror. He was... I don't think he knew I was there. He was like...crying or something."

"Crying?" She tried to remember the last time she had seen Paul cry. She looked across the parking lot. The girl runners were gone. "What's that mean?"

"How should I know?"

"Oh my God." Her life suddenly seemed to be happening far away, at the end of a long, dark tunnel. For an instant, she pictured the photo in her husband's briefcase, the one crumpled and stuffed in her pocket. "Did you talk to him? How could you *not* talk to him?"

"I don't know. We just didn't."

"We have to call the police." It was odd to hear herself say those words. The sound was another woman's voice.

"That's stupid. He's just gone somewhere. He'll be back."

She watched her son. "Something's going on. What is it?"

"I don't know. I really have to go." He climbed out of the car and turned to lean back inside. "Calling the cops is a big mistake. They'll make it worse. You don't know what you're getting into. Just wait and see what happens." He slammed the door and walked back toward the school.

Annie watched Jesse stride across the parking lot. She wanted a drink so badly she was dizzy. She needed a reward for everything she just heard: the wine going down her throat, hitting that chamber in her brain that numbed her senses. If she drove straight to Safeway, she could buy a bottle of the Stevens Creek rosé, the one in the clear bottle, and drink to the label, even if she did it in the car. She'd stop at the label, and keep that promise no matter what. Then she'd get a Starbucks to make herself even. But right now she didn't have the energy to do any of it. She couldn't remember the last time she slept through the night. She rested her head against the seat back and closed her eyes. She thought: *My eggs are tired.*

Chapter Three

(i)

(WEDNESDAY, 10:40 A.M.)

"Technically, it's a rapier, not a sword." Evan Buckley held up a large plastic evidence bag. Inside, the steel blade stuck to the plastic where the blood had dried. "Longer and thinner than a sword. This one's forty inches."

Barbara Prater, another detective on the Narcotics Investigations team, took the bag from Buckley to examine it more closely. "Have to admit, don't often see one of these." She winked at Frames, who sat with his bandaged leg resting on a stack of boxes.

The table in the evidence room held a second bag with an identical-looking weapon and a smaller bag containing a leather wallet.

"Seventeenth-century-style weapon, but this is a knockoff," Buckley said. "I checked on eBay. You can get one for less than a hundred bucks."

Prater swung the rapier back and forth. "Dueling weapon, right?"

"Yeah. Self-defense and fighting, mainly. Not combat." Buckley turned to Frames. "You're lucky the guy didn't have a Scottish broadsword. One of those takes your leg off."

"I wouldn't have gotten stabbed at all if someone had been doing their job." Frames repositioned his leg on the boxes.

"You know about swords?" Prater handed the bag back to Buckley.

"Little bit. Always had a thing for fencing."

"Hey, no kidding? Me too. We were meant for another era, Evan. On my way over here, I was thinking the department should have fencing in its weapons training. How cool would that be?" Prater looked again at Frames. "What do you think, Detective Frames?"

"I think you're an idiot, Prater. But I'm just the guy who shot the asshole with the swords."

Buckley held up one hand. "Like I said, technically, they're rapiers, not swords."

Prater stepped back from the evidence table to face Buckley. "Okay. Favorite fencing scene in a film?"

"Errol Flynn and Basil Rathbone," Buckley said. "*Adventures of Robin Hood*. Classic. You could tell they were both professionally trained."

"I know it. Great scene," Prater agreed. "Fighting on the stairs of a castle, isn't it? I prefer the 1995 film *Rob Roy*. The whole Scottish thing. Liam Neeson and Tim Roth have this sword fight at the end, and Neeson—"

Buckley jumped forward. "Grabs Roth's blade with his bare hand. You're right. I forgot that one. I should watch it again."

Frames put two fingers in his mouth and whistled. "Yo, geeks. Could we get the fuck back to business?"

"Sorry, Steve." Buckley smiled at Frames. "Thanks, by the way, for your help this morning. We appreciate it. How's the leg anyway? I meant to ask earlier."

"Sore." Frames flexed his leg several times to test it. "The ER doc put in stitches and gave me an antibiotic. She said it would have been worse if the blade hit an artery, not a muscle."

"I hear the Sheriff's Office is investigating the shoot," Prater said. "Did they talk to you already?"

"At the scene, briefly. Took my gun. They'll talk to me after they interview everyone else."

"Yeah," Buckley said. "Lonnie and I are scheduled to meet with them this morning. Cervantes too." Buckley waited for Frames to look at him. "Don't worry, Steve. We'll back you up. It was a good shooting. You'll be fine. Plus, they've got the footage from our car cameras and body cams. I don't know how you could have done anything else."

"We'll see. Always the chance they find something."

"But you're not on administrative leave, right?"

"Not yet anyway." Frames shook off the conversation. "Who's the dead guy? Do we know?"

Buckley pointed to the wallet. "Miguel Gonzalez. Forty-two. Pronounced dead at Memorial. Took one to the gut and three to the chest. Nice pattern, Steve." Buckley saluted Frames.

"Thanks," Frames said. "So what's he doing at Cervantes's house? And why's he have rapiers?"

"Don't know," Buckley said. "But judging by the guy's body, he's doing meth, and I'll go way out on a limb and say the autopsy'll find a shitload of PCP in his system. Once you do PCP, the reason for the rapiers could be anything. Probably never know."

"So why was he there?" Frames asked.

"After you shot Gonzalez, we talked to Ms. Cervantes. She

said Miguel had been living in her garage for the past two weeks because he needed a place to stay. She didn't know why he had the rapiers. This morning was the first she saw them. He came in the kitchen waving the swords and screaming nonsense about her being the devil. She thought he was going to kill her. The most useful thing she told us was that Miguel is the cousin of Emilio Medina, which means he probably works for the family. So that's something."

Prater saw Frames's blank look. "Okay. Sorry. I didn't know how much Lonnie and Evan already told you. Six months ago, EMTs were called to an apartment off West Steele Lane for an overdose. OD was Jazmin Taylor, thirty-eight years old, Caucasian. When the techs arrived, Ms. Taylor was unconscious. Usual thing: shallow respiration, weak pulse. They administered naloxone. She opened her eyes, and they thought they had her. But she died in the van on her way to the hospital."

"We have a deal with the ER docs," Buckley said. "They call us when the cause of death is drug-related. This one was obviously heroin. We looked around Jazmin Taylor's apartment and found black tar, which we could trace back to the Ramirez-Medina family."

"There's a family?" Frames asked.

"Crazy, right?" Prater said. "Been in business for nearly two decades. Grandparents, parents, two sons, cousins, uncles. Operate around Olive Park. Network of street dealers. The heroin comes from Mexico, through Fresno and sometimes East Palo Alto. Whenever we see black tar, it's usually the family."

"And this time we got lucky," Buckley said. "The packaging of the heroin in Taylor's apartment had prints belonging to Jorge Lopez. Lopez works for the family. So that's why we're looking for him."

"The other thing..." Prater said. "Taylor's autopsy showed

she actually died of an overdose of fentanyl. She took her usual shot of heroin, but the fentanyl was much more potent and killed her. It's a new thing. Comes from China. So we're trying to get this stuff off the streets."

"By the way, if you're interested, we're shorthanded for another surveillance this afternoon. We got word from one of our CIs that a courier is arriving from Fresno. We need a second car to watch and take pictures. Around four if VCI can spare you for a few hours, and you're…up to it."

"I'm up to it." Frames stood and felt his legs under him. "I'll talk to Eddie."

Prater suddenly clapped her hands. "You know, Frames, this'll be in your personnel record. Stabbed by a rapier. You've got to be the only cop with that injury in the state. At least in this century, you know, since what's-his-name…Zorro. Hey, that's what we'll call you, man, Zorro." Prater pulled out her phone. "This is fucking made for Instagram."

Frames plucked the phone from her hand and held it out of reach. "Prater, don't make me talk to your sergeant."

(ii)

(WEDNESDAY, 10:45 A.M.)

Perfume.

A woman hurrying out of the deli had brushed past Mahler on his way in. He hadn't seen her face, just a gray-haired figure. Even so, a faint, sweet scent lingered—a few molecules let loose in the air. In that instant he had seen his mother, forty years ago, looking at him across the kitchen. In the little house on Bell Street, where they lived in those days. It was her smell, unmistakably. A flower, although he didn't know its name—an intimate detail about her that had filled his life for just six years.

Bone cancer. The adults talked about it. To his child's mind, a strange, hard-sounding disease. How did something get into your bones? And how could you get rid of it? You didn't, as he found out. His mother lost weight until the skin stretched tight around her neck and wrists—places where nightgowns couldn't hide them. At six, he thought it was a bad kind of disease to take so much.

Your mother is...gone. His father knelt low and tried to embrace Eddie and his sister, awkwardly pulling them against his body. For once, the great lawyer was at a loss for words, undone as much as anyone by the mystery of death. Gone—as if she had walked out the front door one last time. For a while Eddie thought of her that way, a few steps from the house, turning around to catch his eye.

Now, a half hour after leaving the deli, Eddie Mahler sat in his office, looking out the window. It had been years since he'd thought of his mother. Odd how things came to you, without reason. He'd read somewhere the average person has fifty to seventy thousand thoughts a day, thirty-five a minute. And here was Eleanor Mahler, née Holmberg.

He remembered so little of her. Photo albums stacked in the garage, full of old stiff prints, losing color year by year, fading like his own memory. A pretty, slender woman smiling back at him from the 1970s. The images made her a stranger he'd never known.

He marveled at his mother's means of coming back. A scent—the most ephemeral of senses, a delicate, gentle presence in the world. Exactly like his mother, not wanting to intrude. How many women still wore perfume? Medical offices now had signs declaring themselves scent-free zones. Perfume seemed a fashion from another era, when women wore hats to church.

What would his mother think of him now? She'd certainly be surprised at his becoming a police officer. His father thought it a mediocre career, inferior to the practice of law, too close to life's squalor. But Mahler remembered his mother, in their few years together, as less judgmental. She was curious about him, eager to hear the stories he invented about his toys, to make him part of her adult life. Once, after her cancer started, her fingers reached from the bed to trace a line around his eyes and mouth, as if trying to learn something she couldn't find any other way.

Would she understand the man he'd become? Did all men want that—to see themselves at least once through their mother's eyes, to have their path forgiven by her loyalty?

The main thing he would tell her was that she had never gone away from him. He had taken a Princeton course in modern poetry because of the volume of Mary Oliver on her bookshelf. In his first years as a street cop he saw, as she would have seen, the meagerness with which people lived on the bottom rung, and that a place existed in his profession for her sort of kindness, even though it might be bounded by brutality.

He'd wanted her to be proud. But, after seventeen years, he no longer knew if he was a good officer by his mother's standard, because the terms of knowing were never simple. Despite the evasions in his own life, it turned out he'd inherited her talent for listening—in his case, sitting across a table from suspects and witnesses, and understanding the moment they revealed the things hidden from themselves.

He could tell his mother that in the past six months he'd managed to diminish his migraines through new medication and—even if it surprised him—talk therapy. He could predict her smile at that news.

Then the present intruded, and his mind raced on. Thirty-five thoughts a minute. He realized he had not bought lunch. Had he left the deli empty-handed?

He saw Eden in his doorway, an iPad in one hand. He wondered how long she had been watching.

"Sorry, Lieutenant." She looked startled. "Didn't mean to bother you. Are you okay?"

Why wouldn't he be okay? Had he been talking to himself? He forced himself to focus. "Officer Somers, tell me something. Do you wear perfume?"

"Not on duty, sir." Eden stiffened, imagining a challenge. "Has someone complained?"

"No, of course not. I was just curious, as a...general matter, if women today wear perfume." Mahler suddenly thought he might have blundered across a personal boundary. Was this question covered in the sexual harassment policy he had never finished reading?

"Sometimes I do, but I don't know if I'm typical of women." Eden frowned. "Are you trying to find a gift for someone?"

"No. Nothing like that." He gestured toward the tablet. "What do you need?"

Eden took two steps inside the office. "Missing person. A woman walked into the lobby and reported her husband missing. Paul Behrens. Forty-seven years old."

"How long?"

"Just since this morning. A teacher. Didn't show up at the school where he works. But—" Eden looked down at the tablet. "He left behind his phone and lesson plans. His wife's worried, thinks something might have happened."

Mahler considered it. "And he's never done something like this before?"

"No. Sounds like a responsible guy."

"All right." Mahler stood. "Let's talk to her."

Eden stepped in front of him. "One more thing. The admitting sergeant said Ms. Behrens may have been drinking."

Mahler followed Eden into the hallway toward the interview room. At the doorway, he hesitated. He was pretty sure what was coming. Missing persons were loser cases—lonely, dead-end assignments that officers dodged, where you searched for what you didn't want to find.

As they entered, Annie Behrens glanced up. Her eyes were puffy and red. She raked a hand through her hair. Dressed in a baggy sweatshirt and jeans, she had a rumpled, sleep-deprived look.

Mahler introduced Eden and himself. They sat facing the woman. "I understand your husband is missing?"

"Yes. Paul—that's my husband—didn't go to his job this morning and didn't call the school where he works. I know it hasn't been that long, but this isn't like him." She leaned forward to make her case.

"Tell me," Mahler said, "since he left home this morning, you haven't heard from him at all, is that right?"

"No. In fact—" Annie found a cell phone in her purse and laid it on the table. "He didn't take his cell. He's never without that thing. On it all the time. Oh. And I brought my husband's laptop." She reached beside her chair and put the computer beside the phone. She looked at the two devices as if she expected them to speak.

Eden waited a beat for the woman's attention to return. "When's the last time you saw Paul?"

"It was... What's today?" Annie frowned. "Wednesday? I think it was Sunday night. We work different shifts. Paul works days. I work second shift. But we had dinner together Sunday, with our children. We have two: Claire's thirteen and Jesse's sixteen."

"How'd Paul seem then?" Mahler made a note on the pad in front of him. "Did he say or do anything out of the ordinary?"

"Not that I remember. After dinner he graded papers, like he always does."

"Okay. Good." Mahler took the moment to change course. He leaned back and spread his hands in a gesture of invitation. "Mrs. Behrens, could we offer you some coffee? It's not Starbucks, but it's pretty good."

Annie's eyes filled. Tears ran down her face. "I had half a glass of wine before I came in…to get through this." Her voice was determined.

Eden left the room to get the coffee. Mahler passed a tissue box to Annie.

Annie wiped her eyes and straightened in her chair. "We're ordinary people, Lieutenant. I'm not used to this." She watched Eden return and accepted the coffee.

Mahler tried to steer her back on track. "Tell me about your husband. He's a schoolteacher?"

"Paul teaches English. Brookwood Middle School, the last eight years. Two years ago, the district named him teacher of the year." She smiled, trying to catch a happier time.

"And he likes the work?"

"Loves it. He worked in insurance for a while after he got out of college. But then he went back to Sonoma State and got his credential. It was like his life's dream. And the kids… He's very popular."

Eden waited to see if Mahler was done. Then: "Has anything changed in the last few weeks at his job? Any problems?"

"A couple of girls were challenging Paul. I don't think it was a big deal."

"Challenging him how?"

"Not doing assignments. Seeing if he'd punish them. Middle school stuff."

"How about the two of you? Were you getting along? Any arguments recently?"

"No. You know, little things. Nothing out of the ordinary."

Mahler watched her look away. Something to come back to another time. He changed the subject. "Does Paul have any other family that he might have talked to?"

"His sister, Beth, lives in Santa Rosa. She's taking care of their father. I spoke with her this morning, and she hadn't heard from Paul. His brother, Michael, lives in a group home in Windsor. He had a brain injury in Afghanistan. I haven't talked to him."

"What about friends? Are there friends Paul might have contacted?"

"Friends? I don't know. Other teachers, maybe. I can give you a list."

"Are there any places where he might have gone?" Eden asked. "Favorite places he goes to get away? A park?"

Annie looked puzzled. "He likes the river. Do you think he's out there?"

"How'd you find out Paul didn't go to work this morning?" Mahler asked.

"The principal texted me. Around eight thirty."

"And Paul had already left the house by then?"

"Yeah. His car was gone. It's a 2015 silver Elantra." Annie was suddenly busy with her phone. "I'll have to look up the license number."

Mahler kept at it. "So you didn't hear him get out of bed and leave?"

Annie took a deep breath and let it out. "I slept downstairs in the family room last night. I do that sometimes when I get home late, so I don't disturb Paul."

"When did you get home Tuesday night?" Eden heard the shortness of her question and wished she had worked up to it.

"I don't remember. Is that important?" Annie's face reddened. In her eyes, Mahler saw a narrow calculus of how far to answer their questions without letting some deeper truth leak out. He stepped in. "We're just trying to get a sense of Paul's movements before he left home. Your husband didn't leave a note to say where he was going?"

"No. Not that I saw."

"Does he usually do that? Leave a note to say where he's going and when he'll return?"

"Sometimes. If it's outside his normal routine."

"You told the sergeant downstairs your son, Jesse, saw Paul this morning," Eden said. "Is that right?"

Annie looked at Mahler, wary now. "Yes. He saw Paul at six o'clock in the bathroom. They didn't talk, but Jesse said Paul was dressed up. Jacket and tie. He doesn't usually wear clothes like that."

"And you don't know why he did today?"

"No. Unless he was going…somewhere." Annie traced a small circle with one finger on the tabletop.

"Mrs. Behrens," Mahler said, "are there any other reasons to think your husband's leaving this morning is out of the ordinary? You said he didn't go to his job or call the school. He didn't tell you where he was going and didn't leave a note. He left behind his phone. He was dressed differently than usual. Anything else?"

"Yes," Annie said. "When Jesse saw my husband in the bathroom this morning, Jesse thought Paul was crying."

"Crying? Did Jesse say why?"

"No. That's all he said. I mention it because my husband's not an emotional man. And I found this in Paul's briefcase." Annie took a manila envelope from her purse and emptied the friendship bracelet on the table.

For a moment, the three of them looked at the bracelet. "Where did you find it?" Eden asked.

"Sealed in this envelope in Paul's briefcase. By itself."

"You haven't seen it before, and you don't know where it came from?" Eden used a nitrile glove to put the envelope and bracelet in separate evidence bags.

"No. I mean it could be nothing, but—"

"But you think it might mean something?" Mahler asked.

"No. I don't know."

The room fell silent. Mahler watched the woman gingerly put her hands back in her lap, as if it was a foreign act. She was a marionette on loose strings. Whatever she had once been was broken apart, into bits lighter than air, ready to float away.

Mahler started again. "Mrs. Behrens, I have to ask. Do you have any reason to think your husband might harm himself?"

"No. I don't think so. He wasn't unhappy as far as I know." Annie looked down at her hands. "What do you do now?"

"If it's okay with you, we'll see if there's anything on your husband's phone that can help us." Mahler passed the phone to Eden and stacked his papers. "We'll want to search your house for anything that can tell us where Paul has gone. As soon as possible, we'll also want to talk to Claire and Jesse, of course. We'll need a recent photo of Paul, if you have one. And we'll take a complete statement from you, go over what you told us. Can you stay a little longer?"

"I guess so. I...called in sick." For a moment Annie looked lost. "We took each other for granted. It's just something that happens. You're both working. There's no time. It's like that for everyone, isn't it?" She smiled weakly and settled back in her chair.

Chapter Four

(i)

"Can we focus on this missing person for the next twenty-four hours and put the other stuff on hold?" Mahler looked at the case lineup whiteboard.

Rivas, Frames, and Eden stood in a row in front of the board, leaning on their desks.

Are we a good team, Mahler wondered for the thousandth time, *this group of mine with their different talents and eccentricities? They're effective, but does any of it have to do with my leadership?* The police department's long-standing policy was to rotate officers through different investigative teams, giving them all chances at a range of assignments and avoiding burnout in any one area. But for the past six months, this group of detectives had been together and had proven themselves in two homicide investigations and dozens of assaults.

At the end of the row, Rivas rubbed his face. He'd been at

a crime scene all night and needed sleep. The oldest and close now to retirement, Daniel Rivas gave the team a memory bank of local criminals. Beside him stood Steve Frames, one of the department's military veterans. Frames had come into VCI with weapons skills and an eagerness to learn investigative techniques. Last in line, Eden Somers bent over her phone. She was newest to the team, someone who brought a background as an FBI analyst, a heads-down investigator who looked at every case as a puzzle to be solved. Missing from the room was Martin Coyle, who Mahler remembered was testifying this morning in a court case. Coyle had earned his role as a kind of unofficial office manager, who pulled together computer systems and research tools.

Were they good? Every day you found out, Mahler thought.

"The Powell murder is in limbo." Rivas spoke first. "We talked to the wife and the business partner, and we're waiting on forensics. For the two Roseland robberies, we're looking at security footage, and the Oakland PD called us with a possible suspect."

Mahler waited. "So the answer's yes? We can focus on the missing person case?"

"Yeah," Rivas conceded. "I mean, we can't really take our eyes off everything else, and Steve's on part-time loan to Narcotics."

"In a sword fight, no less." Eden smiled.

"I heard," Mahler said. "You okay, Steve? Need some time off?"

Frames waved it off. "I'm good. My interview with the Sheriff's Office is scheduled in an hour. They'll make a decision on administrative leave then."

"This your first time?" Rivas asked. "Always strange being on the other side of the table."

"All I can do is tell them what happened." Frames turned to

face Mahler. "But on this missing person thing, do we know for sure this guy is even missing? Do we know he didn't just drive away and forget to tell his wife? Doesn't that happen with couples?"

Rivas laughed. "Oh, man. I'm going to say a prayer right now for your future wife."

Maybe he just wakes up and hates his life, Mahler thought. *Tired of his wife not understanding him, the unrelieved messiness of every room in his house, the entitled kids in his classes. On a whim, he drives alone out to the west county, blasting old Nirvana through the speakers. Gets a burger in Guerneville. Finds himself back home to reality by four. It did happen like that. But sometimes it was like Kevin Farrell.*

Eight years ago, a successful real estate agent named Kevin Farrell had disappeared from the home he shared with his wife and three daughters. His car was found a week later on a rural road in Lake County, his body on the back seat with an empty bottle of Nembutal. The story stopped there, without a real ending. The only detail still in Mahler's memory was Coyle's offhand remark as he dismantled the evidence board: "You park in the middle of nowhere and take all those pills, something is seriously wrong."

"You're right," Mahler said. "We don't know for sure he's missing. But his wife thinks he is, so we have to take it seriously. Let's focus on this for twenty-four hours and see where it goes. He sounds like a person of habit and routine, and this isn't typical for him. Mrs. Behrens said her husband loves his job. So why does he suddenly not go to it? I'm also concerned he left behind his phone and things for his classroom—like he's not coming back and has nothing to lose." Mahler looked at Rivas. "Which reminds me. Give a photo of Behrens to a couple of uniforms and send them over to the school in case he shows up."

"There's also that bit about the son seeing his father crying this morning," Eden said.

"So—possible suicide?" Frames asked.

"At this point, we don't know enough to go there. But it's a possibility."

"Whatever Paul Behrens is up to," Eden said, "he didn't share it with his wife."

"I agree," Mahler said. "I think we're going to have to find out what Mrs. Behrens doesn't know. Steve, look at Paul Behrens's financials. If he's using a card right now, maybe we can see where he is. By the way, you already put out the BOLO, right?"

"Fifteen minutes ago," Frames said. "We also entered Behrens's information into the MUPS database and posted a Stop and Identify bulletin on the Field Services briefing board."

"So we literally have no idea where this guy might have gone?" Rivas asked.

"We might know more when Martin searches his phone and laptop," Mahler said. "When's Martin coming back from court, by the way?"

Eden consulted her phone. "Back in an hour. Eddie, remember Behrens's wife says he likes the river."

"That's right," Mahler said. "Let's have the sheriffs do a check of parking lots and turnouts from Forestville to the coast. And when Martin comes back, have him do a search on the car's GPS."

Eden held up the evidence bags with the manila envelope and friendship bracelet. "What do we think of these? Maybe Behrens took the bracelet away from a student who was disrupting class?"

"It could have been a gift from a student to him?" Rivas said. "When my boys were that age, girls were always making those things and giving them to teachers."

"It's a little creepy, though, isn't it?" Frames asked. "Also, why's the bracelet in a sealed envelope, and why's it in the teacher's briefcase?"

"His wife thought it was important enough to show us," Mahler said. "Eden, I doubt we'll find anything, but have the envelope checked for prints."

"You know what's weird to me?" Frames said. "The missing guy dressed up. Wife says he never dresses up. Is he meeting someone he's trying to impress?"

"That's a good angle to follow," Eden agreed. "If he is meeting someone, who is it?"

"On the other hand, if you're going to off yourself, why put on a sports jacket?"

Eden considered it. "Actually that's not unusual."

"Oh, Christ. I knew you were going to say that."

"In some circumstances, it's common for people to dress up before committing suicide."

"There's probably a study on it, too."

"In fact there is—a paper written by Woolright and Johnston on the apparel of Golden Gate Bridge jumpers."

Mahler stepped in front of the others to cut off more chatter. "Eden, let's do a search of the Behrens house. We have Mrs. Behrens's permission for that. Take Bailey with you. Bedroom, home office if they have one. Look for anything that can tell us why this guy decided not to go to work this morning. See if he left a note the wife overlooked. If he keeps a written calendar in addition to his phone, we might find out why he dressed up. When you get back, I want you to interview the daughter, Claire. Get her mother to bring her in."

Rivas raised his hand. "I can go out to Brookwood. My kids went there, and I know Jennifer Steeley, the principal."

"All right. Mrs. Behrens told us a couple of female students were challenging Behrens. Ask the principal about that. And interview his fellow teachers while you're there. Maybe he talked to one of them even if he didn't tell his wife what he's up to."

Eden handed a sheet of paper to Rivas. "Here's a list of teachers his wife gave us."

Mahler looked at Frames. "Steve, after you look at Behrens's credit cards, do a broad search. Government databases, social media. What do we know about Paul Behrens? Employment history. Arrest record. Whatever. When the son, Jesse, comes in, you talk to him. He's last one to see Behrens."

Mahler looked at the notes from the meeting with Annie Behrens. "I'll talk to Paul Behrens's sister and brother. Let's try to find this guy today."

(ii)

(WEDNESDAY, 12:10 P.M.)

Claire ate lunch alone at one of the outdoor picnic tables on the broad breezeway between the two halves of Cable Middle School. On a cold day like this, she had the outdoor space to herself and was enjoying the quiet, away from the cafeteria. Her meal, a double order of McDonald's fries, was spread on greasy paper. She took a salt shaker from her backpack and poured extra salt on the fries. She ate them one at a time—holding up each long fry, biting it in half, and chewing the two halves.

She was halfway through the pile when the Bitches came outside. Usually there were five of them, but today just two—Bri and Katrina. They stood for a moment at the door. Then they saw Claire and headed her way.

Bri led the way. "Hey, Clairsie." She sat across the table and hunched toward Claire.

Katrina, who wore headphones, sat on the bench next to Claire. She closed her eyes and hummed tonelessly. Her head bobbed, and now her lips moved without any sound coming out.

Claire looked back at Bri. She felt her body tense as she waited for the other girl. In the last few years, Claire had watched Bri's meanness harden on her face like the mask of a prowling animal.

Bri mocked a smile. "What're you doing out here all by yourself, girl?"

Claire waited. She wished the Bitches would leave before her fries got cold.

"Did your mommy buy you that top? I had one like it—in fourth grade."

"What do you want, Bri?"

"Well, that's not very friendly."

Katrina reached across Claire and grabbed a couple of fries.

Claire saw the other girl's dirty fingers and blue nail polish. She cupped her own hands over the fries to guard them.

Katrina chewed with an open mouth. Then she closed her eyes and hummed again. She opened her eyes to look at Claire. "I'm going to be a backup singer for Beyoncé."

Claire tried not to stare at Katrina's eyes. There was something wrong with them. The lids didn't open all the way. The rumor was that Katrina had taken a handful of white doves at a party in seventh grade and it had scrambled her brain.

Katrina swayed her head. "My dad knows somebody who works for Beyoncé. Her truck driver."

Claire backed away from Katrina's wobbling head. It was scary being so close to her. "Beyoncé has a truck driver?"

"Duh. For, like, when she's on tour. And this truck driver is a woman. Which is cool, right? A woman truck driver."

"Sure."

"Anyway, my father sent her a download of me singing, and she liked it."

"The truck driver?"

"No, you dope. Beyoncé."

Claire saw how the rebuke left spittle on the front of Katrina's lower lip. She wondered what it would be like to have scrambled brain cells from too much Ecstasy. When she and Katrina were in second grade, Katrina brought Smarties to school and gave Claire the brown ones. Maybe Katrina mistook the white doves for Smarties.

Katrina moaned, "Oh, oh, oh."

Bri slammed her open palm on the tabletop. "HEY, TRINA! FOCUS!"

Katrina smiled crookedly, still jerking her head to the music in her headphones.

Bri sighed. "So, Clairsie, you know our Facebook page, Little Secrets?"

Claire had heard of it. It was a page where the Bitches posted private messages they stole from other students' phones to embarrass them. She watched Bri and waited.

"You know Hector and that kid Reagan, the one with the Harry Potter glasses? They're real smart, and they can hack people's phones if they just have the number. Cool, huh? Well, they're hacking phones for us and getting stuff to put on our page."

"Why would they do that for you?"

Bri stiffened and looked away. "We have something they want."

"We let them touch us," Katrina giggled.

Claire stared at her. "That's disgusting."

"Hector's not so bad." Katrina considered it. "Kind of shy."

"So here's the deal, Clairsie," Bri said. "Last weekend, our boys hacked your mommy and daddy's phones and downloaded some interesting stuff." She winked at Katrina.

"What kind of stuff?"

"Nasty nasties. Your mom being slut-ty. Who-wee. And your daddy's into something twisted with girls."

Claire felt her stomach lurch. "That's gross. I don't believe you."

"No?" Bri waved her phone in the air. "Want to see? Gotta say, your mom is smoking hot. Here, I can show you."

Claire held up both hands. "No. Stop. Why're you doing this?"

"Why do you think? Mo-ney."

"What do you mean?"

"I mean, you give us two hundred bucks by Friday, and we won't post Mommy and Dada."

"I don't have two hundred dollars. I just get an allowance."

"Ask your mommy. Tell her if she's saving for something special, this is special."

"What happens if I don't pay you?"

"We post the messages, and everybody gets to see a whole lot about Mommy and Daddy." Bri stood to leave and waited for Katrina.

Katrina reached across the table and grabbed another handful of fries. She put several in her mouth but spit them out. "Gross. They're cold."

"Remember. Two. Hundred." Bri held up two fingers. "Otherwise we post your shit, and you're going to want to eat your lunch under this table."

The Bitches walked back toward the cafeteria.

Claire sat still. She tried to imagine what awful things her mother and father had on their phones. Once, when they had gone together to the women's hot tub at the club, she had seen her mother naked, her large breasts hanging down without a bra. Her father was the smartest man she knew. If he had something on his phone, it was a mistake, something he hadn't meant to download. Now her parents were in trouble because of her, because Bri always hated her.

She picked up one of the fries, now limp and cold. Then she grabbed the paper wrapper and threw the rest of her fries across the playground. A swarm of pigeons descended on them as they hit the ground.

Then, as if her thoughts conjured it, she saw her mother's car arrive on the pickup loop on the far side of the playground.

Chapter Five

(i)

Coyle loosened his tie and sat wearily at his desk. The VCI bull-pen was empty. He'd just returned from Courtroom 4 of the County Hall of Justice, Criminal Division, where he'd testified as the arresting officer in a road rage case.

As always, after leaving the courtroom, he felt weighed down with the malevolence that pervaded the trial rooms. It was as if everyone who gathered in the courts came expecting a balancing of the scales, or a return on pain suffered, and was searching for its object.

Oddly, the one place where venomous intent didn't seem to exist, Coyle thought, was in the dock. There, men waited in orange jumpsuits for their hearings. They were a rough-looking bunch—heads shaved, arms densely tattooed. But surrender also ran through them, like survivors of a blast, shorn of something essential. When Coyle looked at those men across the room's wide divide, he wondered if they were searching for an escape, not from jail or the courtroom but from life inside their own skin.

This time, Coyle also came away with the thoughts that had filled his head while he testified.

It was only by coincidence he'd been the arresting officer for the case. At lunchtime, going downtown to buy a sandwich, he happened to be on the sidewalk when the incident unfolded in front of him. One driver, Joseph Tallent, claimed the other driver, Trent Keller, cut him off on the freeway exit ramp. When the two vehicles reached the busy intersection where Coyle stood, Tallent drove his car into the rear bumper of Keller's car. Keller emerged from his car and shoved Tallent backward onto the pavement.

Tallent then took a 9mm handgun from his glove compartment and shot Keller.

The exact site of the wounding was the left buttocks, as proven by a poster-sized photo of Keller's bare rear end that stood alarmingly throughout the trial on a large display pedestal.

When Coyle was called to the stand, the prosecutor, Deputy District Attorney Michael Slater, asked him to describe the confrontation. As Coyle prepared to speak, his mind brimmed with ideas that had been forming for months about the life he witnessed day after day. Coyle did not think of himself as a philosopher, but Eddie Mahler once said all homicide detectives are forced to be philosophers. Lately, Coyle had developed a kind of philosophy about criminal proceedings like the present one and its place in the larger world.

But in the moment Coyle put aside his thoughts and focused on Slater—describing what he witnessed the day of the incident.

As Coyle finished, Slater smoothed his necktie and approached the stand. "Officer Coyle, was it your observation that Mr. Tallent fired his gun at Mr. Keller because he feared for his safety?"

"No, sir. Mr. Keller was walking away at the time of the shooting."

At this point, Coyle wanted to address the court and tell those assembled—the judge, the lawyers, the aggrieved and relatives of the aggrieved, and even the orange-jumpsuited men in the dock—what the proceedings were missing. He wanted to say that this case occurred because people in this country today are angry. They feel disrespected, their needs unmet. Around them, others appear to be gaining an advantage. One day, another car pulls in front of you, as if you don't exist, as if they're entitled to get ahead of you. For once, you decide, you'll get back at them. You take what's yours.

"Did Mr. Tallent say why he shot Mr. Keller?" The prosecutor turned around and gestured toward the defendant.

"He said it was because of the type of car Mr. Keller was driving."

"His car?"

"Yes, sir. That's what Mr. Tallent said."

"What were his exact words?"

Here Coyle really wanted to say that in the hospital on the north end of town, a six-year-old girl or a forty-year-old woman or an eighty-year-old man is dying of leukemia or ovarian cancer or heart disease. They will die tonight or tomorrow or the day after that. Everything we think or say in this courtroom is meaningless to them. What's our injustice in the face of their waning hours?

Instead Coyle looked at the judge. "Your Honor," he said, "the remark contains an obscenity."

"Tell us the exact words," the judge sighed. "But let's not dwell on it."

Of course not, Coyle thought. But what they should be dwelling on is that two miles from where they were sitting is a hillside, easily reached by anyone, that is as beautiful as anything in this world. Across its upper reaches are perfect rows of grapevines. Some days the clouds make dark patterns on the hillside so that the colors of the vines change and the rows appear to be moving. Isn't such a place, like hundreds of others around us, a gift? Why do we allow ourselves to pass by without seeing it?

It was a fair question. But in the moment, Coyle shifted in his chair and addressed Slater. "Mr. Tallent said that Mr. Keller drove a Volvo and was, therefore, a dick."

The gallery broke into laughter, and the judge banged his gavel for silence.

In the commotion, Coyle looked around the courtroom. The problem is, he thought, our lives are filled with trivia— text messages, tweets, Facebook posts—nothing more than flyspecks. We never step back and see our place on this earth with the sense of scale it requires. We end up doing unnecessary things—like ramming our cars into other cars. These things, in turn, set into motion a whole string of unstoppable reactions involving cops, lawyers, judges, courtrooms—all of it, every last bit of it, a waste of time.

Coyle's concentration was broken by Deputy District Attorney Slater stepping into view. "Is it your testimony, Officer Coyle, that the defendant did not discharge his weapon in self-defense but because of the type of vehicle Mr. Keller drove?"

"Yes. And because, as I said, he believed Mr. Keller was a… dick."

More laughter from the gallery. At the defense table, Tallent smiled and enjoyed his brief popularity. The judge frowned. Slater thanked Coyle and returned to the prosecution table.

As he stepped down from the witness chair, Coyle felt a

disappointment in the gulf between his legal testimony and his unspoken thoughts—between the narrow good of his public witnessing and the hope captured in his own ideas. If, as Eddie said, his experience as a homicide investigator made him a philosopher, he wasn't paid to be one. He was paid, at least as far as his time in the courtroom was concerned, to accurately describe the act of human stupidity he had witnessed and to let the legal system sort out the consequences.

Now, in the VCI room, Coyle looked down at his desktop and several sealed bags from the Behrens case that he had signed out of the evidence locker. He was grateful the VCI room was empty. He didn't want to talk to any of the other detectives about what he'd thought in the courtroom. Eden would diagnose him. Frames would make a joke. Rivas would pretend to be busy. He needed to do something ordinary and useful.

The first evidence bag contained Paul Behrens's cell phone. Using the PIN provided by Annie, Coyle opened the phone and clicked the icon for the home security camera, scrolling through dates until he came to today. At 7:15 a.m., the motion-activated camera filmed Paul Behrens's car pulling out of the garage. The man's face was briefly visible through the front windshield. Coyle paused the video to study Behrens's face but could see nothing out of the ordinary. Behrens looked like any other person leaving his house in the morning to go to work. Coyle sent a copy of the video to his own computer for storage and printing.

He made a record of Behrens's incoming and outgoing calls for the past six months, then clicked on a website that allowed him to reverse-search the numbers to identify the people behind them. He made a few notes on patterns and frequency of specific numbers, to be shared later with the VCI team. A sudden decrease in the number of outgoing calls three days ago told Coyle the missing man had probably purchased a second disposable phone at that time. The other phone was probably with Behrens now and could contain important evidence.

Coyle also made a record of Behrens's use of phone apps, including which apps were used most, and the subjects of Google searches.

He found Google Maps searches for Dillon Beach, Bodega, and Salmon Creek.

Under Google searches, he saw Malvolio, Viola, Shakespeare, Salinger, Dickinson, Mission Pizza, Richard Ford, Hardy's Brewhouse, Nothing False, Cummings, Nick Adams—there were too many terms to read. Coyle highlighted the list and printed a copy.

Then, as he was about to put the list aside, Coyle noticed that in a forty-five-minute period on March 14, Behrens had run three Google searches on sexual assault, Child Protective Services, and molestation.

Coyle looked up at the empty room. *What the fuck was this guy up to?*

He opened Behrens's laptop. The teacher appeared to use his laptop less than his phone, and its usage was focused on record keeping for classes, lecture notes, student evaluations and grading, and personal writing.

Coyle printed a list of folder names. Then he clicked on folders at random and read several documents. Most were notes for classroom presentations and gave the impression of a conscientious teacher who prepared thoroughly for his classes. After twenty minutes of reading, Coyle saw a single document labeled "School District" and dated March 16. He clicked on it:

I am writing to announce my resignation, effective immediately, from my position as teacher at Brookwood Middle School. I am doing so to spare the district, my faculty colleagues, the parent body, and most especially my students from whatever pain may be caused by the alleged incident earlier this month. Once the allegations against me are made public, it will be difficult for an objective view of the facts to prevail. But I want to state here that I am innocent of the charges as alleged.

Throughout my career I have tried, to the best of my abilities, to provide a quality education in literature. This work has always involved challenging my students to delve into the issues that lie behind works of art and to see how those ideas play a role in their own lives. For me, literature has been a lifelong passion. I believe it is worthy of our attention for its own sake, but that it also helps us to understand the feelings that lie in our hearts and to create the moral compass that guides us.

Maybe something good will come of this incident. In any case, it is my sincere hope that this one event does not define me and become my legacy, and that I will be remembered for the work that I have done for more than eight years, and for the love of stories that I have instilled in the students I have been privileged to teach.

Coyle sat back. He would reread the document in a minute. But for now, he savored the moment. He thought again of his musings in the courtroom. Sometimes, he told himself now, you make sense of the world one small piece at a time.

(ii)

(WEDNESDAY, 12:50 P.M.)

"This place is empty, right?" Bailey paused in the foyer of the Behrens house and looked back at Eden.

"We've got it to ourselves," Eden said, "and we have the owner's permission to search."

Bailey pulled a camera from her evidence case and shot photos of the family room.

Standing in the doorway of the room, Eden snapped on a pair of nitrile gloves. When Bailey finished, Eden moved slowly around the room. She found the blanket on the sofa, where Annie had slept for the night. She pictured Annie Behrens watching TV early Wednesday morning after her shift. Wet eyes and a fifth glass of wine. Around Eden the room buzzed. Laughter, raised voices, loud pop music. She saw it through the eyes of the missing man—the world left behind. *Was it not enough, or too much? Had he set the universe in motion, watched it change year by year until it excluded him? Had leaving been the easiest thing he'd done?*

This was Eden's first missing person case, though she'd researched the subject in college. According to the National Crime Information Center, the majority of persons reported missing in this country were located alive—missing in one place, present in another. However, behind the numbers in Eden's reading were histories that proved leaving was never simple—or only as simple as you wanted to believe.

Eden herself had wanted to run away just once, during her boarding school days. Even then, she remembered imagining what an investigator would make of the things in her dorm room.

In the adjoining living room, Paul Behrens's briefcase lay beside the recliner exactly as Annie described it. Crouching, Eden opened the case. Inside lay a file folder marked "Assignments" and a thick notebook of lesson plans. She flipped through the pages to the present day. The lesson was a continued discussion of Shakespeare's *Twelfth Night*. A pocket in the briefcase lid held a daily planner. Eden looked at Wednesday, the day of Paul's disappearance. On the line for 11:00 a.m. was a note that said "Jean." A 3:00 p.m. entry read "Staff Meeting." Nothing indicated a reason for Paul Behrens to take the unusual step of wearing a sports jacket and tie. Eden closed the briefcase and put it into a large evidence bag.

Bailey appeared in the doorway. "Okay, Professor. Why'd this guy leave? I mean, I know why I'd do it. I live in a crappy apartment, my job is processing what dead people leave behind, and the last guy I dated had a tattoo of his car. But Behrens lives in a nice neighborhood. Big house—TVs in every room. Wife, a kid of each gender. Steady job. I mean, if you're sick of it, why not get a divorce like millions of other desperately unhappy Americans? Why just drive away?"

Eden stood. "In most cases of adult voluntary disappearance, the reason they leave is they feel trapped and don't see a solution. Their instincts take over, and they run."

"But what are they running from? This guy Behrens has a good life, doesn't he?"

"Sometimes it's a crisis they've never faced before. Maybe they've committed a crime—something as simple as a DUI—and they can't imagine how their life will go on. Other times, it's a deepening depression that gets so bad, they can't stand being where they are."

"What about the family?" Bailey shook her head. "You just leave them?"

"It's not rational," Eden admitted. "It's about fear—the human flight response."

"And they don't leave notes, like with a suicide?"

"Sometimes. Not usually. The impulse is to get out."

"Well, so far, I don't see anything to run away from."

Eden picked up the evidence bag. "Were you serious before? That guy you dated really had a tattoo of his car?"

"Yeah." Bailey smiled. "Chevy Malibu. It was kind of cute."

They climbed the stairs to the second floor. In the master bedroom, Eden saw the mussed bed where Behrens slept Tuesday night. The walk-in closet held Annie's clothes on the left, Paul's on the right. His rack was a jumble of polo shirts, flannels, and khakis—the wardrobe of a typical schoolteacher.

Bailey came out of the master bath with several bottles. "Check out these. Prescriptions in his name: Ativan, Zoloft, Xanax, Valium. Enough downers to put the city to sleep. Guy must have some issues."

Eden walked down the hallway and met Bailey in Claire's room. The bright pastel walls held posters of Ariana Grande and Timothée Chalamet. The room was tidy, bed made. Eden looked quickly through the closet and turned to leave. Bailey stared at the Grande poster. "Hope that's not who she wants to be."

"Leave her alone. She's thirteen."

In Jesse's room, the curtains were closed. The floor was covered in dirty clothes, and the room reeked of stale cigarette ends. Arrayed around the room were concert posters of indie bands. Bailey turned on the overhead light and shot several photos. "Jesus, two kids on opposite sides of the universe."

In the bedside cabinet, Eden found thirty new watches, some still in their cases. "Wow. High-end. Piaget, Breitling. For the son of a schoolteacher, the boy has expensive tastes."

Bailey knelt in front of the closet and shone a flashlight inside. She pulled a plastic storage box from inside. As she popped open the lid, Bailey took a deep breath. She held the open box for Eden to see. "Twenties. Hundreds of them. Kid saves his allowance."

Eden stared at the bills. "Why twenties?"

"If I had to guess, purchase price of whatever he's dealing."

Bailey put a hand on top of the bills. "Probably weed. Street price for a gram is about twenty bucks."

"Count them now and take pictures. Otherwise his lawyer will raise a stink later."

Bailey sat cross-legged on the floor, counting. After a few minutes she looked up. "Three hundred seventy-three. Which is what? Seventy-five hundred dollars?" Bailey closed the lid and placed the box in an evidence bag.

"So, Bailey." Eden smiled. "How're we doing with that image of a father walking away from his perfect life?"

The last door along the second-floor hall opened to a home office. Eden waited in the hall while Bailey took photos from several angles. Inside, Eden headed first for the desk and went through the drawers.

Bailey stared at the shelves lined with books. "This guy's an eighth-grade English teacher, right? Look at these books. They're still reading the same crap I had to read."

"That's why they're called classics."

"Okay. *Catcher in the Rye* and *The Great Gatsby* are harmless enough. But *Lord of the Flies*? What kind of book is that for kids to read?"

"It's to teach us how to behave if we're stranded on an island."

"The ones that really bothered me were the YA novels about misfits. They were always kids dressed like goths and smoking weed."

"That's funny. I had you pegged for a misfit at that age."

"I was."

"But you wore nice girl clothes and discussed the Bill of Rights?"

"No. I dressed like a goth and smoked weed. But what does some suburban forty-year-old author know about me?"

Eden picked up the evidence bag that held Behrens's

briefcase. "Wait a second. I have an idea." She took out the Assignment folder and handed it to Bailey. "Look at the list of assigned books and find copies of them. Let's see if there's anything in them that might help us."

Bailey quickly located the recently assigned titles and made a small pile. She picked up the top book, *Twelfth Night.* "This's the cross-dressing one, right?"

"Yeah, I'm sure that's how Shakespeare thought of it. Your eighth-grade teacher would be so proud."

Opening the front cover, Bailey read, "'To Paul, Then come kiss me, sweet and twenty.' Signed Jean. Who do you suppose Jean is?"

"I don't know, but her name's in his planner. And I remember that line. It's a quote from the play."

"Yeah, I'm sure that's how Jean thought of it."

Chapter Six

(i)

Beth Rigney led Mahler through her house to the kitchen and gestured toward an empty chair at the table. "Is it okay if we talk here? I can see Dad while he's napping on the deck." She stole a look out the window. "He's…stage four. Prostate."

"I'm sorry to hear that." Mahler laid a notebook on the table in front of him.

Rigney's eyes were rimmed with dark circles. "You get through it."

"Thank you for seeing me on short notice. We're trying to find your brother as soon as we can."

"I'm not sure I can help. If my brother's not at work, I honestly don't know where he'd be."

"He doesn't have a favorite spot where he might go to be alone?"

"If he does, he never told me."

"When'd you last talk to him?"

"Yesterday. We talk every day at twelve thirty, when he takes his lunch. But we mainly talk about our father—how Dad's doing, what the doctor's saying."

Mahler thought of this sister and brother who talked every day. He tried to imagine his own sister, Diane, calling him every day now in their middle age. What would they talk about? It was hard to think of Diane as anything but the sullen, rebellious teenager she had been when she died. "Did Paul sound different then? Did he say anything out of the ordinary?"

"Not that I remember. But the guy has a lot on his plate. There's Dad, obviously, and there's Annie's drinking. From what I can tell, that's gotten worse lately. She used to go through a bottle at dinner. Now she always has a glass in her hand. Paul's tried to get her to stop, took her to AA. A couple months ago, he told me he thought Annie got involved with someone at the hospital, one of the staff doctors."

Rigney smiled thinly. "He asked me what he should do. As if I know anything. My husband and I are separated."

"Did he confront his wife about his suspicions?"

"They had it out. Back in March. He went to the hospital one night unannounced and saw them together. She denied it. Made up some wild-ass story. The saddest part? When Paul told me, his heart wasn't in it. It was like he didn't care anymore."

"He didn't care his wife was unfaithful?"

"My brother's in love with one thing—literature. It's the object of all his time, all his...affection. Annie tried to compete, but she doesn't stand a chance. He's in love with poetry, novels, writers, words—and with watching his students follow his path."

Rigney stared across the room. "It's harder when their passion is for a thing, not another person. My husband, the great

Mark Rigney, is in love with money—making it, having it, never letting it go." For a moment Beth Rigney seemed lost in thought. "That kind of obsession's worse than infidelity. You can't threaten a thing with a lawsuit, tell it to stay the fuck away from your husband. When they fall for a thing, it's their whole world, and it takes over their brain and heart and soul."

Mahler waited for the woman to return. He thought how none of us, no matter how apparently ordinary, has a simple life. He saw Rigney's expression seem to search back through her own words for solace, trying to find a way to recover a younger hope. "Earlier you said Paul has a lot on his plate. Is there something else, besides his wife's infidelity?"

"Yeah." Rigney looked relieved at the change of subject. "Something changed the last few months—at school."

"Do you know what it was?" Mahler watched Rigney's eyes glance out to the deck to see her father.

"Paul didn't say, but he's always done this thing with his classes. He's excited about the books they're reading, and he wants the kids to be enthusiastic. He has them write their own short stories, dress in historical costumes, read speeches in front of the class, put on plays. Every year, a handful of students, mostly girls, take it to another level. They get—there's no other word—infatuated. They're enthralled when he reads aloud. They write extra-credit poems to him. One of the other teachers told me the faculty even has a name for these girls: Behrens's Brats. At the same time, each year a few other kids flat out hate his teaching and refuse to read assignments. It's a lot of drama."

"But something different happened this year?"

"He didn't tell me the exact circumstances, but it involved their reading *Twelfth Night* about a month ago. Something went wrong."

"And Paul was worried about it?"

"It was like a puzzle he was trying to work out."

Mahler checked his watch. "Mrs. Rigney, do you think Paul is likely to commit to suicide?"

"He can't." Rigney turned to face Mahler. "What would happen to us?"

Mahler stood to hand Rigney one of his cards. "If Paul contacts you, or if you think of anything else, please call me."

Rigney stared at the card. "You should go see Michael, my other brother. Paul visits him every morning before he goes to work. Paul would have seen Michael this morning. Michael has TBI, traumatic brain injury, from Afghanistan. He doesn't talk a lot, but he understands what you tell him. Maybe Paul told him something that can help you." She crossed her arms and forced a smile. "In some way, Paul's closer to Michael than to me. Brothers, you know."

(ii)

(WEDNESDAY, 1:30 P.M.)

"You can't imagine how awful this is." Jennifer Steeley looked at Rivas from behind her desk. The principal's office at Brookwood Middle School was a narrow room in a prefabricated modular building. The desk was covered with piles of paper and half a dozen desktop toys.

"A school like this—a teacher doesn't show up, the rumors start. You've got text messages flying, social media, all of it. The kids, of course, jump right to the worst case: cancer. They're suspicious when you don't tell them anything. Then, to find out Annie doesn't know where he is?" She rolled her eyes.

Steeley was a large woman with a thin streak of purple

running through a wave of black hair. She hunched over the desk, fingers playing on the surface.

Rivas perched uncomfortably on a plastic chair sized for a child. "First things first. I just want to confirm that Paul Behrens has not been here at the school today, at the start of school or since then. Is that correct?"

"That's right."

"And you haven't received a phone call or text from him?"

"No, I haven't."

"And you don't know where he might be?"

"No. I hope he's safe."

"Okay. Tell me about Paul Behrens, as a teacher here at Brookwood."

"Paul's having a good year. As usual. Kids doing well, mostly. Parents happy, as far as I know."

Steeley suddenly stared at Rivas. "Daniel Rivas. I remember you. Your wife's Teresa; your son's…Alex. Right?"

Rivas smiled. "That's right. We were here two years ago."

"How's Alex? Still driving the girls crazy with those beautiful brown eyes?"

"He's taller than me now. Plays guard on the varsity squad."

"Good student. Good boy." Steeley looked past Rivas, remembering.

In his own middle school years, Rivas had not fared well. He had grown faster than his classmates—a bulky, looming boy, with clumsy hands and feet, banished to the back of classrooms to receive whatever teaching reached that far. His dyslexia, not yet diagnosed, made every lesson a puzzle. A sense of his slowness settled into his broad shoulders and thick middle, so that even now, forty years on, he felt himself the last one on the VCI team, weighing down investigations.

Rivas raised a hand to catch Steeley's attention. "Paul's wife,

Annie, said a couple of girls in one class were challenging him. Do you know about that?"

"Yeah. If it's what I think it is. Two students. I'm not allowed to give you names. Didn't do the assignments, and naturally their grades suffered. They decided to get back at Paul by testing the boundaries."

"What's *that* mean?"

"Disrupting class, using obscenities, anything to force Paul to discipline them. Most teachers don't like to take disciplinary measures, but they're forced to or the whole class pays a price."

"What happened?"

"Paul gave the girls several chances, but I finally suspended them. We brought the parents in. One family took responsibility; the other blamed us. It's the kind of unfortunate thing that happens. But my sense was that Paul was handling it."

As a student, Rivas had spent many hours in an office like this one. Penalties for fights mostly. The principal, Mrs. Wendy Sanchez, who had risen on her own hardened path, reigned with a theory reliant on the benefits of deprivation. On his first time in her office, as if to clarify an issue he hadn't raised, she told Rivas she wasn't his friend or his mother, *tu madre*. That last part puzzled him since he had a loving mother at home and wasn't looking for another. The second time, Mrs. Sanchez told him he could sit in silence or read the book she gave him, a volume of Emily Dickinson, with a page turned down at "The soul should always stand ajar." When he asked her if that was his punishment, she said it was up to him. For a boy who became a cop, it was his first lesson in justice.

"Do you know of anything else that might be bothering Mr. Behrens?" Rivas asked.

"Nothing I know of. He's overworked, but that's not new. Paul seems to thrive on it."

"Was there any indication Paul was thinking of leaving his job?" Rivas decided not to show Steeley a copy of the resignation letter found on Behrens's computer. If the missing man were to return, he might not want the letter revealed to his employer.

"He didn't say anything to me. To the contrary, we talked about plans for the end of the school year."

"Did anything out of the ordinary happen with his classroom in March?"

"March? No. Not that I'm aware of."

"So no student complaints have been made against Paul Behrens?"

"Complaints? What do you mean?"

"Complaints about his teaching style…inappropriate behavior."

"My goodness, no. I don't know where these questions are coming from."

"Ms. Steeley, we have a man missing, who might be in some harm," Rivas said. "We need to ask any questions that might help us find him."

Steeley tightened her hands in front of her. "I've been in this job for thirteen years, an assistant principal before that, a classroom teacher before that. I know what inappropriate behavior is. It's abhorrent. There's no defense for it. I've seen it, reported it. But I also know this. Male teachers, good male teachers, can be ruined by the false claims of one student. It happens."

Rivas watched her. He was losing patience. "What're we talking about?"

"Paul's the most popular teacher in the district. Parents from other schools want to transfer their kids here just for Mr. Behrens. But the thing about Paul is, he's teaching English. He has the kids reading stuff about feelings. You've got Salinger and Cummings and Edna St. Vincent Millay—you know, 'what lips my lips have kissed and where and why.' All that…impressionable stuff. It hits them where they are. But sometimes, some kids—"

"Some kids *what*?"

"Some kids don't have anyone in their lives who cares for them. They are unloved. They want so badly to feel something, to have something. So they go off track. They imagine things that aren't there." Steeley took a deep breath and let it out. "But in this case, I'm not aware of any incident involving Paul Behrens. If it occurred, I wasn't told of it."

"And you had no idea he'd go missing like this?"

"Of course not. On Friday, we talked about a class trip scheduled for the end of the month."

As Rivas stood to leave, Steeley held up her hand. "Before you go, there's one other thing I should tell you. The normal morning routine here is that teachers unlock the doors to their own classrooms. When I found out Paul wasn't coming, I went to unlock his classroom so his homeroom students wouldn't be stuck outside on a cold morning. But I found the door already unlocked. And one of my other teachers told me she saw a strange man leaving Paul's classroom."

Rivas sat back in his chair. "Do you know who this man was?"

"The teacher couldn't see his face."

"How'd a stranger enter the school property? Isn't someone at the front gate?"

"Mrs. Thompson says she didn't see anyone unusual come in. But sometimes, when the buses arrive, a lot of people come through the gate at once. Also, it's possible for someone to climb over the fence in the back."

"And how would this stranger have a key to Paul's classroom?"

"We don't know."

"But, in any case, you didn't go into lockdown?"

"Maybe we should have. It all happened so fast. In a few minutes, we determined he wasn't on campus."

"Do you have security cameras?"

Steeley picked up her phone. "I'll arrange for you to see the feed." She sighed. "It's funny. When you go into education, you think it's going to be about teaching, and then it isn't."

Chapter Seven

(i)

Eden couldn't believe how small Claire Behrens was. Up close, in the doorway of the VCI interview room, the thirteen-year-old's legs, clothed in skintight, floral-pattern leggings, looked like two wrapped PVC poles.

With no siblings and a small extended family, Eden had little firsthand experience of children. They were as foreign to her as tropical birds. Searching her memory for information relevant to the gender and age, she recalled reading the Marston and Levy paper on preteen psychopathic killers and the University of Michigan study of fatal shootings by adolescent girls. Neither seemed appropriate to the girl in front of her.

Claire paused in the hallway. She held a backpack with one hand, just off the floor, a look of martyrdom on her face.

"Hello, Claire." Eden reached to shake the girl's free hand, which felt cold and weak. "My name's Eden Somers." She waved Claire into the room. "Come sit here."

Claire shuffled around the table and unceremoniously dropped the backpack, which sounded like a bag of bricks hitting the floor. She fell into the chair and leaned forward on the tabletop.

"Can I get you something?" Eden asked. "Water? Soft drink?"

"Shouldn't you be looking for my father?" Claire squeezed her fingers together. "I mean, like, right now?"

Eden looked across the table and met the girl's eyes, which were clear blue against her white skin. They held a startling unguardedness. "Actually we *are* looking," Eden said. "We've been at it since your mother spoke to us this morning. We're also gathering information so we know better where to search. That's why I'm talking to you."

"Okay, but you don't have to talk to me like that. I'm not a kid."

"Good to know. I'll remember that," Eden said. "Let's start with this. Where do *you* think your father is? He got in his car this morning and drove away. Where'd he go?"

"I don't know. My parents don't always tell me where they're going."

Eden heard the note of abandonment. She remembered herself at thirteen: beginning her first year of boarding at Deerfield—homesick, friendless, barely passing chemistry, playing a game of counting how many days could go by without hearing herself speak out loud. Had her legs been as skinny as Claire's?

"But you must have ideas. Like you say, you're not a kid."

"A coffee shop." The words came out quickly. "Down in North Beach, in the city."

Eden picked up a pen and rolled it in her fingers. "Which one? Caffe Trieste on Vallejo Street? Caffe Greco on Columbus? Or the place with cannoli—Cavalli Cafe?"

"I don't know names. The last one with the cannoli."

"Cavalli." Eden made a note on the pad in front of her. "So why do you think he went there?"

"He always says if he had more time, he'd go there and drink one of those little cups of coffee and read a book."

"Good. That's a start." Eden watched Claire. The girl's tiny nails were painted purple and chewed below the fingertips. "Your father sounds like an interesting man."

"He's smart. He can recite all of Valentine's speech from *Two Gentlemen of Verona*. He taught it to me. 'What light is light, if Silvia be not seen? What joy is joy, if Silvia be not by?'"

Eden smiled. "'Except I be by Silvia in the night, there is no music in the nightingale.' Had to learn that one myself. Good thing to know by heart. So, when's the last time you saw your father?"

Claire blinked in surprise at Eden's recitation, then returned to the question. "I don't remember. Couple days ago, I guess."

Eden caught a hint of something in the girl's face, a dawning fear at the meaning of her own words. How long before this child, who was racing so fast toward adulthood, would let go of the role she was playing? Eden pressed on. "So you didn't see him last night?"

"He came home late."

"Do you remember what time?"

"Around nine thirty, I think. I was already in my room. But I—" Claire's face reddened.

"You what?"

"I went out in the upstairs hallway, and I heard him down in the family room on a phone. I wasn't trying to listen."

"I'm sure." Eden waited.

"He was talking to someone, and he sounded serious."

"Was it your mother? Could he have been talking to your mother?"

"No." The answer was definitive. "He sounded different. It was someone else."

"Do you remember if the phone rang before he talked?"

Claire frowned. "Yeah, it did. That's why I came out of my room."

"Okay." Eden made a note. "Do you remember anything your father said?"

"I don't know. He was downstairs. It's not like he was shouting or anything."

"I understand." She waited a beat, remembering what Eddie had taught her about spaces in interrogations. "It's okay to tell me if it helps us find your father."

Claire considered this. "He said, 'It'll be all right. Give it time. It'll be all right.' That's what I heard. I know because he says that to me sometimes when I'm worried about a test or something." Claire sat back, looking worn out.

Eden wondered at what any child knows of her parents, at how someone as young as Claire could distinguish her father's voice speaking to her mother from him speaking to anyone else. We are aware of the most intimate details about the people who share our homes, and at other times, we understand no more about them than a random woman or man in the street halfway around the world. Eden could see her own father, Dr. Donald Somers: white lab coat over dress shirt and tie, neat part down the left side of his hair, sad eyes behind wire-rim glasses. Radiologist by trade. A lifetime spent staring at shadows on film.

Once or twice a month seeing in the outline of a breast the irregular white space he was trained to find. "Let's go get lost," he'd say on their Sunday afternoon drives, winking at Eden, alone beside him on the front seat of the Lincoln Town Car. Only later did she think that, after forty years living in the same county in northeast Connecticut, he would never get lost. Later than that, she tried to understand the reason for the sadness in his eyes. She saw him now, staring at an empty point ahead on the rural road. "Malignancy. Do you know the word, Eden? From the Latin *male*, meaning badly, and *gnus*, meaning born."

Eden leaned back, trying not to be too obvious in use of the mirroring technique. "Does your father ever take you for drives in his car?"

"What'd you mean? Like shopping, to Target? Stuff like that?"

"No. I mean, just for fun."

Claire shook her head. "He doesn't have time. He's a teacher. He has to prepare for classes. He's a good father, but he has to work. He—"

Seeing the girl close to tears, Eden stepped in. "I know. I know. Teachers work hard. It's okay." She leaned across the table. "We're trying to find your father. Okay? We're doing everything we can. And you've been very helpful. You really have."

"Once he took me to Goat Rock." Claire's eyes filled and tears ran down her cheeks. "Do you know where that is? We stopped at a little restaurant and had clam chowder. It was just the two of us—not my mom and Jesse. On a Sunday, when he usually does his lesson plans. He said—" She wiped at her cheeks. "He said we were runaways."

(ii)

Coyle made notes on an evidence board—a brief profile of what the team knew about the missing man.

Paul Behrens (47). Schoolteacher. Married. Wife (Annie) nurse (45). Two children: Jesse (16); Claire (13). Brother: Michael (40). Sister: Beth Rigney (42). Small DMV and Facebook photos of each taped to the board.
Left behind: phone, lesson plan, friendship bracelet. No note. Clothes: White dress shirt, khakis, dark necktie, tan sports jacket. 2015 silver Elantra. CA license 6LDG429.
Three credit cards. Balances paid off. No unusual purchases. No activity in last 12 hours.
Employment history: Gregg Insurance—9 years. Brookwood Middle School—8 years.
House: 6th year, 30-year mortgage. Joint account = $12,000. $600 debt. Two car payments.
No arrest record. No domestic abuse. Problems in classroom? Health issues? Wife = alcoholism, infidelity? Son = drugs?
Phone: One call the night of May 2 to be traced. All photos deleted—why?
Social media: Facebook, Instagram, Twitter. Most frequent comments—Jean Cummings, Patty Aguilar.

Cases only came alive for Coyle once he mapped them on the evidence board. Something about physically writing the words made things real. At the start, the pieces on the board were flat: all the names, details equally important. Even after more than twenty cases, he had never found a magic key to them, like starting with the straight-edge pieces of a jigsaw puzzle.

The middle evidence board listed a timeline:

March 14:	Google search on sexual assault, Child Protective Services, molestation.
March 16:	Resignation letter. Not delivered?
April:	Classroom problem—12th Night play.
May 2:	ATM withdrawals $600 x 2. Why so much? Gasoline $42.

May 3:	Disappears. Why now?
6:00 a.m.	Jesse sees father.
7:15 a.m.	Behrens leaves. (home security camera capture of Behrens's face behind windshield)
8:32 a.m.	Text from principal to Annie.
8:45 a.m.	Annie calls principal.

Coyle had long resisted the new electronic evidence boards used on TV cop shows—giant, high-definition touch screens with pop-up windows. In Coyle's mind, VCI cases were about the darkest impulses of man. For that, you didn't want pixels; you wanted handwritten notes, scraps of paper—reminders you were human.

The third board contained leads:

April classroom problem?
Phone call Tuesday night. Awaiting caller ID.
Message: "It'll be all right. Give it time. It'll be all right."
Patty Aguilar: Most frequent called # on cell. Who is she?
Jean Cummings: Note in daily planner at 11:00 a.m. Inscription in book.
Friendship bracelet. Who is it from? Why does B. have it?
Unidentified man in classroom Wed. morning. Get security photo.
Cavalli Cafe? No.
Google Maps searches: Dillon Beach, Bodega, Salmon Creek.

As often happened, Eddie's voice ran in Coyle's mind: *All you need to know in a missing person case is where the guy is— coordinates on a map. You don't have to understand the man's marriage, why he hates his job, or his private thoughts or sexual preference. But you never know which of those other things will tell you where he is.*

Coyle had seen Eden face an evidence board without moving or speaking for thirty minutes. Everyone else was a little less intense. Rivas stood at the back wall and squinted across the room. Eddie was known to talk to a board. Some of Coyle's own best moments in VCI had been late-night sessions alone, writing notes, adding arrows—the parts of a case ping-ponging around his brain. The board became a Venn diagram with intersecting words, a still frame suddenly plucked out of a film racing past your eyes, a giant painting that engulfed you.

Early in the case, the information was young. Later it would grow up: witness statements, phone calls, credit card purchases, denials, confessions, lies. (That was the lesson of eight years of being a cop: everyone lied.) When it was over, if you succeeded, what you were chasing would be exposed—impossible plans, mistakes that couldn't be undone, thoughts about pulling a trigger. Then, Coyle thought, the stuff on the board, originally a list of facts, had the quality of signposts, all of them leading to answers if only you'd recognized them.

Now Coyle stared at one line on the middle board. "ATM withdrawals $600 x 2." Lot of cash. *What was the guy doing with it? Was it a key?* Coyle texted a note about the withdrawal to the team.

The VCI room phone rang, jolting Coyle from his concentration. He reached across two desks to pick it up.

The voice on the other end identified himself as Deputy Robert Dunfries of the Sheriff's Office. "I have information on your BOLO for Paul Behrens."

Was it over? Was it this easy? Coyle grabbed his laptop.

"I just now saw the BOLO. But before you issued it, I spoke with an individual who identified himself as Paul Behrens out near Valley Ford. It was (keyboard clicking)…9:12 a.m."

They weren't looking for a ghost after all. Behrens was alive. Or, at least he had been at nine o'clock. Coyle realized he'd stopped breathing. He covered the phone to mask his gasping for air. "What were the circumstances?" The question came out as a wheeze.

"Car pulled over. Driver on cell phone." Dunfries sounded younger than Coyle—not as many years listening to people lie. "Freestone Valley Ford Road. Narrow stretch, blind curve. Unsafe place to stop. I'll send you an incident report on the stop, but I wanted to call you first."

"But you spoke to him?"

"Yes, sir. He disconnected his call when he saw me. Gave me his driver's and registration."

"Did he say anything?" Coyle asked.

Keyboard clicking again. "I asked if he was having car trouble, and he said no. I also asked if he was lost, and he said no to that, too. Said he had an appointment."

"Appointment?" Coyle hated when other cops repeated one of his words, like he'd been imprecise. Still, he had to be sure. "That's the word he used?"

"Yes, sir. Appointment. Didn't say what or where it was."

"Which direction was he headed?"

"South. Toward Highway 1."

Coyle pictured the location in his mind—rolling hills, country road, intersection with Highway 1. Memory of a drive two years earlier with a college friend from the East Coast. "So from there, he could go east to Valley Ford or west to Bodega and the coast?"

"Correct. I didn't follow him. It took me a few minutes to add notes to the incident report. When I got to Highway 1, he was gone."

Mind racing, Coyle had one more thought. "Did you happen to see anything on the ground after the car pulled away?"

"No. But I didn't take a close look. The GPS coordinates are in my report."

Coyle thanked Dunfries and hung up. He stood and walked across the room to collect himself. As he paced, he texted Eddie with the news and made a request to the sergeant on duty to have a unit check the spot where the car was stopped. Back at his desk, Coyle read his notes. The description of Behrens using a cell phone confirmed Coyle's guess about a second pay-as-you-go phone. Who was Behrens talking to when Dunfries drove up? Patty Aguilar? Coyle added "9:12 a.m. Valley Ford" to the timeline.

Coyle found a county map in his desk drawer and opened it. Pinholes from a previous case made a kind of constellation. Suspects? Victim bodies? He couldn't remember. He taped the map to a wall and put colored pins at the Behrenses' house, Brookwood Middle School, and the location near Valley Ford.

He held a finger on the last pin and looked at the roads east and west. West, he thought. He ran his fingers from Valley Ford to the coast. From there, Behrens would have two choices—south to Bodega Bay or north to Jenner. But five hours had passed since the stop. Miles of roads in either direction. Turnouts, parking lots, stores, restaurants. He looked at Behrens's Google Maps searches. All the locations were on the coast, from south to north.

Coyle ran his finger across the map, searching for something on the paper's surface.

Chapter Eight

(i)

Frames watched Jesse trying to look at ease in the interview room. The detective had known kids like Jesse in high school—the ones who skipped growing up, appropriated some part of adulthood, like sex or pills, and acted like they had shit figured out. Frames conceded some admiration for the guys—they were always guys—for the work they put into it.

"Your mother suggested we talk." Frames spread open a notebook. "She gave us permission to talk to you alone. That okay?"

"I guess. It's not like I know stuff."

"Maybe you'll remember when we talk."

Jesse shrugged, not committing to it.

"Has your father done or said anything unusual in the last few days?"

"Like what?"

"I don't know. You tell me. Has he been worried or nervous?"

"Over the weekend, he was, like, pissed off a lot. On Saturday morning, he flipped out because he couldn't find his car keys."

"Did he say what was wrong?"

"No. Why would he tell me?"

The kid sounded as if he was defending against an accusation that hadn't been made. *What was that about?* "Who would he tell?" Frames asked. "Your mother?"

"I don't know." Jesse shook his head. "I mean, I doubt it. They don't talk much."

"Someone at his school?"

"Maybe. There's a teacher—Jean Cummings. He talks about her. And another one—Patty something." Jesse met Frames's eyes for the first time.

Frames weighed the boy's look. Was he taking some satisfaction in helping out a cop or just metering out what he knew? "What else did you notice?"

"I went downstairs last night about ten. He was sitting in the living room. Not reading or watching TV. Just sitting there."

"Did he say anything?"

"Not really. He looked at me like he wanted me to get lost."

"Do you remember what time your mother came home?"

"She wasn't around when I went to bed at twelve thirty."

"What about this morning?" Frames looked at the open notebook. "You saw your father at six in the upstairs bathroom. Is that right?"

"Yeah. He was dressed up, which was kind of weird."

"And he was crying?" Frames consulted the notebook again.

"I said I *thought* he was crying."

"What else?"

"Nothing. That's it." Jesse sat back, done.

"Really? That's it?" Frames glanced at the time on his phone. He was in a grouchy mood. He'd spent the last two hours doing online research on Paul Behrens, as ordered by Eddie. His least favorite part of VCI work. Pulling together the bits and pieces that may or may not help you find a missing person. When Frames complained, Coyle, of course, told him recent studies showed data analysis was now law enforcement's number one tool, over surveillance and interrogation. Frames didn't buy it. Of all that kind of work, he hated researching social media the most, he said. It reminded him of searching a suspect's pockets—putting your hands on stuff you wish you hadn't.

At that point Eden told a story about Sacramento homicide cops finding a serial killer using Facebook. When Frames asked her how Paul Behrens's Facebook recipe for kale salad was supposed to help locate the missing man, Eden told him to look harder. She said every TV cop show has a scene where the detective stares into space and suddenly figures out who the killer is or, in this case, where the missing man is. According to Eden, the phenomenon was called *anagnorisis*, a Greek word that comes from Aristotle. It meant recognition and described the moment in any story where the character sees the meaning of what's happening. Frames said in real life a guy disappears, and a week later a citizen finds his rotting body in a field. Case solved. But now as he recalled it, Frames hated the frequency with which Eden was right about things.

Frames looked at Jesse. "Do you know who Aristotle is?"

"Aristotle? What…" Jesse frowned with impatience.

"Greek philosopher. No last name as far as I know."

"The fuck you talking about?"

Frames started again. "So…your father goes missing, and you don't have any idea where he is or what he's doing?"

"I told you. I don't know." Jesse was frustrated now, his voice rising. "I'm his son. He doesn't tell me things."

"Okay. Okay." Frames held up his hands. "How about this?"

He reached under the table and grabbed the evidence bag containing Jesse's storage box of twenty-dollar bills. He laid it on the table, slowly aligning it parallel with the table edge.

Jesse snuck a look at it and then faced Frames.

"Uh-oh." Frames laid one hand on the bag.

Jesse glared back silently.

"Oh, come on." Frames smiled. "That's what you're going with? Really?"

"You're not allowed to take shit like that."

"Actually we are allowed to take shit like that. That's why it's here."

"You're an asshole."

"I get that a lot. Usually right before guys go to prison. The thing is, I'm the one with the seven grand, and you're not." Frames shook his head. "Jesse, what's happening here is, your philosophy—the Everyone-But-Me-Is-Stupid philosophy—it's not working."

Frames had a gripe about entitled kids who dug themselves into holes. Raised by a single mom, scraping through high school, joining the Marines, he believed in the toughness he earned. Guys like Jesse had contempt for that route, his class. "You need to get over that," Frames's girlfriend, Natalie, had told him. "You're missing the big picture. The entitlement of middle-class teenagers is a symptom, not the issue. What you should be worried about is sea-level rise, economic inequality, income stagnation." Natalie was a poli-sci major at the JC and always quick to go one-on-one with Frames.

"I don't see income stagnation every day." Frames started every argument with Natalie on solid ground. "What I see are upper-middle-class kids dealing weed, because they can."

"But what's at the core of that?"

"Income stagnation?" Frames was unconvinced.

"You want me to show you the data?"

This was the exasperating thing about Natalie. She had an eyebrow stud she couldn't justify, a tat on her left bicep that took forever to explain, and bangs cut perversely too short. But then she'd run her fingers through those bangs that he was powerless to fix and offer to show Frames the data. Show you the data? His whole life, people had been offering to show Frames the data.

Frames let his focus come back to Jesse, who was staring at his hands on the table. "The important point for you to remember is that we know you're selling weed. Once we find it, we can charge you with selling without a license and selling to minors. That last one's a felony that'll get you five to seven years."

"That's crap."

"You're pretty sure of yourself, aren't you." Frames arched his back and stretched. "Since it's your first offense, you probably won't serve time. But it'll still be a pain. Your family's going to have to hire a lawyer. That costs a fortune. The case will take months in the courts. And even if you get off, it'll stay with you forever. Every school application, job interview. Cops come to your house unannounced for parole checks, bust you for having a beer. Like I say, a pain." As he finished, Frames liked the sound of his own words, even as he imagined Natalie pointing out the injustice of the court delays and the stigma of a conviction.

Jesse looked back with determined disinterest. "Fuck you."

"Yeah. Fuck you," Frames said. "That's great. That's...profound. I hardly ever hear that. Tell me what you know about your father, and we'll try to keep you out of juvie."

"This whole thing is crap, you know that?"

"Probably." Frames suddenly felt bone-tired, like after one of those five-mile runs in the mud back in Basic. He had nothing to show for the last ten minutes. From the start, he'd let the kid get under his skin. Then he'd gone old-school, heavy-handed. *Tell me, Steve,* the voice of Eddie Mahler rang in his ear, *when does that work?* He wished he could begin again.

Jesse broke the silence. "A guy was stalking my dad."

Frames wasn't sure he heard it. "How'd you know?"

"I saw him. Across the street from our house, the last couple weeks."

"You're sure the guy wasn't after *you?*"

"My dad told me. He said the same asshole had been there before."

"Who was he?"

Jesse shook his head. "My dad didn't know, but he said he knew what it was about and he'd take care of it."

"When he told you that, did your father sound frightened, angry? What?"

"I don't know. Determined, I guess. One night I saw the car across the street. I took a knife to talk to him, but he drove off."

"What'd he look like?"

"I never saw his face."

"You get a license?"

"There wasn't one. It was a Honda Civic, a couple years old, dark gray."

Frames made a note and tapped his pen against the pad. "Okay, Jesse. My gut tells me if your father told you about this…stalker, he was willing to confide in you. He treated you like an equal. So I'm thinking he also talked to you this morning. He wasn't just standing at the sink crying, was he? What'd he say?" Frames tried to will Jesse to look up at him. "You understand we're trying to find your father? Make sure he's safe? You want that, don't you?"

Jesse snorted. "You guys…you're good at threatening people. But you don't always get what you want."

"Okay. Good for you." Frames sighed. "You got that off your chest."

A minute went by, the wheels in Jesse's head clearly turning. Finally he spread his fingers on the tabletop. "This morning my dad said this thing. He said, sometimes it's like there isn't enough air in the world for all of us to breathe. The air you need is the same air the guy next to you needs, and you both can't have it."

Frames squeezed his pen, unable to write. In the quiet of the room, the only sound was the air conditioner's hum.

"Then he reminded me of a night when I was little and he read me a bedtime story. When the story was over, I asked if that was the *real* story." Jesse smiled thinly, remembering. "So this morning, my dad said, 'What you'll hear about me isn't the real story. Wait for the real one.'"

Frames watched Jesse look up and saw in his eyes the small boy, propped up in bed, waiting for his father.

(ii)

(WEDNESDAY, 2:41 P.M.)

The sign at the gate read Aurora Manor: A Residential Care Facility. Inside the gate, at the end of a curved driveway, lay a one-story ranch-style house. The house was fronted with evenly spaced Japanese maples and an overall air of guardedness.

Parking close to the house, Mahler read Coyle's text about the report of Behrens's car near Valley Ford. It was good to know the missing man was alive at nine o'clock and to have at least a modest narrowing of his possible location. Mahler thought of one of his favorite mystery novels—Kate Atkinson's *Started Early, Took My Dog*. In that story, the detective, Jackson Brodie, is on a missing person case. Early on, Brodie muses that although his specialty is looking for people, his gift is not necessarily finding them. Still, Brodie decides, in his typical self-effacing style, half the equation is better than none.

Maybe, Mahler thought, that's all his team was doing—looking for Paul Behrens, not necessarily finding him.

The young woman who met Mahler at the door introduced herself as Franny Hastings. She had brown hair trimmed in a boyish cut and wore white trousers and a baggy, untucked shirt with the sleeves rolled up. She looked at Mahler more directly than anyone else in his memory, as if trying to make up her mind. Her eyes were russet-colored and striking. Then she smiled, and for an instant Mahler forgot why he was there.

Just inside, they paused in a small reception alcove and sat facing each other in a pair of brocade wing chairs. "I'm the house manager, or the chief officer, as the guys call me." Franny pushed her sleeves farther up her arms. "In your phone call you said you wanted to talk to Michael Behrens about his brother, Paul? Is that right?"

"Yes. Paul's wife reported him missing."

Franny's face lined with concern. "I'm sorry to hear that. Paul was just here early this morning to visit Michael. The brothers are close." She turned and looked down the building's long corridor, then back at Mahler. "Before you talk to Michael, I need to give you some background. He's one of nine service veterans who live here, all with traumatic brain injury, or TBI. Are you familiar with it?"

"A little bit," Mahler conceded. "I've seen it on TV."

"Yeah. It's all too common with soldiers fighting in Iraq and Afghanistan. When their vehicles hit a roadside bomb, the explosion can be unbelievably powerful, capable of driving an engine block through the hood of a truck. For the soldiers inside the vehicle, the explosion generates a blast wave that literally shakes their brains against the inside of the skull. It causes irreversible neurological damage."

Franny checked that Mahler was following before she continued. "Michael has moderate TBI. In Afghanistan, he was riding in a military vehicle, an RG-31. It's like a super-heavy armored vehicle, specially built to survive mine explosions. Michael's RG-31 ran over an IED. The vehicle was blown in the air, and Michael sustained a severe concussion. TBI is rated on something called the Glasgow Coma Score, or GCS. Michael's GCS is 9. He lost consciousness for more than thirty minutes and had post-traumatic amnesia for more than twenty-four hours."

"So how's that show up?"

"Good question. Bad headaches and memory loss, mostly. It's subtle. You look at him, you talk to him, he seems normal. But he has trouble remembering what he did an hour ago or yesterday."

"Is he able to answer my questions?"

"Maybe, maybe not. It's hard to say. After I got your call, I told Michael his brother is missing and that you wanted to ask a few questions. So he's ready for you."

"Any advice?"

"Don't patronize him. These guys have a kind of antenna for that. They don't want your pity. They're smart and tough. Be honest. You try to spare Michael, he'll see through it. His rank is sergeant, by the way."

"Okay. Good to know. Anything else?"

"Don't try to stop him from calling you sir. He calls me sir. It's ingrained in these guys. It's also a sign of the respect he has for you and that he expects you to have for him."

As a police officer, Mahler had known men and women damaged by violence. But he hadn't spent much time with service members with serious head trauma. He believed the country owed these wounded men and women more than they received, and he found it an irony of modern war that so many of them returned with their bodies intact but their minds devastated.

Michael Behrens sat alone on a redwood deck at the back of the building. His head was bent over an open book.

When Franny and Mahler approached, Michael stood. He was a tall man with a shaggy black beard and an erect bearing.

Franny introduced the men, and Michael squeezed Mahler's hand. "CO said you were coming."

Mahler pointed to the book. "What're you reading, Sergeant?"

"Beginning coding—HTML and CSS." Michael put in a card to keep his place. "Have to start somewhere, don't you?" He winked at Franny and returned to his chair.

Franny smiled back and excused herself.

Mahler sat in a deck chair beside Michael. "I understand you saw your brother, Paul, this morning?" He pulled a notebook and pen from his jacket pocket.

"Yes, sir. Zero seven thirty hours. He always comes by early, before work. He knows I don't sleep much."

Something in the former soldier's words sounded unusual, although Mahler couldn't quite put his finger on it. The rhythm, the space between the words, was slightly off. "How'd he seem this morning? Did you notice anything unusual?"

"He was nervous, kept checking his phone."

"Did he say why? Was he late for school or an appointment?"

"No, sir. Nothing like that. I think a problem came up in the last few days that was…new."

"Do you think the problem was at home, with his family, or at school?"

"Paul didn't say, but I had the sense it was one of his students. If it was Annie or the kids, he would've told me. We talk about that stuff all the time. He can't tell you about students because of the whole privacy deal. And it's gotta be something out of the ordinary. After teaching this long, he knows how to handle most of the crap that comes up."

"Did your brother tell you where he was headed when he left here?"

"No, sir. I assumed it was to school."

"Paul withdrew a large amount of cash yesterday. Do you know why—what he was planning to do?"

"No. Sorry. He didn't tell me."

Mahler made a note on his pad. "Did Paul say anything else this morning? Anything at all?"

"He said he knew I was going to get a place of my own soon and have a car. He said it just like that—like he wouldn't be here for it."

Mahler saw the young man's face suddenly tense, his eyes focused in the distance. Watching him, it was possible to see something playing across the soldier's mind. His expression flinched. In another instant it was gone, as if erased. Mahler waited for Michael's attention to return. "What'd you say at that point?"

For a moment, Michael couldn't answer. "I don't remember right now." He looked out at the yard behind the house. "I think I—I probably said I wanted him to help me pick out a car. We did that together when I was in high school."

"Your brother helped you buy a car?"

"Yeah," Michael laughed. "It was a little Volkswagen Jetta. Six-speed. The color was called Black Pearl. And the kids who had it before me lowered the frame and rebuilt the engine. It was small and underpowered, but I loved that car."

Mahler smiled. "Tell me, Michael. When your brother wants to be alone, what does he like to do?"

"That's it. He likes to go for drives. Out in the country. Play crazy music. He listens to the same music as his students. Plays it loud, just like they do. Helps him think, I guess."

"You're close to your brother, aren't you?"

"He always watched over me. Made sure I did my homework. Woke me for Saturday soccer." Michael looked at Mahler. "Even now he keeps an eye on me."

Mahler stood and handed Michael a business card. "One last question, Sergeant. Where do *you* think your brother went?"

Michael raised himself from his chair to read the card. "I don't know for sure. Like I said, he didn't tell me. But right now, I think he's in the ocean."

Mahler waited to see if Michael would say more. "The ocean? In the ocean?"

"Yes, sir. You asked me, and it's just what I think."

The two men shook hands, and when Mahler looked back from the doorway, Michael had already returned to his chair and book.

Mahler met Franny in the corridor near the front door.

She stood, arms crossed, facing Mahler. "Anything helpful?"

"Interesting young man. Thoughtful."

"Michael's a great guy. He's made a lot of progress. He could be a programmer if he keeps at it."

"It sounds like Michael interpreted Paul's comments this morning to mean his brother's not coming back."

Franny nodded. "These men have been so often confronted with the reality of a fellow soldier not returning from a mission that they've come to expect it. Even if a friend or family member leaves for a short time, they can interpret it as permanent, final. I realize that may sound odd, but it's part of a psychological reaction to death."

"I can...imagine it," Mahler said. As he listened to Franny, for an instant he felt himself again in one of the smooth leather chairs opposite the department's psychologist, the only sound behind their voices, the slow-moving paddles of the ceiling fan. In the air, the minty fragrance of the doctor's tea.

> **Dr. Schafer:** Your mother died when you were, what, six?
>
> **Mahler:** That's right. She was sick for a long time before she passed.
>
> **S:** Do you remember how you felt?
>
> **M:** After she died, people said it was for the best. I think they meant she didn't have to suffer. But at the time, I thought it meant she decided to die.
>
> **S:** How did you feel about that?
>
> **M:** I felt someone made a mistake and forgot about Diane and me. In the back seat of the car driving home from the funeral, I looked out the window and thought we didn't have a home to go back to.
>
> **S:** Your father was there, wasn't he?
>
> **M:** Not a lot. He worked in the city.
>
> **S:** So you felt alone?
>
> **M:** I remember one day using a whole loaf of bread to make sandwiches so we didn't run out.
>
> **S:** You thought it was up to you?
>
> **M:** I thought there were no more days in front.
>
> **S:** Days in front?
>
> **M:** It was just the way the words came to my child's mind. It was the future. I didn't think there was a future.

Mahler pulled himself back to the present and looked down at his pad of paper. "The weird thing is," he told Franny, "at the end, Michael said he thinks his brother's in the ocean. Not *at* the ocean, *in* the ocean. And he said it like he was serious."

"I'm sure he was serious," Franny said. "Michael's very intuitive.

His job in Afghanistan was as an IED hunter. What the guys call a 'window licker.' He sat at the forward window in an RG-31 and looked for explosives buried in the road ahead. Men in that assignment learn to see ordinary sticks or rocks in the road that are disguised pressure plates. Michael was good. Most crews had incidents in the first three months. Michael's direct blast didn't happen until his tenth month in the country. He has a highly developed skill for sensing what you can't see."

"Even with his TBI? Is he talking literally?"

"Yes. Literally. Lieutenant Mahler, you have to understand. These guys don't do metaphors. Wouldn't occur to them. They were in a world more real than you and I will ever see. When they say something, they mean it. You know what? If I was looking for Paul Behrens, I'd drive out to the coast."

Mahler reached out his hand. "Okay. Thanks for your help, Ms. Hastings."

"You're welcome, Lieutenant Mahler." Franny shook his hand, then held it. "By the way, if you're going to stare at my eyes so much, you might as well say something nice about them."

"Wow." Mahler's face reddened at being caught staring at a woman for the second time that day. "Guilty as charged. I didn't know I was being so obvious."

Franny laughed and let go of Mahler's hand. "Occupational hazard. I live with nine guys who don't talk much. My job is to notice what's not being said."

"You'd make a good cop."

"Tell you what." Franny opened the front door. "When you think of what you were going to say, why don't you come back and tell me."

Chapter Nine

(i)

Eden saw the visitor in the ground-floor lobby. Black suit, starched white shirt, briefcase at his feet. He stood when he saw her and extended his hand. "Jonathan Macon. Phoenix."

Whatever you felt about the agency, you had to be impressed by the consistency of training. The guy had studied her file, seen photographs, made himself able to identify her now even with shorter, lighter hair and casual clothes.

Macon was clean-shaven, with the same taut posture she had come to associate with all young FBI agents. It was as if each possessed an internal winch that stretched them tight every morning. His face was young, freckled, straight off the prairie. Eden guessed somewhere west of Wichita. Criminal science degree, master's in psychology. Someone in his family had been a cop. That last part was in his eyes: belief in the "mission."

Eden shook his hand and led him upstairs to the second-floor interview room.

Macon waited for her to sit first. He laid his briefcase on the table between them.

Eden wondered what he knew about her, how much he'd been told. Had he been read in on her failure? Or did the FBI hold that back? "Your email was not specific about the purpose of our meeting."

Macon smiled. "We thought it better to explain it in person."

Eden thought about that "we." She imagined Macon's briefing—four to five senior agents around a table, her own name somewhere in a slide deck.

Macon leaned toward her. "I grew up in Garden City, Kansas, Detective Somers. Western part of the state. Of course, when I say that to anyone in law enforcement, they always think of the *In Cold Blood* murders. Actually that incident happened in a small town just west of us called Holcomb. Anyway, the Macons have always been wheat farmers. Except my granddad—he was a cop. And what you learn in wheat farming is timing. Timing's everything—from tilling to planting to harvest to selling when the price is favorable. A few days either way is the difference between a good year and a lousy year. And right here—this is about timing. It's the whole reason I'm here now."

It was a practiced gambit. Eden imagined him coming up with it while he gazed out the window on the two-hour flight from Phoenix. All part of a setup for her.

"Agent Macon." Eden raised her hand. She waited a beat. "Jonathan. I appreciate all this. But I can save you some trouble. I'm not interested. Whatever it is, I'm not interested."

"It's funny." Macon smiled. "They said you'd say those very words, and now to actually hear them, it's...funny."

"You could take a day or two before you head back, enjoy

the local attractions. Go out to the coast, see the Pacific. Taste some wines. The old-vine zinfandel along the Russian River is worth—"

"This is about the Highway 60 serial killer—your case." Macon blinked. He looked like he hadn't meant to say it this way. "Nine women killed in five states along that highway from 2013 to 2016. Same method of killing in each one: asphyxiation from dirt stuffed in the mouth. Chief suspect a truck driver named Albert McKinley Jory. Four days ago, New Mexico State Police arrested Jory for the murder of Cassie Stanton, one of the New Mexico victims. Indictment's expected tomorrow, maybe later today."

Eden found herself nodding, struggling to control her expression. She had expected something like this eventually, although she might have guessed he'd say the arrest was only planned, not already executed.

"We'd like to ask your help with some recent developments. But we understand you're settled in here. We're not asking you to do anything that would detract from your duties here. I believe Director Kinsella spoke with Lieutenant Mahler."

Eden let thirty seconds of silence pass while she looked across the table at the young agent. After twenty, she saw him give up and look toward the door. When she finally spoke, Eden asked, "Do you know what I did on this case?"

Macon hesitated, unsure if he was expected to answer.

"The Highway 60 Killer. Did they tell you what I did on this case?" Louder this time.

Macon cleared his throat. "I believe you discovered several… aspects…regarding the victims in New Mexico and Texas."

"Did they also tell you what happened to me?"

"No." Macon looked at the tabletop. "I mean yes. They said you were…affected by…the evidence."

How much did Macon know? She looked at Macon's

briefcase lying on the table in front of her. Did he know about the Mount Holyoke semester she worked on the Jory case— esophageal spasms in the dining hall, screaming in the North Rocky shower, the dead women visiting her dreams? Or was it just the time at the Bureau—panic attacks, Ativan prescriptions, weight loss, sleeping with a gun, submitting her resignation a year and a half into the job?

Eden stood and backed away from the table. "I can show you out."

Macon looked up at her. "He knows your name. Jory...he knows your name. He said it during questioning. He has your personal information, and he said something about you." Then he added, as if to clarify, "On Sunday."

The room swam in front of Eden. She reached for the chair- back to steady herself. "How could he possibly know my name? I was an analyst reviewing investigation notes. I never met him. My name doesn't appear in the case reports. Unless someone made copies of the emails and Jory's lawyer saw them."

Macon swallowed, unnerved at how quickly Eden was talking. "We don't know. It may have been someone on a state task force. There wasn't always good...discipline."

A loud roaring filled Eden's head. She thought of all the work she put into breaking her mind and heart free from the case: nine months of therapy (first with the guy, then the woman), meditation exercises, biofeedback, early-morning distance run- ning, more Ativan.

The room seemed suddenly too small. She walked slowly to the door, feeling the way with her feet, then turned back to the table. "What personal information? What'd he say? What'd Jory say about me?"

Macon puffed his cheeks and let the air out. "I'm afraid I can't discuss that kind of detail unless—"

"I come back." Eden looked again at Macon's briefcase and knew it was empty.

"Unless you agree to come back," Macon repeated. His shoulders relaxed for the first time and he smiled. "The Bureau would like you to come down to the San Francisco Field Office and meet with Senior Agent Raymond Chalmers. Agent Chalmers can bring you up to speed."

"What's it about, Macon?"

"I can't say. But you're going to want to do this, Detective Somers. It's for your…safety."

Eden sat again. After a moment she caught Macon's attention. "When I first arrived at Quantico, I remember being amazed at what you guys know. The surveillance, the data, the labs, the history…all the…incremental detail. It was unbelievable, like something amassed by a room full of computers. But by the time I left, what really surprised me was something else, something more important. It was everything you didn't know."

(ii)

(WEDNESDAY, 3:52 P.M.)

The whole meal was odd. First Jesse brought home a pizza without being asked to do it. The three of them—Annie, Jesse, and Claire—were together at the kitchen table. Too early for dinner. Pizza with strange toppings, like artichoke hearts and purple onions—although Annie had to admit it was delicious. And she was hungry, on her third slice. When was the last time she'd been hungry—and sober?

They ate in silence for a long time.

Finally Claire spoke. "Should we save a couple of slices? You know, in case—"

"In case what?" Jesse reached into the box. "In case he comes back?"

"Yeah. He probably hasn't eaten all day. Right?"

"If that happens, we'll get another one." Annie looked at the other two. "To celebrate."

Annie felt the disconnectedness. They were three people whose husband and father was missing. It was the worst day of their lives. But here they were, like actors in a scene, playing characters eating pizza. As if nothing had happened.

Claire poured more Coke in her glass and reached across the table to fill her mother's glass. "This afternoon, when we got home, I thought I saw Daddy in the hallway. Just for a second. Then he wasn't there. Is that like a ghost?"

"No. I know what you mean." Annie raised her glass to thank her daughter. "But it's not a ghost. It's like an after-image thing. I don't know what it's called. We're so used to seeing him that our memory, something in our brain, puts him there. It's because we want to see him. We expect to see him."

"You two are nuts, you know that?" Jesse snorted. "I haven't seen an after-image or anything. He's not here. And you know what else? The cops don't have a clue. Not A Clue. You could tell by the way the cop talked to me."

"What'd they ask you?" Claire turned to Jesse. "The woman cop talked to me. I forget her name. She wanted to know where I thought Daddy went. I said that coffee shop he loves in North Beach, and she wrote it down." Claire replayed the way Eden had watched her while they talked, like the cop lady was trying to pick up signals from Claire's mind across the table.

"I had the guy with short hair who was trying to act all street." Jesse's anger returned at Frames for reaching under the table to grab the box of twenties, proud of getting a jump. "A real asshole."

The two of them waited for Annie to describe her interview. "Don't use that word. I don't like it." Annie felt herself fighting the shakes. "And let's not talk about the police." She wanted to go back to the surreal scene where they were three characters eating dinner. She dropped a half-eaten slice on her plate.

Claire watched her mother. "Where do you really think he is? I mean *really*. Do you think he left us?"

Annie took a deep breath. Playing this part was an effort. "I don't know. Your father wouldn't leave us. I think he wanted to be alone. Something happened in his classroom, and he wanted to be alone."

Jesse shook his head. "No. That's not right. Why wouldn't he leave a note? He always leaves those little Post-its on the kitchen table when he's going to be late. Remember?"

"Yeah. With those goofy cartoons he draws at the bottom." Claire laughed. "Like, if he was going to be in a meeting, the cartoon would be him sitting in a chair, with Z's coming out of his head like he was asleep."

Jesse joined in. "Or, that one he drew when it was play practice, and the cartoon man had his mouth open real wide."

"What would you do if he walked in?" Claire narrowed her eyes at her brother. All the things in her head were spilling out. "Like right now? Would you, like, flip out?"

"I'd say, what the fuck? I mean, really? Are you kidding me?"

"No you wouldn't." Claire kicked him under the table. "You wouldn't say that if Daddy walked in right now."

"We'd be glad to see him." Annie stood and shoved back her chair. "We all would. And he's coming back. I know he is. Let's stop talking about it." Tears formed at the corners of her eyes. She grabbed the plates off the table and carried them to the sink.

Claire joined her mother, taking the plates her mother scraped and stacking them in the dishwasher. She watched

Annie until she saw her mother stop crying. Leaning close, she whispered, "Mommy, could I have two hundred dollars for something?"

Annie sighed. "That's a lot of money, sweetheart. With your father being gone, we need to... I mean, we just have to wait before we spend money."

"I know, I know. But it's actually for something I need right now. Clothes for this thing at school Friday."

"What kind of clothes? Two hundred dollars? Really, Claire?"

"It's not for clothes," Jesse called across the room. "It's something else."

"How would you know?" Claire hated the way her brother always figured stuff out. Jesse was like a spy. Even when she was his age, she probably wouldn't know what he knew.

"I just do. Your daughter's buying drugs. The kids at her school are dealing tabs of Oxy."

"No. It's not drugs. *You're* the one's dealing drugs."

"Claire, tell me the truth." Annie turned from the sink to face her daughter. "What do you need the money for?"

"Clothes. It's a school dance. You can look on the website. I don't have anything to wear."

Annie went back to wiping the countertop. She felt sick now. The pizza on top of her withdrawal left her nauseated. "Well, I'm not giving you two hundred dollars for clothes. You'll have to make do."

"Then you'll be sorry."

"I get it." Jesse stood and approached Claire. "You really don't want drugs. It's something else. Something to do with your old friend Bri Bennett. Right? I know those kids. They're into all kinds of bad shit."

"Just shut up, okay? Just shut up." Claire felt the conversation spinning out of control. Jesse was wrecking everything, as usual.

"Claire, tell us why you need the money." Annie tried to hold her daughter's shoulders but let her pull away. "Why will I be sorry?"

Claire backed herself into a corner of the kitchen to face what was left of her family. "Bri said she and her friends hacked into your and Daddy's phones." She squeezed her fists and struggled to get the words out between gasps for air. "They got pictures of you and Daddy doing stuff."

"What stuff?" Annie felt a sudden chill. "There's nothing on my phone."

"I don't know. They wanted to show me, but I didn't want to see. They just said you were…hot. That's what they said. And Daddy's into something twisted. And if I don't give them two hundred dollars by Friday, they'll post the pictures on this Instagram site called Little Secrets."

"Oh shit." Jesse whistled. He pulled out his phone and tapped the screen. "I know that site. Everybody knows it."

Annie sat back at the table. "I'm not going to pay them. I don't care what pictures they have. That Bri's always been a nasty little piece of work. I won't give her money. We…this family has enough going on right now."

Jesse looked up from his phone. "I'll take care of it."

"No. You will not lay a hand on that girl." Annie faced her son. "That'll only mean more trouble."

"I won't touch her. I promise." Jesse smiled. "I know what to do. Those kids are punks. You won't have to pay them, and they won't post the pictures. Trust me."

Chapter Ten

(i)

"Who's the fat guy on the steps?" Frames looked through a pair of Leica binoculars at the address under surveillance. He and Prater had been sitting in an unmarked car in the Olive Park neighborhood for an hour and a half. They were waiting for the arrival of a white Tahoe and a dark-colored F-150, which according to a CI were bringing drugs from Fresno and East Palo Alto. Buckley and Noah Hernandez, the head of the NIT unit, were waiting in a car at the opposite end of the block. The two cars were connected with wireless mikes.

"You'll have to be more specific," Prater said. "They're all fat." Her head rested against the driver-side window. She didn't bother to open her eyes. The two vehicles were late, and all four detectives were well past their shifts.

"Nearest to us. White T-shirt. Gray hair."

"Luis Ramirez," Hernandez said. "One of the uncles.

Wholesale guy. Once the drivers get here, Luis will handle receiving the drugs. The other guy is Ramon Cruz. Muscle. Arrested for assault last year."

"Who's at the top of the chain?" Frames wished he had a notebook and pen to take notes. Or would Prater tease him about that? He imagined a kind of family tree. Like the kings and queens of England. In this case, the drug dealers of West Santa Rosa.

"The grandfather's Francisco Medina, but he's been out of the picture the last few years. Had a bout of colon cancer two years ago. His son is Julio Medina, El Jefe. Styles himself a businessman. Dresses in suits. Owns an insurance agency without any customers. We might see him today. He likes to stay involved in the day-to-day, keep everyone on their toes."

"So where's our friend Jorge Lopez?"

"Good question. No one on our team has seen him for three days. Before that, he was everywhere. Took care of the street dealers."

"Starting to worry about the guy," Buckley said. "Something's wrong. Especially since he's not bonking his girlfriend Cervantes."

"He'll turn up." Hernandez again. "By the way, Steve, I noticed VCI is looking for someone named Paul Behrens. We track street dealers, and one of them has come onto our radar with that name—Jesse Behrens."

"Yeah. He's the missing man's son. Deals weed. I interviewed him a few hours ago."

"I hope someone talks to him. Guys like him in the trenches are pretty expendable. They're the ones who do time."

Frames looked back at the address and watched Luis light a cigarette and stand to stretch his legs. "What's the plan when the vehicles arrive?"

"Watch and take lots of pictures." Prater gave up on her nap and squinted down the street.

"Not making arrests?"

"It's not that simple. We have to make sure we know what we got, that we actually see the merchandise."

Frames felt himself the student on the team. It was like watching a new sport, like curling, for the first time and having the rules explained.

"How'd your interview go at the Sheriff's Office?" Prater asked.

Frames's mind ran back to the small interview room and the impassive face of the deputy sitting across from him. "A lot of questions. They didn't tell me anything, of course. It'll all be in a report. But I think what I said matched Evan, Lonnie, and Cervantes. They're still reviewing the camera footage. The main thing is I'm not on administrative leave, and they gave me my gun back. Which must mean something."

"You'll be okay, Steve," Hernandez said.

"By the way," Prater said, "one of our informants told us a little more about the swordsman, Miguel Gonzalez. A couple weeks ago Gonzalez was promoted to be part of the family muscle, and it went to the guy's head—such as it was. He started telling the crews he was descended from Aztec warriors. He wanted to carry around one of those ancient wooden swords with embedded razor-sharp stones that the Aztecs used to decapitate the horses of Spanish soldiers. But, since no one's made that kind of weapon in four hundred years, he settled for the rapiers that he used to stab you. With the PCP in his blood stream, he must have mistaken Lucia Cervantes and you for enemies of the Aztec Empire."

Buckley sighed loudly into his mike. "That right there is part of the failure of discipline under Julio. Francisco wouldn't have permitted that stuff. The old man was all about not attracting attention."

Frames looked back down the street. "I wish that fucking Durango wasn't parked there. I can't see the front of the house."

Prater smiled. "Maybe you can go over and ask Ramon to move it."

"Okay. Heads up." Hernandez marshaling the troops. "We've got a Tahoe coming this way. It's behind you, Prater. Driving slowly. White. California license 6BGJ788."

Prater waited until the vehicle had passed her car and then shot photographs of the Tahoe while it parked in front of the address.

The two men on the steps of the address watched the car without moving. Once the vehicle had stopped, the driver emerged: a tall, slim man in jeans, plaid shirt, and straw cowboy hat.

Prater took photos of the man as he turned toward her and walked to the rear of the Tahoe. "Anybody recognize this guy?"

"Not a local," Buckley said. "We can check with Fresno PD or the feds."

Luis and Ramon walked slowly to the Tahoe and shook hands with the driver. The three men talked for several minutes. The driver rested one of his boots on the Tahoe's bumper and glanced up the street in the direction of Frames and Prater. He said something that made the other two men laugh. Luis took out his phone and made a call.

"Nobody's in a hurry, are they?" Frames said. "Not exactly FedEx."

"Relax," Prater said. "Wait for it."

"You sure this guy brought drugs? Where are they?" Frames had always been an impatient student. Whatever it was— literature, history, algebra—he wanted it to move faster.

"They're there."

All three men leaned against the Tahoe and smoked cigarettes. After five minutes, a red BMW parked in front of the Durango. A young man in baggy jeans and leather jacket emerged. He walked back to the trio, where he exchanged hand grabs with Luis and Ramon.

Prater shot photos of him. "You know this guy, Noah?"

A pause while Hernandez studied the new arrival. "No. Have to ask our snitches. But if I had to guess, I'd say a cousin. Obviously known to the other local boys."

While Frames looked through the binoculars at the men standing behind the car, he saw the newcomer bend over, which lifted his leather jacket to expose a handgun shoved in his belt behind his back. "You see that?" he asked Prater.

"Yeah." Prater shot more pictures. "Leather jacket has a gun," she told Hernandez and Buckley.

"Don't see that every day," Hernandez admitted. "Let's find out who he is."

Prater turned to Frames. "These guys don't usually have guns. They sell drugs. They don't shoot each other. Like Evan says, it could be another example of the changing regime under Julio."

After another ten minutes, a black Chrysler arrived on the street and parked in the driveway of the address.

"El Jefe has arrived." Buckley mouthed the sound of a trumpet fanfare.

A middle-aged man in a dark suit and tie climbed out of the car. He made a curt gesture with one hand that made the men push themselves off the SUV, and he said something to the driver.

The driver unlocked the back of the Tahoe and reached inside the cargo space. He pulled a car tire and wheel to the rear edge of the cargo compartment.

Julio looked at it and said something to Ramon, who lifted the tire upright.

Buckley sighed. "Anyone know what the fuck is going on?"

"Are they in the tire business?" Frames asked.

"I know what this is." Hernandez awakening to the idea. "It happened in Salinas three months ago. The drugs are in the wheels."

"You're kidding." The scene in front of Frames looked unreal.

"No. In Salinas, the PD found heroin and meth in metal boxes bolted inside the wheels."

The driver now reached farther inside the Tahoe cargo space and pulled out five more wheels.

"Holy shit," Frames said.

"Yeah. Holy shit."

For the next five minutes, Ramon and the driver lifted the wheels out of the Tahoe and transferred them to the Durango.

In both NIT vehicles, Prater and Buckley shot photos of the operation.

Julio stood on the sidewalk, hands in pockets, and watched the men at work. When the Tahoe had been emptied, the driver closed the rear gate, climbed in the driver's seat, and drove away.

"Now what?" Frames asked.

"Now we wait for the F-150," Hernandez said.

"Then we make an arrest?"

"No. Then we follow the Durango."

(ii)

(WEDNESDAY, 4:32 P.M.)

"The last time I saw Paul Behrens was Friday, during lunch period." Jean Cummings held court behind her desk. Rivas sat in one of the student chairs. "He was…busy with a student."

"Did you speak to him?"

"No. As I said, he was preoccupied." Cummings looked at Rivas for a long moment.

In the teacher's eyes, Rivas saw her losing the battle to summon the earnestness from the start of her career. All that was left now was impatient defiance.

Rivas's chair jammed his knees into the desktop. He looked behind Cummings to a corkboard. The words "The Crusades," cut out of red construction paper, were pinned above an illustration of a figure clothed in body armor. Rivas remembered staring at similar pictures as a boy in class, gauging the weight of the armor across his shoulders, imagining the coolness of the mail around his face. But such fantasies didn't save him in school. He failed test after test, his essays covered with the teacher's disappointed scrawls. He never understood the "why" of history. The reasons behind the broad sweep of events were lost in the dense fog of time.

Ironically, in the VCI, Rivas was known as the historian. He was the Google search engine of local crime. He remembered the names and faces of men and women arrested, serving time, or on bail. He memorized their crimes, choice of weapon, victims, addresses, sentences, associates, wives and husbands, children, tattoos. He knew their voices, favorite obscenities, style of clothes, makes of their cars. Seeing the back of a figure twenty yards away, Rivas could say Oscar Loiaza, two years served for heroin possession, on bail for parole violation, wife Ilsa, drives a red Altima, block leader for Sureños, suspected in the shooting of Rolando Morales.

Rivas saw Cummings waiting for him. "So you didn't see or talk to Paul Behrens yesterday or today?"

"No. I think I already said that. He's one of twelve teachers at this school. It probably seems odd, since his class is two doors away. But we don't share classes, so sometimes days go by when we don't see each other."

"And you don't know where he might have gone this morning?"

"No." Cummings frowned. "Why would I know that?"

"You've worked with him for seven years. You might know where he's likely to be."

"I mean I could guess. But that would just waste your time, right?"

Rivas took out his phone and scrolled through the screens until he came to Eden's photo of Behrens's planner. "Ms. Cummings, your name is written in Paul Behrens's planner for today at 11:00 a.m." He held his phone toward Cummings. "What's that refer to?"

"Honestly, I have no idea." Cummings squinted at the phone screen. "It's not on my schedule. I can show you, if you like. Maybe he forgot to tell me. It could be anything."

Rivas watched the teacher shift in her chair, trying to reclaim her comfort. From the quickness of her denials, he sensed the teacher was lying, but he also knew to confront her on bigger lies still to come. He scrolled through several more phone screens. "How about this? A copy of *Twelfth Night* we found in Mr. Behrens's house this morning. There's an inscription on the title page." Rivas held up his phone again, this time to the photo of the page where someone had written: "To Paul, Then come kiss me, sweet and twenty. Jean."

Cummings's face reddened. "It's a joke. The kids were rehearsing, and they... I mean, I know what it looks like under the circumstances." She smiled weakly. "This is all so crazy."

"Why don't you tell me about it?"

"It's nothing. Really. I have no idea where Paul's gone. That's what you want to know. Right?"

Rivas sighed. He wished he could stand and stretch his legs. He looked across the room. A large map on the wall showed the Louisiana Purchase. Rivas remembered, as a student, making a model of the same map out of plaster of Paris—thinning the plaster in an empty margarine tub, adding food coloring, and shaping the regions of the country on a sheet of Masonite. The purchased territory was yellow against the green of the eastern states, the colors so vivid on his stained fingers that he still imagined the landscape of the midwestern states to actually be yellow.

"We have Facebook postings of you inviting Mr. Behrens to dinner and the movies. If you have a relationship with Mr. Behrens, you may know something that could help us find him."

"I'm not sure what you mean by—"

"Ms. Cummings, we're in a hurry. We need to find this man. Do you understand?"

"I don't *have a relationship* with Paul Behrens. I don't even know what that means. We work in the same school. We're colleagues. We share interests in literature and film. His wife works nights, my husband sits in front of the TV. So once in a while, Paul and I have dinner or see a film together. I don't see—"

"Has Mr. Behrens been worried about anything?"

"Worried? Of course he's worried. Working here is nothing but worry. You worry your students will fail the state exams, if you'll have a job next year, if some kid's going to bring a gun to class, if you—"

"Something specific, lately, that would cause him to disappear?"

"Maybe. I don't know."

"Something with his family?"

"He's worried about Annie's drinking. It's not a secret. But he never talks about it with me. That would be a betrayal."

"So what's the maybe thing?"

"He said he'd miss his classes today because he had to meet someone."

"Who was he meeting? About what?"

"I don't know. He didn't say. Paul always wants to shield me from messy school stuff. He knows I'll try to help out if I can."

"When'd he tell you this?"

"This morning. He called me."

"You spoke to Paul Behrens this morning?" Rivas stood, knocking over his chair. "Why didn't you tell me this at the start?"

Cummings jumped at the sound of the chair clattering across the floor. "Because it doesn't matter." She glared at Rivas. "Paul's not lost. He hasn't disappeared. He's with his girlfriend, Patty."

"Patty who?"

"Patty Aguilar. She's a reading specialist at the school." Cummings shook her head. "When Paul didn't show up at school this morning, I knew he was with her. I texted him, told him I knew. He called back."

"What time was this?"

"Ten ten. Right after first period. He said I was wrong. He wasn't with Patty. That's when he said he was meeting someone."

"Did he say where he was?"

"No. But it was Doran Park."

"How do you know?"

"He told me."

"How'd he call you? He left his phone at home when he left."

"He had a new one, a prepaid phone."

"Can I see your phone to get the number he called from?"

Cummings took the phone from her purse and handed it to Rivas.

Rivas made a note and watched the teacher look across the

room, searching for help from one of the historical displays, as if some nugget of information from the twelfth century would extract her from this problem. He imagined Cummings, before the start of the school year, decorating the room, cutting out letters, finding pictures and timelines, filling the space with evidence of the past, trying to make real what was long faded away.

"I don't know why I believed him. He's no different from other men. He's nothing but a boy." She faced Rivas again. "He said I was his friend. He said I'd always be his friend."

"What else did he say?"

"That was it. After that, the call dropped out. When I tried to call back, it went to voicemail."

Rivas turned to leave.

"I didn't mean that thing about Paul being a boy," Cummings said. "I don't know why I said it. It's just that the man can be so frustrating. He helps everyone else but himself. I think he doesn't know what he really wants."

Chapter Eleven

(i)

"Dinner is served." The last to arrive in the VCI bullpen, Frames carried a large plastic bag to the room's center and emptied a pile of wrapped tacos on the table. The room suddenly filled with the smell of grilled meat, cilantro, and chiles. The detective waved a hand for the others to join him.

"The food truck on Sebastopol Road?" Rivas opened the end of a taco. "I love that place."

Between bites, Coyle saluted Frames. "I always said you'd make a good detective."

"Find this on social media?" Eden smiled at Frames, who returned a middle finger.

As they ate, the team stood in a semicircle in front of the evidence board.

"By the way, Martin," Mahler said, "I called Annie and asked her why Paul withdrew twelve hundred dollars from an ATM last night. She said she didn't know and sounded genuinely surprised. She said it was a lot of money for them and usually they talked it over before making withdrawals of that amount."

"It has to be something to do with his disappearance," Coyle said. "It's a lot of cash for anyone."

Mahler pointed to the timeline. "Okay. What else do we know? Our guy's stopped in Valley Ford at 9:12, and he makes a call from Doran Park at 10:10. That's a beach on the coast. From there, he can only go north or south on the Coast Highway."

"I called the number of the disposable phone he's using," Rivas said. "It just rang. He must have disabled voicemail."

"I can try to run a GPS search on the number, but it's hard in a rural area," Coyle said.

"Why's he out there in the first place?" Rivas peeled back more of his taco's wrapper. "He told the teacher, Cummings, he had a meeting."

"I can add a little something," Eden said. "I spoke to Patty Aguilar a few minutes ago. Remember her? The most frequently texted and called number on Paul Behrens's phone? She's a reading specialist for the district. Verified she spoke to Behrens last night for four minutes. Said they talked about scheduling." Eden looked down at her notebook. "When I pressed her, she said she could tell from his voice that Paul was worried. Apparently a while back, a female student accused Behrens of something. She thought that might be what was on his mind. I asked what the accusation was about. She declined to say. Said she was prohibited by school privacy laws."

"Which is bullshit, by the way," Rivas said.

"Yeah. I know," Eden said. "I pushed back, but didn't get anywhere. She did say Behrens told her he was going to help a student with a difficult problem."

"A difficult problem?" Frames unwrapped another taco. "But

what's that mean? Why didn't this guy just tell someone— anyone—what he's up to? Is he leaving bread crumbs for us?"

"According to Aguilar, once the problem was resolved, Behrens promised he'd tell her about it. By the way, when he was speaking to Aguilar last night, Behrens did not use the phrase 'It'll be all right,' which Claire overheard. So that must have been a different caller."

"Do we believe what this woman says?" Mahler asked. "What was your sense of her?"

Eden shook her head. "I don't know. I had to drag every bit of that out of her. She was not exactly cooperative. The whole time a couple kids were screaming in the background. She's a single mom. I tried to find out what her relationship with Behrens is, at which point she got very quiet. My impression is that Aguilar wanted to be something more than colleagues and Paul Behrens didn't. She said they're simpatico. I don't think you say that about a person if you're sleeping with them."

Rivas laughed. "Yeah. I'm simpatico with my car mechanic."

"Speaking of Aguilar and being simpatico," Frames said, "I tracked down the stalker who was parking outside the Behrens house, according to Jesse. I found the Honda Civic on the tape from the Behrens security camera. The license on the car belongs to Ricardo Fernandez. Works as a serviceman at Dorsey Tires. Turns out Mr. Fernandez is a sometime boyfriend of Patty Aguilar. He suspected her of cheating on him and found Behrens's texts on her cell. Tracked Behrens to his house. He admitted to parking outside three times but claims he never left his car. Says he was seen by Paul Behrens once and chased by Jesse, which matches Jesse's story. The thing is, he was at work at the tire store this morning when Behrens disappeared. There all day. Owner confirms it."

"So dead end for our purposes?" Mahler said.

"Pretty much. I cautioned him about stalking. But I think he's out of the picture."

"Eddie, Aguilar said she thought Behrens was worried about something," Eden said. "Remember Behrens's sister, Beth, told you something happened this year that he was worried about? It had to do with the class reading *Twelfth Night*. Maybe Behrens is meeting with a parent or a school official about that?"

Frames snorted. "What the hell's that mean? He meets someone about a play. It *is* a play, right?"

"Yes, Steve, it's a play." Eden smiled. "But what if it's not the play but something that happened in the classroom? His sister said it was like a puzzle Behrens was trying to work out. Sounds like a problem to me."

Rivas pointed at the right-hand board, with its list of leads. "And...Behrens dressed up for the meeting. Doesn't that mean it's what Steve said this morning—that Behrens is meeting a stranger or someone he needs to impress?"

Mahler walked across the bullpen to the map. "Yeah, but let's go back to the question Daniel asked a couple minutes ago. Why's Behrens way out on the coast?"

"So he won't be seen," Coyle said, "or whoever he's meeting with won't be seen?"

"But there're a thousand ways to stay out of sight without making that drive." Mahler sighed. "Martin, drive out there and look around. Doran Park north to Salt Point, Timber Cove. Especially any points where the road's close to the ocean."

"You think he drove himself over the edge somewhere, Eddie?"

"I don't know. His brother said Paul's in the ocean."

Rivas walked across the room and taped two dim black-and-white photos to the leads board. "These are security camera images of a male breaking into and leaving Behrens's classroom this morning." The photos showed a dark figure in the classroom doorway. "The man—he's clearly a male—enters the classroom at 7:27 a.m. and comes out six minutes later. As you can see, he's wearing a baseball cap and baggy sweatshirt and pants. The cap and shirt have no distinctive markings. The brim of the cap partially obscures the man's face, but enough of the facial profile is visible for identification."

"Have you shown the image to anyone at the school?" Eden asked.

"Not yet. I just pulled it up a few minutes ago. I'll take it back to the school tomorrow."

"Aren't the grounds secure?" Frames asked. "How does someone get into the school and into a locked classroom?"

"Normally nobody but faculty is on the grounds at that time. The front gate doesn't open until seven forty-five, but he could have come over the fence at the back of the school."

"Do we know why this guy broke in?" Mahler asked. "Did he take anything?"

"It's hard to tell from this angle. He doesn't appear to have anything in his hands when he goes in or comes out." Rivas looked down at his notebook. "I spoke to a teacher named Pamela Keegan who witnessed the man leaving. She was thirty feet away and didn't recognize him. She thought he might be one of the HVAC repairmen who have been working at the school. But those workers wear company uniforms. And I called the HVAC company. None of their men were on-site this morning."

Rivas consulted his notes again. "I also asked Ms. Keegan what someone might find worth taking from a classroom. She said her classroom has folders of upcoming assignments, test scores, grades, and written student assessments that aren't shared with parents. The confidential stuff's in a locked filing cabinet, but the lock's her own since the district doesn't supply them. She doesn't know what Behrens might have in his room."

"Ms. Keegan said another interesting thing. When I pressed her on why she thought someone would go to the trouble of breaking into a classroom, she said—get this—a parent might steal something about a student who's not their own. Over the years, the school has had issues between students and between families involving competition and revenge."

"Wow," Frames said. "So even middle schools are cutthroat?"

"Guess so." Rivas stood back with the others. "I'll look for this guy on the school's Facebook page, but I think my best bet is to take the security image out to Brookwood tomorrow and see if Principal Steeley or any of the teachers recognize him."

"You know what else you can ask the principal about again is this resignation letter." Mahler walked up to the evidence board and untaped a copy of the letter. "Listen to this: 'Once the allegations against me are made public, it will be difficult for an objective view of the facts to prevail.'" He turned to Eden. "What did Aguilar tell you? A student accused Behrens of something. I think our Principal Steeley is lying. I think she knows all about this resignation letter and the 'alleged incident in March.' When you go back to her tomorrow, Daniel, ask her again. Maybe she remembers this time."

For a minute the room was quiet. Then Mahler raised a hand. "Okay. Good work everyone. We all know what we're doing next? Let's talk again tonight." He pointed to Frames. "Thank you, Detective Frames, for dinner."

After Frames, Rivas, and Coyle had left, Eden sat still, staring at the left-hand evidence board, where photocopied images of the Behrens family were taped in a line across the top.

Mahler sat beside her. "Something on your mind?"

"It's Mrs. Behrens. She said she didn't remember when she got home last night." Eden looked at her notebook. "She said, quote, 'I don't remember. Is that important?'"

Mahler smiled thinly. "They always say that."

"Okay, but I called the hospital shift supervisor. Annie Behrens signed out from her ward at 11:20 p.m. It's a fifteen-minute drive home. Jesse told Steve his mother wasn't home when he went to bed at 12:30. So where was she between 11:20 p.m. and 8:45 a.m., when she called the principal?"

"Could have been anywhere. Stopped at an all-night to get a bottle of wine? Went to a movie?"

"Well, exactly. But shouldn't we know where Paul Behrens's wife was the night before he disappeared? She came in late enough that she slept downstairs so she wouldn't wake him."

"You're right. I'll talk to her." He checked his watch. "But I think I'll wait until tomorrow. She's had a long day, and I don't have any news for her."

"From your experience, Eddie, how's it look?" Eden asked. "Are we going to find this guy?"

"We'll find him," Mahler said. *Problem is*, he thought, *it almost never ends there.*

Leaving the bullpen, Mahler felt the familiar early signs of an impending migraine—a growing pain behind his right eye, stiffness in his neck muscles, and nausea. In the past six months, he'd decreased the frequency and painfulness of his headaches. But they still recurred, especially when he was focused intently on a case, as he was now. He walked slowly back to his office, found the pill container in the top drawer of his desk, and took two Advil and a single dose of a new migraine medication. He sat back in his chair, closed his eyes, and waited for the medicine to work.

(ii)

(WEDNESDAY, 5:16 P.M.)

Bri looked up from her phone to see Jesse approaching her table in the rear of Starbucks. "What do you want?"

Jesse smiled and sat across the table. "Shouldn't you be asking, where's my money?"

"I don't know what you're talking about."

"No? How about if we pretend to be smart for a few minutes. Think you can do that?"

Bri shoved back her chair and stood. "So now you're doing errands for your little sister? Good luck, asshole." She pushed past his chair.

"Go ahead and leave." Jesse held up his phone. "I was just about to call your friend T.J. I'll tell him you said hi."

Bri stopped and looked down at Jesse, her face pale.

"I was going to tell T.J. you're using the website he set up to run your own game. Or, maybe he already knows. You *were* going to share my sister's money with T.J., weren't you?" Jesse smiled again.

Bri slowly sat back in her chair and watched Jesse.

"Here's the thing." He turned his phone slowly in one hand. "T.J.'s a weird guy. The man has no sense of humor. None. Funny stuff, really funny stuff, doesn't make him laugh. I mean, the deal with my sister is funny. I can see it's funny. You can see it's funny. But T.J.'s just not going to see the humor."

"What do you want?"

"What do I want? I want you to go over to the counter and buy me a large Americano. Then we'll have a talk. How's that?"

Scowling at Jesse, Bri pulled out her purse and wove her way through the tables to the counter.

Jesse looked around the coffeehouse and felt his contempt for the place. It was just coffee. Why make such a big deal about it? Even worse were the customers. Acting like they were busy with something on their laptops or phones. What were they doing? He wanted to stand on his chair and shout, "Who the fuck cares?"

He was startled back to reality by a barista calling "Jessica" with his Americano order. He saw Bri glaring across the room, proud of getting him to look.

She slammed the cup in front of Jesse and sat again across the table.

Jesse tasted the coffee, taking his time. "The deal is, from now on, you and your little posse leave my sister alone. If I hear you're bothering her, I'm going to make a call. You understand?"

Bri looked back with sullen defeat.

"And I want copies of the images you have of my parents. You text them to me now. All of them. I know you'll have copies. But if I ever find them on a website, whether you or someone else put them there, I'm coming after you."

"You're crazy. How am I supposed to do that?" Bri raised her hands, a gesture of helplessness. "They're already out there. A bunch of people know about them."

"That's your problem, isn't it? It's called management." He drank more coffee and looked around the room. He felt his mastery of the moment. A year selling weed behind the high school was like a training camp. It had given him mad skills. He knew how to weigh people, intimidate the weak, dodge the strong. He knew things the poseurs in this coffeehouse would never know.

When he looked back at Bri, she was staring at him. He wiggled his phone in front of her face. "Come on. Wake up. Text me the photos."

Bri worked her phone, her thumbs flying over the screen. After a minute, she looked up. "That's all of them."

Jesse verified the arrival of the text message but didn't open the photos.

Bri stood to leave, rocking back and forth behind her chair. "That it? We done?"

Jesse finished his coffee and looked up. He watched Bri swipe a strand of hair from her face, impatient. He saw the toughness in her eyes and knew it to be affected. He remembered Bri coming over for playdates when she and Claire were seven or eight. Chubby-cheeked girl with freckles. Some monster had fucked with her. "What the hell happened to you?"

"Screw you." Bri shook her head. "What happened to *you*? Fucking high-school drug dealer." She said the last words loud enough for a couple at the next table to turn around.

The insult missed her mark. Jesse smiled placidly. "It's business. But this?" He held up his phone. "It's pathetic. Claire's a kid."

Bri bent toward Jesse. "Look at those photos, genius. Then tell me about pathetic. Your family is seriously fucked." She swung her handbag over her shoulder and stomped away.

Pushing aside his empty cup, Jesse bent over his phone and opened Bri's text message. The photos were contained in a single folder named "behrens." As the folder opened, Jesse drew a sharp breath. It was a photo of his mother, but the only familiar thing in the picture was her face. She was dressed in her underwear and sitting with a strange man. Jesse stared, trying to understand the juxtaposition of images. The scene wrenched together an impossible combination. How had it been done? He used two fingers to zoom in, to try to discern any obvious signs of image manipulation, of cutting and pasting. But it all appeared real.

He glanced around him, suddenly afraid everyone else in the coffeehouse could see the photo. But the rest of the tables were intent on their conversations or electronics.

On his phone, he flicked to the next picture, another angle of the first. This one seemed proof the other image was real.

The third snapshot showed his father seated on a bench beside a girl Jesse didn't recognize. It was the first time he'd seen his father since early that morning. The face held a familiar expression of fondness. For an instant, the image on the phone was almost like finding his father. *He's not missing,* Jesse thought. *He's here with a young girl, maybe one of his students.* They're both smiling. Relief flooded him.

Then he thought something was wrong with the picture. Why did Bri have it?

He scanned the room again. The scene had turned unreal, peopled by actors hired to pretend to be minding their own business. He searched for Bri, but she was gone.

He flicked quickly through the remaining photos—nine in all, more of both parents. He clicked to the first picture of his mother. Holding the photo away from the glare of the ceiling lights, he noticed his hand shaking. He'd been holding his breath.

He sucked in air and breathed deeply for a few seconds. He clicked off the file and laid the phone on the table.

A strange feeling ran through him. He felt a foreignness. It was impossible to believe he and the photos could both be real, as if he had fallen into a strange place where their existence meant he was erased.

He longed for a deep hit of weed to slow him down, to let him breathe normally.

Had he done the right thing, after all, in getting the photos back? When he foresaw his encounter with Bri, he'd pictured himself approaching the table, rehearsed the first couple things he'd say, even practiced in his mind his voice and gestures. But he hadn't gone to the end, envisioned seeing the photos.

Was everything that he'd done wrong now taking its revenge on him, righting some larger balance? His confidence, which had got him this far, had taken him off course. Would his mother want to see the photos? Would the police? He thought of the crazy detective, Frames, leaning over him, demanding the photos.

He wanted to smash the phone, to pull the pictures back out of his eyes. But those pictures seemed now to exist in an infinite world, floating beyond his reach in a weightless, timeless universe where they would live forever.

He sank into his chair in the dim, hateful coffeehouse and for the first time in years was unable to move.

Chapter Twelve

(i)

Eden pulled a small notebook from her desk drawer. For six months she had thrown things on top of the book—articles she meant to read, budget spreadsheets, case notes. Had she been covering it up? She put the notebook delicately on the desktop. Moleskine Classic. Five by eight and a half inches. An elastic strap holding it closed. Black cover worn from use.

She felt wariness in opening it, unsure what she might find. After a full minute's wait, she carefully pulled away the elastic strap and opened to the first page. A four-years-earlier version of herself had confidently written her own name in all caps: EDEN SOMERS.

The book was her personal summary of the FBI's Jory serial-killer investigation. The complete evidence file filled dozens of Bankers Boxes. From the beginning, though, this handwritten book was the little piece she kept to herself. She carried it day and night—at the bottom of her purse or briefcase, on her bed-side table. It became her talisman, a touchstone to make sense of a giant case as the thing grew ever more massive and tore open her heart and left her alone and afraid.

She ran a palm over the open page, feeling a connection to the Eden who'd written there.

Eden needed the book to refresh her memory in preparation for tomorrow's meeting with the FBI—to find the fine line between recollection and plunging herself back into the full nightmare.

The second page contained a list of the nine women, killed in five states, in order of geographic location, from east to west:

Lily Alison Hayes	Missouri
Macy Olivia Coleman	Oklahoma
Bobbie Ann Ramirez	Texas
Veronica Grace Morehead	Texas
Cassie Marie Stanton	New Mexico
Karen Louise White	New Mexico
Kai Alaney Jerome	Arizona
Allyson Jane Earnhart	Arizona
Denise Rose Simmons	Arizona

Beneath the list, she'd written the old mnemonic invented to remember their surnames: HCRMSWJES. "Her Courage Rallies Muted Souls Watching Justice Eternal Served."

A few months later, of course, her trouble would not be remembering the names but trying to get any of them out of her head.

On the third page lay the map. All but one of the bodies had been found along U.S. Highway 60, a major east-west highway that zigzags twenty-six hundred miles from Virginia Beach, Virginia, to southwestern Arizona and the little town of Brenda.

In her mind, the highway would always be a black line drawn across a paper map of the United States, pinned for a year to the wall of her FBI cubicle. The dark line slid state to state, a snake hugging the center of the country.

The highway starts at the south end of the resort strip of Virginia Beach and runs along the Atlantic Ocean shoreline, then serpentines north through historic Williamsburg and the capital of Richmond. From there, it climbs the Blue Ridge Mountains, splits the Shenandoah Valley, past Charleston, West Virginia, across the entire state of Kentucky, through Lexington and the north side of Louisville, and on to cross the Ohio River south of Cairo, Illinois, into Missouri. That much of the highway was thought by the FBI to be benign, although Eden spent two months searching unsolved murders in the cities and towns along the route.

But then the body of Lily Hayes was found in the small town of Sikeston, just north of the Missouri Bootheel, killed in the local Veterans Park, home to a full-size Vietnam-era F-4 Phantom jet. Lily Hayes—the easternmost victim and third in chronological time.

From there, the highway forges into Ottawa County, Oklahoma, across the flat, red-dirt plains at the top of the state, above Tulsa. It drops south through Enid, Oklahoma, a place named after a character in Alfred, Lord Tennyson's *Idylls of the King* and founded during the Land Run of 1893. There Macy Coleman was last seen walking home after watching *Guardians of the Galaxy* with two friends at the Oakwood Mall Cinema 8.

The highway crosses the dry, windy Texas Panhandle, through downtown Amarillo, where Bobbie Ramirez was killed near Plains Boulevard and Veronica Morehead was found in a south-side parking lot along Hollywood Road.

Sometimes Eden wanted the black line to end before it

reached the victims in the Southwest, as if she could have an impact on the evidence—even after the deaths were recorded and the facts collected.

But the highway sweeps westward, passing into New Mexico, through Clovis and Fort Sumner. Karen White was killed in Socorro in the Rio Grande valley, and Cassie Stanton, the only victim not found on Highway 60, was killed in Gallup on Interstate 40.

After Socorro, Highway 60 passes the Very Large Array, the field of giant radio telescopes on the Plains of San Agustin and runs over the Continental Divide into Arizona. In the eastern part of the state, the asphalt climbs through the high desert towns of Globe and Springerville. Allyson Earnhart was found on an unmarked road outside the mountain town of Show Low. Then, where the highway becomes part of the local commuter freeway system and pitches into metropolitan Phoenix, Denise Simmons and Kai Jerome were killed.

There the black line ended.

The following notebook page was devoted to the method of killing: asphyxiation from dirt stuffed in the mouth. Duct tape sealing the lips, limbs bound with strips of cotton sheeting. The text amounted to what the Oklahoma coroner called the horror show. Here were descriptions of soil types, brands of duct tape, and cotton thread counts, and a summary of five different coroner notes on oxygen deprivation, unconsciousness, and times of death.

Then came a written portrait of the only suspect: truck driver Albert McKinley Jory. Middle-aged, large acne-scarred face, hair pulled into a ponytail. His record included two assault arrests, one conviction with an eighteen-month sentence, and one DUI. Previously he had been employed as a warehouseman, local van driver, and journeyman carpenter. At the time of the killings, Jory worked as a long-distance hauler with J&J Trucking of Tulsa, Oklahoma, driving a twenty-six-foot, unrefrigerated box truck for shipping dry goods to motel chains and fast food restaurants.

In the Highway 60 case, Jory was arrested on two occasions, in 2016 and 2018, and charged with the murder of four women. On both occasions, the evidence was deemed insufficient to proceed to trial, and Jory was released.

In her memory Eden saw again her PowerPoint presentations in the darkened third-floor conference room of the FBI's Behavioral Analysis Unit in Quantico, Virginia. The faces of the victims blown up on the screen. Kai Jerome, part Navajo, long black hair, brown eyes the color of deep, loamy soil—eyes used to staring thirty miles across the desert, staring fiercely out at the room, blaming the world for letting her die. Bobbie Ramirez, the youngest, on a sofa in a family photo, tiny beside her older brothers. Eden saw herself pressing the wireless clicker through the crime-scene photos—tire tracks in the dirt outside Show Low, Arizona, and beside them a discarded empty bottle of Fitz's Root Beer. The Amarillo parking lot with its faded sign advertising Southside Dry Cleaning.

After the presentation, there were questions: Was there a pattern to the time of the killings? Did any of the victims know each other? How did the killer choose the victims? Were the victims of the same economic class? Then, in the front row, old Eric Howland, who had identified the Saint Paul ice-pick killer and worked on the task force for the Atlanta child murders, cleared his throat. "Are we certain, Agent Somers, there aren't more than nine victims?"

She turned to the notebook section on the case to be reviewed the following day—that of Cassie Stanton from Gallup, New Mexico. Aged forty-three. Divorced. Lived alone.

Waitress at Applebee's. Last seen getting into her car to go home after the restaurant closed. In 2018, Jory had been arrested for her murder only to be released later for lack of evidence.

How can we be certain of anything? Eden thought. She took her time reviewing the detailed notes. The evidence included a partial fingerprint of Jory's on the console in Stanton's Mitsubishi Mirage, along with a statement from a witness who observed Jory outside the restaurant on the night of Stanton's disappearance. There was also an issue of timing, of whether Jory could have been in the area at the time of the abduction and murder.

Eden looked up from the book to the cluttered corkboard on the wall of her VCI cubicle. One by one, she pictured the parts of the Stanton case that were not in the notebook but jammed somewhere in the Bankers Boxes. First, the photographs of Stanton's face, her bound arms, her car, the console, the parking lot, the restaurant, the field where her body was found. After that, the affidavit from the witness, all in a looping childish cursive that mentioned the yellow glow from Applebee's neon letters and described Jory's aquiline nose as looking like a bird. Then the timing: Eden's explanation for how enough time did exist for Jory to drive from his last stop in Arizona to reach Gallup and match the murder's timeline.

Extracting herself from her reverie, Eden realized the Stanton killing was one of the nine cases with at least three points of evidence, the so-called "three-legged stool." She didn't need to prep herself with the notebook, because every bit of the death of Cassie Stanton was lodged in her memory like a film loop stuck on repeat.

Eden closed the notebook and laid her hand on top. She thought of what Macon had told her—that the meeting in the San Francisco Field Office was for her safety. The words of the mnemonic ran through her mind: "Her Courage Rallies Muted Souls Watching Justice Eternal Served." Was her name to be added to the end of it? Was the dark line of Jory's trail, the snake that hugged the center of the country, coming for her?

(ii)

(*WEDNESDAY, 6:30 P.M.*)

"What'd he do?" The convenience store clerk held the photo of Paul Behrens and looked over the top of his glasses at Coyle. He stood on a raised platform behind a cash register. The checkout space was crowded with cardboard displays of beef jerky, ChapStick, and energy bars.

"Nothing. We're just trying to find him. Did you see this gentleman today?"

"I'm going to say no." The clerk handed the photo back to Behrens. He wore a trucker's cap that said West Coast Crab Shack.

"What's that mean? Did you see him or not?"

"If I say yes, and you catch this guy for selling meth or jerking off in public or whatever, then I'm a witness. It goes to court, I sit in a courtroom in Santa Rosa for six hours until the case is dismissed. You'll be there, but of course, you get paid for your time. I don't get jack shit."

Despite the clerk's irritating belligerence, Coyle felt a measure of sympathy. After all, earlier that day, he'd spent three hours in a courtroom, probably as fruitlessly as the clerk implied, on a road-rage case of no consequence.

Coyle gave himself a moment to start over. "Sir, it's important we find this man as soon as possible. Did you see him or not?"

"No, I haven't seen the poor dumb bastard. That good enough?"

Coyle tucked the photo back in his shirt pocket. In the parking lot, he leaned against his car and looked across the street at Bodega Harbor, where several dozen small fishing boats rocked beside the docks. He had started this search an hour earlier five miles south at Doran Park, where Paul Behrens had made a phone call at 10:00 a.m. Coyle checked for Behrens's Elantra in each of the park's seven public parking lots, then drove slowly north on Highway 1, the only route the missing man could have taken.

For the past thirty minutes, he'd scoured the grounds of a hotel, a condominium complex, an abandoned store and, just now, the Harbor Grocery and Deli.

GPS tracking on the Elantra turned up nothing—not surprising in a rural area.

The approaching sunset was an orange band along the western ridgeline. In another hour, it would be dark, and everything about the search would be harder.

As he considered the difficulties of his search, he thought of how his girlfriend, Adrienne, might approach it with her intuitive powers. Now as he stood in the deli's parking lot, he heard Adrienne's voice: "Visualize what you're trying to find, Martin. Close your eyes and concentrate. See it with your heart chakra, your intuition. That's more powerful than all your senses."

Coyle closed his eyes and pictured Behrens's face—the missing man's sad eyes, clean-shaven cheeks, and graying widow's peak. *Where the fuck are you?* Were you allowed to say "fuck" in a visualization, or did that kill the whole thing? He waited. Nothing. Probably did it wrong. He opened his eyes. He missed Adrienne.

She was a Reiki master practitioner with a small clinic in

Santa Rosa. She healed her patients by treating their qi, or "life force." Once early on, as he lay in bed, Adrienne demonstrated her technique to Coyle. Her hands hovered, palms down, over his bare chest. She told him she was shifting the electromagnetics of his biofield to improve his relaxation. He wanted to say he felt something, and maybe he did. Mostly he liked watching her thin, delicate fingers, the blue veins in pale skin, balancing above him.

He listened to her explanation of the practice. It made a kind of sense to him, although he was a little spooked by the black-and-white photo of the Japanese Reiki master framed and mounted above the incense altar in her apartment. He envied her belief, faith that her practice was real, though it couldn't be proved.

When she asked what he believed, he said he had been raised Catholic but lapsed in his sophomore year at the community college in favor of *Assassin's Creed*, JavaScript, and C++. When she pressed him, what he remembered from all those years in ten-thirty Mass was Christian reciprocity, *Do unto others*, which just sounded like common sense. What he didn't tell her was that seven years in the department had winnowed his faith to the liturgy of law enforcement embodied in the California Penal Code. At the academy, he committed it to memory until he knew the major section numbers by heart without looking at the laminated crib sheet in his jacket pocket and could recite the penal code with more confidence than the Twenty-Third Psalm.

Coyle thought of telling Adrienne the philosophy he tried to explain that morning to the courtroom gallery. He realized now that the courtroom had been the wrong audience. Adrienne would stop whatever she was doing while he explained the philosophy's parts: our mistaken focus on the modern world's trivialities, our failure of empathy for those approaching death, and our blindness to the physical world's beauty. It was less esoteric than Adrienne's Reiki, more born of Coyle's lived experience, but nonetheless a coherent, valid philosophy. Though committed to her practice, Adrienne was open to other points of view, able to listen without interrupting. What's more, after they discussed religion and philosophy, he and Adrienne always made love. Coyle didn't understand the connection, but his Catholic childhood had taught him when to stop asking questions.

Coyle walked across the street to the large dockside restaurant.

"Is he the one started the fires?" The hostess squinted at the photo. Behind her the restaurant dining room was empty but for one couple sitting beside a broad window with a harbor view.

"No. He didn't start the fires. We're just trying to find him."

The hostess took a step backward. "How do I know you're a real cop? You're not dressed like one."

"I showed you my badge and ID card. I'm with the Santa Rosa Police Department." Coyle pointed at the photo, hoping to recapture her attention.

"I read online that guys buy those badges on eBay and pretend to be cops." The memory of this revelation caused an angry frown. "You could be doing that right now."

"Ma'am, did you see this man earlier today? He might have come in here at lunchtime."

"Was he with a woman? There was a guy with a woman at lunchtime."

"Was it this man?"

"I don't know. It could have been him, but he looked way different. Kind of weird, with tattoos and stuff. Do you have a photo of this guy's arms?"

"No. Sorry." He reached for the photo. "Thanks for your help."

"If you wore a uniform," the hostess said, "people'd know you're a cop."

As he walked back to his car, Coyle checked his phone for texts from other members of the team. Mahler's voice sounded in his head: "What's the logic of it? If this guy's meeting someone, the location has to be a place they can both find— something clearly named and defined, a landmark. It can't be just a random spot on the side of the road."

Coyle looked ahead along the highway. If you were going to meet someone, would it be at a real estate office? A saltwater taffy shop? A gift store? None of them made sense.

Behrens dressed up for a meeting, drove forty minutes out to the coast, left behind his phone. What was he expecting? What was he prepared for? An out-of-the-way spot where he and the other person wouldn't be recognized together?

Behrens's brother, Michael, said Paul was in the ocean. Coyle wondered if he should be scanning the coastline, checking parking spots close to the water.

Why didn't Behrens tell his wife or someone else where he was going? Why was it a secret? Couldn't Behrens imagine the worry and fear he was causing his family? Coyle remembered a suicide two years earlier: a middle-aged father hung by his belt from a bedpost, face gray, mouth open. Discovered in the late afternoon by his nine-year-old daughter coming home from school. A spirit inside Coyle silently screamed at the slack body for the indelible vision his last act planted in the young girl's memory.

Coyle heard Eddie's voice again: "You won't find answers to every question. Look for the answers you need. Where did Behrens and the other party agree to meet? Where's the location simple and unambiguous enough for a text message? For the time being, forget the rest."

Coyle tried to picture the path north on the highway. He ticked off the possible coastal landmarks over the next ten miles: Goat Rock, Salmon Creek, Jenner, Timber Cove. He climbed back in his car and headed north.

Chapter Thirteen

(i)

(WEDNESDAY, 7:25 P.M.)

At the red light Frames looked across the car at Lonnie Wiggins in the driver's seat. Wiggins drummed his fingers on the steering wheel to an irregular beat. His lips moved silently.

"Why're you doing that?" Frames asked.

Wiggins looked back at Frames, his eyebrows raised. "What's that, Steve?"

"Not talking."

"I thought you hated it when I talked too much."

"I do. But when you don't say anything, I keep waiting for you to start. Then when you don't talk, I imagine what you would have said. And when you do that stupid silent drumming thing like right now, I've got your imaginary words running around my head."

"You're very moody, you know that?" Wiggins's voice took on a sympathetic, solicitous tone. "Have you ever considered medication? There are some wonderful herbal remedies, like Rescue Remedy. Comes in a lozenge or tincture that you add to water. It's made up of the essence of five flowers chosen by a British doctor, Dr. Edward Bach. The basic formula includes impatiens for impatience, clematis for grounding and anchoring back to reality... I'd be happy to share some with you."

"No thanks. Just go back to pretending you're Dave Grohl or Ringo Starr or whoever."

Wiggins accelerated through the green light and continued his drumbeat on the steering wheel. "Neil Peart. Drummer for Rush. Always wore a tubeteika—you know, one of those small, round cloth caps they wear in Central Asia? Remember their song 'Red Barchetta'? Late seventies, I think. It had that—"

Frames leaned his head against the passenger-side window and closed his eyes.

Frames and Wiggins had been in the station when Hernandez called to tell them the body of the drug dealer Jorge Lopez had been found. The dealer had been shot and his body left in the parking lot of a derelict strip mall in the South Park neighborhood. Hernandez asked the detectives to meet him at the site to discuss their next steps.

By the time Frames and Wiggins arrived, the parking lot had been framed in perimeter tape, and half a dozen police cars were lined together on the street. Standing lights were set up where Lopez's body lay in a narrow patch of high weeds and trash between a former dry cleaners and an abandoned fast food drive-through. Two coroner technicians in full-body suits were crouched under the lights beside the victim's body. A uniformed officer logged Frames and Wiggins into the crime scene and directed them to walk along a narrow path that had already been searched by the evidence techs. The smell of the body greeted the two detectives when they were fifteen feet away.

Hernandez turned to meet them. "The techs guess the body's been here two days. We'll know more when they do the autopsy."

"We heard he was shot?" Wiggins peered around Hernandez at the body.

"Three times in the chest. The killer got close. Maybe someone who knew him."

"Find any casings?" Frames looked across the parking lot to where Bailey was taking photos of something on the ground.

Hernandez shook his head. "I don't think the shooting happened here. Not much blood under the body, and there are drag marks through the high weeds." He pointed behind him. "He was probably killed somewhere else and dumped here."

"Which means the killer had help," Wiggins said. "Jorge's a pretty big guy."

"Yeah. You're right. We found a wallet in his pants pocket, with bills and credit cards. Wearing a new-looking watch. No drugs on him."

"Where'd the tip come from?" Wiggins asked.

"A homeless guy. Found the body this afternoon." Hernandez opened his notebook. "Robert Landsman. Guy's pretty freaked. We've got someone talking to him now." Hernandez gestured across the parking lot to where a uniformed officer squatted beside a man sitting on the pavement. "Smelled the body, probably. You wouldn't see it from the sidewalk. No reason to come back here."

"Do you think his killing's related to your investigation of Lopez for the overdose death?" Frames asked.

"You mean do I think someone in the family did this to take him off the street?" Hernandez shook his head. "I doubt it. I've never seen that kind of thing before."

"What do you guys know about Lopez?" Frames asked.

Hernandez looked at Wiggins. "Nothing special, really. If we hadn't found his prints on the dead woman's packet, we wouldn't have been looking for him. He's been around for a couple of years. We picked him up for dealing a few times."

"He sold around West Steele, Apple Valley," Wiggins said. "Usually out of his car. Small packages. He knew his junkies, and they knew him. They called him El Oso, the bear."

"He doesn't look like it, but Jorge was something of a ladies' man." Hernandez smiled. "You remember last year when we were watching him, he was with one woman after another? Maybe we should talk to Cervantes. See if her boyfriend was up to something."

"You're right. The number of rounds close-up looks personal. Maybe jealousy."

"Yeah," Hernandez agreed. "Also, Lonnie, talk to the dealers and your CIs."

"How's this shooting affect our surveillance of the Medinas?" Framed asked.

"Just added on top of it. Prater and Buckley are still at Francisco's house. If they see any evidence of the product moving, we'll jump on it. If you're available for it, we appreciate your help."

"Sure. Just let me know."

When the coroner technicians had stepped aside, Frames pulled on a disposable safety mask and gloves and knelt next to Lopez's body. The dead man, who was lying on his back, was dressed in a flannel shirt over a white T-shirt, baggy jeans, and work boots. His body had been handled roughly by his unofficial pallbearers. His clothes were stained, his hair flung in a messy tangle.

Careful to avoid touching anything, Frames leaned close to examine the wound sites on the chest. Lopez's shirt front was unbuttoned and the bullet holes were marked on the man's T-shirt. He thought of the loud sound of the gun close-up—*pop, pop, pop*. The barrel rising up with each firing. He thought of Lopez's surprise, puzzlement if there was time, and the uncontrollable force flinging his body backward onto the ground.

Frames rocked back on his heels and looked at the body again. He didn't see anything of use. The dead man was a disappointment.

Then, just as he was about to stand, Frames saw it—a long, straight scratch across the back of the victim's right hand. The wound looked recent.

Frames turned to Hernandez. "Was the body on its back, like this, when he was found?"

"Yeah." Hernandez joined Frames beside the body. "The homeless guy didn't move him, and we only lifted him to find his wallet. Why?"

"It might be nothing, but look at this." Frames pointed to the scratch.

"Happened when they dragged him across the pavement?" Hernandez asked.

"Or something else." Frames gestured toward one of the coroner techs and stepped away from the body. "Could you please turn over the right side of the body?"

The technician grabbed hold of the dead man's shirt and jeans and tilted the body.

"What's that?" Frames pointed to an object on the back pants leg.

A second technician took a photo of the object. Then gently picking the thing off the pants, the technician dropped the object into a plastic evidence bag and held it up for Frames and Hernandez. It was a small silver buckle.

"What do you think?" Hernandez asked. "Scratched the

victim's hand when the body was being carried? Ripped off something, like a jacket sleeve?"

"Maybe," Frames said. "I've seen jackets like that. Worth looking at."

"Good work." Hernandez stood. "Don't know how we missed that when we took the wallet."

Frames knelt again beside the body. *Not as useless as I judged you earlier,* he silently told the man. He looked at Lopez's face. The skin was swollen, tinged gray-blue. His eyes were closed, and dirt had collected around his nose and mouth. Frames noticed where a few days earlier Jorge Lopez had trimmed his whiskers and shaved to make a short, even moustache and goatee. It was a cheerful look. Jorge. George. The cheerful drug dealer. El Oso, the bear. Had he been a talker? What made him a ladies' man?

Frames reflexively felt a sadness, not for this man but for everyone. Although the dead man was a dealer, responsible for at least one overdose death, was it sad that anyone ended up here, in the high weeds amid discarded food wrappers and soda cans? Was there such a thing as a deserved ending? Who decided it?

Behind him, Frames heard Hernandez crouch behind him again. "My mother had a saying," he said quietly. "*Mira lo que hace el diablo.* Look what the devil has done."

(ii)

(WEDNESDAY, 10:12 P.M.)

Jesse pushed his phone across the kitchen table toward Annie. "Those are the photos from Bri. You don't have to pay her anything."

Annie stared at the phone. "What'd you do? How'd you get these?"

"Does it matter?" He popped a can of Coke and sipped it. "You should look at them. They're going to be a problem for us."

"Us?" Annie looked at Jesse. When had her son become this stranger telling her what to do? Had that happened when she wasn't paying attention?

"Us. The Behrens family of 3700 Oak Crescent—Paul, Annie, Jesse, and Claire. Just look at the fucking pictures. Can you do that?"

Annie pulled the phone toward her and tapped the screen. Suddenly she saw her own face looking back.

In the photo, she was dressed in panties and bra and seated on a man's lap. One of her hands held a glass, the other the phone that was taking the photo. She was looking straight ahead and smiling, although the effort of the smile was evident. The man, who was wearing surgical scrubs, had turned his head to one side, as if unaware or uninterested in the selfie.

It was the photo she had been expecting since Claire mentioned compromising pictures, but Annie was still shocked by the reality of it, and by the knowledge it had been viewed by her son and daughter and the juvenile delinquent extortionist Bri and who-knows-how-many strangers. She saw how old she appeared in the photo's unforgiving digital clarity. The shadows under her eyes were dark, and the lipstick was smeared from kissing. Worse, her underwear wasn't sexy, as she had felt at the time, but worn and pathetic for her figure and age. She felt sorry for the woman in the picture but didn't know how to help her.

"His name's Greg. Greg Winter. Dr. Gregory Winter." Annie heard the dry rasp of her own voice. She continued examining the photo. "An orthopedic surgeon at Memorial Hospital. I met him back in February."

"A rich doctor?" Jesse snorted.

"He's not rich. That's the thing." She looked up at Jesse and saw the coldness in his eyes. "Divorced twice. Paying a ton in alimony and child support. Lives in a crap apartment, drives a Corolla."

"So what is it then?"

"What is it? We keep each other company. Your father and I haven't—"

"Come on. I don't want to hear this."

"No? Then you've no right to judge me." A wave of nausea suddenly gripped Annie. She wished she had some wine, but knew it was a mistake to drink in front of Jesse. She took a bottle of tonic from the refrigerator and poured a glass. "Your father's idea of love is reciting poetry. He remembers more lines of poems than anything I say to him."

When they first married, Annie recalled, Paul's dreaminess had been romantic. For a couple years, he wrote his own poems and even talked about publishing them in a small book. He was enthralled with a famous poet. Roethke? Berryman? She couldn't remember. He read lines aloud to her from a notebook he carried around. Still vivid in her memory now was Paul's face, full of happiness in those moments at discovering something in his own heart. He wanted her to be proud of him; she could see it when he looked back at her. How could she explain to Jesse how it felt then, and how it changed year by year, overshadowed by the busyness of making a living, their declining love life, and the infrequency of even a kiss? How could she explain the expression on her young husband's face, and the loss of it, to Jesse, parked as her son was in his own disillusionment, opaque and angry about everything?

Jesse smiled. "You sure Dad's idea of love is just reciting poetry?" He took a long draw of his soda.

"I'm not sure of anything. I have no idea why he took off this morning. Whatever it is, it's not about Greg. Your father found out about us months ago. He came to the hospital once because he forgot his keys, and he saw me talking to Greg. He knew then."

"And you and Dad just went on as if nothing happened? Wow. I mean, this guy Greg looks disgusting. That gut and the beard. Jesus."

"He's not disgusting. He's kind. A good man." The tonic burned down the back of her throat.

"A *good* man? He's involved with a married woman."

"I don't have to explain myself to you. You couldn't possibly know what my life is like."

"No? Why's that?"

"Because you're a guy. Because you don't care about anybody. You know how to get things, but you don't know anything about people."

"Yeah, well sometimes it's important to get things. Look at the rest of the pictures."

Annie swiped to the next photo. In it, her husband sat beside a teenage girl on a bench. The girl had her hand on Paul's shoulder, and the two of them were smiling at each other. The next photo showed them laughing. "Who is she?" Annie whispered.

"No clue."

"And Bri hacked this off Dad's phone?"

"Presumably. That's the way it works."

"Does Bri know the girl?"

"I wasn't about to ask."

Annie turned the phone to view the photo in landscape. Tapping the screen, she spread her fingers to focus on details of the image. "Where is this?"

"A school?" Jesse guessed. "Not Dad's middle school. But the wall behind them looks like one of those modular buildings at a school."

Annie looked at her son. "Someone took this photo. It's not a selfie."

"Yeah. How about that?"

She pushed the phone toward Jesse.

"There's more," he said, shoving the phone back.

"I don't need to see them."

"No? Okay, but my father, your husband, is into something. I don't know what the fuck it is. But when the cops find him, they're going to have a shitload of questions. And then social media'll get interested." He squeezed the empty soda can in one hand and crushed it flat.

Annie closed her eyes and pressed her fingers against the lids.

"You and Dad are going to need to get your acts together, or all this…stuff is going to come out in the open."

"What about you? I know about your…drugs. What about that?"

"Really? We're going to do some equivalency thing here? The thing is, I have my shit under control. You and your husband don't. And whatever Dad's doing this morning could be the next bombshell."

Annie stood and walked slowly to the family room. When she returned, she tossed a crumpled paper on the kitchen table.

Flattening the paper, Jesse saw a selfie of a teenage girl sitting on a bed. The girl smiled at the camera. The sheets were pink with a pattern of clouds and rainbows. The girl's body was nude from the waist up. Jesse sighed. "Fuck. Where'd you get this?"

"From his briefcase. This morning."

"Who is *she*? She's not the one on the bench."

"No. I don't recognize her."

"This is just too fucking weird. Have the cops seen this?"

Annie shook her head. "I took it out of Dad's briefcase before they got here."

Jesse stood and leaned heavily against the table edge. "Is this why Dad's gone, why he's taken off?"

"I told you I don't know," Annie said. "He hasn't talked to me."

"Yeah? Good for him. I hope he doesn't come back. I hope he just keeps driving. Oregon, Mexico, wherever."

"Don't say that." Tears rolled down Annie's face. "Not *now*. Don't say that now." She wiped at the tears with the flat of her hands.

Turning to leave, Jesse saw Claire watching from the open doorway. As their eyes met, she backed silently away from him and ran through the dark family room and up the stairs to the second floor.

Chapter Fourteen

(i)

Frames yawned. Across the bullpen, Eden sat with her head lying on the desktop, eyes closed. "Officer Somers, you can go home and sleep if you want. Señor Rivas took off half an hour ago."

Eden slowly raised her head and blinked. "At Mount Holyoke, I once stayed awake for four days during finals." Reaching over Rivas's desk, she dipped her fingertips in a glass of water and wiped her eyelids. "I ate nothing but fried eggs with sriracha sauce three times a day."

"Sounds disgusting." Frames stared at the glass.

"It kind of was. But I aced those tests, even biochem, which was a bitch—all those premed overachievers." Eden rose to stand behind her desk and stretch. She ran in place, raising her knees high with every step.

"I stayed awake for a week in Fallujah." Frames yawned again. "It was the bullets hitting around my head that kept me awake."

"Seriously?" Eden stopped jogging.

"The bullets? Yeah. They seemed serious at the time. People shooting at you tend to be literal-minded."

Eden smiled. "Well, I'm glad they didn't hit you."

"Me too." Frames pointed to Rivas's water glass. "You're going to throw that water away, right? You're not just going to leave it there?"

Ignoring him, Eden stood at the whiteboard and pointed to the posted map. "At 10:10 this morning Paul Behrens made a call from Doran Park. After that—nada. Martin's been looking for five hours."

"So basically we've got nothing."

"It's not nothing. We know a few things."

Frames raised his hands in frustration. "Okay, sure. We know Behrens is somewhere. Aren't you going to tell me Newton's fourth law of physical matter, or some shit, says everyone's somewhere? Also, he's not on the moon. NASA would've called us by now. The point is, we haven't found the guy—which is our job. And the longer we don't, the more it doesn't look good for him."

"Or us," Eden agreed.

Frames looked at Eden's workspace. "So what're you working on? What's the notebook?"

Eden held up the small black Moleskine. "My record of a serial murder case I worked on in college and at the FBI. An FBI agent showed up here this afternoon and asked—or sort of demanded—that I meet with them tomorrow in the field office in San Francisco. The suspect was rearrested a few days ago. It turns out he knows who I am. The agent said the meeting was for my own safety."

"Wooo," Frames said. "That doesn't sound good."

"You ever wish you were good at something else? I'm good

at analyzing information. But sometimes I wish it was vacation resorts...or hair."

"Hair? Really? You'd be bored."

"Would I? The first word of this team is violent. I hate violence. My job is to look at killers and what they do. It's never... not awful. Sometimes I even hate the victims—what they make me look at. There were guys at the Bureau whose specialty was BPA, bloodstain pattern analysis. Imagine those guys on Bring-Your-Father-to-School Day?"

"You're lucky to be good at something, to use your talents. Not everyone can do that." Frames waved at the evidence boards. "Look at all that."

Eden pushed off from the chair and plucked the photo of Claire from the whiteboard. "This girl is the only one in the family who's not fucked up. You know that? If something's happened to her father, it's going to hit her the hardest."

"Are you sure? Maybe it's going to be hardest on the wife or Jesse. Maybe their deviant behavior is based on insecurities that'll be challenged by the loss of continuity in their lives."

Eden stared at Frames.

"All I'm saying is, things don't always fit a pattern." He saw Eden waiting. "My father left when I was eight. One day he was there, the next he wasn't. I didn't find out why. My mother just said he wasn't coming back."

"Did she know or wasn't telling?"

"I don't know. I was just a kid."

"You must have missed him."

"Maybe. Maybe not. He wasn't that great a father when he was there. Besides, my mother hung in there and did okay. She worked as a waitress in one of those overpriced restaurants in Healdsburg, made great tips. I was raised on the kindness of strangers."

"Wait." Eden frowned. "You know that play?"

"What play? I've read all those studies of fatherless boys growing up: Kraus and Enderlin, Stems and Wadsworth, Frobisher et al."

Eden blinked. "You read Kraus and Enderlin?"

"Did I pronounce it wrong?"

"No. I mean yes. But—"

"The thing is, none of those studies account for the anomalies, people like me. They miss the margin of error. What's the margin of error in most multivariate studies? Two percent?"

"Actually I believe it's 2.4."

"That, right there, is who you are, Officer Somers." Frames pointed to Eden. "You couldn't just say two. You had to say 2.4."

"What? That's the number. You want me to make up a number?" She taped the photo of Claire back on the board. "Could we just go back? You read Kraus and Enderlin?"

"You're surprised I read? You're not the only one who went to college. Get over yourself."

Eden dropped into her chair and stared at Frames as if he'd entered her field of vision for the first time.

"Tell me, Officer Somers, who are the people we deal with every day?" Frames waited a beat. "They're ordinary men and women, going about their business, who don't know psychology from a ham sandwich. All they want from us is to help them when they're in trouble. What do studies give you that you couldn't get just by listening to them?"

"All kinds of things. Forensic science has improved criminal investigations in a thousand ways. Shelby and Founder proved a murderer's mental state can be revealed in crime-scene evidence. Kincaid showed how to interpret patterns of speech in suspect interviews. Don't you think we're better now than we were fifty years ago, or ten years ago?"

"Maybe. But in a small town like this, it's pretty basic. Usually we just find the guy with the right blood type on his clothes."

"Okay," Eden conceded. "I just think we should use what we know."

For a minute, the two of them looked at the whiteboard.

"How about you?" Frames spoke first. "Did your father stay or leave?"

Eden took a deep breath and thought for the second time in twenty-four hours about her father. "Yeah. He was there. He was a doctor, a radiologist: Dr. Donald P. Somers. But he…passed away while I was in college. Myocardial infarction, heart attack. Which is ironic, isn't it? Wouldn't a radiologist know the signs? I remember I found out in a religion seminar on early Christian mystics. We were discussing Hildegard von Bingen, who had these incredible visions of… It doesn't matter. Anyway, a girl came to the classroom door with a note for me to go to Counseling Services. They gave me the news from my mother."

Eden faced Frames. "I think he loved me. He did all the dad stuff. He helped me make decisions—where to apply to college, which courses to take. Biochem was his idea. He told me once I looked like Margaret Cleaves." Eden smiled and, seeing Frames's blank face, added, "Nineteenth-century physician, invented brachytherapy—it's this cancer treatment that inserts a radioactive implant into the tissue."

"So you're a disappointment?"

"For being a cop?"

"What would the old man think?"

"He'd worry for my safety. But he'd probably never say it. As far as I can tell, all fathers are mysteries. Their inner life, if they have one, is buried. Whatever they think or feel is locked inside, even when they sit across the table from you every night. My own theory is, fathers are thinking all the time—the billions of neurons in their cerebral cortex firing away with opinions about you, ideas to tell you. They may even think they *have* told you, but the neural pathway to their language center is, I don't know, just not there or something."

"So you never got to know him?"

"I always thought I would when I was older—when I learned more science or something he respected. Then he'd open up. But we ran out of time." She looked down at her desktop. "My field is understanding people. Kind of screwed up that one, huh?"

"Maybe not. You just ran out of time. The life your father left behind is still there."

Eden looked up, surprised. *Had Frames actually said that, or did she imagine it?* She found herself wanting to connect with this new version of Frames. "How's the Narcotics case going?"

"It's good." Frames looked a little surprised at being asked. "Learning a lot of new things. How street drugs are moved. How NIT operates. So far, it's been outside work, less research—which, as you know, drives me crazy. When I was in the service, especially when I was deployed, I liked the action, being where the bullets were flying." Frames was getting into it. "For a while, I think I was addicted to it. There was something about being that close, two inches from where the last bullet landed. Now—"

"You think about it differently?"

"It's definitely changing. A few hours ago, I saw the body of a dealer who'd been shot. I see that, I wonder. Be crazy not to."

"You're right," Eden said. "Be crazy not to."

For a moment neither of them spoke.

Frames broke the silence. "But right now we've got this guy Behrens. We're here, right? You want to work?"

"Sure. Sure." Eden brightened.

"You know what I think we should do? We have Eddie talk to

Patty Aguilar. See if he can get her to tell us about that student who accused Behrens of something."

"So, what you're saying is, Aguilar'll tell him because Eddie's what? A man? Or, scarier than me?"

"You're kidding." Frames laughed. "Eddie's scarier than everybody—except that goalie-mask guy in the *Halloween* movies. I'm sorry, Officer Somers, you're smart and...tall and...smell good. You're just not scary." He saw her watching him. "Okay, sometimes you are scary, but not all the time." He pointed again to Rivas's glass. "Seriously. You're going to throw away that water, right?"

(ii)

(THURSDAY, 12:10 A.M.)

A photo of Paul Behrens, taken from the evidence board, looked back at Mahler from the top of his desk. Thoughtfulness captured in the missing man's eyes—a rare trait, in Mahler's experience. He remembered an interview with Michael Caine in which the British actor described how film actors' eyes are the keys to the characters they play.

Then again, photographs, along with actors, could be deceptive.

Mahler imagined the thoughtful-eyed man waking on Wednesday morning, picking out his shirt and tie, crying in front of the bathroom mirror. *Why?* Mahler asked the photo. *What happened the day before or the night before? Why leave behind your phone and climb into your car without telling your wife or principal where you're going?*

Behrens stared back with the same thoughtful look, considering Mahler's questions.

Mahler tried to picture himself in the other man's life, dressing and driving away without telling anyone. Speeding down Interstate 5 south all the way to Los Angeles or north to the Oregon border. Something about the freedom and anonymity of that simple act appealed to him. Wasn't it the purest of American dreams? A ribbon of road stretching ahead as far as the eye could see. In his case, though, a sense of responsibility always held him back. Or was it the instinct to show up, drilled into him courtesy of the Army Rangers? *Maybe I didn't have enough to escape,* he told the man in the photo, *or something worthwhile to find at the other end of the road.*

Mahler thought of Eden's question about whether they'd find Behrens. Apart from the suicidal real estate agent Kevin Farrell, Mahler had worked three other missing persons. A twelve-year-old boy, Jeremy Vaughn, who disappeared from his home in Santa Rosa and ended up 250 miles away in a cannabis trimmers camp in Humboldt County. Returned on his own after six weeks, mind-addled and half-starved. Marilyn Lisle, mother of three, left her shift as a nighttime stocker in a supermarket. Marilyn and her car were never seen again. Mahler imagined the woman driving into a small town in Idaho or Utah, still dressed in her store smock, and starting life over from scratch. Harriet and Charles Pool, on a Sunday afternoon outing, drove their car over a steep wooded hillside on Petrified Forest Road. They went missing for six days, pinned in the front seat of their crushed car, surviving on a bag of trail mix, spotted alive by a cyclist who fell by chance exactly where the car descended the hillside.

Happy ending in two of four. Was that a good average?

You played no useful role in any of them, Mahler's own father pointed out, another judgment on his son's value. James David Mahler was a lawyer who made a career of prosecuting class-action police brutality cases. He believed law enforcement, by its very nature, was destined to fail, that a police department did not protect the public but made life worse for most citizens. Ex post facto. Mahler remembered his father's smile as he pronounced the Latin. You arrive after the thing's happened, and you arrest or kill the suspect. *How does that help the victim or the victim's family? What's your motto, Officer? To protect and serve? Have you ever done that, Eddie? Or are you always too late?*

Mahler: When we were kids, after my mother died, my father came up from the city a couple times a month to make sure Diane and I were behaving ourselves.

Dr. Schafer: Were you? Behaving?

M: Mostly. Not that he knew what to do if we weren't.

S: Why do you say that?

M: In my sophomore year I failed chemistry. My father asked me what happened. I said I couldn't understand it. He asked if he needed to hire someone to hold my hand.

S: What'd you say?

M: I learned to say less and less. Anyway for him, that was good. Usually when he was angry, my father stopped talking. For a couple weeks or a month.

S: That's a long time.

M: He made his point. You don't get to be a lawyer without knowing a lot about silence.

S: What'd your father think of you joining the police force?

M: He said cops were dogs.

S: Dogs?

M: Yeah. When I got my uniform, he said, now you can be as mediocre as you always wanted to be.

S: Did he change his mind when you were assigned to VCI?

M: By then he was dead.

Mahler dragged his mind away from life's failures. He walked down the corridor to the men's restroom. There he splashed warm water on his face and pressed against the pain point above his right eye. In the past seven hours, he had experienced no scotoma, the visual auras that had previously accompanied his headaches and distorted his vision. This time, there was just the dull ache that persisted in his head and weighed down his thoughts. Did his success in reducing his migraines qualify as some kind of accomplishment? Did it mean he was finding ways to diminish the conflicts in his life? Or was it just a manifestation of the better meds?

Back in his office, Mahler refocused his attention on the work at hand. Who was the man who broke into Behrens's classroom? Was he involved in the teacher's disappearance? Somewhere a security video held the man's identity. Had the man found something that Paul Behrens was running away from?

Identify the man, locate the stolen item, find the teacher.

What about Patty Aguilar? What wasn't she telling them? What did she have to hide? Had her flirtation with Paul Behrens exposed the man to trouble, or was he trying to escape it? Did Behrens want out or all the way in?

Am I getting warmer? Mahler asked the photo. *Or still cold?* Behrens's eyes maintained their thoughtfulness.

There were Eden's questions about Mrs. Behrens. Where was she the night before her husband's disappearance? Had she come home earlier, argued with her husband, killed him, dragged his body to the car, driven to the country, and dumped Behrens where the remains would be found in a month?

The lesson of police work was that the life of every person, no matter how ordinary on the outside, held dozens of threads. Pull on each of them and pay attention to what shows up. That was the job—pull on threads and see what happens.

Luck played its part, too. Coyle searching the coast would speak to someone who saw the missing man. Then Martin would follow one tiny fact to another like a children's connect-the-dots puzzle, until he found Behrens asleep in the back of his car in a drive-by on a remote coastal road.

Or, Behrens would call home from a motel in Siskiyou County and apologize for the worry he'd caused.

Or—and this had to be considered seriously, given Mahler's own fifty-fifty history with missing persons—ill luck had played its hand.

Paul Behrens might never be seen again on the face of the earth. Like Marilyn Lisle, he drove to a small town in Idaho or Utah and started life over from scratch.

Or, the teacher's body, still clothed in his necktie and sports jacket, would wash up on the beach at Goat Rock.

Mahler looked back at the photo of Paul Behrens. The missing man's brother, Michael, had Paul's eyes, but in the soldier's case, they were searching, puzzled. Did the lostness in Michael's eyes have anything to do with his brother's disappearance? Was Paul searching for something on Michael's behalf?

How would the outcome of Paul's disappearance affect his brother? Would it strengthen the brothers' bonds? Or, be another tragedy in the soldier's life?

Mahler's mind drifted away from the rehabbing soldier, down the hallway from the Aurora Manor common room to the office of the manager, Franny Hastings. He imagined her trimmed hair, her smile, the dark-brown eyes watching him. What would Michael Caine make of those eyes? She was a distraction, an unnecessary complication, in the middle of an investigation that filled his head.

He returned to the threads in the life of Paul Behrens. What about a classroom incident? An assignment taking a wrong path? Misunderstood words? Misinterpreted gestures? The hormones of a thirteen-year-old girl and the chemical reaction when mixed with a lonely middle-aged teacher and his unfaithful wife? Did that really happen?

How could his team uncover such a thing? Would they need to interview every student in the presence of their parents? What harm would come to the students by simply asking those questions?

The face of Franny Hastings reappeared with a smile for Mahler.

The thoughtful eyes of the man in the photo had questions for Mahler, too. *Who's that, Eddie? Why her? Why now? Are you really over your migraines? What are the threads in your life?*

Chapter Fifteen

(i)

(THURSDAY, 12:33 A.M.)

"I was just reading about the Louisiana Purchase." Rivas looked up from the laptop and saw Teresa in the kitchen doorway. "Did you know we bought it from Napoleon for fifteen million dollars, which works out to four cents per acre?"

"Sounds like a deal." Teresa yawned. "Why're we talking about this at twelve thirty in the morning?"

"Sorry. Did I wake you?"

"No… Actually yeah. I heard you down here and saw the light. What're you really doing?"

"I interviewed a middle school teacher today as part of our missing person case. Looking around the classroom, I remembered building a plaster of Paris model of the Louisiana Purchase when I was that age. My mom helped me. She didn't know what the model was or why I was doing it. But she spent hours working on it."

"That's terrific. I can't imagine Paula actually doing that. But is there some reason you're reading about it now?"

"Talking to these teachers and the principal reminded me what a poor student I was in middle school. I had undiagnosed dyslexia. After the first few years of school, the teachers stopped expecting much of me."

"But you made a good career for yourself. Aren't you proud of that?"

Rivas wasn't sure how to explain to Teresa what the Behrens case was making him feel. As with every missing person case, it was like chasing a ghost. He and the VCI team were always a few steps behind the phantom of Paul Behrens, with only glimpses of the shadows left behind. Rivas thought of the unique personal history everyone builds over the course of a life—memories, pictures, words. In moments of crisis, like this one for Behrens, we're boiled down to that history, all of it listed and taped to the VCI evidence board.

As much as he and the team had spent the day chasing Behrens's past, some undercurrent of the investigation was forcing Rivas to confront his own. Two weeks earlier he'd filed the paperwork for retirement. When that day came six months from now, Rivas knew he'd disappear from his life like Paul Behrens. His cop self would be gone for good, as hard, or maybe harder, to find than this teacher who climbed into his car this morning and drove to the coast.

What would the evidence board for his life look like? He pictured his photo and those of Teresa and his sons. The lists in Coyle's handwriting of what he'd accumulated and left behind. Rivas knew not to expect too much meaning when he looked back. Police work taught him a few lessons, grayed the lines of good and evil, and imprinted half a dozen snapshots of anguish. What he wondered about were the secrets in his life, like the ones being unearthed in Paul Behrens's life.

"What's this really about?" Teresa poured herself a glass of juice and sat at the table opposite her husband.

"I don't know. I couldn't sleep. I was lying there thinking how we interview people every day, ask them all sorts of questions. We force people to tell the truth, maybe for the first time. We take them apart, layer by layer. It exposes them. We end up knowing...secrets."

"That's your job, sweetheart." She reached across the table to take her husband's hand.

"Yeah, but this schoolteacher, Paul Behrens, the one who's gone missing? Turns out there're things he wasn't telling his family. On top of that, his wife has a drinking problem. His son's selling weed. According to Eden, his daughter's a lonely kid. It's all come tumbling out."

"Okay, but knowing about Behrens's family might help you find him, right?"

"Maybe. But it's not clear how much the poor guy knew. It made me think about my retirement and if I'm any different from this schoolteacher."

"In what way? Are you planning to disappear?"

"No. Of course not."

"Because if you are, I'll find you." Teresa narrowed her eyes at her husband. "They won't need VCI. You know how good I am at finding things in this house when you and the boys can't find them?"

Rivas smiled. "I'm not going to disappear." What he felt was confused in his mind. He didn't know if he could get it out. "I'm making a major change in my life. I'm going to retire from the only job I've had."

"Are you rethinking that decision?"

"No. Not really. I mean, it's a tough choice. I won't lie. But the injury in the Thackrey case made me shorten the timeline, even though we'll have to pay for the boys' college. I'm not a kid, like Frames. I can't take the physical punishment like I used to."

"All right. So what's your retirement have to do with this missing schoolteacher?"

"I feel sorry for the guy, for all the things he didn't know about his family and all the things he wasn't telling them. Is that what retirement's going to be like for me? Are all the secrets going to come out?"

"Secrets? What secrets? I don't have a drinking problem. Although I'm thinking of changing this juice to scotch if we keep talking."

"What about the boys?"

"Your sons are just fine, Danny. Alex asked Veronica Lunardi on a date. You know how he got to know her? They're in a calculus study group. Daniel Junior's AP physics teacher encouraged him to apply to Caltech."

"Why don't I know these things?"

"You're too busy worrying. The boys think your worrying's funny. They tease you by not telling you things." Teresa studied her husband. "But then there's you, Daniel Rivas. What aren't you telling me?"

"That's just it. I won't know until I retire."

"Maybe they'll be good things. Glass half-full."

"Driving back from Brookwood today, I remembered I flunked algebra. Twice. Did I ever tell you?"

"I want a divorce." Teresa laughed. "I think the consequences of that ran out a long time ago. Unless you want to tell Eddie."

Rivas smiled back. "It's going to be different, you know? Retirement's going to be different."

"We'll figure it out. We always do. I'll help you make another plaster of Paris map of the Louisiana Purchase since it sounds like that was the high point of your youth." She stood and kissed her husband. "But, Monsieur, if you want to know my secrets, you have to come to bed."

"Okay, I'm coming up." Rivas closed his laptop. "Just tell me, was the Louisiana Purchase a good idea?"

"It's too late to sell it back to the French, if that's what you mean."

(ii)

(THURSDAY, 12:53 A.M.)

Coyle found a sheriff's unit parked next to a silver Elantra on Bean Avenue in the Salmon Creek neighborhood of the Sonoma coast. It was a one-lane, winding road, with run-down summer cottages on one side and broad wetlands on the other, where the mouth of the creek meets the ocean.

As he threaded his way down the road, Coyle's headlights caught the responding officer, Denny Telford, leaning against the patrol unit. Coyle recognized Telford's boyish face, squinting into the light, and remembered playing softball with Telford's brother.

The call came from Dispatch. A little after midnight, a local citizen out for a walk had noticed a car parked illegally on the narrow road. Shining a flashlight into the car, he saw someone in the front seat and what he described as "a lot of blood." At twelve thirty, Telford identified the car as Behrens's Elantra and found no pulse on the man. Dispatch called Coyle.

Climbing out of his car, Coyle pulled on gloves and vinyl shoe covers and took a small flashlight from his jacket pocket. The air blew cold and damp, and the spot was close enough to the ocean to hear the waves hitting the beach.

"You got here fast." Telford pushed off his vehicle.

"Been out on the coast all day." Coyle looked past Telford at the Elantra.

"I think he's your guy. Definitely his car. I watched where I put my feet. I'll leave you to it. Let me know if you need anything."

"Appreciate it." Coyle felt something sinking inside him. He walked slowly toward the car.

"Single gunshot wound to the head," Telford called after him. "Right side. Your field techs are on the way."

Coyle shined the flashlight in the driver-side window. Smeared blood on the window had already started to dry. Through the dark stain, Coyle could see the head and shoulders of Paul Behrens. There was at once a feeling of relief at reaching the end of the search and sadness at seeing this end of a man and knowing its meaning for his wife and children. Coyle held up his phone and took photos.

He walked around the car to open the passenger door. The metallic smell of blood filled the interior—for Coyle, the familiar sensory signal of violent death. Careful not to touch, he balanced on the balls of his feet just outside the open door and played the light inside. Behrens's body sat upright in the driver's seat, head tipped toward the window. The face was white with the marbled stillness of every body at every crime scene Coyle had witnessed. The eyes were open and looking ahead, seeing forever whatever had been in view in that last instant. The lips were parted. The wound lay above the ear, a dark hole burned at the edges. Coyle let the light stay on that spot for a few seconds, taking in its finality.

Across Behrens's chest, the seat belt was still fastened. The right hand rested on the console, where it had evidently fallen after firing the gun. The handgun, a midsized semiautomatic, lay on the passenger floor mat. No shell casing was visible. The techs would find it. The console and dashboard were empty—no phone, no note in sight. That last bit bothered Coyle. Wouldn't an English teacher write something?

Coyle shifted his weight to lessen the pressure on his lower back. He took a few more pictures with his phone. Then he smelled something else in the car—the briny odor of seawater. Looking at Behrens again, he noticed the man's clothes were wet. A small puddle of water lay at his feet. "What the fuck?" he whispered. He pointed the light to Behrens's face again, as if the dead man might explain it to him.

Coyle closed the car door to preserve the scene and tapped his phone. Mahler answered on the second ring. "It's him." Coyle shoved his free hand in his jeans pocket to keep warm. "Looks self-inflicted."

"Okay." Mahler's voice was soft.

Coyle pictured his boss in his office. He waited to see if Mahler would say more. "Not exactly where I expected this one to go. I thought we'd come across him driving around or asleep in his car."

"Yeah, me too. Something must have gone sideways in a hurry."

"One thing, Eddie. Remember the brother saying Behrens was in the ocean? Well, the body's soaked."

"What do you mean?"

"I mean soaking wet. And it hasn't rained out here all day. Somehow he got wet. I think he's been in the ocean."

"In his clothes?"

"Yeah. In his clothes, and it must be fucking freezing on the beach."

For a moment the two men were silent. Coyle looked across the road, where Telford sat inside his car typing on the laptop. "Will you talk to the wife?"

"Yeah. We need to get to her before this thing hits social media."

"Got a text saying the field techs and the coroner are on their way. So I'll hang on here."

"You didn't find a note, did you?"

"No. Nothing. Maybe the techs'll find something."

Coyle turned toward the sound of the waves. Although it was too dark to see, he knew the road dead-ended in a parking lot a quarter of a mile farther, where a footpath climbed over the dunes to the beach. Once in high school, Coyle had gone across that stretch of sand with a girl he knew to be too pretty for him. He remembered her gold necklace and the shy and gentle way she retreated when he leaned forward to kiss her. He could feel the wind in his face then, too. Cold but different when he was younger. It was a lonely spot to take your life. Maybe that's what you wanted in the end. "Can't believe we find Behrens here. I checked this road around eight o'clock, drove all the way to the dunes. Car wasn't here then."

"Give yourself a break," Mahler said. "You were covering a lot of ground. Besides, it gives us the start of a timeline."

"What do you need me to do?"

"Have the sheriffs help you put up some tape. Let's keep the public back. When the press shows up, don't let them get close. I don't want a bunch of pictures online. And nobody talks to the neighbors, reporters, anybody."

"Got it. So—Eddie, you have any ideas about this thing?"

Mahler stared again at the photo of Paul Behrens on his desk. "Only that the more I learn about our victim, the less I understand him."

PART II

Chapter Sixteen

(i)

(THURSDAY, 6:00 A.M.)

"He's not alive, is he?" Annie sat across from Mahler at the kitchen table in her home. As she spoke, she nervously tugged at the edges of her bathrobe. Her eyes were dark from lack of sleep. "When you called and asked to come over here, I figured it wasn't good news."

"No. No, it's not. I'm sorry, but we found Paul last night in his car on the coast. The first indications are your husband took his life." Mahler let the words sink in.

"Oh my God. It's true then." Annie pressed her hands to her face and sobbed. "I just thought he'd come back."

"I know," Mahler said. "I realize this is a lot to take in. The chaplain who came with me is available to talk to you at any time in our conversation. Just let me know. As I said earlier, her name's Elaine Jacobs. She's very experienced. I asked her to wait in the living room until you and I talked. But I can have her come in if you need her."

"I'm okay," Annie said, wiping at her tears.

"I also want to caution you. The determination that Paul's death was by his own hand is preliminary, pending the coroner's review."

"You mean someone else—"

Mahler cut her off. "At this point, we just don't know."

"What did he... I mean, how—"

Mahler shook his head. "I can't give you that kind of information yet. The coroner will determine cause of death. Later today or tomorrow. Is there someone who can come and stay with you? Your in-laws?"

"No. I don't want to see them just yet. My children are here. They'll—" Annie ran her hands over a table mat in front of her. "Paul didn't seem depressed. He didn't say anything to me." She looked at Mahler. "Can you tell me if he left a message? A note?"

"Our officers didn't see one. But the car is still being searched."

"You'd tell me if there was a note, wouldn't you? No matter what it said?"

"Yes, ma'am. We'd tell you."

Annie tilted back her head as tears ran down her face. "Oh God. It doesn't make any sense. Is that what people always say?"

Mahler reached to the kitchen counter for a box of tissue and handed it to Annie. He waited while she wiped her face and collected herself. "Can I get you some water?"

Annie looked back without answering.

Mahler found a coffee mug in the cabinet, filled it at the tap, and set it in front of Annie.

Annie wrapped her hands around the mug and held it still.

"Mrs. Behrens, we're trying to understand what happened to Paul," Mahler said. "Why he went to the coast yesterday. If he was meeting someone. Do you have any ideas?"

"He didn't tell me," Annie said. "He didn't say anything to the kids. And it's not like him. My husband's... He *was* a very organized man, a planner. He wasn't...spontaneous."

"Okay. Even though he didn't tell you, can you think of any reason for him to go out there yesterday, to not go to his job?"

"His job, those classes, were everything to him. He never missed them, never even took a sick day."

"So why'd he do it yesterday?" Mahler paused and watched Annie lift the mug and take a drink. "If you can think of anything, even if it doesn't seem related."

"I can tell you one thing. Jesse said my husband was dressed in his sports jacket and tie. Paul hated to dress up. He only did it on important occasions—when he was trying to look professional, when he thought he was being judged. A minute ago, when you asked if he was meeting someone, that's what I thought of."

Mahler wrote in his notebook: "Meeting someone? Being judged?"

Annie stared at her hands, lost in thought.

"We're still trying to find out," Mahler said, "why Paul withdrew twelve hundred dollars from an ATM Tuesday night."

"I know. I know." Annie looked weary. "Like I said yesterday, I have no idea why Paul did that, what he needed the money for."

"Did Paul own a gun?"

"Dear Lord. Is that how—"

Mahler held up his hands. "I'm sorry. I can't tell you more right now."

"This is all so confusing. But Paul didn't own a gun. It's not something he'd have."

"Tell me about your husband," Mahler said. "Tell me about Paul."

"I already did," Annie sighed. "He was a teacher. He loved his job. He was named—"

"Teacher of the year. I remember. But what else? Did he have problems with students, with parents?"

"Yes. But no more than normal. All teachers do, especially in middle school. Kids act out."

"What about recently? Has he talked about any problems with students?"

"You mean with girls in his classes?"

Mahler made a mental note of the clarification. "Any students."

"I don't know. He didn't discuss it with me. But we didn't talk about work. We didn't talk about anything...except Jesse and Claire."

"Your sister-in-law told us that some of Paul's female students became infatuated with him."

"Behrens's Brats? Yeah. I heard those stories. But I think the other teachers made too much of that. Paul was a serious teacher. He required a lot of his students."

Mahler tapped his fingers lightly on the tabletop and thought of how to play his next card. "Mrs. Behrens, we interviewed someone yesterday who told us that earlier this year a female student accused your husband of something. We also learned Paul may have been meeting with someone yesterday on the coast."

"Who told you that? What student?"

"I can't tell you who told us, and we don't have an identity for the student."

"I don't think it's true. It doesn't sound like my husband."

"So does that mean Paul never said anything to you about a student or meeting someone?"

"No. Nothing. But a lot of time, Paul only told me something when it was over. It was his way of being in control."

Annie stood. "I can show you something. I'll be back in a minute."

When she returned to the kitchen table, Annie laid a phone and a piece of paper in front of her. She swiped at the screen until she came to the photo of her husband and a girl seated on a bench. She turned the phone toward Mahler. "Some kids in my daughter's school hacked this photo off Paul's phone and threatened to post it on social media."

Mahler studied the photo. "Who's the girl? Do you know her?"

"No. It could be a student at Brookwood. Years ago I knew his pupils, but now… One year after another, I can't keep track."

Mahler looked up from the phone. "And you said this photo was hacked from your husband's phone? When we searched his phone, we didn't find any photos."

Annie returned a blank look. "I believe it was a while ago. I don't know exactly."

"And what do you mean by 'hacked'?"

"It was the game of some children. I don't understand it. My son, Jesse, can explain it. All I know is the photo came from Paul's phone." Annie passed the paper photo of the semi-nude girl to Mahler. "I found this in Paul's briefcase yesterday morning after he left."

"Again, do you know who this girl is?" Mahler smoothed the paper to study it.

"No. No idea. But when I took it out of his briefcase, I crumpled it up before your people searched my house."

Mahler looked up from the photo. "And why'd you do that?"

"It surprised me, scared me. I thought you'd find him before this, and the pictures wouldn't be necessary. I didn't want them to be…misinterpreted. I thought they were a mistake."

Mistake? Mahler wondered at the word but let it go. "But you're showing them to me now? You changed your mind? Do you think these photos might be related to your husband's leaving?"

"Yes." Annie shook her head. "No. I don't know. When I first saw them, I thought maybe something had gone wrong. Paul had gotten into some trouble and needed to…get away. Then when you said that thing a minute ago about Paul being accused of something, I thought I should show them to you. I don't know…what they mean."

Annie glanced toward the living room where the chaplain waited and lowered her voice. "Couldn't these photos be a… I mean, in your experience, Lieutenant Mahler, couldn't there be something…an innocent explanation?"

Mahler had never liked the phrase. Most explanations lost any claim to innocence after the first dozen words. Innocent according to the California Penal Code? In the eyes of God? Mahler supposed we'll all find how innocent we are when, as his mother used to say, our life is over and we stand before the Father. "At this point we need more information, to understand the circumstances." He held the paper photo and handed the phone back to Annie.

Annie tapped at the phone. "I'll send you a copy."

Mahler watched Annie work the screen. "Mrs. Behrens, when we spoke yesterday, you didn't remember what time you arrived home Tuesday night. But we talked to your shift supervisor. She said you signed out at 11:20 p.m. Is that correct?"

"That sounds right." She looked up from the phone.

"Your son, Jesse, told us you weren't home when he went to bed at 12:30. Could you please tell me where you went after you signed out from the hospital ward and what time you arrived home?"

"Where I went?" Annie frowned and looked away from Mahler.

"Yes. Where you went when you left work Tuesday night."

"I was…with a friend."

"I'll need a name."

"Greg. Dr. Gregory Winter."

"And where were you and Dr. Winter last evening?"

"In my car."

"In your car? You were with Dr. Winter in your car?"

"That's right."

"And when did you arrive home?"

"I'm not sure. Around 1:45. Something like that."

"You were in your car with Dr. Winter for two hours?"

"Why do you need to know this? It doesn't have anything to do with Paul."

"Mrs. Behrens, we're trying to understand what happened to your husband." Mahler pushed gently. "We need to know the whereabouts of every member of his family."

Annie lowered her voice again. "We were...intimate. Greg and I...in my car. That's all. He's not involved in...this."

"Did your husband know about you and Dr. Winter?"

"He knew... Yes. He knew I'm seeing Greg."

"Have you spoken to Dr. Winter today?"

"No... I called him. He didn't pick up."

"Is that unusual?"

"Sort of. Normally he texts. I called his office, but they said he didn't come in...or call." Annie frowned. "He missed a couple of appointments and a surgical procedure."

"So you don't know where Dr. Winter was this morning when your husband left?"

Annie's face expressed bewilderment. "No, but look... Greg's not involved in this. I know he's not. This is wrong. I know it."

Mahler let the woman play out her confusion. Which man was she devoted to? he wondered. "I think you'd better give me Dr. Winter's contact information." He pushed a pad across the table.

(ii)

"The gun's a nine-millimeter Glock." Coyle pointed to a photo of a handgun taped to the whiteboard in the VCI bullpen. "One shot fired. Shell casing on the floor of the car between the seats. Only prints on the gun are the victim's."

The whiteboard held photos of Behrens's body, with close-ups of his face and head wound. Other photos showed the car's interior and the site on Bean Avenue.

Mahler stood in his usual spot, leaning against the filing cabinets on the edge of the bullpen. He felt the difference in the room's air. The focus of the investigation, Paul Behrens, belonged to the team in a way he hadn't the day before. Yesterday he had been lost, a runaway, a target to be pinned on a map. Now he was dead, the sort of ending the team always inherited. Ghosts, Tommy Woodhouse called them. Closed-eye faces on a whiteboard, restlessly waiting for answers.

"The serial number's been filed off," Coyle continued, "so there's no record of registration. According to the state DOJ database, Paul Behrens has no gun registered in his name. So... basically, the registration's no help."

"We need to know where the gun came from," Mahler said. "Annie says her husband didn't own one."

"Eddie," Rivas said, "are we treating this death as a suicide? If it is, it's not our case anymore, right?"

"Yes, but something doesn't look right," Mahler said. "Normally, with a suicide, family and friends describe the victim's depression prior to the act. When we're asked to locate a missing person, the family often brings up the possibility of a suicide. That didn't happen here. None of his family or colleagues mentioned it." Mahler turned to Eden. "This morning, when I broke the news to Annie, she said her husband never gave any indication he was depressed. With suicides, aren't there usually signs?"

"Usually," Eden said. "Sometimes they come out of the blue, and the family recognizes the clues only after the death. But you're right. In this case, we haven't seen a lot to indicate Behrens was about to take his life."

"Which means," Mahler said, "there're enough questions to justify our taking the rest of today and looking at this some more."

"Okay," Frames said. "I see where you're going. But there *are* a few things that could've pushed Behrens over the edge. This morning his wife told you she's cheating on him, right? Maybe Behrens found out and couldn't stand it. Felt humiliated. Or depressed over the loss of his marriage."

"I don't know," Mahler said. "Yesterday Beth Rigney, Behrens's sister, told me Paul confronted Annie about the affair back in March. She said Paul didn't seem to care. She said his heart wasn't in it. This morning, when Annie told me her husband knew of the relationship, she made it sound like it wasn't a big deal."

"But there's something odd about Annie's companion, Dr. Winter." Mahler paged through his notebook. "She said he didn't return her calls all day yesterday. He also didn't come to his office." Mahler tore a page from his notebook and handed it to Coyle. "Here's his contact info. Find him. Let's see where he was when our victim disappeared."

"Also, what about the girls in the photos Annie Behrens gave you?" Frames asked. "What's going on there? Was our Teacher of the Year acting inappropriately or, worse, with the girls?

Maybe he learned he's about to be exposed, arrested. It's going to wreck his career, his marriage—his life basically. He can't face it, so he drives out to the coast and shoots himself."

"But if that's true, what exactly happened with those girls?" Mahler asked. "We need to find their identities. Daniel, show the photos to Principal Steeley and see if she can tell us who they are."

"It's odd, though, isn't it?" Eden said. "In some ways, that premise doesn't make sense. Behrens is a successful, experienced teacher. He'd know how to handle students and parents. He also loves his job, and is good at it. Why's he suddenly take a left turn?"

"He got in trouble," Frames said. "Started small. Good intentions. Snowballed out of control."

Mahler turned to Coyle. "What else do we know? Do we have a report from the coroner?"

Coyle scrolled through his laptop screen and read out loud. "Single gunshot wound to the head. Time-of-death estimated at 9:00 to 11:00 p.m. GSR on the victim's hand. No other significant markings on the body. Only thing in the victim's pockets was his wallet and a little cash. Clothing was damp. Clothing and shoes had evidence of sand, consistent with the victim being on the beach and possibly in the ocean prior to his death. That's the full report for now." Coyle looked up from his screen. "Autopsy's scheduled later this morning."

Mahler walked to the center of the room. "If Behrens was on the beach, and in the ocean in his clothes, someone might have seen him." He addressed Frames. "Drive back out there, Steve, and do a canvass."

"Okay, but where? I mean, the guy called Jean Cummings from Doran Park and ended up in the Salmon Creek neighborhood. That's a lot of oceanfront."

"Start at Salmon Creek. Behrens left a puddle of water on the floor of his car. Maybe he was in the water not long before he took his life."

"Eddie, you see this?" Coyle turned his laptop screen toward Mahler. "The press has photos online of the car on Bean Avenue. Identified it as belonging to Paul Behrens. Also, Sergeant Glasser down in Public Information says she's already received inquiries from the paper and a couple TV stations."

"Write something for the department to release. Keep it simple. No details on the death."

"How's the wife doing, Eddie?" Rivas asked.

"In shock. Not sleeping. I tried to find family or friends to stay with her. She didn't seem to want her in-laws. A chaplain is with her now."

"She's at risk," Eden said. "She wasn't in good shape before we found her husband. It'll be worse once it sinks in."

"I'm also worried about Claire," Mahler said. "She probably won't talk to the chaplain. Why don't you go out to the house and talk to her—alone, if possible. You'll need to get the mother's permission."

"The forensics team made an initial report," Coyle read from his laptop. "Outside the car—tire tracks not matching the Elantra. Techs say they're not sure those are relevant. That road gets a fair amount of use. Inside the car, they found mud and sand on the passenger-side floor mat. Partial footprint. Floor of back seat—takeout carton and a half-empty bottle of Jameson's. Nothing unusual in the trunk. Car's been towed to our garage, and they'll dust for prints there."

"Tell them to dust the seat belt," Rivas said. When Coyle looked up, Rivas added, "You decide to off yourself, why'd you leave the seat belt on? Whenever I'm sitting in my car, the first thing I do is take it off."

"Where's the phone?" Eden asked. As the others turned to look at her, she said, "He had a phone. Probably a burner. He talked to Jean Cummings. Where is it?"

"I didn't see it in the car last night." Coyle looked back at his laptop. "No mention of it in the forensics team's report."

"Which means he lost it or threw it away," Rivas said.

"Or someone else was in the car and took the phone," Mahler said. "Which changes everything. This morning Annie said her husband only dressed up when he wanted to look professional and thought he was being judged. If Behrens did meet someone, that means we're looking for whoever was in that car."

For a moment, the bullpen was quiet, the thought settling in.

Frames broke the silence. "Another thing, isn't it surprising the techs didn't find a note in his car or in his clothes? Guy's a literature teacher and a writer. A month ago, he wrote a resignation letter. You'd think he'd write something?"

"I agree," Mahler said. "Plus, given the circumstances, wouldn't he want to explain himself? To his wife and especially his kids?"

"Sometimes they don't," Eden said. "Depends on the level of despair. They may feel they can't explain it, or they're just unable to write. Nationally, the percentage who leave notes is only something like twenty-five percent. For Behrens, maybe the meeting with whoever went south. Also sounds like he was drinking."

Mahler walked slowly back and forth, staring at the whiteboard, as if in conversation with the taped images. "What's that right there?" Mahler leaned close to a photo of Behrens's wound site. "Martin, can you enlarge that picture?"

Coyle worked his tablet and a minute later pulled a sheet of paper from the printer.

Mahler taped the new print on the whiteboard. "There." He pointed to a spot on the print. "What's that look like?"

"Contusion." Rivas stood and squinted at the photo. "Bruise. Probably the end of the barrel pressed against his head."

Frames nodded. "He was nervous, freaking out. He shoved it too hard against his head."

"Or something else," Mahler said. "Did forensics find any fibers or evidence on the passenger seat?"

Coyle leaned close to his laptop. "Like I said earlier, mud on the floor mat. Partial footprint. Nothing about the car seat."

"Tell them to look again." He walked toward the door, then turned back to the group. "Call me if anything comes up. I'm going to talk to the victim's brother."

Chapter Seventeen

(i)

"Julia Guerro. Her name's Julia Guerro." Jennifer Steeley ran her fingers carefully along the edge of the plastic evidence pouch and looked down at the selfie of a young topless girl. "She's a student in one of Paul's classes."

"You don't seem surprised this photo was found in Paul Behrens's briefcase."

"Surprised? No. No. I'm…not surprised." She let go of the photo.

"Why not? Why would this be in his briefcase?" Rivas made a note on his pad.

"Is it true Paul's dead? There're stories on Twitter you found him."

"I can't comment at this time."

"Which means it's true." She massaged her eyes.

"Let's get back to Julia Guerro. Why aren't you surprised Paul Behrens had this photo?"

Steeley looked back at Rivas without speaking.

"We're trying to find out what happened to your teacher. This might—"

"What difference does it make now? If he's dead, what difference does it make?"

"We're trying to understand the circumstances behind his disappearance yesterday. It's important for—"

"Back in March, Julia posted the photo on Instagram. She deleted it after a couple of hours, but a lot of people saw it. She said Paul took the photo and was intimate with her. None of it was true, of course. It's a selfie. Julia took the photo herself. No one else was involved. But it led to rumors, kids talking."

"What'd you do?"

"I brought in Julia with her mother. Julia admitted she made it up. She was head over heels. Writing poems to Paul, telling stories to her friends. This kind of thing doesn't happen often, but it does go on. Look. I'm just a school principal, obviously not a psychologist. But I'm around these children all the time. Have been for years. So I'll say this. The hormones of these girls are raging, their bodies are changing, and they don't understand a lot of it." Steeley took a deep breath, trying to gain equilibrium. "Julia's parents are divorced. She's one of five kids living with her mom. I think she just needed to be seen."

Rivas looked at the photo of the girl again. Was it easier now than years ago for things to go wrong? Or, was it really no different? Born into the wrong family. Walking home the wrong way, at the wrong time. Talking to the wrong person. Ending up caught in a photograph—on a phone, online, clicked on, seen. "What about Paul Behrens?" Rivas asked.

"He was shaken. Scared, frankly. Nothing like this happened before. He believed in what he was doing. He adored his students. But this—"

"So you talked to him about it?"

"Of course. Several times. He denied anything was behind it. But he started second-guessing his teaching methods. You know, had he done anything to encourage Julia's stories? And after that, he couldn't focus. He was all over the place. He missed appointments."

"What about this?" Rivas handed Steeley a copy of Behrens's resignation letter. "We found this on Behrens's computer."

Steeley picked up a pair of eyeglasses and read the letter. When she finished, she threw the glasses back on the desktop. "Paul never showed me this. This is the first I've seen it."

"Does it surprise you?"

"Absolutely." Steeley returned the letter to Rivas.

"So is the Julia Guerro photo the incident he refers to in his letter of resignation?" Rivas asked.

"Yes. But I never saw that letter. He never said anything to me about resigning."

"Why didn't you tell me this yesterday when I asked?"

"Because I didn't think it was relevant to his being missing."

"Not relevant? You just said Paul changed after the incident. He couldn't focus."

"I know. I know. But it happened months ago. I thought Paul was getting better."

Rivas heard a lot of stories, got lied to a lot. It was always a waste of time. "So you didn't report the incident with Julia Guerro?"

"No, I did not. Because we addressed the situation head-on when it happened. We put it behind us. The child, the parent, and the teacher."

"Are you sure about that?" Rivas looked down at his notebook. "We also know that at the end of that month, Paul Behrens ran Google searches on the terms sexual assault, Child Protective Services, and molestation."

Rivas watched the principal look back silently, calculating her next move. Something in her eyes told him that Steeley was trapped on the wrong side of whatever was going to come to light with Paul Behrens. As happened a hundred times in his job, he could foresee a person being undone by the unexpected wave of circumstances headed toward them. In six or eight weeks, this woman with her streak of purple hair could be out of a job, out of her profession. And how it happened would always be a mystery to her. Whatever part of it could be labeled good intentions, she'd still be searching for a long time to find the starting point, that place in the rearview mirror where the unraveling began. "Ms. Steeley, you know you're required by law to report incidents of possible child abuse, and that failure to do so is a criminal offense."

Steeley stared back at him. "I don't appreciate your telling me what's a criminal matter."

"That's *my* job."

For a moment neither of them spoke. From outside came the sound of students, a young girl's voice calling the name Ellie over and over.

Rivas picked up the photo of Julia Guerro. "This photo was in Paul Behrens's briefcase yesterday when he went missing. We need contact information for Julia Guerro and her mother."

Steeley turned to her computer screen and tapped on the keyboard. After a minute, she wrote on a piece of paper and slid it across the desktop to Rivas.

"This'll only make things worse. You know that, don't you? For the girl, for Paul's memory, for his family."

Rivas ignored the question. He reached back into his folder and showed Steeley the photo of Paul Behrens sitting next to a girl on a bench. "This photo was found on Paul Behrens's phone. Do you recognize her?"

Steeley held up the photo and frowned. "Her name's Zoe

McFarland. She's in Paul's eighth-grade English class. One of our top students. Good family."

"Do you know why the photo was taken, and why it was on your teacher's phone?"

"No idea. Kids take photos all the time. As I said before, Paul was popular with his students. In this case, I don't know why it would be on *his* phone."

Steeley handed back the photo. "But—" She turned to her computer and tapped at the keyboard. "Maybe it's a coincidence, but Zoe McFarland didn't come to school this morning. We called the parents. They thought Zoe was with friends. We're trying to track it down."

"So the school and the parents don't know where the girl is?" Rivas asked.

"No. Mr. and Mrs. McFarland are making more calls before... contacting the police. With another student, I'd suspect truancy. But not Zoe. If there's nothing else, I should get back to the McFarlands'."

"One more thing." Rivas gave the principal the security camera images. "Here's the man who was seen coming out of Paul Behrens's classroom Wednesday morning. Do you recognize him?"

Steeley squinted at the printouts. "I don't understand. That's John McFarland. Zoe's father. But why—"

"You're certain?"

"Absolutely. But I don't know why he'd be there."

Rivas gathered his files and stood to leave.

Steeley leaned over the desk. "Will you report the Guerro case to Child Protective Services?"

"It's not up to me."

"Whoever takes this job won't be as dedicated to the children as I am. You know that, don't you?" Steeley shook her head wearily. She looked up at Rivas. "The people who make those decisions? It's about spreadsheets."

Rivas waited to see if the principal would say more. Then he pushed his chair back in place. "We'll be in touch if we need anything else."

(ii)

Mahler hesitated in the doorway. The window shades of the care facility's common room had been closed, leaving the space in a dark shroud. The room was empty but for a barely visible couple in the far corner. As his eyes adjusted, Mahler could make out a seated Beth Rigney facing her brother, Michael Behrens. She was holding his hands and appeared to be speaking, although her words didn't carry across the room.

Mahler tapped lightly on the doorframe and waited until Michael looked up. "Sorry to disturb. I'm wondering if I might ask a few questions."

Michael nodded and whispered something to Beth.

Pulling a folding chair from a nearby table, Mahler sat close. "I'm sorry for your loss." He spoke softly, as if to preserve the room's quiet. "I know we were all hoping for better news."

Michael looked back silently. His sister sat still, not lifting her head.

Mahler took a pad from his jacket pocket. "Sergeant, you told me yesterday your brother, Paul, didn't say where he was going when he left here. Is that right?"

"That's right, sir. He didn't say."

"He didn't mention anything about a meeting? About the people he was going to see?"

"No, sir." Michael frowned. "But that wasn't unusual. He didn't talk about his work with me."

"You also remembered that when Paul was here yesterday morning, he kept checking his phone. Was it the phone he always had, or did it look different?"

Michael jumped at the question. "It was different. It wasn't his iPhone. I notice things like that."

"Was he making calls or—?"

"Texting. He got a couple texts. I heard the phone go off, and he read them. A couple times he excused himself and responded. He didn't say who they were from or what the messages were."

Just like the day before, Mahler heard the unusual pattern of the former soldier's speech, as if he was checking each word as he spoke it. "Okay. That's helpful. Another question: when I asked you yesterday where you thought Paul went, you said he was in the ocean. Do you remember?"

"Yes, sir. Although I believe I said I *thought* he was in the ocean."

Mahler looked down at his pad. "I'm sorry. You're right. Those were your words."

"Was he?" Michael asked. "Was my brother in the ocean?"

"We don't know yet. But it appears he might have been. That's why I wanted to speak with you again."

Beth sat up. She brushed the hair from her eyes and faced Mahler. "The chaplain who spoke with us said Paul was found in his car."

"That's right. But there were indications he may have been in the ocean. We're just—"

"What kind of indications?"

"I'm afraid I can't go into the details. We're trying to understand what Paul might have been doing in the time before he... was found."

Beth winced at Mahler's hesitation.

"Which is why I wanted to ask you, Michael, what made you think Paul was in the ocean? *Why* did you think that?"

"I get these things. Pictures. In my mind. I can't explain it, but I see them. When I was deployed, somebody in the APC had to look ahead in the road. That was my job. I got good at seeing things."

"So, with Paul, what exactly did you see?"

"He was running in the waves. That's what I saw."

Beth watched her brother and squeezed his hand.

"Was he by himself?" Mahler asked.

"I believe so. Yes, sir."

Mahler made a note on his pad.

"Lieutenant Mahler, I know what I can't do." Michael leaned toward Mahler. "Some people think I don't know because of the damage to my brain. But I know."

"I believe you."

"Good," Michael said. "I'm glad you do—as an officer asking the questions."

Mahler noted the soldier's trust in an officer. For an instant, Mahler was transported back twenty years to Army Ranger School, Fort Benning, Georgia. In front of him—students assigned to his command, waiting in the rain for his instructions. Their faces young, most just out of high school, ready to do whatever he commanded.

Beth held up both hands, as though framing something in the air. "Did you talk to Annie? I mean, did she tell you anything?"

"We've spoken to Mrs. Behrens several times. I can't tell you what she said."

"She knows something about Paul going away. When she called me yesterday morning, she was super weird. Remember I told you that when you came to the house? Looking back, I think she had an idea about where he went." Beth looked up at Michael. "I'm sorry to be saying this now, given what's happened. But Annie has secrets. You know it, right?"

Michael shrugged. "I don't talk that much with Annie."

"In some cases, you never find answers, do you?" Beth asked Mahler. "You don't figure out what happened or why."

Mahler shoved his pad back in his pocket.

"I heard this podcast," Beth said. "A guy was killed, and they thought his girlfriend did it, but they couldn't find enough to know for sure."

"We'll do our best." Mahler stood to leave. "Thank you both for your help."

He left the common room and walked down the main corridor of the care facility to the front lobby. As he signed out on the visitors' log, he saw the house manager, Franny Hastings, sitting in her small office.

"How're they doing?" she asked.

"It's still fresh," Mahler said. "Michael just told me he knows what he can't do. He wanted to be sure I knew that."

"These guys are in a tough spot," Franny said. "Their own damaged brain is all they have to understand their thoughts... themselves. It's like looking at yourself through a cracked lens. Some of them, like Michael, are very aware of that. On top of the brain damage, most of the men in this facility have PTSD, which acts in a particularly cruel way to fuel their fears. It's like a repeating echo of whatever awful things they experienced."

"I know," Mahler said. "I have my own experience with it." The words came out before he planned it and caught him off guard. He tried to explain himself. "Several years ago there was a homicide in the city. A young woman. It stayed with me more than some others."

"Then you know what it's like." Franny studied Mahler. "I'd

be happy to talk about it with you sometime if it would help. It's one thing I do have experience with."

> **Dr. Schafer:** You said you felt responsible for the murder of Susan Hart. Why?
>
> **Mahler:** Because we didn't act quickly enough after the murder of Michelle Foss.
>
> **S:** But at the time Michelle Foss was killed, no one knew the killer would act again. No one knew it wasn't a onetime act. Is that correct?
>
> **M:** Yes. But we should have. If we had, Susan Hart wouldn't have died.
>
> **S:** But you didn't kill her.
>
> **M:** No. Of course not. But I left her there in the park.
>
> **S:** *You* left her there?
>
> **M:** She was alone when she was killed.
>
> **S:** And that was your fault?
>
> **M:** I thought it was.
>
> **S:** Is that why you returned to the place where she was killed?
>
> **M:** I guess so.
>
> **S:** And is it why you talked to her after she was dead?
>
> **M:** I thought she was lonely.

Mahler felt the awkwardness of having drifted into this personal area. "Thank you for the offer. I didn't mean to—"

Franny saw his embarrassment and changed the subject. "You realize, Lieutenant Mahler, with this investigation into Michael's brother, you're an important person in Michael's life."

"Me? What do you mean?"

"Michael trusts authority. It's been his entire adult life. The military—and by extension, law enforcement. He trusts you.

After you left yesterday, he said he knew you'd find Paul. And you did."

"I'm sorry it wasn't with a better result."

"Yes, but you did find him. For someone like Michael who's been in battle, that's a big deal."

Mahler turned to leave, then came back. "Actually, I was going to ask, Ms. Hastings, if you'd like to get together for coffee or...something. Dinner?"

"To talk about your PTSD?"

"No." Mahler felt himself suddenly tongue-tied. "Just...to talk."

Franny smiled. "Sure," she said. "How about tonight?"

Chapter Eighteen

(i)

Coyle thought about the VCI team's caseload and what awaited them once the Behrens homicide was resolved. On any given day, the team had dozens of cases—stabbings, assaults, robberies, occasional shootings. There was never a slow season. Holidays. Storms. Blue skies. Bad economy. Good economy. Nothing made a dent in the reports. In the VCI bullpen, it was possible to believe violence was as natural as breathing or the beating of a heart.

Coyle's car was parked behind a building in Medical Row, a section of downtown Santa Rosa known for its successive blocks of physician suites. The vantage gave him a clear view of cars entering and leaving a one-story brick complex that housed the office of Dr. Gregory Winter. So far, he hadn't seen the doctor's five-year-old white Corolla.

To distract himself from his dark thoughts, he scrolled

through his texts. A message from Rivas identified the girls in Behrens's photos as Julia Guerro and Zoe McFarland. A text from Frames documented his lack of progress in a canvass of houses near the coastal Salmon Creek site where Paul Behrens's body was found.

Coyle's mind returned to his work and his thoughts in the courtroom the day before. What was his own purpose in the midst of the baseness of the VCI caseload? Was it the merest sorting of puzzle pieces to know what happened? Was that worth what he saw day to day?

"According to Dogen Zenji," Adrienne told him, "the reason we exist is to allow God to experience the universe. We provide the eyes and ears for God."

"So, in this case, I'm helping God to know what it's like for a man to beat another with a hammer?" Coyle had tried for a tone of skepticism, not sarcasm, but wasn't sure he achieved it. He guessed there was more to it.

"There's more to it," Adrienne said. "Everything around us— buildings, sky, cars, people—is constantly expressing the truth of the universe. Therefore, Dogen says, it's our sacred responsibility to hear and see so that the ineffable reality of the world can be revealed."

Coyle stretched his arms and tried to feel himself open to ineffable reality. He was more likely, he thought, to experience f-ing reality.

The building's tenant list identified the doctors who shared the office building. The sign held six names and the doctors' specialties—four family practice, two orthopedics. Beneath the names were two dark bars on the sun-faded panel where other names had been removed. An hour earlier, the lobby receptionist had greeted Coyle with a smile that disappeared when he mentioned Dr. Winter's name. She told him the doctor was not in but was expected soon. She said it all with the pinched, warning expression that you got from servers in a restaurant when you ordered the calamari, and their eyes said you'd be better off with the wings.

Coyle had once believed all physicians to be equally on top of the social pyramid due to their expertise and income, and to the public's dependence on doctors to repair bodies and save lives. In recent years, though, he'd begun to recognize hierarchies within the profession. At the pinnacle were neurosurgeons, who use robotic-assisted techniques to repair delicate neural tissue, along with interventional cardiologists, who perform myocardial revascularization. Further down, orthopedic surgeons were cruder, more strong arms than fine motor skills, the hardware guys, the carpenters who drill holes in the broken carpal bones of teenage skateboarders and insert screws into the hips of the fallen elderly. In other words, neurosurgeons were Mercedes E-class; orthopedic surgeons were Corollas.

As if on cue, the Corolla in question arrived in the parking lot. Coyle waited for Winter to climb out of his car. After a few minutes, when the doctor didn't move, Coyle approached the open driver-side window. From the car's interior came a rancid odor of things unwashed and empty takeout cartons.

Coyle held up his badge. "Dr. Gregory Winter? I have some questions. Could you step outside the car please?"

Winter stared ahead at the back wall of the office building. "All right, if it's absolutely necessary." He pulled himself from the driver's seat and leaned against the car.

Coyle took out a small notebook. "We're investigating the death of Paul Behrens. I have a few questions for you."

"Paul Behrens? The schoolteacher in the news?" Winter seemed to awaken from a spell.

"That's right. Can you tell me where you were yesterday from 8:00 a.m. until midnight?"

"Yesterday? The whole day? I was here." Winter gestured toward the building. "In my office. I mean, for part of that time."

"With all due respect, Dr. Winter, we know that's not true," Coyle said. "Your office manager told us she hasn't seen you since Tuesday morning. You haven't called in. You may as well just tell us the truth. We can easily check everything. Lying is wasting your time and ours."

"I went to see my children." Winter looked down at his hands. "They live with my ex-wife in Forestville."

"Your kids aren't in school?"

"They're young—two and four."

Coyle made a note. "When did you arrive, and how long did you stay?"

"Nine or so. I stayed for lunch and left after that."

"I'll need your ex's number to verify that."

"Is that really necessary?"

"I'm afraid so."

Winter scrolled through his phone and held the screen toward Coyle.

"What'd you do after that?"

The doctor frowned, deep in thought.

"Come on. It was yesterday. Wednesday. What'd you do?"

"I drove out to the coast."

"Where exactly?"

"I took 116 through Guerneville to Jenner, at the mouth of the river, and then north from there."

"Why'd you go there?"

"I don't know. I just drove. I wanted to be alone. My wife—my ex-wife—and I are going through some things. The visit didn't go well. We argued. The kids were… I couldn't go back to my practice as if nothing happened."

"Did you meet anyone? Did anyone see you?"

"Did anyone see me? I don't know. What kind of a question is that?"

"Is there any way of proving you were on the coast when you said you were?"

Winter reached through the car's open window to the back seat. He pushed around a pile of food cartons and took hold of a small paper bag. "I bought some takeout at a restaurant in Timber Cove. Here's the receipt." He handed the slip to Coyle.

"When did you come back from the coast?" Coyle read the receipt and made a note on his pad.

"I didn't. I mean, I stayed out there all night." Winter rubbed his eyes. "I had a sleeping bag. I came back this morning. Right now."

"Did you see Paul Behrens?"

"Behrens?" Winter roused himself and looked back at Coyle. "No. Why would I? I've never met him."

"Where were you Tuesday night?"

"Why'd you ask? Annie told me you people talked to her. You already know where I was."

"Just tell me."

"I worked on charts at the hospital until eleven. Then I met Annie. We had sex in her car in the parking garage. I went home and slept. In the morning I went to Forestville like I told you."

Winter watched Coyle writing in his tablet. "Look. I know how it sounds, given what's happened. But Annie said she was leaving Paul. She doesn't love him. Or, didn't love him. Whatever. Anymore. It was something that…happened. Annie feels bad. We didn't plan it."

Coyle heard the rationalization but had no personal or professional opinions on the guy cheating with the dead man's wife. Seven years of listening to suspects across the department's small interview table had made him stop wondering about people and their cautionary choices. What did register was that Winter was with Annie Behrens hours before her husband disappeared and that part of the timeline was Coyle's job.

Coyle flipped through the pages of his tablet. "You said you slept in your car Wednesday night? Where was that?"

"I don't remember. One of those rest areas. Past Salt Point maybe."

"Could it have been farther south? South of Jenner? Bodega?"

"I told you I don't remember. I wasn't paying attention. My ex-wife is talking about taking our kids to Oregon. I had a lot on my mind."

"If we go through that pile of paper in the back seat, are we going to find receipts from other places?"

"I don't know. I don't know." Winter's face reddened. "I don't think I went there, to Salmon Creek, or whatever you said."

"I didn't say Salmon Creek." Coyle felt something shift. He remembered his old mentor Tom Woodhouse saying, "Look for the facts, but be bright enough to know when the facts find you." Or, was this more of Adrienne's ineffable reality that he was experiencing for God?

Coyle closed his tablet. "Dr. Winter, I'm going to ask you to come into the station where we can talk."

"Wait. Please. Listen to me. I can't afford to have a disruption like this. My practice is in a fragile state. We're reorganizing. One of my partners left. I had nothing to do with Paul Behrens's disappearance. I swear."

"Okay. Then let's get it over with." Coyle turned toward his car and waited for the doctor to join him.

(ii)

(THURSDAY, 11:00 A.M.)

"Do you want to go back to school?" Eden kept her voice quiet, just above a whisper.

"Yeah, I guess so," Claire said. "It's better than sitting around here."

"You'd rather be with your friends?"

"I don't have any friends."

In the Behrens's living room, Eden sat on one end of the sofa with Claire on the other. Eden watched the girl, legs tucked under her body, making herself into the smallest possible profile. *Why is it so hard to be a teenager? Do any young girls grow up unscarred?* She remembered her own nights at Deerfield as a first-year, lying awake in the dark dorm room, listening to the other girls whispering outside the door. Could she make herself die just by wishing for it?

"I know this is a hard time for you, Claire, with the news about your father."

"You didn't find him, like you said you would, before he—"

"No. No, we didn't, and I'm sorry about that. I really am. Now, though, we're trying to understand what happened."

"It's too late."

"You're right. Still, it's important to find out, if we can, exactly what happened to your dad."

Eden paused to see if Claire would say anything. The girl sat silently, looking at the floor. Eden waited another ten seconds. An array of family photographs hung on the wall behind Claire: a younger Jesse in soccer jersey and shorts, Annie and Claire with their arms around one another laughing at the camera, the four of them at a picnic table in front of a lake. The wall was like a terrible memory of happiness. Eden could understand Claire's restlessness and desire to leave. The house had a lonely emptiness, an unbearable silence.

"What's your favorite subject in school?" Eden tried to restart the conversation in a different direction.

Claire didn't respond.

"Is it English, like your dad taught?"

"No. Algebra."

"Algebra? Really? I'm not sure I've ever heard anyone else say that."

"Our teacher told us the word 'algebra' means the 'reunion of broken parts.'"

"I didn't know that."

"Everything fits together, if you do it right."

Teenage girls need solutions, Eden told herself, equations that make sense. This girl especially.

"And it doesn't have any words. Sometimes I get tired of words. It's about x."

"Solving for x. I remember that."

"There's a boy in my class named Eric who goes around saying 'x the unknown,' 'x the unknown,' in a fake deep voice, like it's a character in the Avengers, or something."

Eden smiled. The young girl glanced at her for an instant to see if she was smiling, then looked back down. None of us knows how we'll survive loss until it comes, Eden thought. We imagine it'll call on our faith or our hardiness or our powers of distraction, but we have no idea in advance what those things really are and if they're any match for the loss. *What resources did this girl have in the face of her father's death?*

"You told me yesterday about your father's phone call that you overheard Tuesday night. Do you remember?"

"Yeah. So?"

"We're trying to put together a picture of what your father was thinking and doing the last few days. Now that you've had a little more time to think, I'm wondering if you remember anything else your father said or did recently."

"He talked about normal stuff. He talked about the Giants and how their pitching wasn't as good as last year. Sunday night he bought fresh pappardelle for dinner and said the name came from the Italian word that means 'to gobble up.'"

Eden smiled again. "Your father was a word person, wasn't he?" She watched Claire nod and saw in her eyes the adjustment to the past tense.

For a minute they sat silently. Eden looked back at the wall of photos and noticed a picture of Paul Behrens. He had been walking away from the camera but, just as the photo was taken, turned back to look over his shoulder and raise one hand in a wave.

"A week or so ago, my dad and I went grocery shopping." Claire licked her lips. "When we finished, we were sitting in his car in the parking lot. I told him how sometimes I had feelings about another person that I didn't want anyone to know. I'm not sure why I said it. It just came out. My dad always listened to me. He asked me what kind of feelings, and I said I couldn't tell him. I mean, I wasn't ready then."

Eden wondered what feelings could be trapped inside this sweet, young girl. "What'd your father say?"

"He said in philosophy there's this debate thing about whether we're responsible for what we feel in our hearts, even if we don't act on it. Some people believe we're only responsible for feelings we act on. Others believe what's in our heart is our truth."

"Your father sounds like a smart man." Cops, Eden thought, didn't get to bother with the heart's true intentions.

"He said it had taken him forty years to learn this, and he hoped it wouldn't take me as long."

"What did he mean by that?"

"I don't know. My dad just said, as adults we need to decide what to reveal and what to keep to ourselves. Sometimes revealing a secret can cause harm to ourselves and the people close to us. Other times, keeping secrets can be more damaging. He said he was helping someone deal with secrets she'd learned."

"She? Did he say who?"

"I could tell he didn't want to say. He told me this French writer—I forget his name—said that man is what he hides. My dad said we should always try not to hurt other people with our secrets."

Eden suddenly realized she had been holding her breath, and she gulped at the air.

Claire didn't seem to notice. She turned to face Eden. "Officer Somers, I read in a book somewhere that the dead can hear us. Do you think it's true?"

Eden owed her career to the factual discipline of police investigation, scientific study, the statistical research on human behavior. She saw the girl's clear blue eyes watching. She thought of the thirty or more dead bodies she'd seen in her short professional career—many of them young women, not much older than Claire—faces stiff, eyelids closed, with nothing in their appearance of a sentient, listening being. Even so, she remembered three or four times, alone with them, telling them how sorry she was, saying it without expectation of their hearing, but willing the words to go somewhere. "Maybe. I don't know."

"People say it's impossible. A dead person's brain has stopped functioning. The sensory organs in the ear aren't working. But how does anyone really know because no one has actually died and come back, right? Maybe the person's soul can hear?"

Eden tried to think of something comforting. Here were the limits she had wondered about earlier, of this young girl's resources for coping with the loss of her father. Should she tell Claire that once or twice a month she spoke to Dr. Donald Somers, whose body had lain for the last nine years deep in the frozen earth of northern Connecticut? Was that proof of anything besides her own loneliness? "Many religions believe those who have passed can hear our prayers."

The girl pressed on, unsatisfied. "But there are so many things I want to tell my father. And there will be for the rest of my life. I mean, like forever. How will I tell him?"

Eden reached across the sofa and took one of the girl's hands in hers. "Something inside will let you know how to do it. Your connection with your father will never end. You'll always be able to talk to him."

Chapter Nineteen

(i)

Frames held up his badge to identify himself.

In the middle of the doorway, a fifty-year-old man stood with his arms folded across his chest. He wore a T-shirt and drawstring sweatpants. "Are you looking for a donation? Jesus, isn't it enough I have to put up with your phone calls every damn week."

"I'm here about something else." Frames took out his phone and opened it to a photo of Paul Behrens. "Did you see this person yesterday? He may have been walking on Bean Avenue or the beach."

The man glanced at the phone and returned to Frames. "You know what pisses me off about you cops? You go around like you're acting under some unquestioned authority, some almighty principle. The letter of the law. But it's an illusion. All you have—"

"Sir, please."

"No. You listen to me. All you have is what's on your belt. Without it, you're no different from me. But because there's that weapon, you think you can tell me what to do."

Frames started over. He turned his phone toward the man again. "Did you see this person yesterday? It's important we talk to anyone who saw him."

"I didn't see the guy. Okay? Can you take that fucking thing out of my face?"

Frames looked more closely at the man—face flushed, pin-sized pupils, toxic juju in his veins. Was there any point in trying to engage? At another time, Frames would have jumped at the argument—the legitimacy of law enforcement in today's world. In the back of his head, he heard his girlfriend Natalie's voice: *If not now, when?*

In his imaginary argument, Frames told the man he'd been a member of two institutions: the Marine Corps and the Police Department. He was used to being lumped together, taking the blame for the idiots. But no body of people is entirely homogenous. The SRPD includes headbangers, placeholders, and a lot of people trying to figure out how to do a complicated job.

But was it true? Or, if you were in the institution, were you brushed with the devil, to use Natalie's words? Was the darkness inside even you?

The man in front of him, consumed with grievance, already had his answer.

Frames shoved the phone back in his pocket. "Thanks," he said. "You've been very helpful."

Once the door slammed shut, Frames took out a paper tablet to make a note of the address and response. For more than hour, he'd been knocking on the doors of the beach houses within a mile of where Behrens's body had been found. The modest one-story bungalows in the Salmon Creek neighborhood were former summer cottages for San Franciscans but were now year-round residences. So far, no one had seen Paul Behrens.

Frames walked fifty yards farther down Church Street, which fronted the ocean beach. He limped slightly, adjusting to the pain in his calf, where he had been stabbed with a rapier the day before. To the west, a low fog bank darkened the sky, but under it he could see waves coming ashore, slapping against the rocks and sand.

The next beach house was quiet, but he saw a light inside. He climbed to the porch and pushed the doorbell. When he didn't hear a sound, he knocked on the door. An elderly woman appeared in the doorway. She had gray hair pulled back from her face and wore a flannel shirt and corduroy slacks.

Frames took out his badge and started to introduce himself.

"I thought you'd come," she interrupted. She smiled at Frames, her blue eyes taking him in. "Well, not you specifically, but someone. After what happened on the road last night. Come in, young man. My name's Dorothy Fellows."

"I just wanted to ask if you—"

"Do come in and sit down, won't you? It's cold with this door open."

Frames followed the woman into a dimly lit sitting room with a sofa and large stuffed chair. A fire burned in a cast-iron stove. The room smelled of woodsmoke and flowery perfume. He waited for her to settle into the chair. Then he sat on the sofa across from her.

"Thank you for agreeing to see me." He took out his phone and passed it to the woman. "Did you happen to see this man yesterday?"

She held the phone and raised her glasses to peer at the screen. "I don't think so." She handed back the phone. "I didn't see that face. But I noticed something. Last night about nine, I went out on my porch to look at the stars. That's when I saw two people—they may have been men—running on the sand. After I heard about the poor fellow on Bean Avenue, I wondered if it might be related. Shall I make us some tea?"

"No. No. Thank you. I just—" Frames was in a hurry to hear more about the two people running on the beach, the first possible sighting by anyone in his canvass. But he saw the old woman's eyes waiting, and in an instant, he thought of Alice. For the last fifteen years of her life, his grandmother lived alone in an old Victorian in Cloverdale, half an hour north of Santa Rosa. "Stevie, when Nana asks if you want a cup of tea," Frames's mother reminded him, "she's not asking you if you actually want to drink tea, she's asking if you'll keep her company for half an hour."

"On second thought, tea would be great." Frames relaxed on the sofa. "I'd like that."

Dishes clattered in the kitchen. "As I say, I went outside to look at the stars," the old woman shouted. "I go out every night before I go to bed. Do you know the night sky? It's a wonderful show. For the next night or two, in the southeast sky, you can see Mars above the gibbous moon."

Gibbous moon? Was that real? "I always promised myself I'd learn the stars," Frames called into the kitchen, "but I never got around to it. They seemed too large to know, and all of it changing, season by season, before you could get your head around it." He wasn't sure the woman heard him but went on anyway. "I remember, when I was deployed, one morning before dawn outside Mosul. I was returning from patrol and looked up at the sky and realized it was the same back home in California. Even though I didn't know the names of the stars, it was somehow more familiar than the ground under my feet in that place."

Frames looked at the sitting room walls, covered with framed needlepoints, two commemorative plates, one the Liberty Bell, the other Mount Rushmore, and photographs—nearest him a young girl standing stiffly, arms at her sides, solemn face toward the camera.

"Shareen, my youngest." Returning with a tray of a teapot and cups, which she positioned on a low table between her chair and the sofa, Dorothy Fellows gestured toward the object of Frames's gaze. "Passed a long time ago. Sweet as honey, that one."

"Shall I be mother?" the woman asked, sitting again in her chair. "That's what the English call the one who pours the tea." She filled two cups. "Lapsang souchong. Smoky tea. Doesn't deserve milk, if you ask me, but you're welcome to it, of course. Now then, I've kept you waiting long enough. What did you want to ask me?"

Frames blew across the top of his cup. "Tell me about the two people you saw running on the beach last night."

"Not much to tell, when it comes to it. Too far away to see clearly. I noticed them because it's rare to see anyone on the beach that late. It's cold out."

"Were they wearing coats?"

"Not that I could see. Funny, that."

"But you said you thought they might have been men, is that right?"

"Maybe." Dorothy Fellows wrapped her fingers around the middle of her cup. "I may be saying that only because I heard about the man you found in the car."

"Could you see what they were doing?"

"Running. That way—north." She pointed a finger to her left. "Close to the surf. One ahead of the other. Then the second one caught the first and they fell."

Frames finished his tea. "Were they fighting?"

"Oh, I don't know, dear."

"Could you hear if they said anything?"

"You ask very good questions, young man. But, no, I couldn't hear anything."

"That's okay." Frames handed the old woman one of his cards. "If you remember anything else, please call me."

"Did you know this area was sacred for the Miwok? They called it *Pulya-lakum*. Some historians believe it was a point of departure for the newly deceased traveling to the spirit world. Maybe those powers assisted the poor man who died here last night."

Dorothy Fellows looked thoughtful. "You know, I should have mentioned this earlier. Last night I also saw another person outdoors, walking a dog. He was much closer to the beach and might have had a better view of the couple on the sand. Walked right past them, I expect. He's the one you should talk to."

"Do you know him?"

"No. But I see him all year round, so he must be local. Always the same route—from the top of the hill all the way to the parking lot. If he sees me, he waves. With him, there's this little white dog he calls Larry." She smiled. "Not that the dog's name helps you. I only know it because the man has one of those retractable leashes, and he shouts when the dog goes too far."

Frames stood to leave and followed the woman out of the sitting room. At the door, he turned to her. "Thank you for the information—and the tea."

"Oh, you're welcome. I hope you learn what you need to about the fellow in the car. Funny what happens to us, isn't it? How we all make our endings?" Then, as if intuiting Frames's earlier thought, she said. "Start with one constellation's name. The others will come."

"I'll try that." Frames stepped onto the porch and took the path toward his car.

(ii)

Annie Behrens sat on the deck behind her house. The sun shone faintly through the gray cloud cover. It was cold for May. She wore Paul's down jacket, with the collar turned up. It was one he wore on ski trips to Tahoe and had a tear on the right sleeve where he had snagged it on a branch. In her hands, she cradled a mug of coffee. A splash of Maker's Mark gave the coffee a sweet aroma that she breathed each time she lifted the mug to her lips.

She could see the harlequin flowers blooming in a bed at the back of the yard under the mulberry tree. The flowers appeared every year the second week of May—bright crimson and yellow petals bursting out of green, spear-shaped stems. It was a predictable routine. "Did you notice the harlequins are out?" Paul would ask. Then they'd stand side by side, looking out the kitchen window at the promise kept in their backyard.

Now the flowers were crowded with weeds. For an instant she thought of reminding Paul to weed the bed on the weekend if it wasn't raining.

Why didn't she sit out here more often? When Sara, their real estate agent, first showed them the house, the deck was Annie's favorite feature. She remembered lingering after Paul and Sara had gone back inside to see the second floor. She pictured a table and chairs, guests over, cocktails in highball glasses, talking casually about their children's achievements. Did they know Claire had started the violin? Did they see Jesse make that pass in front of the goal last Saturday?

She began to cry, tears running down her face too fast to catch. She wiped at them with her left palm and took a long drink of coffee.

The sliding glass door opened, and Jesse flopped onto the wicker chair beside Annie's. He wore a tank top and flannel pajama bottoms. He rested his bare feet on the deck railing.

"Couldn't sleep?" she asked.

"Not really. Not after the cop left."

What he's not saying, Annie thought, *is how do I sleep when I keep falling through trapdoors?* They would live this way now—by all the things they wouldn't say. *Lacunae.* Unfilled spaces. Paul taught her the word. What would she do for words now Paul was gone? "I thought Lieutenant Mahler was very kind—the way he spoke to us."

"I guess so. It's his job. Probably does it all the time."

"Still, he was careful, especially in front of Claire."

"There's no good way, though, is there?"

"No. No, you're right." Had Jesse seen her crying? She reached toward him but realized he was too far away. Her arm stretched in the air until she withdrew it. "Aren't you cold?"

"I'm okay. I'm not staying. You sound funny."

"I took a little Xanax. I thought it might help me sleep."

"Be careful, Mom. With the alcohol and all. You know that, right?"

"I'm fine. It's only half a milligram. Just for today."

They watched the wind stir the leaves that packed around the flower beds. She heard a new gentleness in Jesse's voice, his anger stilled overnight.

"Did you know Dad was going to do this?" Jesse asked.

"Take his life? No. Of course not. I mean—"

"What?"

"I did think about it. That's why I went to the police. The thing is, your father struggled with anxiety—and fear."

"Fear? Of what?"

"Not having enough money. Losing his job. You kids getting hurt. Not living up to his father. Frank Behrens is a wonderful grandfather, but he was a hard-ass to Paul. Dad grew up never good enough for your grandfather."

"I never saw him afraid of anything."

Annie drank her coffee. "No. He was pretty good at keeping it to himself. When you and Claire were young, there were panic attacks. He'd wake up at two, three in the morning with these awful adrenaline rushes."

"I didn't know that."

"He didn't want you to know. Your father has…had a wonderful imagination and passion. He knew so much about literature, biography, history. That's what made him such a good teacher. But he wasn't…realistic. He believed too much in emotions, feelings. You work in a hospital like I do, you know better. Sometimes your father didn't have the resources to deal with adversity. I thought he was doing better. But maybe…not."

Annie leaned forward to make sure Jesse was listening. "You can ask me anything. If I can, I'll tell you."

Jesse looked back silently.

"It's crazy what goes through your mind." Annie sat back. "After Lieutenant Mahler left, I was thinking the funeral home will want me to pick out clothes for your dad."

"That's what you were thinking? Now?"

"I know it's weird. But I remembered when my grandfather passed away, my grandmother gave the funeral home his best suit. Poor Grandpop died of liver cancer. In the last eight months, he dropped something like sixty pounds. He looked lost in those clothes, like the important part went missing before he died. But nobody knew what to do."

"That was before I was born, right?"

"You were two. Anyway, I was thinking about Grandpop, and it made me remember the shirt I bought your father for Christmas three years ago."

"Oh God," Jesse snorted. "The blue one?"

"Yes. Yes," Annie laughed. "With the pattern."

"It was hideous," Jesse laughed out loud. "When he opened the wrapping, the look on his face—"

"He looked like he wanted to hide." Annie shook with laughter and struggled for breath. "I felt so sorry for him."

"Why'd you buy it?" Jesse laughed again at the memory.

"It looked nice online."

"You're not thinking of having him wear that thing now, are you?"

"No. Of course not. No. I just thought of it. That's all." She smiled. It felt good to laugh.

"By the way," she said, "you and Claire should take off from school for the rest of the week. I'll call the administration. You okay with that?"

Jesse nodded.

"Come on." She reached a hand toward him again until he took it. "When Claire comes down, I'll make pancakes."

"Yeah. That's fine." Jesse looked out across the backyard. "What's going to happen to us—I mean, the three of us?"

"You don't have to worry about that, sweetheart. We're still a family. We'll be fine."

"Will we? Really? I know you have a mortgage. You've only got one income now. You just said Dad used to worry about money. I'm not a kid."

Annie ran her fingers over the back of her son's hand. "I know you're not a kid. But it's up to me, not you, to figure it out. I promise. It'll be okay."

Jesse gently pulled his hand away to face Annie. "Mom, I

want to believe you. I do. But now, with everything, I...don't know. Is it true, or just something we say?" He slowly climbed out of his chair and went inside.

Watching him, Annie suddenly felt the air leave her, as if she was losing herself inside her skin, like her grandfather shrinking with his cancer.

Chapter Twenty

(i)

"Okay, see this guy?" Coyle stood at one of the VCI evidence boards and pointed to a photo of Gregory Winter. "There's something about him. He's not telling us what he knows. He pretty much lied about everything I asked him a couple hours ago."

"Like what?" Mahler walked toward the evidence board from his usual vantage point in the room beside the filing cabinets.

"He said he visited his wife yesterday. I called her. He wasn't there the whole day. She hasn't seen him in two weeks. He said he drove out to the coast and went north from Jenner. But according to his car's GPS, he first drove south from Jenner, all the way to Doran Park, and later doubled back up the coast to Salt Point. His credit card record shows a charge last night for the Bay Shores Motel, which is two miles from the Salmon Creek neighborhood where we found Paul Behrens's body."

Mahler looked closely at the photo. "Did he say *why* he was at the coast?"

"He wanted to be alone," Coyle said. "Claimed he didn't meet Behrens and in fact has never met the guy."

"What was your take on him?" Mahler faced Coyle. "I mean, when you were talking, what'd you think of him?"

"I don't know." Coyle looked surprised at the question. "I guess I thought he wasn't taking me seriously. It was like he didn't want to put a lot of effort into answering my questions."

"I understand we have an interview with Winter in an hour?" Mahler said.

"Yeah. By the way, Eddie, have you walked past the interview room lately? Winter's got a lawyer. It's Kate Langley."

"Kate? Really? That'll be interesting." Mahler tried to remember the last time he'd seen his former girlfriend. Months? Weeks, at least. For an instant her face appeared in his mind's eye. He heard her voice sarcastically mocking his attempts at online dating. Then beside her face, he saw Franny Hastings, the woman from the rehab facility the day before.

He shook himself free of these thoughts and studied the evidence boards. On the timeline, Coyle had added:

10:10 a.m.	Behrens calls Jean Cummings from Doran Park. Meets with someone? Where?
8:00 p.m.	Car not on Bean Avenue.
9:00 p.m.	Two men seen running on beach.
12:30 a.m.	Dispatch call. Body found on Bean Avenue.

Under "Leads" were five more lines:

Meeting on coast—who?
Gun—ownership?
Cause of death: suicide/homicide—evidence?

Gregory Winter?
Photos of students?

Mahler looked at the other detectives. "Coroner's report?"

Coyle shook his head. "I'll text them again."

"Okay," Mahler said, "apart from this guy Winter, do we know any more about why Behrens left or who he was meeting?"

"I spoke to Claire again." Eden read from her notebook. "She didn't know where her father went, but she said he told her sometimes revealing a secret can cause harm to ourselves and people close to us. Other times keeping secrets can be more damaging. Apparently Behrens told Claire he was helping someone deal with secrets *she'd* learned. He didn't tell Claire who she was."

"A lot of secrets with this family. Behrens's sister thinks Annie knows why her husband left yesterday, and she's not telling anyone."

"You think that's true?"

"I don't know. My guess is Mrs. Behrens's alcoholism has made her secretive, but she's also pretty unstrung right now. Hard to know what she's capable of."

Rivas stood and approached the evidence boards. "I found out more about the two photos of Behrens and the girls." He pointed to one of the photos. "This topless girl is Julia Guerro. She took that picture herself and posted it to Instagram. Then she started a rumor Paul Behrens was with her when she took the photo."

"When was this?" Eden asked.

"March. Seven weeks ago."

"About the time Behrens wrote the letter of resignation?"

"That's right. Anyway, turns out it was all a prank. The school investigated and met with the parents. Julia confessed she made up the whole thing. It blew over, but it shook up Behrens."

"Isn't it strange Behrens kept a copy of that photo in his

briefcase where his wife could find it?" Coyle asked. "If the incident blew over, wouldn't you get rid of the photo?"

"Good point, although we may never know," Rivas said. "Principal Steeley also identified the girl in the other photo—the one sitting beside Paul Behrens on a bench. Her name's Zoe McFarland. Another student in one of the guy's classes. We're still trying to figure out how and why it ended up being part of a scheme to blackmail the Behrens family, and under what circumstances the teacher and student were sitting together. For that matter we don't even know who took the photo."

Mahler turned to Coyle. "Isn't there some way to search the digital characteristics of the photo and find its origin?"

"I can take a look. My guess is, the image's been copied and transferred so many times, the digital fingerprint's been lost."

"Couldn't there be a simple explanation for them sitting together?" Eden asked. "I mean, is it really that unusual?"

"Maybe not, but complicating all this are two other things." Rivas held up two fingers. "First, Zoe didn't go to school today, and her parents don't know where she is. Last night she told her mother she was going to a friend's house a few blocks away and staying the night. When she didn't show up at school, the parents called the friend and found out she never arrived. She's currently missing. Field Services put out a Nixle and a BOLO, and they're talking to her friends and looking at social media."

"Well, that's not good," Mahler sighed. "When and where was she last seen?"

"She left her parents' house at 775 Wedgewood Way in Fountaingrove last night about six. She was supposed to walk three blocks to 330 Newgate Court. That's the last time she was seen. All this comes from the principal. I'm meeting with the parents in thirty minutes."

"Did someone pick her up? A friend?"

"Her parents don't think so. The girl's thirteen, pretty young to have driver-age friends."

"How about a cab? Uber?"

"I'll check both."

"So what's this missing girl have to do with Paul Behrens?" Coyle asked. "Was she with Behrens?"

"We don't know," Rivas said. "The sheriff who stopped Behrens Wednesday morning on Valley Ford Road said he was alone. The second thing is, I pulled the school security footage of that man who broke into Paul Behrens's classroom this morning before classes started." Rivas turned to a blurred black-and-white photo of a figure in the classroom doorway. "I showed the image to Principal Steeley. She identified the man as—are you ready for this?—Zoe's father, John McFarland."

"Are you kidding?" Mahler raised both arms in frustration. "The father of the girl in the photo breaks into Paul Behrens's classroom the morning the teacher disappears? It can't be a coincidence, can it? What's it got to do with Behrens?"

"And why does anyone break into a classroom?" Eden asked.

"Steeley didn't know of any issue between the teacher and student," Rivas said. "She described Zoe as a top student, quiet, doing well academically. I'll find out more when I meet with the father and mother."

"Why's that name McFarland familiar?" Coyle paged through his notebook. "On the night of May 2, Behrens received a call. I traced it to a number owned by Zoe McFarland. I just remembered."

"Another reason the name's familiar," Rivas said, "is that John McFarland's in the news a bunch, and you've probably seen ads for his houses. He's a developer in the county." Rivas returned to his desk and looked at his laptop screen. "Age forty-seven. Wife

Charlotte. Zoe's their only child. As I said, they have a home in Fountaingrove."

"So, money," Mahler said.

"Yeah, money. But it's an old family business. John's father, Arthur, starting building houses in the county during the seventies and eighties. Tract homes, nothing special, handful a year. John's on a whole other level—a hundred or more buildings a year, big developments, expensive homes. McFarland Custom Homes. So the son's moved up in the world. Donor to charities, political campaigns. Even bought an interest in a vineyard in Alexander Valley."

"With all that money, why's his kid going to public school?" Mahler asked.

Rivas shrugged. "Blue-collar roots? Kid has friends there?"

"So where are we?" Coyle stood in front of the boards to face the others. "Paul Behrens wakes up Wednesday morning, leaves his house, doesn't show up at his job. He doesn't tell his family where he's going. He drives all the way out to the coast, calls a fellow teacher and says he's meeting someone. Fourteen hours later, we find him in the front seat of his car in the Salmon Creek neighborhood, dead from a gunshot wound to the head by an unregistered gun. Suicide or by someone's hand. His car wasn't on Bean Avenue at eight last night. At nine o'clock, two men are seen running on the beach. That's all we really know for sure. We have no idea what happened with this guy from 10:00 a.m. to midnight. We also don't know why he went to the coast, if he met anyone, who he met, and whether he or someone else pulled the trigger. Right?"

"Yes, but"—Eden raised her hand—"to be fair, Martin, we also know Behrens's wife was having sex with another man the night before her husband went missing. That man was out on the coast yesterday. Behrens himself was in the ocean sometime during those fourteen hours. His son is selling weed and maybe more. One of his students is missing, and that student's father broke into Behrens's classroom."

Rivas snorted. "Yeah. There's that."

Mahler waited for the team to return to their desks and then approached Eden. "You're meeting with the Bureau in the city this afternoon?" he asked quietly.

"Yeah. Three thirty." Eden stacked folders into her briefcase. "Have to leave in a few minutes."

"Want one of us to go with you? Moral support?"

"I'll be fine," Eden sighed. "It's just a routine debrief on a couple lines of inquiry I uncovered with the Jory case when I was back at Quantico."

"Okay." Mahler watched her eyes seek a middle distance across the room. "If you change your mind, let me know."

(ii)

(THURSDAY, 1:52 P.M.)

As Mahler and Coyle entered the interview room, a woman in a dark business suit seated beside Dr. Winter looked up and smiled. She shook their hands across the table. "Lieutenant Mahler, Detective Coyle. Kate Langley representing Dr. Winter." She handed a business card to the two men.

"Afternoon, Counselor." Mahler took the card, recognizing it as a gesture on Kate's part to maintain a professional appearance in front of her client. Even knowing in advance he was to see her, Mahler felt a frisson of surprise at suddenly being close-up across the table from his former partner. Quickly recovering himself, he switched on the tape recorder, noted the date and time, and identified the four people in the room.

"I understand you have a few questions for my client in connection with the case of Paul Behrens?" Kate looked back and forth from Mahler to Coyle.

Coyle started it off. "Dr. Winter, what's your relationship with Annie Behrens?"

Winters cleared his throat. "We're colleagues at Santa Rosa Memorial Hospital. She sometimes works shifts on the B Ward, where I have postsurgical patients. We've also developed a personal relationship."

"A personal relationship?"

"As I already told you this morning, we developed a close relationship and recently were intimate."

"Yes. That's right. As you explained earlier, you were intimate with Mrs. Behrens on Tuesday night in her car in the hospital parking lot. Is that correct?"

"It was a spontaneous thing. Just happened. It's embarrassing to talk about in this…setting."

Mahler exchanged a glance with Kate. A few years ago this would have been a story they'd share.

"What time was that?" Coyle went on matter-of-factly.

"Around eleven thirty. Twelve."

"And it just happened. Spur of the moment?"

"We didn't plan it."

"This intimacy was a change in your relationship?"

"Yes."

Mahler took out his phone and scrolled to Bri's blackmail photo of Annie unclothed on Winter's lap. He held the phone for Winter and Kate to see. "Mrs. Behrens told us this photo was taken about five weeks ago. So your relationship with her has been going on for longer, isn't that right?"

Winter's face reddened. "Yes. To be accurate, Annie and I have been seeing each other for…some time."

"How long?"

"Several weeks. Months. I don't remember."

"All right," Coyle said. "Go back to Tuesday night. What'd you do after you and Mrs. Behrens met in your car?"

"We went home. I mean, separately, to our own homes."

"What time did you arrive home?"

"Around one."

"Let's talk about where you were yesterday, on Wednesday. Earlier today, when we spoke in your car, you said you visited your ex-wife in Forestville from about nine to lunchtime. Is that right?"

"No. I believe I—"

"When I spoke to your ex-wife an hour ago, she said you never visited yesterday, and she hasn't seen you in several weeks." Mahler bore down. "Is it your intention to keep lying?"

"Come on, Eddie," Kate sighed. "Dial it back."

Winter raised both hands in surrender. "No. No, he's right. I was lying." He stared at the tabletop.

Kate put a hand on Winter's shoulder. "Greg, just tell them what you told me."

"All right. When I woke up yesterday, I couldn't stop thinking about the thing with Annie and what happened. I wanted to talk to Behrens. I didn't feel right about it. I wanted to be out-front, to say I was in love with Annie. So I called Paul, and I—" Winter addressed himself to Coyle. "I didn't tell you this earlier because I didn't want to get involved with everything that happened with Paul being missing and all."

"You called Paul Behrens yesterday?" Coyle looked incredulous. "He didn't have his phone with him."

"He had a disposable cell, and he was picking up messages from his other phone."

Coyle made a note to check the phone log. "What time was this?"

"Nine thirty. Thereabouts. I said I wanted to meet him. I said it was about Annie and it was important. He answered right away, said he wasn't in town. He was on the coast, on his way to see someone."

"Did he say where on the coast he was?"

"No. But I said I'd drive out to the coast and talk to him there. I wanted to get things out in the open as soon as possible. Anyway, he said his other meeting was at ten and we could talk at eleven. We arranged to meet at Doran Park."

Mahler watched Kate, who was focused on her client. He thought of how she had changed when she was out of his sight. Her hair was shorter than the last time he'd seen her. It made her look simpler, less encumbered, as if she could run away from him and be gone.

"And *did* you meet him there at eleven?" Coyle asked.

"Yeah. We met in the park. When I arrived, his car was in one of those pullouts. He was standing outside the car, leaning against the fender."

"How was he dressed?" Mahler asked.

Winter frowned. "Sports jacket and tie. Right away he said the person he was supposed to meet never showed up."

"Did he say who it was?" Coyle again.

"No. But he seemed upset. He kept checking his phone, and he sent several texts while we were together."

"Did he say why he had a disposable phone?" Coyle asked.

"Not directly. But he kept fumbling with the screen like it was unfamiliar. Once he got frustrated and said he was doing all of it because someone made him. I assumed he meant the person he was meeting. Anyway, I told Behrens I was seeing Annie. I tried to be gentle about it. I was pretty sure Annie hadn't spoken to him. He was—"

"He was what?"

"Angry. He said he knew his wife was unfaithful. He said it was a terrible thing for his children and that I must have no sense of decency. He kept asking what I expected him to do. Did I expect him to say it was okay, to forgive me? He asked if I had kids and what they'd think of me."

"What'd you say to that?" This poor bugger, Mahler thought, has been squirming under pressure for twenty-four hours.

"What could I do? He was ranting. I left. I drove north on the coast as far as Salt Point. But then I stopped there and thought I wanted to tell him that I only wanted what was best for Annie. The three of us could talk and find the best way forward. I decided to go back. I texted him and asked if we could meet again. I wanted to say I was sorry, that I hadn't meant to hurt him."

"What happened? Did you see him a second time?"

"No. He didn't answer my texts. When I went back to Doran, he was gone. I texted Annie, but she didn't reply. Finally I just pulled into a motel in Bodega Bay. I didn't feel like driving all the way back."

"Was that the Bay Shores Motel?" Coyle inserted himself.

"Yeah."

"So you didn't see Mr. Behrens after your meeting at eleven?" Mahler asked.

"No. And obviously he was alive when I saw him." Winter dropped back in his chair, as if spent from his account.

Kate gently laid a hand on Winter's arm again and said something Mahler couldn't hear. It was odd to see Kate in this role, familiar and strange at the same time. Who was she to him now? Someone he once told secrets to, someone he cried in front of, someone he lay next to for three years. Would she ever be just a friend he'd known, a professional he'd shake hands with, someone whose very name wouldn't awaken a melancholy, a woman he wouldn't miss when she left a room? Whatever happened with his new dating, she would be a picture in his memory, a smile at one of his jokes, a whisper beside him in bed—all those things that, while his mind betrayed him in a thousand ways and wiped away this or that memory, would be the last ones to remain.

> **Dr. Schafer:** Tell me how you and Kate ended your relationship.
> **Mahler:** We argued for months.
> **S:** About what?
> **M:** Everything. The main thing was I was preoccupied with a case, with the death of Susan Hart. I wasn't talking to Kate. I wasn't home a lot.
> **S:** What about your level of intimacy.
> **M:** We weren't intimate at all.
> **S:** What happened?
> **M:** One day she packed her clothes and moved out.
> **S:** Back up. What precipitated this?
> **M:** I told her I didn't think we should be together.
> **S:** So it was your decision?
> **M:** Yes.
> **S:** But you described it as Kate leaving you.

Mahler went back to the reality of the case and directed himself at Winter. "When you met Paul Behrens in Doran Park, were you inside or outside his car?"

"Outside." Winter awakened himself. "The whole time."

"Did you see inside his car?"

"No."

"Did Paul Behrens have a gun?"

Winter blinked at the question. "Not that I saw."

"Did you have a gun?"

"Absolutely not. I don't…own one."

Kate suddenly peered at Mahler. "Is VCI investigating this as a homicide?"

"We're investigating Mr. Behrens's death." Mahler returned her look.

"Dr. Winter." Coyle consulted his tablet. "In our search of your office, we found a notice from the state medical licensing board regarding an upcoming hearing. Can you tell us the subject of that hearing?"

"You don't have to answer that, Greg." Kate's voice was firm.

"Why's that, Counselor?" Mahler asked.

"Because it's not relevant to this interview or to Mr. Behrens. You'll have to get a court order. Anything else?" Kate stood and held her briefcase. Her eyes flashed with anger.

Mahler shook his head. "We'll be in touch."

Chapter Twenty-One

(i)

Agent Macon met Eden in the hollow, echoing lobby of the FBI Field Office in San Francisco. He waited stiff-backed on the other side of the security screening station. "Detective Somers, thank you for making the time." Unlike the day before in Santa Rosa, Macon's face was now smileless and solemn, as if the cold steel and concrete of the field office required a certain reverence. "We're upstairs. Senior Agent Chalmers wanted to meet before the conference call."

Macon turned and walked farther into the building's atrium toward the elevators, the long stride of his brogues forcing Eden to jog behind. On the third floor, they followed a corridor to Chalmers's office.

A large man in white shirt and tie, Chalmers shook Eden's hand. He pointed to a chair in front of his desk. "Probably don't remember, but we met in Quantico two years ago." Chalmers smiled. "Long table. Lots of men. All looking alike."

"Your wife just had a baby," Eden said in a flat voice. "Hazel. First child. Named after your mother. Or, no, mother-in-law."

Chalmers let out a low whistle. "Ah, that's right. You're the one with the memory, aren't you? Should have known."

The senior agent turned serious. "I believe Jonathan told you. We have a video call at 4:00 p.m. with Jory's lawyer, Anthony Dunbar. We'd like you to listen to Mr. Dunbar regarding your role in the development of evidence in the case of Cassie Stanton."

Eden saw the woman's face in her mind. Curly red hair, freckles across her nose. Eyes closed forever in a coroner's photo.

"I know you're the expert on this thing." Chalmers raised a file in one hand. "But just so we're all on the same page, let me lay it out. Albert Jory was arrested on two earlier occasions, 2016 and 2018. Charged with the murder of four different women in the Highway 60 case. One of those victims was Stanton. On both occasions, the evidence was deemed insufficient to proceed to trial and Mr. Jory was released."

"Last week, Jory was rearrested in New Mexico and charged again in the Stanton case, based on new evidence, including the timeline, plus fingerprints, a witness statement, and a number of other items. Apparently Dunbar and his team filed a motion in court over the weekend to challenge the evidence. Down the line in Virginia, everyone noted your comprehensive approach. I've worked on this thing for six months, but frankly no one knows the details on all nine women as well as you. No one's studied it with your…intensity."

Eden waited.

"We can give you a copy of the motion, obviously," Macon said. "But we'd like you to listen to Dunbar and see if you can help us in any way."

"That's it?" Eden ignored Macon and held steady on the

older man. "Aren't you forgetting something? Yesterday I was told Jory has my personal information and said something about me. I wasn't to know what he said unless I came down here."

"Yes. I was going to discuss that." Chalmers settled back in his chair. "When Jory was arrested, state police searched his home and truck. They found a notebook containing certain... facts about you."

"Facts? Like what?" Eden remembered Jory's notebooks. Wire-bound journals recording his daily activities dating back fifteen years—calorie intake, bathing schedule. All the books smelling like the Lemon Pledge he applied to every surface in his apartment.

"Your driver's license, your cell, and...home address in Santa Rosa."

Eden drew in a sharp breath. "What'd he say about me?"

Chalmers glared at Macon. "Agent Macon misspoke. That wasn't intended to be shared with you."

"I have a right to know."

"It's not meaningful to Mr. Jory's case."

"You want my help?"

Chalmers let go of the losing hand. "He said he liked your name and...wondered if you've already tasted from the tree of life."

The two men looked away from Eden.

Eden absorbed the words. She let several seconds go by. In the room's silence she watched Chalmers fold and refold his hands on his desk. "How did Jory get my license and cell?" she asked.

"We don't know."

"Yes, you do."

"We have to—"

"Tell me."

"Look, I've seen your work. I admire it. But a lot of folks worked the nine murders in this case. Not just the agency. State police, local police, task forces. Six private investigators. Somewhere along the line, you might have rubbed someone the wrong way, showed them up, declined an offer for a beer. Who knows?"

"Really? You're saying a local cop took offense?" Eden realized Chalmers couldn't recognize his own insult. "I work for a city police department. None of my fellow officers would release private information. No one, except the Bureau, ever had access to it."

"You can't accuse the Bureau—"

Eden waved away his protest with one hand. "Let's be serious. I do anything on this case, I want your assurance that the FBI and you, Agent Chalmers, investigate how Jory got this information. If not, I go to your supervisor. Then I'll talk to a reporter."

Chalmers took a moment to collect himself. "Okay," he said. "I hear you. The Bureau will conduct an investigation into the leaked information. But right now we don't have enough to keep Jory in custody. You know him. He looks careless, but he's not. We need to work together."

The conference room was a long rectangle with a gigantic video screen the length of one wall. Chalmers typed a number into a laptop at the center of the room's table. Ten seconds later, a life-sized image of a man seated at another table appeared on the screen. A note in the bottom corner of the screen read Anthony Dunbar, Albuquerque, New Mexico. Dunbar looked to be in his late forties, head shaved, deep tan, dark Italian suit.

Chalmers spoke first. "Good afternoon, Mr. Dunbar. Agents Chalmers and Macon here in San Francisco. This is Detective Somers, formerly with the Bureau, who worked on this case."

Dunbar looked straight ahead and smiled. "Nice to meet you, Detective Somers, via video as it were. After reading your work for the past few days, I confess I feel as if I already know you."

"Hello," Eden said quietly.

"As I'm sure the agents told you, I represent Albert Jory in the Cassie Stanton case. Last week, my client was charged in Ms. Stanton's murder in light of new evidence presented by the Bureau. Over the weekend, my associates and I filed a motion in court to challenge the evidence. Agent Chalmers can share a copy of the motion with you, but I'm happy to summarize it for you." Dunbar looked up and waited for Eden's assent.

"In the case at hand, Ms. Stanton, a waitress at Applebee's in Gallup, New Mexico, was killed on the night of July 12, 2016, after she left work at midnight. The timing is important, isn't it, Detective Somers? When I first took this case, I heard about Eden Somers's timelines. That's all the other attorneys could talk about. Apparently you're famous for them—minute by minute, footnoted. In my own experience, timelines aren't always useful. Crimes don't take place on schedules. But let's leave that aside, shall we?"

"At the time of his first arrest," Dunbar continued, "Mr. Jory's previous defense lawyer presented Jory's own daily log book, which showed he stopped that night for a delivery at the Chevron station in Window Rock, Arizona, at 11:15 p.m. His lawyer pointed out, since the great state of Arizona does not observe daylight saving time, that time was really 12:15 a.m., which would not have given Mr. Jory time to drive to Gallup to murder Cassie Stanton. Isn't that right?"

"That's correct," Eden said.

"However, since then, Detective, your own review of the case noted that, because the town of Window Rock is part of the Navajo Reservation, and therefore on federal land, it does observe daylight saving time. So Mr. Jory's stop was indeed at 11:15 p.m. and would have given him ample time to drive the thirty minutes to Gallup and kill Cassie Stanton. Correct?"

Eden felt herself being led along a path. She stared back silently at the lawyer. She remembered the hair ties Jory wore in his ponytail. The kind preteen girls wear. A different color for each day of the week—Monday yellow, Tuesday green...

"But what you didn't take into account is Mr. Jory's employer, J&J Trucking, installs software on all its vehicles. The program records both the time the liftgate on the rear of the truck bed is lowered for a delivery and the GPS coordinates of the delivery. And—this is important—the software is programmed to Arizona state time whenever the vehicle's onboard GPS indicates the vehicle is anywhere in Arizona. We've obtained a printout for Mr. Jory's truck, which shows that my client was indeed in the town of Window Rock at 12:15 a.m. the night of July 12."

Dunbar leaned his elbows on the table in Albuquerque and smiled at Eden. It was a smile not born of happiness or joy, Eden thought, but conceived somewhere in the man's bile duct to express advantage over another person.

"Mistakes are part of forensic investigations." Eden heard Professor Hiatt's voice now, from a lecture during senior year at Mount Holyoke College. "You can be diligent. You can triple-check every scrap in your file. And still they happen. You overlook a detail. Or, you see that detail, but don't know what it means. Often the mistake is inconsequential, trivial. No one notices. But sometimes...a mistake is like a parasite that eats everything else. It leaves nothing untouched in its path, and your case is"—here the professor threw open the fingers of one hand—"gone."

"What's more," Dunbar said, "the fingerprint evidence in the Stanton file has been corrupted. It was a partial print on the console of Stanton's car, and now the lab admits the analysis methods were flawed. The witness who said she saw Mr. Jory outside the restaurant the night of the murder has recanted her testimony. When we showed her a photograph of Jory, she said she couldn't positively identify my client—that she would have remembered the ponytail. There are other issues, too, which I've summarized in my filing. The point is, based on the lack of evidence, we've been granted a hearing next Thursday before a judge in the Tenth Circuit. We'll be seeking a dismissal of charges and the release of Mr. Jory."

Eden watched Dunbar looking back at her on-screen across a thousand miles. She thought of a dozen things to say. She could tell him his tie was too narrow for a man of his size, that a lecture at Quantico included a slide deck on the detriment of attorneys' facial expressions in legal proceedings. She could ask if he'd ever heard the aphorism "Truth is the daughter of time." Did they teach that in law school? Something about the witness statement was off, but she couldn't think now what it was.

Did Dunbar know what former homicide detective Tommy Woodhouse told Eden—that the souls of victims are at work to help law enforcement solve their murders? Had Dunbar looked in the file of Macy Coleman, Jory's Oklahoma victim, and seen a photo of the woman's three-year-old daughter, a little girl with a single pigtail sprouting from her head and a homeless look in her eyes? Eden wanted to tell the lawyer a story she'd heard over drinks late at night with a couple of Bureau old-timers about a defense attorney for a serial killer who found the fabric of his suits, even new custom-made ones, took on a sulfurous smell.

Eden didn't say any of those things.

"Thank you for your presentation, Mr. Dunbar," she said. "The Bureau will offer rebuttal evidence before next Thursday's hearing."

"I look forward to it, Detective Somers." Dunbar's smile remained undiminished, although a hint of doubt flickered across his eyes.

Chalmers switched off the screen and turned to Eden. "We can request a continuance from the judge. Under the circumstances, the chances are—"

Eden again saw the closed eyes of Cassie Stanton. "Send me the files," she said. "Overnight."

"Which ones?" Macon looked alarmed. "There're sixty Bankers Boxes."

"All of them." Eden stood and picked up her notebook and purse. "By tomorrow 10:00 a.m."

Macon looked at Chalmers, who nodded.

Eden walked out of the conference room without waiting for an escort.

(ii)

(THURSDAY, 3:43 P.M.)

The view from the floor-to-ceiling glass wall of the McFarlands' living room was of the city of Santa Rosa below, houses and streets spread out across the valley in miniature. No effort was required to see the whole of it. No hiking to the top of a peak. No driving to a remote lookout. The panorama was given to anyone standing in the room. Never before had Rivas understood how a view might seem to bestow ownership. The people who lived in this house owned the whole of what lay on the valley floor below.

The house was built on the side of a hill in the Fountaingrove neighborhood of Santa Rosa. Charlotte McFarland had met Rivas at the front door and led him along a curved hallway, past a large, gleaming kitchen, to the living room. The space they entered had dark cherrywood floors and U-shaped white leather sofas facing the glass wall. Standing in the front of the wall with his back to Rivas was a tall man in a dark business suit. He turned to face Rivas and extended his hand. "John McFarland."

Abruptly waving Rivas toward one of the sofas, McFarland stayed where he was, feet spread apart and making no secret of his impatience. "Can't this wait? Right now our priority is finding our daughter."

Charlotte McFarland hovered at the end of the sofa, pacing back and forth. "This is a very bad time for us. Zoe's disappearing like this is so unlike her. It's very worrying."

"I'm sorry." Rivas took out a tablet and pen. "These questions can't wait. As I explained on the phone, every member of the department is doing all they can to find Zoe." He looked back and forth between the two parents. "We need to find out as soon as we can why Paul Behrens drove to the coast yesterday, who he met there, and how he died."

"Do you think this man's death and our daughter's disappearance are related?" Charlotte squeezed her hands together. "Is there a chance Paul Behrens took our daughter?"

"There's no evidence of that. But we don't know." Rivas opened his tablet. "First, can you both please tell me where you were yesterday, from 8:00 a.m. to midnight?"

"I was here most of the day." Charlotte spoke rapidly, anxious to finish. "I met a friend for lunch in Healdsburg at noon and was back here by two."

"I was in my home office here until about eleven," John said. "Then I went to a building site in Windsor. I was there about an hour. I had a meeting downtown. I got back here about six, and we had dinner at seven thirty."

Rivas made a note in his tablet. Then he took a folded piece of paper from his jacket pocket and showed it to John. "Sir, the security camera at Brookwood Middle School recorded this footage at 7:27 a.m. yesterday morning. We believe this is you leaving Paul Behrens's classroom. Is that correct?"

John glanced at the paper without taking it in his hand. "I don't know. Yes. It is. But that has nothing to do with Behrens's or my daughter's disappearance. It's just—"

"Just what?"

"A misunderstanding."

"A misunderstanding?"

"Yes. It's not important. Especially now, with our daughter—"

Rivas paused. From his vantage sitting on the sofa, looking up at the tall, broad-shouldered man, he could sense the frustration in John McFarland, a man used to commanding a room. "Mr. McFarland, the school was closed at the time this image was taken. Which means you broke into the classroom."

"I was looking for something that might tell us where Zoe is." Charlotte's hands fluttered in the air. "We've been so worried."

"Principal Steeley told us you didn't learn of Zoe's disappearance until she failed to arrive at school that morning. This image was taken before you knew."

John put his hands in his pockets and shifted his feet. "All right. All right. For God's sake. I—we—had some concerns about Paul Behrens's attitude toward our daughter." He looked to his wife for confirmation. "I went to his office that morning to talk. When he wasn't there, I was…frustrated. I pushed on the door and it opened. It wasn't that difficult to get in. I looked on Behrens's desk. I don't know what I expected to find. I didn't… take anything."

So far Rivas had heard two lies and now an equivocation. Did money let you make your own truth? "What do you mean, Mr. Behrens's attitude toward your daughter?" he asked.

"Her grades were suffering," Charlotte laid it out for Rivas, conceding the subject wasn't going away. "Just last semester two A's went to B's. Children today can get off track so quickly. And, even at this age, the grade counts toward the averages colleges consider. John and I attended top schools, so we know—"

"I didn't like what that teacher was saying to my daughter," John interrupted.

"The class was reading a book," Charlotte said. "*Emma* by Jane Austen and—"

"Behrens compared Zoe to one of the characters in the story."

Charlotte's phone pinged with a text, and she read the screen. "I'm sorry, but we have friends looking for Zoe. So I have to read my messages." Looking up from her phone, she said, "As Zoe explained it to me, two characters in the novel are describing Emma. It's been a few years since I've read the book. But apparently one of the characters says Emma's very pretty but not vain about it. Mr. Behrens asked Zoe what she thought of the passage, and Zoe felt he was saying it about her—that she was pretty but not vain."

"Is that the kind of thing, Detective, you'd want a teacher saying to your child?" John asked Rivas.

Rivas thought of his teenage sons, Alex and Daniel Jr., with their ever-present earbuds and long, limp hair hanging over their eyes. They'd long ago stopped listening to the now-shorter adults in their life and could go days without uttering a full sentence.

"Behrens told Zoe she was no longer a girl but a young woman," John said. "What business does an English teacher have to say that? And when we tried to talk to him, he was cagey."

"You have to be extra careful these days," Charlotte said. "You don't know what's going on with kids, with what they see and hear on social media, how things spread. We don't want our daughter growing up too fast. She doesn't have siblings. She can be…innocent."

"Did you speak to Paul Behrens about your concerns?" Rivas asked.

"We spoke briefly on the phone, but we were still trying to find a time for a meeting. I believe John got frustrated with the…lack of resolution."

"Like I say, Behrens was cagey," John said.

"I see." Rivas flipped the pages in this tablet. "Let's go back. Mr. McFarland, you admit you were at Brookwood at 7:27 a.m. yesterday. Can you tell me again where you were throughout the day?"

"I returned home from the school about eight fifteen. The rest of what I told you is true."

"Which was—?"

"I went to the Windsor site at eleven. There for an hour. Then a meeting downtown. Back home by six."

"I'll need names and contact numbers of people who can verify those movements."

John took out his phone and read several numbers to Rivas.

"So neither of you was on the coast yesterday?" Rivas asked.

"No," Charlotte said. Her phone pinged again and she bent to read it.

John shook his head.

"And did either of you see Paul Behrens at any time on Wednesday?" Rivas looked back and forth as the two parents said no.

"Now, unless there's anything else," Charlotte said, "we really must focus on finding Zoe."

Rivas stood. "It's important that at least one of you stays here in case Zoe returns. Also, obviously watch for incoming calls. And please work with the liaison officer on any information you receive. Our department will keep you informed of our progress."

As Rivas turned to follow Charlotte to the door, he looked out once more on the city and thought of how simple and small it seemed from here.

Chapter Twenty-Two

(i)

"How are Jesse and Claire?" Beth leaned over the kitchen table, her voice grave, as if expecting the worst.

Annie shrugged. "You know how it is with teenagers. Mostly not talking." Was it possible to report how any of them were doing since learning of Paul's death twelve hours earlier? Their feelings seemed to have a physical presence in the house, drifting from room to room without them. Annie had a constant ringing in her ears, another complication.

Her sister-in-law and brother-in-law phoned, then arrived minutes later at the front door. After some tearful clutching at each other, Annie invited them in, offered tea, and led the way to the kitchen. None of them knew how to behave. Paul was always the host for family events, the glue that held them together—keeping Beth from dominating, knowing how to cut through Michael's shyness, explaining Annie's unfamiliar habits—more recently her insobriety—to his family.

"How about you, honey?" Beth put her hand on top of Annie's. "How're you?"

Annie saw Beth watching, trying to measure what the death of her brother meant to an unfaithful wife. How much did Paul's family know about their marriage? What had he said when she wasn't there?

"Not sure, honestly." Annie turned her hand over to squeeze Beth's. "Taking it one hour at a time." Though news of Paul's death was still fresh, Annie felt the pressure for her to get past it, to start living in some magical future.

"Mike and I were just saying it's hard to believe. The reality of it seems to be coming from far away. It still hasn't arrived."

"What's hardest for me is the *way* it happened." Michael spoke haltingly. There was a poignancy to his confusion. Michael's damaged brain struggled harder to find meaning. "Paul never said anything that made me think this might happen."

"I know. I know," Annie said quickly, eager to help.

She glanced involuntarily toward the chair at the head of the table. When Beth had first approached the table a few minutes earlier and reached for the chair, Annie had quickly repositioned her to a different one with an excuse about the chair's uneven legs. The head chair had always been Paul's. She couldn't say that when she came downstairs from her afternoon nap an hour ago, she'd imagined her dead husband sitting there, dressed in his sports jacket, bent over a pile of student papers. She hoped her guests ignored Paul's brown mug that she had put at his place.

"Did Paul leave any instructions?" Beth asked.

"No…no. I don't think so. He always meant to. He wanted to be cremated. He talked about that." *Was that true?* She remembered thinking the day before how for the past year she'd been in the habit of tuning out her husband.

"Mike and I can help with anything. Just let us know."

"I thought I'd call McNeer Funeral Home," Annie said. "We used them for Dad's service. Of course, we'll have to wait for the coroner to release his body. They haven't given us a time for that." It was surprising how easily one adjusted to saying "his body."

Annie paused. Beth and Michael were silent, looking at the tabletop, unsure of the subject.

"I don't know who we'd get to lead the service," Annie said. "I was raised in the church, of course, and Jesse was baptized at St. Rose's. But we haven't been in years. I don't think—"

"Didn't Paul have a friend who taught drama?" Beth looked at Michael. "He'd be comfortable in front of an audience. Glenn something at Piner High?"

"I should write this down." Annie turned to search the kitchen drawers for paper and pen.

"It's all right, honey," Beth said. "We're just talking."

"Paul would want poetry in the service," Michael said. "You know how he was."

Beth smiled. "Paul and his literature. Neruda. One time Paul read 'If You Forget Me' out loud to me. Do you think Jesse and Claire would want to read something?"

"They'd hate it," Annie said too bluntly. The three of them were planning a funeral service like it was a school program. She imagined a portion of the service devoted to readings of love poems by fellow teachers who had wanted to get laid by her late husband.

She felt bone-tired, as if she hadn't slept in days, although she had awakened from a nap just an hour earlier. She didn't have the strength to talk about the plans. Could someone else handle it—someone else closer to her husband than she was?

Who was she now? Grieving widow? Surviving spouse?

Single mother of two? Had she wanted any of those roles, or were they dumped on her by a departing husband who ran away without leaving a note? She thought of standing at the funeral service, looking out on the sea of Paul lovers, to announce: I'd like to thank my sweet husband for leaving me a mess to clean up.

How did she end up at this table with these people? She'd never felt welcomed by the Behrens family. She was Paul's choice, not theirs—another decision they didn't understand. She wasn't like them: less intellectual, more hands-on. She was a nurse who knew meds, who was good at finding a vein for an IV. She wasn't in thrall to Frank Behrens, the family's grim patriarch. She didn't have the Behrens reserve, their caution. She was ready to let go, to run onto the dance floor, do tequila shots, have sex in the back seat of her car with a man who wasn't her husband.

Who were *they*? Beth—a woman closing in on her midforties, who saw life through the lens of the wreckage of her own divorce. Part of family lore held that the Behrens children married spouses who ruined their chances. The main event was an ex-husband leaving her for someone who made him happier. The passing days were lessons in bitterness that sucked away life until her face and limbs were pinched and barren.

Michael—the damaged warrior, who went off to war and came home a stranger. Physically untouched, without a scratch on his body, until you parted his hair and examined his scalp and saw the scar tissue. Somewhere inside there, things were rearranged, furniture thrown around a room. In his presence, you watched a contest, where Michael searched for pieces too fractured and scattered to put together.

Without Paul, the Behrens clan would only get together for Jesse's and Claire's birthdays and graduations. Awkward occasions where they'd all be close to tears whenever Paul's name was mentioned. They'd tiptoe around Annie's drinking and dating. And they'd regret the time their brother wasted on the careless bottle-blond who seduced him.

She looked again at the head of the table, where Paul had raised his head toward her from his student papers. He looked lost, a spirit who'd taken a wrong turn. Still, he seemed in no hurry to explain his own mystery, how he'd ended up dead in the front seat of his car way out on the coast. Did reason no longer matter once you reached oblivion?

"Did you see the harlequins blooming this afternoon?" Paul asked.

Annie smiled. "I knew you were going to say that. A little bit of magic, isn't it? Same time every year."

She turned from her husband to Beth and Michael. "I'll call you," she said. "We can figure out all the details."

(ii)

(THURSDAY, 6:33 P.M.)

Frames drank from a Coke and offered the can to Tom Wood-house. The retired detective took a long drink and squinted down the block at the site of a law enforcement raid an hour earlier on the Olive Park home of Francisco Medina. A dozen police vehicles still remained, blocking both ends of the main street that ran through the neighborhood. By now the suspects were arrested, transported, and processed. The drugs and other seized materials had been loaded into vans and driven away.

They sat on the tailgate of Frames's Tundra, the adrenaline of the raid slowly dissipating. Neither was ready to go home.

"Surprise seeing you here," Frames said.

"Noah called. Asked if I was free to observe."

"Why'd he ask you?"

"I worked Narcotics twenty years ago when the Ramirez-Medina organization was getting started. I met all the players, arrested most of them at one time or the other. I think Noah wanted another pair of eyes tonight to see if he missed anything." Woodhouse smiled. "Unofficial, of course. Officially I was never here. Told me to stay out of harm's way."

"So what'd you see, old man?"

"Not much has changed—the same guys are just older. Julio's in charge now, along with Luis. That's different. Francisco's too sick. Probably just making sure his son doesn't fuck up."

"I was on the team that went inside and arrested Francisco," Frames said. "We found him in a hospital bed in the living room. Weighs about a hundred pounds. Guy could barely get on his feet."

Woodhouse shook his head. "He'll be dead by the end of the year. Colon cancer. Couldn't happen soon enough if you ask me. Man's a monster. Responsible for most of the addicts in the county—fifty to sixty new ones a year. Wrecked their lives, drained them over a decade, until we found their bodies on the street. Made himself out to be the beloved patriarch. On surveillance we watched him at picnics and quinceañeras surrounded by grandchildren."

"You think he'll be charged in this one?"

"Doubt it. The family lets the middle managers and dealers take the fall. The other thing that's changed—more guns tonight. Didn't used to see those so much."

"Speaking of which, you heard we found the body of Jorge Lopez last night? Took three to the chest, at close range."

"I heard. I knew Jorge. Noah told me Lopez was wanted in the death of an addict. Sounded like they had a good case.

The DEA puts you in jail for twenty years if you cause an overdose."

"You think the family decided he was a liability?"

"I don't know. Wasn't their style when I was in the game. But who knows? Could have been a personal matter."

Frames finished the Coke and squeezed the can. The raid had been larger than he expected. More than a dozen vehicles and personnel not just from NIT but also the SWAT team and the Sheriff's Narcotics Task Force. Hernandez had called for it because surveillance indicated the drugs were about to be moved. All in all, the raid found six car wheels loaded with drugs. When Buckley and Prater cut open the tires, they found metal boxes bolted to the wheels, just like Hernandez had guessed. Inside the boxes were packages of black-tar heroin and meth. A simultaneous raid at the home of Luis Ramirez found cash, cell phones, packaging material, and digital scales.

"Yesterday when we were on surveillance, we saw a young guy, early twenties," Frames said. "Had a gun in his belt. The team didn't know him, but Noah told me later they found out his name is Rafael Soto." Frames took out his phone, scrolled for a few seconds, and turned the screen to Woodhouse. "Know him?"

Woodhouse peered at the phone. "No. Might be new. If he's carrying a gun, he could be involved in street discipline or just a cocky asshole. I didn't see him here tonight."

"Me neither. Yesterday we found a small silver buckle that accidentally snagged on Lopez's jeans. A few minutes ago, Prater told me they matched the buckle to one on Soto's jacket when we photographed him during surveillance. So the team's pretty sure he's the killer. Any ideas where we should look for him?"

"Watch the street dealers. If he's out there, he'll make contact. By the way, why are *you* here? Isn't VCI keeping you busy enough?"

"Narcotics was shorthanded, asked me to help out," Frames said. "It's just a onetime thing."

"Is it? You sound a little invested."

"I'm interested. That's all. Tell me something, Tom. You've been around a while. You think we made any difference with this operation just now?"

"Oh sure," Woodhouse said. "People up and down the supply chain will be unhappy. Dealers won't have as much to sell. Addicts will have to make do with whatever they can scrape together. All that product in our custody won't provide a return on investment. Like any businessmen, the Medinas are all about the bottom line. These guys will have to hold off a few more weeks on buying that new pickup or big-screen TV."

Woodhouse looked down and swung his legs back and forth. "Bad news is, there's always more product in the pipeline. Stuff's simple to make, and you can hire some poor dope to sell it. The work generally takes less effort than teaching in a classroom or putting on a roof. And on the demand side, there's no shortage of despair in our world. People you love die. However much you plan, your life doesn't turn out the way you thought it would. Every day, people look around, and all they want is to close their eyes and go to sleep. It's funny, isn't it? We're all afraid of death, but people pay a lot to be in a coma."

Frames raised his hands. "Wow, Tom. You really go dark, don't you?"

Woodhouse laughed. "Sorry. Philosophy's the last refuge of old men."

"Okay, so as a philosopher, when you were doing this job, did you ever think about the big picture?"

"Sure. The work has consequences other jobs don't. Cops see things most people never do. I found it was good to remember we're not healers or social workers. They pay us to make people safer. We find people who hurt others. It's a limited role."

"And sometimes we make things worse."

"Of course," Woodhouse said. "Police officers are in the middle of some serious shit. Wrong decisions are a big deal. By the way, where's this coming from?"

"I don't know. Lately I've been thinking about the people we meet on the sidelines—witnesses, family members, the woman who answers the door when you canvass. You ever think about them?"

The two men looked down the street, where forensic technicians in white overalls took photos of the dealer's Durango.

"VCI once responded to a shooting near the fairgrounds," Woodhouse said. "Young father, twenty-three years old, walking home to his apartment building at night, shot in the head. Mistaken identity. Shooter just thought he was somebody else. When we arrived, the victim's wife was sitting on the floor inside the building lobby, whole body shivering. In shock. I found a blanket and talked to her. Nothing I said was going to make a difference. We caught the shooter the next day, but for that woman and their child, it didn't help. I thought about her for years after. Still do."

Woodhouse looked at Frames. "You have someone specific in mind?"

"You hear about VCI's missing person case?" Frames asked.

"Yeah, I heard. Sad ending. Martin said it might be a homicide?"

"That's what it looks like. Plus, you know how these things sometimes open up other stuff? We caught the missing guy's son selling weed to high school students. Turns out he works for the Medinas."

"Doesn't surprise me. Even with legalization, the street

supply still belongs to the family. Tell you what, though, that kid should get out. Dealers are expendable. Always somebody else to take their place."

"I talked to the kid. Told me to fuck off."

"Kind of the universal response of youth to age, isn't it?" Woodhouse smiled. "I'm sure I said it more than once when I was young. Felt good at the time. So what do you want?"

"That's the thing. I don't know. I mean, you meet these people. They're not in the center of the picture where you're working. But they're there, in the way, not seeing the truck coming right at them. I never know what I'm supposed to do."

"Work usually answers that question. A week after that fairgrounds shooting, we had an armed robbery of a convenience store. You get busy. You move on."

"You still remember that wife shivering in the lobby, though, don't you? Am I going to have all these faces and names in my head in twenty years?"

"Probably. Unless you're lucky enough to develop Alzheimer's and forget everything." Woodhouse jumped down off the tailgate. "Let's just be happy for ten minutes that you guys took a shitload of heroin off the streets. How about that?"

Chapter Twenty-Three

(i)

"First, we've got the gun, right?" Bailey peered over her glasses at Eden and waited for an acknowledgment. She stood on the other side of the evidence table in the dark, windowless technicians' room.

Eden returned the look and nodded slowly. She was exhausted, too tired to see or think. She had driven back from the FBI meeting in San Francisco through rush-hour traffic, bumper-to-bumper for fifty miles. She felt the irony of examining evidence in VCI's missing person case after a lawyer on-screen in New Mexico proved the insufficiency of the evidence Eden had analyzed for six months in the Albert Jory case. The slow drive back gave her time to believe truth no longer existed. It was possible to pile up facts on either side of any scale—to show the sun revolved around the earth, to prove OJ didn't kill Nicole, to deny a truck driver killed nine women along Highway

60. None of it mattered. Not the time Albert Jory stopped in Window Rock, Arizona, on the night he strangled Cassie Stanton. Not the gun in the box that Bailey was now holding in front of her.

Eden closed her eyes and held them closed while she breathed deeply.

"All righty, Detective Somers, while you're taking a nap or whatever, I'll just keep talking." Bailey held up the box containing a gun. "The weapon found in Paul Behrens's car—and used to kill him—is a Glock 23 Gen4, nine-millimeter, semi-automatic handgun. Four-inch barrel, thirteen plus one rounds, made in Austria. Common gun in the United States."

Bailey laid the box back on the table and waited for Eden to open her eyes. "Unfortunately, the serial numbers that normally appear on the frame and the firearm bolt have been filed off. We can send the gun to the state lab, where they use electron backscatter diffraction—I love saying that—to recover the number. That'll take two weeks, which doesn't help you now. But—and this is an important but—before you allow yourself to sink into existential despair, let me tell you the good news."

She picked up a small plastic bag. "This is the shell casing we found under the seat in Mr. Behrens's car. The casing has what's called an extractor mark on it. This mark is made when a small hook inside the gun, called the extractor, removes the cartridge from the chamber. So—while you, Detective Somers, were busy memorizing the poetry of Gerard Manley Hopkins at Mount Holyoke College, and saying things like 'dapple-dawn-drawn Falcon,' yours truly was in technician school reading scientific studies on the adequacy of extractor marks for making identification."

"Why do I care about this, Bailey?"

"Because, my indomitable homicide investigator, the

unique extractor mark on this casing is identical to a casing found in a burglary at a Windsor warehouse two years ago. At the time, the mark was noted by an underpaid county technician in a regional database. In that burglary, the sheriffs questioned, but never charged, Mr. Thomas Hyland. The gun was never found. No gun is registered to Mr. Hyland. But someone, like yourself, might want to speak to Mr. Hyland."

Eden took the casing bag from Bailey and examined it.

"The other thing about this gun is that I found skin cells on the muzzle. The coroner can confirm or dispute this when she makes her report tonight. My own assessment is that the gun was shoved very hard against the victim's temple to leave those cells on the muzzle."

"Meaning?"

Bailey held up her hands. "I'm not a genius analyst like yourself, but my semi-expert opinion is that the victim did not put the gun to his own head. Someone helped him do that."

"So we've moved from suicide to assisted suicide?"

"At the least. Also, as suggested by Sergeant Rivas, we dusted the car's seat belt for prints." Bailey moved further down the evidence table. "The belt itself is too porous to pick up anything, but we checked the metal buckle and guess what? There we found prints belonging to just two individuals: the victim and Gregory Winter. Yikes, right? We also found the victim's and Winter's prints on the Jameson bottle."

Bailey held up a photograph. "Footprints on the car's passenger-side floor mat. Partial print of a hiking or work boot. Several types of dirt and sand. Can't determine how old the prints are. So nothing definitive there."

Moving to the other end of the evidence table, Bailey pointed to a stack of plastic bags. "Fibers on the passenger car seat. Indistinct blue cotton fibers. Could be jeans or a skirt. Also, silk fibers. A dress or a men's business suit. If you showed me an article of clothing, I could match it or rule it out. But without that, I can't tell you the origin. Besides, we have nothing to prove the time of the fiber deposit."

"As far as the victim's body is concerned, you'll have the coroner's report in a few hours. But I was able to examine his clothes. They were drenched, not just wet. There was evidence in the clothing and shoes of salt water, sand, and fragments of seaweed. It would indicate the victim was in the ocean, not wet from rainfall."

Bailey stepped away from the table and crossed her arms. "That concludes my presentation of evidence. But, Eden Somers, before you go back to the VCI room or fall asleep again or whatever, I have a question of my own. Are you going to tell me why you were in such a shitty mood when you came in here?"

"It's not important. I'll get over it." Eden felt old and tired. She was only a few years older than Bailey, but she couldn't remember being eager, happy with the work, like Bailey was with the flotsam left behind by Paul Behrens.

"Love life?"

"No." Eden shook her head. "Definitely not."

"No, you definitely don't have a love life, or no, it's definitely not that?"

"It's not that."

"Does it have anything to do with your appointment in the city with the Bureau?"

"How'd you know about the appointment?"

"In case you forgot, Detective Somers, this is the police department. It's basically a building full of detectives. There are no secrets. I know Matt Holland in Property Crimes wears 49ers boxer shorts and how much alimony Shirley down in Data Processing gets from her second husband."

"All right. Yeah, I had a meeting at FBI headquarters. The evidence in a serial killer case I worked a couple years ago is being challenged in court. I've got until next week to go back through the data or the suspect gets released."

"So let the Bureau handle it. It's not your problem anymore, is it?"

"The suspect has my home address, phone number, even my driver's license."

"Shit."

"Yeah. Shit."

"You think you can figure it out?"

"I don't know." Eden felt her frustration return. "Two years ago, I thought so. Lately I don't know. I mean, this guy was careful."

For a moment, the two women stared at the table.

"You want some help?" Bailey asked.

"No. No thanks. I appreciate the offer."

"What? I'm just a local evidence goofball, not an FBI-trained analyst?"

"Come on, Bailey, you know it's not that. There's the whole chain of custody shit. You know. If anything comes out in court, it could—"

"I won't touch it. I won't even be in the same room. Just talk to me."

Eden looked at Bailey.

"This is all I do. All day. When I go home at night, I read online forensics articles. Unlike you, I don't have a love life. This is all I think about."

Eden smiled.

"I want to help."

"Okay." Eden took a small notebook from her purse. "Here's my personal notebook on the Jory case. That'll give you the broad outlines. But don't go near the case files. Stay the fuck away from them."

Bailey held up her right hand. "I promise to stay the fuck away from them."

"By the way," Eden said as she walked out, "the case files are sixty Bankers Boxes coming from the Bureau tomorrow morning."

"Wait. What? Sixty?" Bailey called after her. "Is it too late to say I'm busy?"

(ii)

(THURSDAY, 7:05 P.M.)

"Tell me how you got into your work at Aurora Manor," Mahler said.

"It's funny." Franny smiled. "When you ask me a question, I can't help but see you as a detective working a case."

"Sorry. You're right. I interrogate people for a living."

"Does it work, your interrogation?"

"Sometimes. The problem is, everyone lies."

"Really? Everyone?"

"In my experience, yeah. Pretty much. We all have secrets."

"So you want to know my secrets?" Franny smiled again.

"Only if you want to tell me."

The table was tucked in the corner of a Healdsburg restaurant—a busy, noisy room, forcing them to lean close, closer than they'd been before, just to hear each other. Mahler watched Franny raise her wineglass and noticed for the first time how long and thin her fingers were.

They were in that early stage of a relationship, Mahler thought, where everything is a question, even the shallowest of things. Would they like the same wine? She suggested a pinot, and they both complimented it. Was the restaurant a good choice? She said she'd always wanted to try it.

Franny took a sip of the wine and looked across the table at Mahler. "Okay, Lieutenant Mahler, to answer your question, I got a bachelor's and master's in psychology. My first job out of school was at the VA Medical Center in San Francisco. Just applied and got it. Didn't really know what I was getting into. But once I got there, I loved it."

"So what was it you loved?"

"It's different working with returning service members. You can't generalize, of course. No two of them are alike. But they have something I don't find in other people."

"Can you describe it?"

"I think so. People in the services receive very specific training. Mostly it's in weapons, but it's also in how to move in a very particular combat setting—literally what steps to take. So they know if x happens, you do y, and the guy beside you does z. It's extremely disciplined and structured. If everyone does as they're trained, they don't die. Obviously they weren't trained for what to do now that they're injured and out of the service. But they bring those same expectations to it—that there's a set of steps they can take to carry on. It's a belief in the power of discipline and order, and that it's up to them to carry it out."

"And you find that interesting? That's what draws you to the work?"

"Absolutely. It's a unique way of looking at the world."

The two of them paused while a server delivered their dinners.

"How'd you get from the VA Medical Center to Aurora?" Mahler asked.

"I wanted to try working in a smaller setting. Do more

one-on-one. The work's the same, but you have more time, so it's more personal."

"If it's not violating the privacy of your treatment, how do you help Michael Behrens, who has TBI?"

"In general terms, without going into details, I help him understand how his mind works now, where his strengths and weaknesses are."

"Is he coping with his brother dying?"

"It'll take a while to process. It's hard enough for you and me to take in a sudden death. For someone like Michael, it's even more confusing. Plus he's got PTSD. He saw a number of close friends killed in combat. So the sudden death of his brother gets mixed in with those memories."

"But enough questions about me." Franny tipped her wineglass toward Mahler. "Your turn. Tell me something about your life. Have you always lived in Sonoma County?"

"I went to school back east. Princeton. Joined the service."

"Which branch?"

"Rangers."

"Tough bunch. Ever deployed?"

"No. Served as a trainer. Fort Benning."

Franny smiled. "How am I doing so far as an interrogator? Softening you up with the easy stuff?"

"Good tactic." Mahler smiled back. "I hardly noticed. But usually when I meet people...women for the first time, they want to know about my job." Mahler thought of Sharon Weyrich, who had stormed out of Café Liguria the day before.

"I think I know what your job is," Franny said. "Besides, we'll get to that. Do you have family here?"

"My sister, Diane, died of a drug overdose when she was a teenager. Parents passed away."

"You've been on your own then?" Franny stared at Mahler,

weighing her thoughts. "And presumably you're not in a relationship. Or we wouldn't be here. Right?"

"That's the general idea."

"Why is that? You're still young." She smiled encouragingly.

"Who knows? Criminal investigations are not ideal for meeting someone, as you know."

Franny ate more of her dinner. "What about those secrets you say everyone has? Am I going to learn yours?"

Mahler took a deep breath. "As the psychologist, I'm sure you know more about this than I do. But in my experience, not all secrets are about deceit. Sometimes it's a personal sense of privacy."

"Isn't that still a kind of withholding?"

"Maybe. But what I don't tell the world informs my personality, not the world's. We all have things we keep to ourselves." For an instant, Mahler remembered Eden reciting Paul Behrens's quote that man is what he hides. "I'm sure you have a few things you're not ready to talk about."

"Is that right? If you're so sure, what do you think they are?"

Mahler paused. "You really want to do this?"

"Really. I'm curious."

"All right. I'd say it has something to do with your interest in discipline and order."

A startled look crossed Franny's eyes. Recovering herself, she slowly smoothed the napkin in front of her. "Maybe we should just leave it there. Stick to the simple stuff. Have you ever been married?"

"Once, in my twenties. Divorced. Wonderful woman. We just didn't have enough in common."

"Since then?"

"Since then I was in a relationship for three years. A local lawyer. Kate Langley. It ended two years ago."

"How'd it end?"

"It was mutual."

Franny snorted. "It's never mutual. In the history of human relationships, no two people decided to leave each other at the same moment."

"Okay. I left. I was going through the PTSD thing at that time and—"

Franny waited to see what Mahler would say. Then she softly asked, "And what?"

"And I guess I couldn't do both—deal with the PTSD and be with her."

"Would Kate say that?"

"I don't know. Kate might say a lot but probably not to me."

"Seriously, Eddie? You were in a relationship for three years, and you don't think Kate would admit to frustration?"

Mahler remembered the anger in Kate's eyes five hours earlier in the interview room. "She's married now. It's... Could we talk about something else?"

"Oh sure." Franny smiled thinly. "Sounds like we both know just when to go to our corners."

They sat in silence for a few seconds.

Dr. Schafer: Are you meeting other women?

Mahler: Usually just once.

S: Why is that?

M: Lots of reasons. I say the wrong thing. Mainly I can't get over the idea it won't work out once we get to know each other.

S: You realize you can't know that until you try?

M: Yeah. It's just that I can't see how we'll make it.

S: You have to know that ahead of time?

M: Something like that. I know it's not logical.

S: Not logical? It's not how life works. Are you at all familiar with spontaneity?

M: I realize it doesn't make sense.

S: You're leaving these women entirely out of the equation. You don't know what they'll feel or do.

M: I have some ideas.

S: But they're your ideas. Jesus, Eddie, do you really want your life to be that predictable? It's called the future because it hasn't happened yet.

M: I think we've already established I have a problematic relationship with the concept of the future.

S: Maybe we need to talk about trust.

"Eddie, listen," Franny spoke first. "Tonight was great. I really like you. I do. It's embarrassing to admit, but a few minutes ago, when we were flirting, I imagined kissing you. I can see waking up in your bed in the morning before it's light and talking. You'll tell me more about your sister, Diane, and that girl you told me about the other day, the one who was killed and you couldn't forget."

"Why do I feel there's bad news coming?"

"I can't do this. It's just not going to work." Franny looked at Mahler and waited for him to return her look. "When you talk about Kate, you get this confused look in your eyes, like you're not sure where the ground is. Which probably means you're holding on to guilt or something like that."

Mahler knew exactly what the something else was—leaning over the precipice, already sure how it feels to fall.

"You interrogate people for a living," Franny continued, "and I'll bet you're good at it. But you've got a lot under your own surface. Maybe I'm making too much of the last twenty minutes. But life's short. I live with service members returning from combat. I know how suddenly a person's world changes. Two years ago, my father passed away. We thought we'd have more time. You know what? All the time we have is right here, right now tonight at this table. So I don't want to take the time while you figure it out, and let me do all the work."

Franny reached across the table and put her hand on top of Mahler's. "Sorry. I said too much, didn't I? Got a little carried away."

For a moment neither of them spoke. Then Mahler quietly said, "A little more than I was expecting. But you're very…clear." He thought of the day before in the café when Carina asked him to tally his failed dates. This one, smart enough to know better, made six. He looked down where Franny's hand still held his. "You're right, too," he said. "When relationships end, it's never mutual."

Chapter Twenty-Four

(i)

They met downtown beside the stone footbridge in Juilliard Park. It was an old city park, with mature redwood trees, grassy lawns, and a small stream running through it. On its fringes, like a frayed edge, was a neighborhood of vape shops, tattoo parlors, and a hangout for the homeless.

Jesse arrived first as always and watched Soto take three tries to parallel park his BMW on Santa Rosa Avenue. Iberian red. Dumbshit color. *Why not just write "drug dealer" on the driver's door?*

When Soto reached Jesse, they waited for a homeless man to move out of earshot and walk his bicycle through the redwoods to the street.

"Haven't seen you in a while." Soto lit a joint and deeply inhaled. When he finished, he offered it to Jesse, who shook his head. "Where've you been?"

"Busy." Jesse sat on the bridge's low wall and jammed his hands in the pockets of his sweatshirt.

"Really? Too busy to text?"

"My father died, okay? You can fuck off."

"Yeah. I heard. Sorry about that, man." Soto took another hit. "Also heard the cops talked to you."

"So what?"

"So our organization got visited this afternoon. Nine arrested. Including Julio and Luis. Cops took a month's worth of product."

"Nothing to do with me. The cops just asked a bunch of questions about my father."

"They take your shit?"

"No. Nothing like that."

"'Cause if they did, it's still on you, man. It's not our problem."

"I just said they didn't take my shit. I've got it." Jesse stood. "Is that all?"

"No. Sit your ass down." Soto trimmed the end of the joint on the stone wall and inhaled again. "It's something else."

Jesse sat on the wall and waited.

"The weed's worthless," Soto said. "The kids can get it anywhere."

"No, they can't. I'm there. I know. Not if they're underage."

"Then they're stupid."

"What difference does it make as long as I'm selling?"

"The difference is we're not making money."

Across the park, a young man and boy played in a meadow with a soccer ball. The man showed off, juggling the ball on the top of one foot. Keepy ups—Jesse remembered the name. Then the man flipped the ball to the boy, who was too little for the ball's size and weight. When the child tried to kick it, he fell backward on the grass, surprised—as if the ball juggling on the man's foot played a trick. During soccer season, Jesse's father used to take him to a nearby field Friday nights for skills practice before Saturday morning games. "Turn your dribbling foot inward," his father called. "Little toe facing the ball." Now listening in the air, Jesse thought he heard his father's voice coming across the meadow, too faint at that distance to make out the words.

"I need you to start selling stamp bags," Soto said.

"Fuck you." Jesse hopped off the wall and backed away. "I'm not selling it. I told you before."

"I don't give a shit what you told me." Soto flipped the joint end into the water below. "A position's opened up. You're the guy."

"What position? Lopez? What happened to Jorge anyway?"

"Didn't keep his mind on business."

"I said I'm not doing it. Find someone else."

"I found *you*."

"What? You going to make me?"

Soto smiled. "You don't think so? We take you off the street one night and shoot you up in the back of a car. Some high-quality hero. After that, you beg us to let you deal."

"You're an asshole. You know that?" Jesse couldn't put much into the insult. He knew Soto held all the cards.

"I'm the asshole little shitheads like you work for." Soto reached behind him to touch something at the small of his back. "Remember?"

Jesse watched him and pressed his hands deeper into his pockets. Soto's breath had a sour garlic smell. Did the man ever brush his teeth?

Jesse looked back across the park to the man and boy with the soccer ball. The boy managed a kick that nearly reached the man, who clapped his hands and hooted. "Push the center of the ball ahead of you," his own father called. "Eyes down field." Jesse remembered running, the ball two or three feet in front, his legs strong under him, every step making him the star in his imagined game. The Friday nights were late, the sun long set, the sky already dark. His father on the sideline, too far away to see, just his voice calling across the length of the field. Had only his voice returned now? Was that possible?

"We going to have trouble, *chico*?"

Jesse shook his head.

"We give you a bundle. You sell ten-dollar bags. Off West Steele. I show you the blocks. The junkies'll find you. The regulars are out every night."

"You mix the stuff you sell?"

"None of your business what we do."

"It *is* my business. Someone dies, I get charged with a felony."

"All you need to know, the stuff's top-of-the-line black tar. Junkies love it."

"I'm talking about fentanyl. Lopez know about that?"

"Who the fuck cares what he knew? Your job is to sell what we give you. That's all."

"What about cops?"

"What about them? Walk the blocks. Keep an eye out for a couple of dickheads sitting in a parked car. What's so hard about that?"

"If I get ripped off?"

"No one's going to rip you off. Just try not to be stupid."

Jesse looked at Soto's eyes, red now from the weed. He watched Soto scan the park again, nervously checking for something. Jesse worried about the other man's hair-trigger jitteriness. Was it meth?

"I do it until you find someone else."

"You do it until I tell you." Soto smiled again. "You make

some money. Buy yourself a car like a man." He held up his key fob and swung it back and forth on its short chain.

"I don't need a car," Jesse said.

"We all need cars, *chico*." He turned to walk across the park grass. "Keep your phone turned on."

(ii)

(THURSDAY, 9:12 P.M.)

As Coyle walked down the Salmon Creek Beach, a small white dog on a retractable leash reached Coyle before its owner. The dog stopped at Coyle's feet and smelled his shoes. It looked up and barked twice, then ran down the path through the sand dunes.

"His name's Larry." The owner puffed from the effort to catch up with the dog. "He's a West Highland. A Westie. Sounds fierce, but he won't bite."

Coyle looked after the dog. He had learned not to trust any dog owner's claims about an animal's tendency to bite. As a law enforcement officer, he was entitled to shoot a dog if he felt threatened, but proving a fifteen-pound dog named Larry was threatening would be a hard sell.

"People think he's named after a famous Larry," the man said. "Like Larry Bird or Larry King. But I just like the name Larry."

Coyle, who didn't recognize either of the "famous Larrys," and didn't care what people named their pets, wished he could have the last five seconds of his life back. He held out his badge and identified himself. "Can I ask you a few questions?"

"Sure thing. Is this about Larry getting off his leash last weekend? I'm amazed they sent you all the way from Santa Rosa. It's too bad he got into that guy's trash. I offered to—"

"It's not about that. It's about the two men on the beach Wednesday night. I understand you might have seen them? Mr.—"

"Ashland. Richard Ashland. Who told you?"

"Please answer the question, sir. Did you see two men?"

"Yes. Why is—"

"What exactly did you see?" Coyle took out his notebook.

"Two men running down the beach across from the parking lot. About nine o'clock. Over there." Ashland pointed to a spot where the surf hit the beach a hundred or so yards ahead of where they were standing. "It was that old woman in the second beach house, wasn't it? She was out on her porch. She always waves."

"Tell me what you saw."

"The first man, the shorter one, ran into the water. I mean, right into it. Fully dressed, but still. That's why I noticed. It's fricking cold, and the guy goes into the water."

"Was the other man chasing him? Is that why he went into the water?"

"That's what I thought at first—that the first guy was trying to get away from the other one. But then—"

"Then what?"

"Then I don't know. The other guy, the taller one, was right there and pulled him out of the water and back onto the beach. So then I thought it was okay. The two of them came up here." Ashland pointed to a spot closer to the dunes.

Coyle looked to the place the man indicated. As he had the night before, Coyle thought again of the girl who had come to these dunes with him the summer before senior year, and how she had leaned away from his kiss. He remembered now, her name was Kaylee. When he drove her home that night and before she got out of his car, she turned and said, "You're sweet,

Martin," which confused him then but which he now knew was exactly how far he had been from that kiss. "Was the first man hurt?" Coyle asked.

"I couldn't tell. He staggered when he walked. Looked out of it. Like he was drunk or something. Is this about the man who died in his car on Bean Avenue?" Ashland squinted into the wind to locate Larry, then tugged on the leash to draw him closer.

"Yes. What happened next?"

"They came up the dunes. The larger man had one arm under the other man's shoulders and was supporting him while they walked. They passed me there by the wooden steps. Larry went right up to them. Nearly got his leash tangled in their legs."

"Did they say anything?" Coyle asked.

"No. I said, 'Good evening.' Neither of them answered. I asked if they needed help. The larger man looked at me and kept walking. Was one of them the man who died?"

Coyle ignored the question. "Where'd they go after they walked past you?"

"They walked from the end of the dunes toward the parking lot. I couldn't see exactly where they went. It looked like they were headed toward the lot or maybe farther on Bean Avenue. So I assume they went to a car."

Coyle finished writing in his notebook and took out three photo arrays he had mocked up that afternoon. Each one held six male head shots. He showed Ashland an array that included Paul Behrens. "Are any of these men the couple you saw?"

"The shorter man I saw might be that one," he said, pointing to Paul Behrens. "I couldn't see him very well because he didn't lift his head. Is that the man who died in his car? I saw it on the news."

"Were either of them here?" Coyle held an array that included Gregory Winter.

"No. None of them."

Coyle held up the last array, which included John McFarland. "Were any of these men the couple you saw?"

"That one," Ashland pointed to McFarland. "Definitely. Him, I'm sure of it. That's the larger man."

The answer and the suddenness of it surprised Coyle. He pictured himself returning to his car and texting Eddie. This was confirmation of McFarland in the presence of Behrens the night Behrens died. The case would change now. They'd have to find McFarland. Coyle watched Ashland. "Are you certain? It's very important."

"Young man, I tended bar for thirty years at the St. Regis in San Francisco. Know it? California Street on Nob Hill? That line of work, you see and remember faces. Your tips depend on it. You remember men's eyes, facial hair, the cut of their suits. Women—you never forget hair color, earrings, shades of lipstick. One of my regulars walked up here this minute, I could tell you his usual time to arrive and the brand of rye he wanted in his manhattan. You put this man in a crowd a month from now, and I'll pick him out."

"You'd be willing to appear in court?"

"Sure," Ashland said.

The two men looked at each other.

"You don't believe me, do you? Okay, listen." Ashland turned away from Coyle. "We've been together what, five minutes? You're wearing a blue-striped oxford shirt, untucked, jeans, some sort of hiking shoes. You're a couple inches shorter than me. So I'd say five ten. Hazel eyes. Brown hair shaved on the sides. I think it's called a fade. Parted on the left, and graying on the temples. Half-inch scar under the outer end of your right eye, a childhood injury, if I had to guess. Lucky it missed your eye. I'll bet it scared your mother. There's a—"

"All right. All right. That's enough." Coyle asked Ashland for his address and phone number and added them to his phone.

"By the way, Larry will remember the tall man's scent, if you need him to. He got a good scent off the guy. I've seen him recall a smell a year after—"

"Probably not necessary." And a little weird, Coyle thought. He looked down the path where Larry lifted a leg to pee on a tuft of beachgrass. For an instant he imagined the dog on the courtroom witness chair where Coyle had been seated the day before. Would Larry be tripped up by Deputy District Attorney Michael Slater? "Thanks for your help. We'll be in touch." Coyle handed Ashland a business card and headed back down the path to his car.

As he walked, Coyle turned to the sea to watch the breakers hit the beach. A chill air blew across the dunes. The water would be cold. Had Behrens been drugged? Ashland didn't mention him shivering. Did that mean something? Did the story of Behrens and McFarland on the beach point to murder, not suicide? Had Eddie's intuition been right? When was Coyle going to learn not to doubt that?

Coyle stopped and let the wind blow in his face. He put aside the case and its mysteries and felt the loneliness of the spot and his own sadness. He wondered how many years would have to pass before this place on the coast no longer awakened a memory of the girl and that failed kiss, and he wondered what message lay in the memory for the grown man he was now.

Chapter Twenty-Five

(i)

Rivas and Mahler walked slowly into the VCI room. Rivas sat heavily in his chair and rubbed his eyes. *Are we a good team?* Mahler asked himself this for the second time in two days as he stood in the center of the bullpen and looked at the others. Frames turned to face him. Eden did, too, with a phone earpiece in one ear and a forefinger raised, needing one more moment. *We were good,* Mahler thought. *Before.* Professionals. Until Eden got here. Overqualified and underexperienced, Eden made them a team, more than anything else. Eden took out the phone jack, put down her hand, and looked to him expectantly.

"Daniel and I just went up to the McFarlands," Mahler said. "No one was there, and both cars are missing. We put out a BOLO for the two of them and called the airports. We also stationed a couple of cars on their block in case they return."

"Any idea where they went?" Eden asked. "Do they have a second home? Relatives?"

"We're looking at that."

"Tell me again what Martin said," Frames said.

Mahler read from his phone. "He talked to a witness who says he saw John McFarland with Behrens on the beach at Salmon Creek the night he died. The witness said Behrens appeared to run into the water. McFarland pulled him out and led him toward the parked cars. The witness is very certain it was McFarland."

"So McFarland was with Behrens Wednesday night," Eden said. "Which makes him the lead suspect, but we still don't know if he was responsible for Behrens's death. Is that right?"

"Yeah," Mahler said. "Strictly speaking, that's all we know. And Dr. Winter is still in the picture."

"When I interviewed McFarland," Rivas said, "he told me he never went to the coast Wednesday. He even gave me the names of several employees to vouch for his presence in Santa Rosa Wednesday afternoon and evening. All of them confirmed he was in town. Which, if we believe Martin's eyewitness, means McFarland and his employees lied."

"But why would McFarland meet Behrens on the coast in the first place?" Eden asked. "McFarland's upset about a school lesson? So he drives all the way to the coast and chases Behrens into the ocean? It doesn't make sense."

"You're right," Mahler agreed. "Something's missing."

"By the way," Frames said, "while you were gone, I got the coroner's report." Bending close to the screen, he read aloud. "'Evidence indicates the weapon used to kill the victim was likely fired not by the victim but by a second party. The force used to press the tip of the gun onto the victim's temple is inconsistent with self-administration.'"

"Self-administration? What an expression." Frames pulled his computer onto his lap and turned his chair to face the inside of the VCI bullpen. "So, we're talking about a homicide, not a suicide. That was your idea all along, wasn't it, Eddie? Good call."

"What else does it say?" Mahler asked.

"'GSR found on the fingers of the victim's right hand suggests he was holding the weapon at the time of firing. However, the region of injured tissue on the victim's temple is sufficiently deep to demonstrate the gun tip was forcefully shoved against the head before firing.' Blah, blah, blah. There's some stuff about ruptured blood capillaries under the skin where the gun touched the temple. Blah, blah."

Frames scrolled further through the screen. "Okay. So the cause of death was a single gunshot wound to the head. But listen to this. 'However, prior to the shooting, the victim ingested a quantity of a Schedule I drug, which would have significantly impaired his physical responses and mental capabilities.'"

"What drug?" Rivas asked.

Frames leaned back until the front legs of his chair lifted an inch off the floor. "Ta-da. Fentanyl," he announced. "'Serum analysis shows presence of 3-methylfentanyl, otherwise known as fentanyl. No needle marks found on victim.'" Frames dropped back on the floor and continued reading. "'It is suspected the drug was administered orally.'"

"Where'd Behrens get fentanyl?" Mahler asked.

"He had a ton of prescription drugs in his home." Eden looked in her notebook. "Ativan, Zoloft, Valium."

"But not fentanyl?"

Eden shook her head.

"I think I know where it might have come from." Rivas held up his phone. "You know the state medical licensing board investigation Martin was looking into—the one on Dr. Gregory Winter? I took a call a couple hours ago from the board. The investigator wasn't willing to tell me much, but he said it was a six-month joint operation with the Sheriff's Office. Winter was about to be charged with theft of Schedule I drugs from his hospital, including—"

"Fentanyl," Frames said.

"Yeah," Rivas said. "And remember the Jameson bottle in Behrens's car had prints from both Behrens and Winter?"

"So Winter put Fentanyl in the scotch bottle?" Eden asked. "Why would he do that?"

"We can ask him tomorrow when he comes in for another interview," Mahler said. "What else do we know?"

"I'm looking at the gun used to kill Behrens," Eden said. "We can tie the weapon to one fired during a warehouse burglary in Windsor two years ago and to a suspect in that case named Thomas Hyland. I talked to the investigator for the burglary, Sergeant Loudon at the Sheriff's Office. Hyland was found with merchandise from the burglary. He denied knowledge of its origin, and no other evidence connected him to the crime. He was never charged, and the weapon was never recovered. Hyland had two prior burglary arrests. Unemployed at the time of the burglary. He previously worked as a journeyman roofer."

"Is there a connection between Hyland and McFarland? Did he work on one of McFarland's construction crews or for a contractor?"

"I'm just getting into it."

The room fell silent as the detectives returned to their desks.

Mahler took a seat next to Frames's desk. "How'd the drug bust go?" he asked quietly.

"Good," Frames said. "I think. We got to them before they had a chance to move the drugs. Nine arrested. Several members of the Medina family, plus couriers from East Palo Alto and Fresno. Noah's still sorting through the confiscated drugs. But it was a lot. Meth. Heroin."

"Sounds like good timing. Any word on the Lopez murder?"

Frames shook his head. "They've got a possible suspect. Guy named Rafael Soto. We saw him with a gun during surveillance, but he wasn't at the drug bust site this afternoon."

"Does Noah's team have a line on the guy?"

"Prater and Buckley are talking to people on the street, see what they know. Prater's going to text me if they turn up anything. When I have a chance, I'm also going to talk to Señor Memory." Frames pointed to Rivas.

"How about you? Don't want to burn you out on double shifts. I can find someone else to fill in with Narcotics, if you need me to."

"I'm okay for now. But I'll let you know."

Mahler stood and walked across the bullpen. Eden caught him before he could leave. "I just got a text from Behrens's daughter, Claire," she said. "She sent me a photo of a receipt she found. It's for a room at the downtown Hyatt Regency. Rented by her father Tuesday night. I called the hotel. They confirmed the reservation, and the card key system says someone's still in there. I called the room. No answer."

She waited for Mahler. "So who is it?" she asked.

"I'll drive." Mahler turned for the door.

(ii)

(FRIDAY, 12:06 A.M.)

"Tell me about the receipt," Mahler said as he pulled out of the police lot, the steering wheel spinning in his hands.

"Claire's father gave her a book Tuesday night," Eden said. "She didn't look inside until now. She saw the receipt and texted me. Now she wonders if her father gave her the book so she'd find the receipt. The reservation was made in person by Behrens Tuesday night. Paid cash. For five nights. Which is why we didn't find a charge on his credit card when we looked, and it accounts for the large ATM cash withdrawal."

"And the clerk you spoke to just now hasn't seen the room guest?"

"No. The desk clerk on duty tonight wasn't there Tuesday. Hasn't seen or spoken to the room's occupant."

Mahler drove through the near-empty downtown streets toward the Hyatt. "So why does Behrens rent an expensive hotel room?"

"And why now, and why untraceable cash?"

"Is this a girlfriend of Behrens's we haven't heard about before?" Mahler asked.

"Maybe. But how many girlfriends can one man have? Also, we know Paul Behrens was at home later Tuesday night and didn't stay at the hotel himself."

The hotel desk clerk greeted Mahler and Eden with an automatic smile. Her expression turned serious when they held out their badges. "You just called, didn't you?" she said to Eden.

The clerk tapped on her keyboard. "As I told you, Paul Behrens made the reservation here at the desk at 8:03 p.m. Tuesday evening. Room 217. Two queen beds with view. Our nonmember rate. Five nights. Paid in advance."

"Have any phone calls been made on that room's phone?" Eden asked.

The clerk studied her screen and shook her head.

"Has any room service been ordered?" Mahler asked.

The clerk looked again the screen. "There's no record of

that. But our guests often go out to one of the restaurants in the neighborhood."

"You'll need to give us a key."

"I don't know." The clerk glanced into the empty office behind her. "I've never done this before. I'll have to call my manager."

"It's urgent," Eden said.

The clerk looked at both Eden and Mahler. "Could I take a photo of your badges for our records? I'm still going to have to tell my manager."

The two officers held out their badges to be photographed. Then Mahler took the key card the clerk held out to him.

They climbed the stairs to the second floor, walked along a dimly lit carpeted hallway to Room 217, and knocked. No sounds came from inside.

Mahler knocked again. "Santa Rosa Police. Please open the door."

No reply.

"We're investigating the death of Paul Behrens." Mahler leaned closer to the door and raised his voice. "We need to talk to you."

After a minute, the room door opened the length of the door chain. A young girl peered out. "Are you really the police?" In the dark doorway, all that was visible was the girl's frightened face.

Mahler held up his badge. "What's your name?"

"Zoe McFarland," the girl whispered.

"The daughter of Charlotte and John McFarland?" Eden asked. "Can we come in and talk?"

"Are my parents with you?"

"No. It's just the two of us."

"Do they know I'm here?"

"No. We didn't know you were here. But we can call them if you like."

The young woman shook her head. Then she backed up and slowly unlocked the door for Mahler and Eden.

As the two detectives entered the hotel room, Zoe faced them in the center of the sitting area. Dressed in tights and a top, she was a tall, thin girl. She squeezed her hands together and looked uncertain how to behave. Behind her, the room was dark and quiet.

Mahler moved quickly past the girl to verify the room was empty.

"Your parents are looking for you." Eden thought the girl looked a lot like Claire Behrens—the same spare frame, thin limbs. A wired intensity in the eyes. *Was it really true, or just her own unfamiliarity with teen girls?*

"I know." Zoe held up her phone. "They left messages."

"Can you tell us what you're doing here?"

"Mr. Behrens brought me. Is he really dead?"

"Yes," Mahler rejoined the others. "I'm afraid so."

"Then it's my fault." The girl dropped onto the sofa and began to cry, letting the tears pour down her face.

"Why's it your fault?" Eden asked, searching the room for tissue. Not finding any, she grabbed a cloth napkin from the dining table and handed it to Zoe. "What happened?" She sat on the sofa facing the girl.

"Did Mr. Behrens hurt you?" Mahler pulled a chair to face the sofa.

The girl wiped at her face with the napkin and shook her head.

"Did he act inappropriately?"

"No. I don't know what that means."

"You can tell us anything," Eden said. "You don't have to worry anymore."

"You don't understand. I *asked* Mr. Behrens to bring me here. I mean, I asked him to take me somewhere safe, and he said I could be here. He helped me."

"Safe?" Mahler asked. "Safe from what?"

"I don't have to come with you, do I?" She looked back and forth at Eden and Mahler.

"I'm not going to lie to you. You can't stay here alone, so you have to come with us," Mahler said. "But, first, tell us why you had to come here. Safe from what?"

"My parents."

The words fell in the room like gunshots. Suddenly the room was silent but for the faint humming of the air conditioner.

"Your parents?" Eden asked, her voice soft, as if not to disturb the silence. "Why didn't you feel safe from them?"

"Because they killed someone. A woman. I found out about it."

"Wait a minute." Mahler edged closer to Zoe. "What did you find out? Who did they kill?"

"My mother did it. It was an accident. She killed the woman. And my father knew about it."

Eden looked at Mahler to see if he'd heard what she had.

"I didn't feel safe." The girl began to cry again. "I didn't know where else to go."

PART III

Chapter Twenty-Six

(i)

Frames stood in the darkness of a cluster of redwoods in Santa Rosa and looked across an empty street at a row of two-story apartments. *Had he gotten the address wrong?* He'd been in the same spot for more than hour, waiting for one car—a red BMW. So far, the car hadn't shown. The windows in the building were dark.

He thought of what Tom Woodhouse had said earlier that night about the despair of drug users. "Every day, people look around, and all they want is to close their eyes and go to sleep." Frames never felt it himself. Had he always kept busy to avoid depression? Or had he dodged that genetic imprint and was just not built that way, as one of his girlfriends said? Still, he'd seen despair in others, even without drug addiction. His mother's deep sadness led her to days of silent withdrawal that shadowed his childhood.

Then there was Woodhouse's story of a young father shot

in the head in a case of mistaken identity. What did anything in your life matter if you died that way? Had you wasted your life learning to play the guitar, falling in love, making plans? Was there something more blameworthy in being killed that way instead of dying peacefully in a hospital bed?

What about Jesse Behrens? Privileged, middle-class, white kid playing at being a drug dealer. Dreams in his head of *Breaking Bad*. Now caught up in the Ramirez-Medina organization. Was it a slow-motion tragedy?

Frames looked toward the southern end of the street and wondered again if he had gotten the wrong location. Prater supplied this address near the Coddingtown mall, a popular spot for drug sales. "A junkie named Milton hangs out around the doorway of 1207 McBride. White guy. Forties. Thin and shaky. Soto makes regular deliveries there. You might find him there."

In his time under the trees, Frames saw zero pedestrians and only one car, a car that was not a BMW. His phone buzzed with a text from Prater. "Need company?" He texted he didn't but would let her know.

Rain started, a thin, slanting drizzle that managed to penetrate the tree cover. In ten minutes, his jacket was soaked.

A text arrived from Woodhouse asking where he was and if his feet were cold. *What was the old man doing awake at two in the morning?*

Two blocks away, a car turned onto McBride, headlights approaching slowly through the rain. Frames recognized the barrel-echoing growl of the BMW engine as the car passed under a streetlight. The car parked thirty yards away in the only available space. Frames watched Soto climb out and walk along the sidewalk toward 1207.

After a minute, a figure emerged from the apartment building and met Soto under the building's overhang.

While the two talked, Frames jogged in the darkness parallel to the street. When he reached a point between Soto and the BMW, Frames broke into the open across McBride.

The two men heard his feet on the pavement. The junkie dove back into the apartment. Soto turned and sprinted up the sidewalk away from Frames and the BMW.

"Police. Stop." Frames jumped between parked cars and followed the dealer.

At the northern edge of the apartment building, Soto disappeared into an alleyway.

Frames ran flat out, all his attention on keeping up. In the dark alley, he lost sight of Soto for a few seconds but heard running steps ahead. The alleyway opened onto a lighted parking lot. By the time Frames reached it, he could see Soto on the far side zigzagging around cars.

In the open now, Frames gained on Soto. *Where was Soto's gun?* Frames's mind raced. *Did he have time to call for help?*

Soto vaulted over a cast-iron fence with spike-topped rails and landed on his feet. He glanced back at Frames and ran on.

It took Frames a few seconds longer to get over the fence, picking his way between the sharp spikes. When Frames hit the sidewalk, Soto was a half block ahead, crossing a street toward a high-rise apartment building.

Frames gave chase, slower now as he felt the pain and stiffness from the rapier wound two days earlier.

For a few seconds Soto vanished, a specter in the darkness of trees and shrubbery bordering the apartment tower. He reappeared silhouetted by the building's lobby lights.

Outside the lobby entrance, Frames took shelter behind a concrete planter and peered inside. Soto was not in sight. The entrance appeared to be the only public way in or out, but the lobby space had a bank of elevators and four visible interior doors.

Frames pulled out his Glock and entered the lobby. No elevator lights were lit, telling him Soto hadn't taken that route. Frames tried the nearest interior door. Locked. He tried two more, one to a stairway, the other unmarked. Both locked. Frames stared at the fourth door, labeled "Employees Only." Without a window in the door, it was impossible to tell what lay beyond. *Was Soto waiting on the other side, or had he run farther inside? Was it time to call Prater?*

Frames gingerly tried the door handle and felt it give. He threw it open and flattened himself against the wall outside the doorway. After a few seconds he turned into the space—a cool, dark corridor filled with a machine hum. As his eyes adjusted to the darkness, Frames could tell it led to the building's HVAC area. He listened for sounds of the other man moving but heard nothing. He walked slowly and silently in the darkness, still gripping his gun. The machine hum grew louder.

From ahead came a piercing metallic screech. Frames stopped, pressing himself against the corridor wall. Then he moved cautiously forward to a dimly lit utility room housing an AC unit and furnace. He bent low to search under piping and equipment. After a minute he could tell the room had no exit other than the corridor.

He steadied his gun in front of him and made his way to the far end of the room. Soto was there—Frames was sure of it— inches away.

Then he saw it. Six feet up the far wall—a louvered window, now spread open. A waist-high steel pipe provided just enough step to reach the window. The screech had been the window bending open.

Frames leaped onto the piping and boosted himself to the windowsill. Through the opening, he heard the soft thud of someone crashing across the ground. Shoving the Glock back in its holster, he dove forward to fall through the opening into the bushes bordering the building.

It was raining harder now. Wind ripped through the trees. For a moment, Frames stood still, listening. To his left, he heard footsteps running over a ground cover of ivy vines and juniper bushes.

He pulled out his gun. Again the swollen, gray face of the dead drug dealer, Jorge Lopez, flashed across his mind.

A hundred yards away Frames glimpsed a figure sprinting through the darkness. He ran toward it. Twice ivy vines snagged his feet, and he fell forward. His clothes were dripping wet, his hands scratched and sore. He gripped his gun and breathed hard.

The dark figure had disappeared. Was Soto farther up the street or in one of the blind passageways between buildings? Frames listened but could hear only wind gusting through the overhead branches. *Had he lost him?*

Suddenly something struck him on the head, knocking him helplessly to the ground and loosening the gun from his hand. He felt an intense pain. The world spun in a tight circle. The earth lifted toward the sky. He grabbed at the ivy to steady himself and closed his eyes to stop the spinning. Nausea flooded through him. He opened his eyes again and threw up, spitting the bitter taste into the ivy.

Where was the gun? He pulled himself up and reached blindly into the ivy. The effort reignited the screaming pain. He let himself slide to the ground.

Someone approached. From his vantage point, all he could see was the shape of legs coming nearer. *Was it Soto? Had Soto hit him and come back?* He waited to hear the rack sliding on Soto's gun. *Would he hear the gunshot that killed him?*

"Steve?" The voice sounded familiar. The figure came closer.

Again. "Steve."

Frames felt arms reach around his upper body and pull him to his knees. He looked into the man's face.

Tom Woodhouse.

"Jesus," Woodhouse said. "I thought you were dead."

For a minute, the rain was furious. They were alone in the noise of it pounding around them, as wet as if they'd jumped in a lake.

Frames gripped Woodhouse's arm to stay upright. "What—?"

"It's okay." Woodhouse spun in a circle as if they were on separate horses of a merry-go-round.

"How did you—?"

"You told me where you were, remember?" Woodhouse said.

"Did you see him?"

"Soto? Was that Soto?"

"He was right here. I almost—"

Woodhouse gingerly touched Frames's head. "We need to get you to the ER."

"Give me a second," Frames said.

Frames looked at the other man and forgot who he was. Was this his father come home? At the thought, a snapshot rose in his memory. A figure stood in a doorway, a straw cowboy hat pushed back on his head. And something else—his father, lifting him in the air, kissing him on the lips, and saying a name. Steve-O.

He blinked and flashes of light burst behind his eyes. Around him was the deep-woodsy odor of the cedar trees. He thought of how good it was to be alive. He remembered Specialist Tinsley, Third Battalion, First Marines, after a day of house-to-house in the Second Battle of Fallujah: "Hey, Lance Corporal, look who didn't get fucking killed." Tinsley grinned, and the cigarette in the corner of his mouth dipped up and down as he spoke.

The words of Dorothy Fellows, the old woman on the coast,

came back to him: "Funny what happens to us, isn't it? How we all make our endings?" Sometimes you didn't get fucking killed, Frames thought.

In front of him he recognized Tom Woodhouse again. Had Woodhouse saved him? Or had he arrived by chance? Or were those the same thing?

After a few minutes, Woodhouse looked up into the cedar branches above them. "Man, it's raining hard, you know that?"

Frames raised his head and felt the rain hit his face. "Yeah," he said quietly, "it sure is." He looked at the night sky like Dorothy Fellows had told him. The storm covered the stars, but there was something wonderful in the vast black dome. Was it benevolent or indifferent? It was hard to tell. But even now, busy with rain and wind, the sky did not seem to wish him harm, as much on earth did. He felt as if he was seeing it for the first time and knew it for the blessing that it was.

(ii)

(FRIDAY, 4:33 A.M.)

"Sorry. I can't sleep." Zoe sat cross-legged atop the comforter on one of the hotel room's queen beds. She looked at Eden, who lay on a sofa in the sitting area. "Can we just talk?"

"Sure," Eden said. "I'll heat some water for tea." She'd been awake for the past hour, making notes for the Jory case.

Before Mahler left to return to the station, Zoe had poured out the story of her mother's accident. She perched on the sofa, legs stretched out to rest on the coffee table. She looked down at her hands, squeezing her fingers together. "It was a little more than a year ago. April 12, 2018. Saturday night. I memorized all this because I haven't been able to get it out of my mind."

Mahler watched Zoe. Sensing a fragility in the girl, he resisted the urge to interrupt with questions.

"My mom and dad attended a winemaker dinner in Alexander Valley. You know, one of those things where a local chef prepares a meal and they match wines with each course? Both Mom and Dad had been drinking, but my mother had less, so she drove home. My father fell asleep in the front seat.

"It happened on Chalk Hill Road. There was a pedestrian, a woman, walking on the shoulder. My mom never saw her until it was too late. She hit the woman with the right front bumper and headlight of the car. They stopped. Daddy woke up, and they got out of the car. They felt for a pulse but could tell she was dead. It was late. Dark. No other cars came by. They moved her body off the road. And they...left."

Zoe looked from Mahler to Eden, as if expecting something. "There wasn't cell phone service where the accident happened. They thought they'd call later, when they got into service, closer to home. But then, you know, they...didn't."

"When they got home, Mom wanted to call the police. Daddy didn't. He said the woman was already dead. Admitting their fault wouldn't change that. No one would find out. He'd have a friend fix the car." She looked across the room into the darkness. "I almost understand it."

"I Googled the accident," Zoe said. "Her name was Melanie Rosen. She was walking home from a friend's house. The CHP investigated the accident as a hit-and-run. It was on TV, in the newspaper. The driver was never found."

Zoe stopped. The room fell silent.

Mahler had listened to every word, impressed by the girl's calmness and clarity. He noted the lack of excuses, rationalizations. It sounded like something the girl had turned over in her mind for days, baring it to its reality. "How'd you find out?" he asked.

"For months, I knew something was wrong. Mom was taking pills, sleeping all the time, losing weight. Then, like, a month ago, I heard my mom and dad arguing. It was late at night, in their bedroom, which is next to mine. Mom was crying. I heard her say the word 'kill.' That's what woke me up. My dad kept telling her to shut up."

"The next day, I asked Mom what happened. At first she denied it. But I knew she was lying. I said I'd talk to Daddy. Then she got really scared. She said she'd tell me what happened if I promised not to tell my father. She made me promise like I was a little kid. She said, 'Promise, promise, promise.' So I did. Then she told me. When she finished, I said you *have* to tell the police." Zoe sat forward and waved one hand as if sweeping something aside. "You can't just hide it."

"She said my dad would freak." The girl fell back and her voice softened. "That if people found out, my mom would go to jail. Maybe both of them. My dad's business would be ruined. All their friends would know and… Even if my dad didn't go to jail, we'd lose the house and have to move somewhere far away. She kept saying I'd already promised not to tell anyone."

"That's a lot to put on you," Eden said. "What'd you do?"

"Nothing. For a few days. But I couldn't stop thinking about it. In English, we were reading *Twelfth Night*. Mr. Behrens talked about secrets and the bad things that happen when we have secrets. After class, I asked him what to do if you knew a really terrible secret."

Zoe smiled thinly. "He thought it was weird, I could tell. That I was, like, being sexually abused or something at home. He got real serious. He closed the classroom door and sat next to me. He said if it was worrying me, I should tell the truth."

"So I told him. The whole thing, everything I knew. How I was afraid to talk to my dad. He said it wasn't my responsibility to contact the authorities. It was up to my parents, and they needed to come forward. It was a legal thing…a moral thing."

"Did you go back to your parents after that?" Mahler asked.

"No. Mr. Behrens and I talked about it three times that week. Finally Mr. Behrens said he'd talk to my father. That scared the crap out of me. Mr. Behrens is nice. My dad… He's not like that. I told Mr. Behrens if he spoke to my dad, I'd run away. He tried to talk me out of it. He said I had to go somewhere safe. That's when he arranged for me to stay here. I got scared late Tuesday night and called him. He said it'd be all right. Just give it time."

"I need to get some water." Zoe went to the room's sink and poured herself a glass.

Mahler and Eden exchanged looks. As secrets go, this one was pretty good. They were getting closer to something. Here was the missing reason for McFarland to meet Behrens on the coast, and the Tuesday night phone call was what Claire overheard her father say.

Zoe returned to the sofa. "I have messages from both my mom and dad. My mom says I should come home. My dad says he knows I told Mr. Behrens. It's going to be okay. He and Mr. Behrens talked. He just wants me home, too. But then I heard Mr. Behrens is dead, and I didn't know if my dad—" Zoe looked at Mahler. "Did my father kill Mr. Behrens?"

"We don't know," Mahler said. "That's why we're trying to find him."

"But wait, Zoe." Eden rose from her chair. "Have you actually talked to your parents in the past forty-eight hours?"

"No," Zoe said. "They texted. I texted my mom back and told her I was okay."

Mahler leaned forward. "Zoe, your parents aren't at the house. Do you know where they are?"

Zoe shook her head. "I mean, they have an apartment in

the city. Mom has a house on the river. They could be at one of those. I can give you the addresses." She tapped at her phone screen.

"It's probably not a good idea for you to be here alone," Eden said. "Is there a relative's house where you can stay?"

Zoe looked up from her phone. "Maybe my aunt Jeannine and uncle Roy. I think they'd be okay with that."

"All right," Mahler said. "We'll contact them. In the meantime, I'd like Officer Somers to stay here with you. Would that be all right?"

Zoe smiled at Eden. "I guess so. I'm not going to off myself or anything."

"We know," Mahler said. "We just need to be sure you're safe."

After Mahler left, Zoe climbed into one of the queen beds and fell asleep.

Eden stretched out on the sofa in the sitting area. She tried several times to close her eyes but kept seeing Anthony Dunbar's face on the video screen from Albuquerque. Finally she sat up and made notes on the Albert Jory case.

When Zoe awoke, Eden heated the electric kettle and poured two mugs of herbal tea. Zoe opened the curtains. They stood side by side, looking out the window at the quiet hotel parking lot and the morning sky.

"Zoe," Eden said, "your parents told one of our detectives they were concerned about Mr. Behrens's attitude toward you. Something about the novel *Emma*?"

Zoe sighed. "It was nothing. Mr. Behrens was trying to make a joke. It bothered me when it happened, and I told my mom. Afterward, I realized it was kind of lame, but he was just trying to be funny. My mom and dad took it the wrong way."

"And your grades?"

"Mr. Behrens was a hard grader. He said he was getting us ready for high school and beyond that college. My essays weren't my best work. That's all. It was me, not him."

Eden nodded and let some time pass.

"I don't understand how I'm supposed to feel," Zoe said after a few moments. "Does that make sense? I love them. I love my parents. But what does it mean that they did this thing, this hit-and-run?"

"People act differently under pressure," Eden said. "Sometimes even people in your family. It's hard to predict. You can still love someone even if you don't understand their actions. You may never understand or condone what they did, but that doesn't mean you stop loving them."

They resumed staring out the window. The night before, Eden had seen similarities between Zoe and Claire, both being the same age—the thinness of their limbs, their bodies coming into womanhood, naivete revealing itself even as they tried to assert their worldliness. Now, with time to watch Zoe, she saw the differences. Where Claire was shy and just beginning to find her adult voice, Zoe showed the advantages of her family's wealth and status. She had adopted from her mother the bearing of the privileged; from her father she had learned how to look for the angles.

"Are you close to your parents?" Zoe asked.

"There's no short answer to that." Eden considered the question. "I was close to my dad, but he passed away nine years ago when I was in college. My mom lives in Connecticut. We talk once a week."

"When you grew up, did your mom and dad have secrets, things they didn't tell you?"

Eden tasted the tea. A car slowly circled the parking lot. She remembered the first anniversary of her father's death. Her mother had opened a bottle of rosé that night after dinner on the screened-in porch behind her parents' home. It was quiet. The sun had set, draining the sky of color but not yet dark enough for stars. "We lost a baby before you were born," her mother said, as if suddenly discovering the occasion for the news. While she spoke, she looked across the quiet backyard, not at her daughter. "Did I ever mention it? Stillborn at six months. A little boy. For a while after that, your father and I didn't talk or, what's the expression, have relations. I believe there was a nurse in his practice at that time. A pretty girl, younger than me. I don't think he loved her. He came back to me after a few months, and we made the best of it, as one does. Then you came along. I named you Eden. Your father had no part in that decision. I liked the name, of course, but really it was because I wanted to remember the innocence from before. My goodness, you were always my lovely innocence." Her mother turned to smile at Eden for a second before continuing her gaze outside.

Eden remembered her mother's thin, liver-spotted hand as it lifted the wineglass to her lips. The porch was silent, which seemed wrong for that moment and the adjustment of history. Eden opened her mouth but couldn't get a word out. In that instant the story both remade her and vanquished what she had known of herself.

Now Eden turned to face Zoe. "I think my parents had their secrets. But they were old-fashioned Yankees. They believed in a kind of New England propriety. There's a Robert Frost poem called 'The Good Hours' about a man walking past cottages late at night in the snow. His very presence is a profanity because it's well past the good hours when everyone else is asleep. My mom and dad believed in that kind of strict, socially accepted sense of right and wrong. There were things my parents didn't say between themselves, let alone share with me."

Zoe swirled the tea in her mug. "I'm alone now, aren't I?" she said.

Looking at Zoe's eyes, Eden could see the girl working out the consequences in her own mind. She wouldn't be taken in by false assurances or hand-holding. "Whatever happens, your parents will always be your parents," Eden said. "But you'll have to spend some time with your aunt and uncle. Someone will take care of you. You won't be alone." *But it will feel that way.* From her own loneliness, Eden knew it was the thinnest of comfort, but she also knew nothing she said now would be a match for the girl's future.

Chapter Twenty-Seven

(i)

"This is the summary of the joint investigation by the state medical licensing board and the Sheriff's Office." Mahler laid the papers on the table in front of Gregory Winter and Kate Langley. "The indictment involves theft of Schedule I drugs from the medical supplies of the Santa Rosa Memorial Hospital. Specifically, the charge refers to the illegal withdrawal of 150 tablets of Abstral, a sublingual form of fentanyl, in 400 microgram doses."

Kate pulled the papers closer and turned the pages slowly.

"The full text of the case isn't available because it hasn't been presented to the district attorney." Mahler imagined the wheels turning inside Kate's head. "But we know it involves the theft and sale of drugs over a two-year period. Your client is looking at fifteen years."

"It's a misunderstanding." Winter straightened in his chair.

The man intended to play the whole nine innings. "The whole thing is a procedural error in how the paperwork was handled."

"Your attorney can argue that in court," Mahler said.

"Why're you pursuing this now, Eddie?" Kate dismissed the papers by pushing them back across the table. "What's this have to do with VCI's investigation of Paul Behrens's disappearance and death?"

"The latest coroner's report on Behrens shows the presence of fentanyl," Mahler said. "We believe it was administered through the whiskey found in the victim's car. Your client's fingerprints were on the bottle."

For a moment the room fell silent.

Mahler watched Kate and Winter absorb the new information. Mahler's guess: Kate hadn't known about the fentanyl.

Winter examined his hands folded on the table, considering how to begin. "When I went back to Doran Park the second time, Behrens was still there. I lied about that."

"What time was this?" Mahler opened his notebook and began writing.

"Around three. Behrens was still sitting in his car, but he was more subdued than in the morning. I think the whiskey calmed him down. Made him more talkative. Said he'd taken his wife for granted and needed to win her back. Told me a story about how they met at a friend's backyard party. She was sitting on the edge of the pool with her feet in the water. When she looked up, she smiled right away even before he spoke. He remembered the way her wet hair fell across her face. It was like he was going back over these old memories, and he needed to tell someone. I just happened to be there."

Mahler tried to remember when he first met Kate. Did it mean something that he couldn't remember the moment? Or had it simply not been memorable? Should he ask her now to remind him? He remembered other moments. The time she came home after midnight from a meeting, woke him with a kiss to make love. The time they drank tequila shots and he told her about the ballroom dance class he failed at age thirteen and they laughed until tears rolled down their faces. The time he heard her crying in the shower and she pulled him fully clothed into the water to hold her while she wept.

The time he came home to find her closet empty and a note under a set of house keys that told him not to call.

Dr. Schafer: Did you try to reconcile with Kate after you separated?

Mahler: It wasn't like that.

S: How was it?

M: You read the reports. I was talking to a dead girl.

S: How do you feel about it now?

M: Regret. Obviously. But there's nothing I can do.

S: Isn't Ms. Langley married?

M: Yeah. That kind of tied my hands.

S: So Kate's moved on and you haven't?

M: I always hated that expression. What does "move on" mean? It seems to me when a relationship ends, the moving part, going from one place to another, isn't the important thing.

S: What *is* the important thing, Eddie?

M: Isn't it your job to tell me? Parts of me changed because of Kate. I can't change back like a chameleon. What do I do about that? Who am I without her?

Winter leaned over the table. "Behrens said he and Annie were happy at the beginning, but they were serious about their careers and put their energy into work and the kids. No time for each other. Then something happened in the last few days that made him rethink things."

"Did he say what it was?" Mahler pictured Behrens sitting in his car, telling the doctor about his wife, the schoolteacher's memory warming with the alcohol.

"No. But he said he was trying to meet another person, and the meeting kept getting canceled. I could see it bothered him."

"Did he tell you who he was meeting and what it was about?"

"No. But he was drinking, so he was kind of all over the place."

"Where does the fentanyl come in?"

Kate raised her hand. "Before my client tells you anything else, has the DA said anything about what Dr. Winter will be charged with? And what's the DA willing to give in exchange for my client's cooperation?"

Mahler met Kate's eyes. In her voice he heard the same challenging tone she had adopted in the last month of their relationship. Its origins had never been clear to him. Was it meant to assert her own strength, to push back against the intractable behavior she couldn't change in him, or to test the boundaries of the give-and-take in their daily redefinition of their relationship? Had he and Kate been doomed from the start? In his job he swam in a world of lies, trying to find truth in the constant misdirection of suspects and witnesses, while, as a lawyer, Kate had a different relation to truth, something guarded behind the shield of privilege. "I haven't spoken to the DA," Mahler said evenly. "I'm just trying to find out your client's involvement in the death of Paul Behrens. Plus Dr. Winter has lied already. How do I verify any of what he's said?"

"It's okay," Winter said. "I'll tell you what you want to know about the fentanyl. Behrens said he was going to reconcile with his wife. As part of that reconciliation, he'd tell her the kind of person I really am. He said he knew the truth about me. He'd talked to my colleagues and friends and knew what I'd done. I asked him what he meant by that, but he just kept saying once Annie knew who I was, she'd leave me."

"You believed him?" Mahler held Kate's eyes across the table.

"Not until I knew he'd talked to the doctors in my office building and my receptionist. I have no idea what they told him, but the other physicians have some knowledge of my financial challenges. He seemed very proud of what he knew. He looked right at me and said, 'I know more than you can imagine. You're fucked, you douche.'"

Winter sat back and closed his eyes, seeing it play out in his memory. "It was ugly. It was awful. I came back to the park. I thought we could talk. Then he goes off on me. I didn't know what to do, but I wanted him to shut up. At one point he left the car to take a call, so I put a tablet of Abstral in his bottle. It wasn't enough to hurt him. The whiskey was a small, half-pint bottle. The fentanyl was just 400 micrograms and was in sublingual form so it wouldn't be fully absorbed as intended. I just wanted to get back at him and make him shut the fuck up. When he came back, he said the meeting was on. He took another drink. The drug was in the whiskey, and I watched him drink it. After a few minutes, he got sleepy."

Since Mahler stared at Kate, Winter looked there, too. "So, okay, I gave him fentanyl. But the important thing is, I very much doubt the drug killed him. I don't know what your coroner found, but the amount I put in the bottle was a small, non-lethal quantity. There's a possibility of an anomalous reaction in combination with the alcohol, but—"

"That's enough, Greg." Kate touched Winter's shoulder.

"All right. All right," Mahler conceded. "Just so we're clear. Behrens didn't tell you who he was meeting?"

"No. I think I even asked. He said it was none of my business."

"What time did you leave him?"

"I don't remember. About four. I didn't look at the time."

"And where'd you go?"

"Like I said last time, I went to a motel in Bodega Bay. You can check my credit card. I didn't lie about that."

Kate stacked her papers and sat straight in her chair. "I believe my client has told you what he knows about Paul Behrens." She looked at Mahler. "Are we done, Eddie?"

Were they done? Were he and Kate done? She was a different woman from the one he'd known. She'd been changed by the years apart from him, by her marriage to her accountant husband, Roger. Roger—less of a puzzle to be solved, less likely to disappoint her. Whatever Mahler had once meant to her was forgotten, overwritten by the thousand times Roger surprised her with a kiss, made her laugh, showed up. Listening to Gregory Winter talk about Annie Behrens, Mahler heard the sadness of its delusion. "Yeah," he said, more and more aware of his own delusions. "We're done. But I am going to place your client under arrest."

Mahler helped Winter to stand and cuffed his hands behind him. "Gregory Winter," he said, "you're under arrest for the illegal administration of a Schedule I drug."

Winter's head dropped as Mahler Mirandized him. "I didn't kill him," Winter said. "I did not do that."

"One thing at a time," Mahler said, glancing back at Kate and leading Winter to the door.

(ii)

(FRIDAY, 9:12 A.M.)

"I was here all night with this thing." Bailey held up Eden's Moleskine notebook on the Jory serial killing.

Eden looked at the notebook, which represented the most significant portion of her life's work, the macabre search for killer Albert Jory. "All night? Really? It's a hundred pages."

"It's not the pages. It's the words on the pages." Bailey reached behind her to grab a laptop. "And I did some research of my own."

Eden sat, unable to compete with Bailey's energy level. "Okay. That's good, I guess." With the window shades drawn, the evidence room was darkened even on a bright morning. Bailey's table was strewn with stacks of paper, DVDs, evidence bags, electronics cords, flash drives, cartons of Chinese takeout, and a paper plate with a half-eaten breakfast burrito.

"I have, like, a million questions." Bailey swept her forearm across the table to make a space for her computer.

"Ask away." Eden stared at her Moleskine across the table. She felt uncomfortable at it being in someone else's possession. She wondered about that, like she'd crossed some line.

This was her third straight day on the Behrens case, forty-eight hours without sleep. She was beyond tired, in a jittery, artificially stimulated state of sleep deprivation. The past night in the hotel room—scribbling notes on the Jory case and listening to the revelations of poor Zoe McFarland—had drained Eden's battery dry.

Looking at Bailey, Eden wondered if it was possible to draft in the wake of the forensic technician's apparently boundless enthusiasm. "Where do you want to start?" Eden asked.

"Let's stick to the Cassie Stanton murder for now," Bailey said. "First, the partial fingerprint on the console of Stanton's car."

"It might be an anomaly," Eden said. "We know Jory wore gloves. We found a box of them in his storage unit."

"Well, I wouldn't give up on it." Bailey leaned toward her laptop screen. "The initial analysis showed a seventy-eight-percent match to Jory. The second analysis was flawed. But if I was in charge of this thing, I'd have a third independent lab check it again."

Eden made a note on a pad of paper in front of her. "We can order that."

"Second, I know Dunbar caught you off guard with that stuff about the trucking company's software and the timing of Jory's delivery in Window Rock. But I did some poking around about the brand of software used." Bailey typed quickly on her keyboard and swung the laptop to face Eden. "I found chatrooms where users are talking about bugs in the program. At the time of the Stanton murder, users were finding errors of up to thirty hours. I also found internal emails at the trucking company between dispatchers and drivers complaining about errors in the software that showed—"

"Wait." Eden squinted at the laptop screen. "Exactly how did you access those memos?"

"Through the company website." Bailey smiled. "Or, at least the backdoor to that website."

"Bailey."

"The point is, you can poke holes in the program's accuracy." Bailey turned the computer back to her side of the table. "And, if you know somebody smart, you could calculate the exact degree of the error and the real time."

Eden jotted down another note. Her exhaustion began to ebb.

"Then there's the witness statement from Virginia Palmer. In her recantation, Ms. Palmer says she can no longer identify Jory as the man she saw the night of the murder because the man she saw did not have a ponytail. But at the time of the murder—"

"Jory didn't have a ponytail," Eden said. "Dunbar's investigator showed her a recent photo."

"You need to go back to the witness."

"Okay," Eden said. She allowed herself a measure of hope.

"Then there's the crime-scene photo. The initial scene photo clearly shows a piece of metal, possibly steel, in the dirt beside the passenger door. But the technicians never identify it among the items found at the scene. What's the story with that?"

"The crime-scene inventory..." Eden sighed. "A local investigation team..."

"You had a problem?" Bailey asked.

"We lost it. Or, I should say, it was lost. I don't know. The object was believed to be a tool from Jory's toolbox. Eight-inch-long steel pliers. They appear in the photos but not in the inventory so they—"

"Okay. Okay." Bailey held up her hands. "The fact that we don't have it doesn't mean it never existed. God, I hate reports. That brings us to the cotton sheeting Jory used to tie the victim."

"Ugh," Eden groaned. "Do we have to do this?"

"Hey, it's your case. You'll be the one who's responsible for letting this asshole loose. The guy who, by the way, kills women like you and has your address and phone number."

"I know. I know." Eden looked at her hands, palms flattened on the table. "It's the part of the evidence I despised the most. I always hated that Jory tied their arms so they couldn't move. When I first got into this, some of the guys on the team thought the sheeting wasn't strong enough to bind the victims. That somehow the women let themselves be tied up. I always knew how strong it was. The most awful thing of all was the women weren't able to move when they died." Eden looked up. "I just hate it."

Bailey sat back and tried to gauge Eden's level of distress. "Okay. I'm with you on that. But can we talk about it as evidence? I think there's a possibility with it. Can we start with what you know?"

Eden puffed her cheeks and let out the air. "Okay. Actually I made some notes about it last night from memory." Taking several pages of Hyatt stationery from her pocket, she read out loud. "All the victims were bound with cotton sheeting. The strips were approximately six inches wide and knotted at the ends. The knots were always a bowline. It's believed the strips were torn from a larger piece of cloth. That much was true in all nine murders."

"And?"

"And…Albert Jory, as a dispatched truck driver, commonly delivered dry goods, including cotton bedsheets, towels, and napkins to hotel chains and restaurants. When Jory was arrested in 2016, the FBI found a box of sheets in his storage unit. That box was traced to a shipment that was delivered to a Hilton Embassy Suites in Amarillo, Texas, but later returned."

"What's 'returned' mean?" Bailey asked.

"The box was flagged by the local manager and subsequently rejected by the Hilton corporate purchasing agent," Eden said. "Apparently, Hilton intended the shipment to be returned to the supplier, but the box never made it there. Instead Jory kept it."

"You wrote that from memory?" Bailey asked.

"Pretty much." Eden felt fulfilled in the work done overnight at the hotel, a slight compensation for a sleepless night. A legacy of her mother's New England industriousness—never waste an hour of time.

"So what happened?"

"Nothing. We could never make a connection between the sheets in Jory's storage unit and the cotton strips found on the victims. No fingerprints were found on the bindings. The sheeting used on the victims also had no foreign fibers. Like I said earlier, Jory probably used gloves."

"Was the same grade of cotton in the bindings and in the storage unit?"

"The fabric is a common, run-of-the-mill cotton sheet." Eden looked back at her notes. "It's a fabric known as American Upland. Short staple fibers. One-and-an-eighth inches long. Found in millions of cotton products in this country."

"So was that the end of the sheeting forensics?" Bailey asked.

"More or less," Eden said. "What's this possibility you mentioned earlier?"

"Let me tell you a story. A couple years ago, I took a semester of evidence analysis at UC Davis. We studied a case involving a hotel murder. The victim was found wrapped in a sheet, and the defense claimed anyone with access to the hotel bedsheets could have committed the crime. No direct evidence connected the suspect to the crime. But forensic analysis found that the sheet on the victim was different from the linens used in the hotel. The sheet on the victim had a specific defect in the cotton weaving."

Eden shook her head. "The sheets Jory used were strong. I told you. They weren't damaged."

"Hang on, Officer Somers," Bailey said. "I'm not talking about torn sheets. These defects are small. You need to know what you're looking for. It turns out defects are not an uncommon thing in cotton weaving. On its website, the industry trade group Cotton Incorporated lists more than a hundred different specific defects. Each is caused by a different glitch in the loom during the commercial weaving process."

Bailey opened a folder from a stack on the table and read from the top page. "For the case in my class, the forensics team found a defect in the sheets called a 'broken pick.' It's a defect where the filling yarn gets tangled on the bobbin while the loom continues to run. It makes a distinctive visible mistake." Bailey looked up at Eden. "The investigators were able to match the defect in the sheet on the victim to the same defect in a sheet owned by the suspect."

"So you think—" Eden said. Maybe she was just overtired, but it seemed the younger woman had opened a door to endless possibilities. A hundred markers that might tie the sheets to Jory? Now Eden's hands were fists.

"Presumably the Hilton corporate purchasing agent rejected the sheet order for a reason. Maybe because—"

"The sheets had a defect," Eden said. "And if we can match the defect in the sheets that the hotel rejected and that were found in Jory's storage unit to the defect in the sheets used in the killings, we can prove that it was Jory who killed the women."

"That's the idea," Bailey said.

"But what's the likelihood a hotel purchasing agent noticed such a small defect?"

"You have any better ideas?"

Eden shook her head. She opened her laptop and peered at the screen. "Okay," she said. "Boxes 43 and 44 contain photos of the sheets used in the murders. Wow. Approximately 700 photos. You up for that, Bailey?"

Bailey rolled her eyes.

"I'll try to track down the hotel purchasing manager. I'm sure that means more boxes." Eden tapped at her keyboard. When she finished, she felt herself revived, good for another twelve hours.

Chapter Twenty-Eight

(i)

(FRIDAY, 9:42 A.M.)

Eden wheeled the hand truck into the evidence room and, one by one, lifted three Bankers Boxes onto the table. "According to the inventory list, these two boxes have photos of the cotton sheeting used in the murders." She looked at Bailey. "You want those?"

"Sure." Bailey pulled the tops off the boxes to look inside.

Eden hauled the third box over to her end of the table. "This box supposedly contains everything related to the trucking company's delivery records and the Hilton purchasing agent, whose name, as I recall, we don't know."

Bailey pulled a handful of folders from one of the boxes. After scanning the contents of several folders, she turned to Eden. "Are you kidding me? What a mess. There's different stuff here from each of the murders. You've got reports on the sheetings, black-and-white printouts of photos, flash drives of photos. There's no consistency."

"Welcome to a multistate serial-killing investigation. Nine murders, nine forensics teams. Somewhere in there is a copy of my summary report. It'll be a manila folder with the Department of Justice seal on the front. Big red letters: 'Authorized Personnel Only. FBI Classified Investigation File.'"

"Oh my God. Here it is." Bailey opened the folder to the first page. "Look at that. You signed it. Agent Eden Somers. May 23, 2017, 15:23." She looked across the table. "You recorded the time?"

"It was required," Eden said. "Turn the page. You'll see my review of each murder's cotton sheeting evidence: folder numbers, forensic technician's name, contents, format, the whole thing. Use that as your key to the folders."

Bailey turned the pages and read silently for a few minutes. "Okay. Now I feel better. Bless your anally retentive self."

Bailey set up two laptops side by side. She used one computer to view the samples of cotton sheeting recovered from the murder sites. On the other computer, she opened the screen to Cotton Incorporated's website of Standard Fabric Defect Glossary. The glossary had photos and descriptions of more than a hundred fabric defects.

Once Bailey had arranged the laptops and stacked the murder site folders, she looked across the table at Eden. "What's the evidence look like on the hotel purchasing agent?"

Eden held up a handful of papers. "All we have in the records is a memo from the Hilton corporate office confirming that in November 2015 a box of cotton sheets was rejected by the regional purchasing manager for north and central Texas. No reason is listed for the rejection. A note attached to the top page says an investigator checked the corporate archive and found no recorded reason. No name is given for the purchasing manager."

"What're you going to do?" Bailey asked.

"Find the purchasing manager," Eden said.

Bailey checked the crime-scene photos of the cotton sheeting used in the each of the nine murders. The photographs were close-ups of the cotton weave as it was produced on industrial looms. With the digital files, she was able to enlarge the photos and examine them at high magnification. For the hard-copy photos, she held a magnifying glass close to the photos.

For the first twenty minutes all the images looked identical. She flipped to the Standard Fabric Defect Glossary and tried to locate the defects shown there in the crime-scene photographs. None were apparent. After forty minutes, she noticed the patterns of the weave appearing to move in waves across the photos.

Bailey closed her eyes and pressed on the lids. "This might be impossible," she said.

"You've only been at it for an hour."

Eden called Hilton's national office of public information, who referred her to the personnel department. The personnel representative declined to search for the manager's name, citing privacy laws. Eden identified herself as a law enforcement officer investigating a serial murder. The representative repeated her refusal to assist. Eden told the representative the case involved cotton sheets purchased by Hilton that were used to strangle nine women in five states. The representative went offline for three minutes and returned with the name of the regional purchasing manager for north and central Texas: Brian Shaw.

According to corporate records, Shaw left the company in 2017 without contact information.

Eden called the offices of the FBI Behavioral Analysis Unit in Quantico, Virginia, and asked for the extension of Josh Hartford. Hartford picked up the phone with a joke about how nice it must be to work in wine country. Eden said she was back on the Albert Jory case and needed a favor. She asked Hartford to run a database search for all males in the United States named Brian Shaw. Hartford tapped on his keyboard and located a list of a hundred and eighty-nine individuals. Eden asked him to narrow the list to individuals aged thirty to sixty. The narrowing reduced the total to forty-seven. Eden asked for phone numbers for the forty-seven. Hartford said they would be in her email box in thirty seconds. Hartford asked if Eden wanted to join the office pool to guess when Paul Gerrard would retire. Eden put twenty-five dollars on November 2021.

Bailey looked up from her laptop. "Why can't I be looking at photographs of something interesting? Italian sports cars? Shirtless men? Shirtless Italian men? I actually have to sleep in sheets tonight."

Eden shook her head. "Are you at all familiar with the typical parameters of a forensic investigation?"

She made her calls on speakerphone, leaving her hands free to take notes. After three hours, she had made sixty-eight calls, spoken to thirty-nine Brian Shaws or relatives of Brian Shaws, none of whom had ever worked for the Hilton hotel chain. She had left messages at twelve numbers.

Bailey asked Eden to join her in front of the twinned laptops. "Okay. I think I found the defect. I can't find it in all the photos, but look at these three groups of photos. They're from the crime scenes for Macy Coleman, Cassie Stanton, and Karen White. See that irregular pattern in the weave?"

"Yeah. In the middle of the diagonal weave, there's a sudden vertical and horizontal pattern."

"Right. Now look at this sample from the Cotton Incorporated's website. Doesn't that look like the same thing?"

"Yeah," Eden said, "it's got that same break in the diagonal."

"It's called 'harness breakdown,' which occurs when the harness straps break on a conventional loom. Apparently the harness stays down, and the warp floats on the back of the fabric. So we're looking a harness breakdown on the rejected hotel sheets."

"Okay," Eden said. "Make copies of the images from the three crime scenes and the image from the Cotton Incorporated's website. Then write a one-page summary of your findings."

Over the next two hours, calls from Eden's messages were returned. The first six were dead ends. Then the seventh Brian Shaw called.

"Hi. I'm Brian Shaw," the caller said. "You left a message for me."

"Mr. Shaw," Eden said, putting the call on speaker, "did you ever work for the Hilton hotel chain?"

"Yes, I did. From 2013 to 2017."

"During that time were you the purchasing manager for the north and central Texas region?"

"Yes," Shaw said. "From July 2015 to November 2017. Before that, I was assistant manager."

"Mr. Shaw, I'm conducting a police investigation. I can't give you any details at this point. But as part of that investigation, we're looking at a shipment of cotton sheets delivered to the Amarillo Hilton in 2015 and subsequently rejected by Hilton Purchasing. Those sheets were later used in the commission of a crime. I realize it's been four years, but do you, by any chance, recall that rejection of sheets?"

"No."

The abruptness and finality of the answer caught Eden off guard. For a moment she was speechless and looked across the table to Bailey, who made a circular motion with her hand to keep the caller talking. "I see," Eden said. "So you have no memory of the incident?"

"Not really," Shaw said. "I handled hundreds of hotel purchases. And as you say, it's been four years."

"I understand." Eden searched her mind for something else to say. "Okay. Thank you for your help anyway."

"However, Officer Somers, I do have records of all my transactions, if that's of any use. I could call you back."

"If you wouldn't mind. Thank you." Eden clicked off the call and looked at Bailey. "What do you think?"

"Worth a shot," Bailey said.

Five minutes later the call came in. "Sorry," Shaw said. "Had to go out to the filing cabinets in the garage. Anyway, here we go. I've got an inventory sheet here. It says, 'One shipment. Box 17. Fifty cotton sheets. Returned to manufacturer. November 12, 2015. Defective quality.'"

"Do you have a record of the type of defect?" Eden asked.

"According to the report, 'the fifty queen-size cotton flat or top sheets in this box were found to have a defect on every sheet eighteen inches from the fourth side or head-of-bed end. Over time, the defect is likely to cause the premature failure of the product during ordinary use and/or laundering.'"

"Is the defect identified?"

"Yes, ma'am. The defect was something called harness breakdown."

Across the room, Bailey pumped her fist into the air.

"Just to confirm, Mr. Shaw," Eden said, her voice shaking, "you rejected this shipment of sheets for a defect of harness breakdown and ordered it returned to the distributor?"

"Yes, ma'am. Looking back at this jogs my memory a bit. If I'm not mistaken, the box itself was damaged, which caused me to inspect the contents. Which is how I found the defect."

"If you don't mind me asking, sir, how did you find such a small defect?"

"Our corporate office gave us a seminar on inspection techniques for hotel linens. They showed us how to look at sheets and how to see possible defects, even gave us inexpensive, hand-held microscopes. But I also had a personal reason. At that time, in November 2015, a room at the Amarillo Embassy cost $116 to $143 per night. For that price, I believed a guest had the right to expect the materials in the room to be of the highest quality. I grew up in west Texas. A hundred dollars is a lot of money. You can tell yourself it isn't, but then you can tell yourself a lot of things, can't you?"

"Yes, sir. Mr. Shaw, would you be willing to testify in a criminal proceedings?"

"My gosh. Criminal proceedings for bedsheets? Why, sure. If it'd help."

"May I ask, Mr. Shaw, why did you keep that record?"

"I keep all my records. Don't you? I mean, you never can tell, can you?"

"No. No, that's right. You never can tell."

Eden clicked off the phone and looked across the table at Bailey. For a moment the two women were silent, letting it sink in.

"Did we just do this?" Bailey asked.

"I think we did," Eden said. "It was your idea."

"You did all the work."

At first Eden didn't hear Bailey. Her mind surrendered to the frustration of criminal investigation and the last five years. Fuck Anthony Dunbar, and fuck his stupid tie. Fuck Albert Jory, too, along with the FBI. Fuck the boxes. Fuck the whole stupid case. Fuck. Fuck. Fuck.

Then she tuned in to Bailey's words. Bailey was right. It was the work. Eden always knew it'd be the work that would end it. Not therapy. Not Ativan. Not time. Just work. She remembered hearing Eric Howland, the FBI old-timer, once say, "The perfect crime's a myth. We just haven't gotten to it yet."

Eden knew she'd be remembered, if at all, for her failure. The solution wouldn't register. It didn't matter whether anyone thought she was smart. Everyone was smart. Failure was always more memorable.

Still, there was satisfaction in the last four hours. It was appropriate Jory would be proved guilty by a tiny mistake in the cotton bindings—imprisoned by his own tool of entrapment. Fitting, too, that the killer was undone by two women.

Eden looked at Bailey. "Thank you, Bailey. No one but me will ever know. But thank you."

(ii)

(FRIDAY, 10:16 A.M.)

"I can give you a copy of the incident report if you want it." California Highway Patrol Officer Pete Gallagher looked across his desk at Rivas. Gallagher's right hand lay on top of a thick stack of papers.

"Sure thing," Rivas said. "Maybe you could just give me the high points of the incident." Rivas mirrored the other man's use of the word *incident* to give the impression of speaking the same language. He'd learned the technique in a workplace training seminar called "Getting Along with Difficult People"—a workshop that convinced Rivas everyone he knew was difficult. Now he put some effort into a smile. *Appear cooperative,* Rivas thought. *See what happens.*

"I think I can do that," Gallagher said.

Rivas waited. He knew he couldn't stop smiling now if he tried. *How long was this conversation going to last? Did the CHP's mandate to stop speeding apply to everything they did?*

"I understand the SRPD has suspects?" Gallagher asked.

"Possible suspects."

"And you haven't made an arrest?"

"We're trying to locate the individuals."

Gallagher considered this answer. In his heavily starched khaki dress uniform and with his ramrod posture, the officer had a stiff, self-contained appearance, as if he were on a kind of permanent parade review. "So in exchange for our summary of the incident," Gallagher said, "we'll receive information about your suspects and participate in their arrest?"

"That's correct." Rivas broke eye contact with the officer to take a look around. They sat in a small cubicle at the Santa Rosa Area CHP headquarters in Rohnert Park. The space had a neat, minimalist quality that matched the officer's appearance. Rivas couldn't find a single personal touch anywhere. Not even a standard workplace photo, which Rivas expected, of Officer Gallagher, spouse, two children, and dog all standing at attention.

Gallagher sighed. He opened the folder and began reading. "The victim was Mrs. Melanie Rosen. Age seventy-four." Gallagher slid a coroner's head shot of the victim toward Rivas, who registered an older woman with close-cropped gray hair whose handsomeness was still visible beneath the dark bruising and broken cheekbone on the left side of her face.

"She was killed in a hit-and-run incident on Chalk Hill Road the night of April 12, 2018." Gallagher looked up, making sure of Rivas's attention. "We believe the accident took place between 11:00 p.m. and midnight. The location was a blind curve approximately a thousand yards south of the intersection with Murphy Road." Gallagher passed a map across the table and pointed to a spot on the paper. He watched Rivas make a note on his pad.

"Our post-incident analysis indicated the victim was likely

struck on the shoulder of the road by a car driving south. No skid marks were found on the road surface, suggesting the driver did not see the victim until impact. The roadway shoulder narrows at that point due to the presence of a steep hillside, which leaves little pedestrian space to walk safely. That fact, plus the blindness of the curve for a southbound driver, contributed to the accident. Our analysis indicated the driver was driving at forty-five miles an hour, took the turn a little too sharply, and drifted a foot or two onto the shoulder. It was...enough."

While Rivas made more notes, Gallagher handed him a pile of photographs. Rivas noticed the officer handled these photographs more gently than the previous items.

Rivas held the photographs in his lap and stared at the top one.

A full-length body lying on a dirt hillside, lit by crime-scene lamps against the nighttime darkness. The head facing into the dirt. The right arm at a painfully oblique angle, as if stretching hopelessly toward something farther up the incline. The left leg broken and bent backwards at the knee.

The single still photo told its own story. The human body as rag doll—the consequence of tissue and bones tossed aside by a five-thousand-pound vehicle driven at forty-five miles an hour.

The other photographs in the stack were different angles and close-ups of the body.

The back of the head with dry leaves caught in the hair.

The chest and abdomen clothed in a bloodstained flannel shirt.

The broken leg close enough to reveal that the force of the impact had thrown the shoe from the foot and left it bare.

Rivas viewed each image in turn, careful to handle them by the edges to avoid marking them with his fingerprints.

As usual, for Rivas, even after twenty years on the job, the sight of a life unnaturally taken halted his thoughts, stopped sounds around him. It always took a lot out of him. He felt trapped for a moment in the dead woman's isolation.

The evidence also let him view Gallagher in a different light. In Rivas's experience, all professionals who encounter frequent death deal with it in their own way—dark humor, practiced indifference, tunnel-vision focus on procedure. Maybe Gallagher's starched shirts and stiff posture were a tactic for being in the presence of mangled bodies without seeing them every night in his sleep.

Gallagher waited for Rivas to finish and replaced the photographs in his folder. "In hindsight, it was not an ideal place for the victim to be walking in the dark. The blind curve and the vehicle speed probably meant she didn't have time to get out of the way."

"From interviews, we learned Mrs. Rosen was returning home from visiting a nearby neighbor, Donna Bishop. Rosen left Bishop's house about eleven and was taking a shortcut back to her house. It was apparently her habit to walk on the left side of the road, facing traffic. She had lived in the area for more than three decades and was very familiar with the road."

"The driver probably didn't see the victim until it was too late," Gallagher said. "Obviously that's not an excuse for the accident or leaving the scene. Evidence indicated one or more persons got out of the car, but we were unable to find usable footprints or other markings. We believe the victim was moved, possibly by the driver, farther off the road from the point of impact. The vehicle then backed up and drove on."

"I assume no witnesses were present?" Rivas asked.

Gallagher shook his head. "No. The incident was reported at 1:30 a.m. by a driver passing the site and seeing the victim. In addition, no inquiries were received." Seeing Rivas's questioning look, he said, "Sometimes you get a guilty party calling to see what we know."

"Do you know what kind of vehicle was involved?"

"Given the vertical reach of the victim's injuries, on the chest and head, the forensics team believed the vehicle to be an SUV." Gallagher looked down at the folder again. "After the accident, we canvassed local repair shops and issued notices to be on the lookout for specific types of automobile damage. No responses were received, which means the driver either had the repair done privately, sold the vehicle out of the region, or just garaged it."

"I remember reading about the case in the press at the time," Rivas said.

"Yeah. We spoke to the media. The accident was covered in newspapers, as well as radio and TV. Obviously that reporting included pleas for public information. We also issued Nixle alerts asking for the public's assistance. We never received anything useful or actionable."

Gallagher turned more pages in his folder. "Considering it was Saturday night, we considered the strong possibility for the involvement of alcohol. We investigated public events that night at two wineries farther north on Chalk Hill Road in Alexander Valley. We interviewed thirty-eight individuals at one event, twenty-four at another. We looked at the vehicles of two individuals but didn't find anything of relevance."

"Sounds like a lot of work," Rivas said.

"Yeah. It's what you do, isn't it?" Gallagher sighed again and closed the folder. "Mrs. Rosen was well liked in the neighborhood. Her husband had died five years earlier. She raised chickens on her farm and sold eggs." Gallagher seemed to run out of a story. He sat back in his chair. "The case is officially unsolved."

Rivas reevaluated his opinion of Gallagher. He had long

bought in to his own department's common antipathy toward CHP officers, which held they were glorified traffic cops, better paid than other law enforcement, and all too willing to give you a speeding ticket. If he still felt no brotherly regard for the officer, he admitted now to a kind of respect. He moved Gallagher out of the "difficult people" column. The other man probably encountered fewer deadly firearm crimes than VCI but was nevertheless confronted with death by that other great American weapon, the automobile.

"So what does VCI know?" Gallagher asked.

Rivas thought how to start. "We have a thirteen-year-old female, Zoe McFarland, who says her mother confessed to the hit-and-run," Rivas said. "According to the daughter, the mother, Charlotte McFarland, was driving. The father, John McFarland, was present in the vehicle. The family has a residence in Santa Rosa, but both parents are currently at large. We have officers searching for them. The child has been placed into the care of relatives. And—just to be clear—John McFarland is also a suspect in the homicide of Paul Behrens, the victim who was found on the coast last night."

"I understand," Gallagher said. "You have any leads on the parents' whereabouts?"

"Two of their vehicles are missing, so we suspect Charlotte and John may be in separate locations. We're looking at second residences in San Francisco and Forestville."

Meeting over, Rivas checked his phone. "One of our team is on his way to the family house in Forestville. I'm going to join him. Why don't you come with me?"

Chapter Twenty-Nine

(i)

Approaching the McFarlands' vacation home in Forestville, Coyle saw a single car in the driveway—the Lexus he knew to be Charlotte's. He pulled his own car tightly against the rear bumper of the Lexus to block its exit.

Coyle paused. On the drive to the property, he'd received a text from Eden. Zoe McFarland said her father kept at least one handgun in a home safe. Coyle had to assume the Lexus driver might be armed and be willing to resist arrest.

From the front seat of his car, Coyle scanned the property. The lot was remote, four miles off the main road and half a mile from the nearest neighbor. It was a dark, densely wooded area, chiefly mature redwood trees. Twenty yards ahead lay the vacation home—a one-story cabin with a narrow porch and shake siding. A light could be seen in one of the windows.

Coyle called Mahler. "Eddie, I'm here at the McFarland

Forestville home. I don't see either of them. But Charlotte's car is here. Do I go inside the house without a warrant? Can we claim fleeing suspect?"

The line was silent for a moment. "Okay. But watch yourself. And remember, if going in is ruled unlawful, anything you find could be excluded."

"Yeah, but I don't think we can wait for a warrant." Coyle clicked off.

Coyle saw no one outside the house. He pulled on nitrile gloves and took his Glock from its holster. Climbing out of the car, he moved to the Lexus and peered inside. The car was empty and held no suitcases or bags.

He sprinted to the house. On the porch he heard recorded music playing inside. He glanced in a window but avoided making himself visible. The front door was open a few inches. He knocked loudly on the door frame. "Santa Rosa Police," he called through the doorway.

The music—classical piano—played loudly inside.

No one answered. *Could anyone hear him over the music?*

Coyle knocked again, this time harder, and nudged the door open a few inches farther. "Santa Rosa Police," he called.

Glancing quickly back, he despaired of hearing, above the music, the sound of someone coming behind him.

Still he hesitated to enter the house alone, considering whether to call for another member of the team. *Were the McFarlands inside? Did they see his car arrive? Were they armed? Hiding in an interior room? Had they already left via a rear door?*

For an instant Coyle thought of Officer Jeff Kittle. Five years with the department. Wife, one daughter. Took a routine Saturday night call and walked into a domestic. Man, girlfriend, twelve-pack of Coors Light, and an argument over who got to sit in the "good" chair. Three seconds after Kittle came through the doorway, before his eyes adjusted to the room's darkness, the girlfriend pulled the trigger of a gun she forgot she was holding and fired a .38 round into Kittle's midsection. The bullet missed the officer's inferior vena cava blood vessel, which would have ended his life, but tore a hole in his colon and large intestine. That sent Kittle to early retirement and left him wearing a colostomy bag for the rest of his life.

It was Kittle's face Coyle reimagined as he held the Glock in a tactical grip, pushed the front door fully open, and stepped into the cabin's large, open living room. Ahead were sofas, soft chairs, coffee table, large-screen TV, and a fireplace.

No one visible. No gun fired. Coyle felt instant relief.

The music blared—a crashing keyboard.

Straight ahead lay an open kitchen. To the right, open doorways to three bedrooms.

Coyle cleared the bedrooms, then ran to the kitchen, where he looked behind the center island and under the large oak table.

He took a deep breath and put the Glock back in its holster.

From the large kitchen windows, he could see outside to a wooden deck and beyond that a view of the Russian River. The river, still swollen by spring rains, zigzagged through the forested valley below.

The music played from an Alexa device on the kitchen counter. He clicked it off and listened for a moment for anything that could now be heard in the vacuum of silence.

The kitchen was clean and tidy and looked unused. On the counter he found a cold, half-filled mug of tea and a discarded tea bag. The large refrigerator was empty. He checked several cupboards and found the shelves bare.

Coyle returned to the other rooms. The beds in each room were neatly made. On the bed in the master bedroom he found a woman's purse. He dumped the contents on the bed. A wallet held a driver's license for Charlotte McFarland, credit cards in her name, and four hundred dollars in cash. He saw no suitcases or other supplies.

In the living room he took the time to look carefully at the tables and sofas but saw nothing that looked recent. The car outside confirmed someone—probably Charlotte—was present on the property. But the scene here made it appear she didn't intend to stay.

Coyle texted Eden. Did Zoe's parents have a favorite spot on the vacation property where Charlotte might have gone?

Then he called Mahler again. "I went inside the house," Coyle said. "No one's here, but I found Charlotte's purse." Coyle could hear traffic on the line. Mahler was in his car. "No suitcases or food in sight, so I don't think anyone's planning to stay. I'm about to walk toward the river and check the woods. Where're you?"

"On my way to the Fountaingrove residence," Mahler said. "Listen. Hold off on looking outside by yourself. Daniel talked to a CHP officer about the hit-and-run. They're on the way. Wait for them before you look any further. And Martin. Be careful."

"I'll wait." Coyle pictured Mahler driving too fast up the curving road to Fountaingrove.

"We got word from SFPD. The McFarlands aren't at their San Francisco condo."

"Christ. How many houses does one family need? Does Zoe have any other ideas where they might be?"

"I asked Eden to check. By the way, Daniel got a name and profile of the hit-and-run victim. Her name's—"

The call failed. Coyle was about to redial when he heard thumps on the roof. Footsteps. One. Two. Three. He stuffed the phone in his pocket and grabbed his gun. He stood in the middle of the living room and listened. The footsteps stopped. He listened intently. From the kitchen came the hum of the refrigerator. The wind gently shook the window screens.

Then again. Three steps in the middle of the living room ceiling. Not an animal. Two legs, not four.

He looked outside. No sign of anyone.

Who was this? And what the fuck were they doing on the roof?

Coyle moved outside to the porch. He listened but didn't hear anything. He wouldn't be able to see the rooftop unless he left the porch, but the open ground offered little cover.

Coyle imagined his own face featured in a training film for the department's force options simulator. "As you can see," the instructor's voice intoned, "Detective Coyle, a seven-year veteran—and exemplary officer to this point—waited too long on the porch. Thus giving the shooter time to position himself on the roof. The memorial service for Officer Coyle was well attended by members of the department and their families."

Coyle picked two redwoods twenty yards from the house and dashed behind them.

He looked back to the building's roofline.

No one visible. No Charlotte or John McFarland wielding a gun. *How had they gotten down?* The roof was at least twelve feet high. *Had they jumped? Wouldn't he have heard them?*

He watched the roof and was ready to leave the tree cover, when he saw it.

A crow. Large body. Black iridescent feathers. Slender bill.

The bird looked back at Coyle and cawed. It pecked at something in the center of the roof. Then hopped. One. Two. Three.

(ii)

Mahler pulled into the Fountaingrove neighborhood of Santa Rosa. The right side of Wedgewood Way offered a panoramic view of the city below. He stopped beside an unmarked police car a hundred yards from the McFarlands' home.

The officer in the driver's seat, Ray Neeley, rolled down his window. "Nothing to report, Lieutenant," he said. "No sign of either the wife or husband's car. You want us to canvass the neighbors?"

"Not at this point. We found the wife's car in Forestville, and we believe she's in that area. We're still looking for John McFarland. Black Lincoln Navigator. I've got a warrant to search the house."

Jay Preston, the other officer in the car, leaned toward the open window. "We heard the couple may have a firearm."

"Yeah. If you see McFarland, assume that."

As they spoke, a white pickup approached the McFarland house and parked out front. On the driver's door was a logo for McFarland Quality Homes.

"I'll take care of this." Mahler closed his window and drove toward the truck.

He met the pickup driver on the sidewalk at the base of the McFarland house. "We're looking for John McFarland." He held out his badge. "Could you please tell me your name and why you're here."

The other man tipped back a baseball cap. "I'm Frank Paymer. One of John's foremen." He wore a T-shirt and mud-covered jeans and boots. In one hand he held a sheaf of papers.

"I need to talk to John about one of his Rincon Valley houses. I take it he's not here? Guess I should have called ahead."

"If he's not here," Mahler asked, "do you know where he might be?"

Paymer leaned against the fender of his truck. "Oh Christ. We've got four sites going on. Could be at any of them. He never keeps to a schedule. Goes where he's needed. Why're you looking for him?"

"It's important we find him."

Paymer tossed his papers back inside his truck. "I can call around if you like."

"Yeah. Do that. But first tell me. How long have you worked for the company?"

"Eight years. Started on one of the crews. Last two as foreman."

"What kind of a person is John McFarland?"

Paymer smiled, with a look that wondered how far to go. "Fair. Tough. Definitely expects you to work. Tight-fisted about overtime. Not one of the boys."

"What if you get crosswise with him?" Mahler asked.

"Crosswise? Oh, he'll go after you. I saw him beat the crap out of a framer for stealing tools. A few years ago, he threatened some guys for trying to unionize." Paymer squinted up the street. "Then again, I've seen worse. I think John sees himself as a big community guy. Supports local charities, one of the Little League teams, gives college scholarships for the kids of the guys who work for him. He'll spend money on that. He's complicated."

Paymer waved a hand toward the house above them. "This was his dream house. Outbid three other developers for the lot. Took two years to build. He loves this place."

Mahler handed Paymer a business card. "Let me know when

you get done calling the construction sites." Mahler walked up the steep driveway. At the top he looked back to the police car and called Neeley. "I'm going inside," he said. "Call me if anyone else shows up."

Mahler slipped on nitrile gloves and used the house key Eden got from Zoe. He walked down a hallway past the kitchen to the living room. Curtains were drawn closed over broad windows. He found the master bedroom, with separate walk-in closets for Charlotte and John. Both appeared full.

Mahler's phone rang. "Eddie, I heard you're looking for John McFarland." Eden. "I don't know if this is relevant. But after you left, Zoe talked about her father. She said he's incredibly stubborn, never admits he's wrong. From conversations with her mother, Zoe believes that while Charlotte's been agonizing over the hit-and-run, John's dug his heels in. Zoe said her father would have strongly resisted any attempts by Behrens to come forward with an admission. He's more likely to double down."

Double down? Did that include killing? "All right. That's good information," Mahler told her.

"Another thing. The gun used to shoot Behrens was used in a Windsor burglary by Thomas Hyland. Last year Hyland worked on a roofing crew for McFarland Quality Homes. That's where McFarland got the gun."

"Also, Boss." Eden was on a roll, taking as fast as she could. "Remember that friendship bracelet we found in Behrens's briefcase? Zoe gave it to Behrens. She wanted the teacher to pass it on to her dad. Remind him she still loved him. She thought it might make him rethink his unwillingness to admit to the hit-and-run."

"Behrens must have just forgotten it," Mahler said. "Where's Zoe now?"

"At her aunt and uncle's house. She asked if she could go home to get some clothes."

"Let's wait until we find her parents," Mahler said.

At the other end of the house, Mahler checked a home office. The desk was covered with papers—spreadsheets, invoices, business letters, thick reports. Inside a closet he found a safe. When he pulled the handle, the door opened. Inside were stacks of paper. No gun.

Mahler looked around, trying to imagine the man here, where he figured things out. On the wall was a framed sign for McFarland Quality Homes. Beneath the company name were the words "Tradition of excellence for thirty years."

He walked back through the house to the front door. Paymer stood on the porch, about to knock. "No one at any of the sites has seen John today," Paymer said. "Also, sounds like he's not picking up calls. Have to say, that's definitely not like John. He always makes a point of taking calls. Day or night."

"Okay. Thanks," Mahler said. "You talk to him or think of anything else, please call me." Paymer walked back down the driveway to his truck.

Mahler's phone rang again. This time, Rivas.

"Eddie, have you found John McFarland?"

"No. I'm at the McFarland house right now."

"I'm headed out to Charlotte McFarland's house in Forestville. Listen, Pete Gallagher, the CHP officer who headed up the hit-and-run accident, is here with me. He started to tell me something I think you should hear."

Mahler heard the phone passing to Gallagher.

"Lieutenant Mahler, I don't know John McFarland." Gallagher spoke quickly. "But I was telling your sergeant a few things we use to identify and locate suspects in a hit-and-run. Studies show hit-and-run drivers fit different profiles. One type involves risk-takers. They're self-confident and believe it's worth the risk of leaving the accident because they doubt they'll be caught."

"Yeah. I can see that," Mahler said.

"Another type involves people with little impulse control. For them, adrenaline kicks in. They act before they think and drive away from the accident. There's no hard-and-fast rule, of course. People don't always fit these categories. Sometimes it's as simple as the driver is with someone they aren't supposed to be with."

"There's even a type called justifiers," Gallagher continued. "They think the accident is not really their fault. Or, even if they know it's their fault, they believe there's a good reason for not admitting their responsibility. They explain it to themselves or to someone they need to believe them."

Gallagher paused. "I don't know if this stuff is useful in your case, but—"

"Did you say justifiers?" Mahler asked.

"Yeah. They're common especially among—"

"Okay. I got it," Mahler interrupted because he finally understood. "It tells me exactly where John McFarland is."

He clicked off the call and ran to his car.

Chapter Thirty

(i)

Coyle met Rivas and Gallagher in the driveway of the McFarlands' house in Forestville. He shook the CHP officer's hand and told them about his search of the house.

"It looks like John McFarland's not here," he said. "This is Charlotte's car, so we think she's on the property." He held up his phone. "Eden just texted me. The daughter, Zoe, says the property has two trails. One starts in the front of the house and goes through the forest down to the Russian River. The other starts at the deck behind the house and follows the ridgeline above the river. Zoe called it the lookout trail. It ends on a hillside overlooking the river about a quarter mile west."

"I understand she might be armed," Gallagher said.

"Possibly." Coyle was still jumpy from the crow's impersonation of a killer hiding on the roof. He wanted to be moving. "I'll take the river trail. You guys search the lookout trail. We can call each other if we find her, but cell service is pretty patchy out here."

Coyle followed the trail through the woods. Inside the redwood forest, it was quiet and dark. He tried to peer through the dense cover ahead of him and stopped every thirty yards to listen for sounds of someone else. After five minutes, he found himself on the edge of the woods, where it opened onto a sandy beach beside the riverbed. The water, fifty feet wide, poured swiftly down the center of the bed. On either side were large, bleached boulders.

Coyle walked out onto the rocks and peered up at the clear blue sky. After the cover of the woods, the sunlight was bright and warm. He looked around to get his bearings.

Then he saw her. High on a hillside above him, a woman stood on a rock outcropping forty feet over the riverbed. She wore jeans and white cotton shirt. Her long hair blew in the wind. She appeared to be staring at something farther downriver.

After a few seconds, the woman turned and saw Coyle. "Are you looking for me?" she called. While she waited for Coyle's answer, she took a step closer to the edge of the outcropping.

Coyle could now see that her feet were bare and that she held a sandal in each hand. "Are you Charlotte McFarland?" he shouted.

"You're too late. My daughter's gone."

Coyle's mind raced. *What was the woman doing on that rock? Should he call Rivas and Gallagher? Was it more important to keep talking to her?* He hunted for a route up the hillside and guessed it would take at least three to four minutes to reach her.

"We found Zoe. She's safe," he called. "I want to talk to you."

"It doesn't matter. You're too late. I've made up my mind." Swinging her arms at her sides, she dropped the sandals over the edge and watched them bounce down the hillside onto the rocks below.

"No. No. It's not too late." As he spoke, Coyle saw twenty feet behind the woman the figures of Gallagher and Rivas quietly approaching. He kept his eyes focused on the woman so as not to alert her to the presence of the men.

On the hillside, Gallagher was in the lead when they saw the woman on the rock. He glanced back at Rivas.

Rivas gestured for Gallagher to go first. "Take off your sunglasses," he whispered. "Use her first name."

Gallagher shoved his glasses in a shirt pocket and stepped forward slowly, quietly. "Charlotte," he said, "my name's Pete."

Charlotte looked behind her and took in Gallagher's uniform. "You're here to kill me, aren't you?"

"No, I'm not." Gallagher's voice was even. "It's going to be okay. We can figure this out." Gallagher took two small steps forward, his arms extended for balance. The rock's surface was loose, sandy gravel. Gallagher searched for firmness with each step.

"What I did was unforgivable." Charlotte looked out over the valley, her voice far away. "I can't go back."

"Yes, you can," Gallagher said. "Charlotte, look at me. You have a daughter. Your daughter needs you. Look at me."

Charlotte turned. As she did, her feet slid toward the rock edge. She raised one arm to right her balance, but the movement threw her farther forward.

Gallagher leaped ahead and grabbed the woman's right ankle as she toppled over the ledge. He held her suspended as her body swung back and forth in the air.

The force of the woman's fall and the swinging of her body pulled Gallagher across the rock surface on his chest. With his free hand, he searched frantically for something to catch his movement.

Behind Gallagher, Rivas dove on the rock and caught one of Gallagher's boots. He braced himself against a rock crevice and held tight.

"Gallagher," Rivas called. "You're not going anywhere. Can you hear me? You're not going anywhere."

"Yeah," Gallagher wheezed.

Rivas shifted his weight, grabbed Gallagher's other boot, and squeezed harder. "Can you hold her, Gallagher?"

"I've got her."

"Martin'll be here in a minute. He's going to help you lift her. Okay?"

As soon as he saw Gallagher and Rivas approaching Charlotte, Coyle jumped across the dry boulders in the riverbed toward the hillside. At the base of the cliff face, he glanced up and saw the figure of Charlotte McFarland suspended headfirst over the rim. He scrambled up the rock wall without waiting for firm handholds.

Reaching the top of the overlook, Coyle ran toward the edge, climbed over Rivas, and threw himself beside Gallagher. The view over the perimeter was a dizzying drop forty feet to the rocks of the riverbed. He looked down at Charlotte McFarland. Her limp body had stopped swinging back and forth and hung still. Her arms were extended forward, as if diving toward the rocks below. Coyle reached into the open void. Twice he tried to grab hold of her left ankle but misjudged the distance. The third time, he caught her foot. Pulling upward, he secured his grip. He took a deep breath.

Coyle glanced at Gallagher. The officer's face was red and tensed from the effort. "Can you pull?" he asked.

"I think so," Gallagher said.

"All right. Now."

They yanked Charlotte's legs up. When the waistline of her body had reached the top of the rock, Coyle grabbed hold of her belt with his free hand and heaved her toward him.

The woman was unconscious now, her body an inert, heavy

weight. Coyle and Gallagher dragged her away from the edge and laid her on her back on the center of the rock surface. Then they pushed themselves upright and knelt on either side of Charlotte.

Charlotte's face was drained of color, eyes closed, breathing shallow.

Gallagher bent over her, ready to administer CPR. But Charlotte's eyes opened. She blinked several times and finally focused on Gallagher. "Did you catch me?" she asked.

"Yes, ma'am." Gallagher was breathing like he'd run a race. "We did."

"Did you really find Zoe?" Charlotte's focus shifted to Coyle. "Is she safe?"

"Yes, she is," Coyle said. "She's with John's sister and her husband."

"I wanted to die. You know that?"

"Yes. I know."

Charlotte slowly sat up and faced Gallagher again. "You hate me, don't you?" She took in the man's torn CHP shirt, buzz cut, and military bearing. "For what I did to that woman? For hiding?"

"No, ma'am." Caught off guard by the questions, Gallagher let his answer stumble out. "This is my job. That's all. I don't... hate you."

"Well, I do," Charlotte said. "Ever since that night. I died that night, too. My husband... Every unfair step takes you further away." She closed her eyes. Tears rolled down her face, and her shoulders shook.

The hilltop was quiet, stilled by the drama of the last few minutes. The only sounds were the wind sifting through the redwood branches at the forest edge and the woman's soft crying.

Gallagher hesitated, aware of Coyle and Rivas watching, unable to move. Then he slowly reached out and took Charlotte's hand.

(ii)

(FRIDAY, 11:05 A.M.)

Turning from the hallway to the kitchen, Annie found a strange man facing her beside the sink. "Who are you?" Her breath caught in her throat. "How'd you get in?"

"The back door was open." The man smiled. He looked unsurprised at being found. "My wife does the same thing. Locks the front door but leaves the back door unlocked."

"What do you want?" Annie's mind raced. *What weapon did she have? Where was her phone?* "I'm calling the police."

The man stood still. He wore an expensive-looking black business suit. "I want to talk to you. That's all. I promise. And don't call the police. Let's try to be civilized." His voice was even, as if used to reassuring.

"Why should I talk to you? Who are you?"

"My name's John McFarland. I knew your husband."

"My husband's upstairs." Annie stared at McFarland, taking in more of his figure. His arms hung loosely at his sides. At the end of the right arm there was a handgun. "He'll be down here in a minute," she whispered hoarsely.

"Now we both know that's not true, don't we? Is anyone else at home?"

Annie took one step backward, her body instinctively blocking the hallway. "No. No. I'm...here alone."

McFarland smiled again. "I've thought a lot about truth the last two days. Whoever else is here, please tell them to join us."

"There's no one else here."

"Please. I'm trying to do this in the simplest way I know."

Annie's shoulders dropped. "My daughter, Claire, is upstairs." She turned to the hallway and called Claire's name.

From the second floor, they could hear Claire's footsteps. Then the girl stopped on the stairs, halfway down. "It's okay," Annie called. Some impulse told her it would be better to follow the man's instructions.

"Before we talk," McFarland said, "do you have anything alcoholic to drink? Wine, beer. Anything will do."

Annie opened the refrigerator and found a bottle of wine. She poured a glass and handed it to McFarland.

"You won't join me?" McFarland asked.

Annie shook her head, fear overcoming her lust for the drink.

McFarland gestured for Annie to lead the way. "Let's find a comfortable place to talk."

They sat in the living room. Annie took Claire's hand to the sofa and shook off her daughter's questioning look.

McFarland faced them on the recliner. He put the wineglass on a table beside his left hand and rested his right hand with the gun on the arm of the chair. He looked around the room. "It's a very nice house," he said. "I'm a homebuilder, so I know a little something about layout. This is a very functional arrangement, the way the kitchen opens to the living room here, the sightlines out to the back." Suddenly reflective, he managed a wry smile.

For thirty-six hours, he'd been living in an alternate universe with different oxygen and gravity. He was an actor unsure of his new character, as if the words being spoken were a script and not his own. It took every ounce of energy to focus on the frightened women on the sofa.

"Claire," McFarland said, "I was telling your mother that I knew your father." His expression turned serious. "Actually, I'll admit to you at the outset that I'm responsible for taking the life of your husband, Annie, and your father, Claire." McFarland paused to let this new idea sink in. "You are, in fact, the first people I've told. It's not an easy thing to say, and I'm sorry for it, of course. But there it is. That is the fact. Do you understand?"

Annie wiped at the tears that ran down her cheeks. Claire stared coldly at McFarland.

"I'm sure you want to know why I'm here. The reason is, I want you to hear my side. In the days to come, I imagine you'll hear many things that aren't true. But I wanted you to hear the truth."

"Why do you have a gun?" Claire asked.

McFarland looked at his right hand and frowned. "I don't know. To be honest, I forgot I brought it with me. But since last night, I just haven't felt...safe."

McFarland kept his eyes on the gun. "When I met Paul yesterday, I tried to have a normal conversation. My wife, Charlotte, killed a woman in an automobile accident a year ago. It wasn't reported. For good reasons. My daughter, Zoe, told Paul. He wanted me to go to the police. Which obviously isn't possible. We—Paul and I—disagreed. I was willing to make certain concessions. He...was not." McFarland recalled his frustration with Behrens. The other man refusing every appeal, making a stupid hand gesture, pointing a finger. Did he think he was lecturing his students?

McFarland stared at the wineglass before taking a drink. "Here's what I told him. I'll let you be the judge to its soundness. I told him I couldn't confess to the accident because I have a responsibility to my family. My company. I'm responsible for the welfare of two hundred employees. Their families, too. My father entrusted me with the business, his gift to me. I've spent twenty years trying to honor that gift. It's a heavy burden. If you've never been in the position, you can't imagine."

He paused, hoping for an interaction, but neither of the

women spoke. "My wife was the driver and would pay the heaviest price. She's not a strong person. She's needed to raise our daughter. Zoe is very close to Charlotte. It would destroy Zoe to lose her mother."

"The last thing—and maybe most important—was what would coming forward achieve after all?" McFarland spread out his arms. "Does it bring back that poor woman? Does it reduce the family's grief in any meaningful way? There simply is no recompense, is there? Nothing gets better if we tell. What's done is done."

Speaking tired him. His words came back to him. *Nothing gets better by telling.* Was there a place upstairs where he could lie down and sleep? He supposed he'd have to kill these women first.

"In any case, I explained all this to Paul. I don't have the luxury of making an admission, simple as that. I have to be practical. But—and I sincerely wish this wasn't the case—he refused to understand. He scoffed at my reasons. He wasn't a businessman."

"You're an asshole," Claire said.

The suddenness of the word made Annie flinch. She grabbed her daughter's hand.

McFarland, who had become used to his own voice, blinked and stared at Claire.

"You don't know my father," Claire said. "You don't know anything about him."

"Your father—" McFarland said firmly. "Yesterday your father was drinking. Maybe on drugs. He wasn't clear in his mind. He thought everything was simpler than it is."

"You don't know anything. You're a pig."

"I see you're angry. I felt sorry for Paul. He was afraid of me. At one point he ran away, straight into the ocean in his clothes.

What's the point in that? He said he just wanted me to leave him alone. But that's no way, is it?"

Claire turned to Annie. "Does this guy have to be in our house? Do we have to listen to him?"

"You're very brave, Claire," McFarland said. "How old are you?"

"Thirteen."

McFarland's face sank in sadness. "My daughter Zoe's thirteen. She's missing. Did you know that? Disappeared. You can't believe how worried her mother and I are." McFarland seemed lost in thought. "You remind me of her. Idealistic. Wanting everything out in the open."

McFarland caught himself. There was so much he couldn't tell the women. He couldn't say how surprisingly easy it was to kill the schoolteacher. Much easier than he thought beforehand. The smallest step. Until the hit-and-run, he hadn't known how good he was at doing these things. McFarland smiled at Annie. "Your mother's more sensible. She knows I can kill both of you right now. I'll already be charged with one murder and a felony hit-and-run. What're two more?"

"Before I came down here," Claire said, "I called the police and put my phone on the stairs, so they're listening to everything you say. They'll be here any minute."

"Ah, yes. Your generation's proficiency with technology. I suppose that was inevitable." He raised his gun and aimed it at Claire. "I guess that means I shouldn't waste any more time."

"No. No." Annie moved in front of Claire. "Wait. Please. Wait."

At that moment, from the hallway behind McFarland came the sound of a door opening.

McFarland swung his handgun toward the sound.

Eddie Mahler quietly entered the room, his hands in the air.

"John." Mahler held steady eye contact with McFarland. "My name's Eddie Mahler. I'm with the Santa Rosa Police. I have a message from Zoe."

Chapter Thirty-One

(i)

"I wanted to let you know," Mahler said, "your daughter, Zoe, is safe. She's with one of our officers." He continued facing McFarland but lowered his arms.

"Zoe? You found her?" McFarland looked puzzled. He held the gun, aimed at Mahler.

"Yes. She's fine. Your sister and her husband have agreed to let her stay with them." Mahler stole a quick look at Annie and Claire, who sat close together on the sofa.

"She left home." McFarland acted like he just remembered. "We didn't know where she was."

"I understand. But she's safe now."

"Good. That's good. Does her mother know? Does Charlotte know?"

"Yes. We told her. She's safe, too. We found her and she's with us." Mahler felt the room wrapped in a delicate skein, holding together the gunman, the frightened women, and himself. The danger lay in pulling or letting go at the wrong second.

McFarland stared at Mahler, absorbing the news. He laid his hand with the gun on the armrest.

"I talked to Zoe last night for several hours," Mahler said. "She's a wonderful girl, John."

"What'd she say about me?"

"She said you'd be mad at her for telling Paul Behrens about the accident."

"I was mad," McFarland acknowledged. "But I'd never hurt her. Not my daughter."

"I know that. I think Zoe was just frightened. All...this frightened her. So she ran away."

"We should have handled it differently," McFarland said. "We made mistakes."

"I know." Mahler stood still, wondering at his decision to enter the room without a gun.

"My daughter will never understand what I've done. She's idealistic. When Zoe learns all of it, she'll hate me, like this girl here."

"I don't think that's true." Mahler let himself glance at Claire. "Did you know Zoe made a friendship bracelet for you? She wanted to remind you that she loved you. She asked Paul Behrens to give it to you, but he must have forgotten."

"A bracelet? I didn't see it."

"No. But we have it and will give it to you. Zoe wanted to find the right thing to do. To help you and your wife, to find a way through this...problem. That's why she talked to Paul Behrens. To help you."

"But I didn't do the right thing, did I?"

"No. But you still can. Hurting Annie and Claire won't help you, John."

From outside came the sound of sirens.

"Who's that?" McFarland asked. "Is it about me?"

"Patrol cars," Mahler said. "But I told them to wait outside. They're not coming in here. Okay?"

"Yeah. Sure." McFarland looked at the gun, newly discovered.

"Annie and Claire have lost a husband and father. They need to heal their family."

Now McFarland's attention went back to Annie and Claire. He peered across the room at them.

"Claire here is the same age as Zoe. Did you know that?"

McFarland raised the gun again. For a moment he pointed it across the room. Then he slowly bent his arm and pressed the tip of the barrel under his chin.

Mahler remained still. He could lose it all now. In his mind, he heard the gun discharge, the bullet blasting the man. "John, this is not the end," he said. "This is not the end."

"I can fix everything," McFarland said.

"No. This won't do that."

"Everyone will be better off."

"No. That's not true," Mahler said. "You don't want Zoe to lose her father. You can't undo what you've done. But you can stop doing harm."

Mahler watched McFarland tighten his grip on the gun, still pointed under his chin. He searched his mind for the next words. "After all that's happened, you can do something good. You need to spare Annie and Claire any more harm."

Mahler took a peek at the two women. Annie had begun crying. Claire covered her eyes with her hands. "John, do you know what Zoe told me last night?" Mahler asked. "Are you listening, John?"

McFarland stared straight ahead.

"She said Mr. Behrens told her that people are complex,"

Mahler said. "There're no easy answers. We need to find our way with what's real, not what we imagine. It's part of growing up. Behrens said that's what he loved about literature. It explores the complexity of our feelings and thoughts."

Mahler let that sink in. After a minute, he said, "It was about you, John. Paul Behrens was helping Zoe come back to you."

McFarland slowly lowered the gun and laid his hand in his lap.

"And I took his life." McFarland looked across the room at the photo of Paul Behrens on the wall.

"John," Mahler said, breaking the other man's concentration, "I'd like you to put the gun on the floor."

"Is Charlotte all right?" McFarland asked.

"Yes. She's fine."

"It was an accident. That's what it was."

"Yes. I understand."

"Charlotte didn't see the woman. It happened so fast. We didn't know what to do." The words seemed to take the air out of McFarland. He bent over and laid the gun on the carpet.

For a moment the room was still. No one spoke. Mahler walked toward McFarland, picking a path through a minefield. He took hold of McFarland's gun, ejected the clip, and put them in separate pockets. Then he reached his hand toward McFarland. "You need to come with me, John."

McFarland struggled to find himself. His bearing exhausted, broken. "Where do we go?"

Mahler helped McFarland stand. "I'm going to place you under arrest. We'll go to one of the cars outside." Mahler turned the man around and attached handcuffs. He laid one hand on McFarland's shoulder. "You did the right thing here," he said.

Mahler checked on Annie and Claire, who sat still on the sofa. "Are you all right?" he asked.

Annie nodded, her eyes looking back with an empty gaze.

"One of my officers will come in to talk to you," Mahler said, turning to lead McFarland toward the door. As he left the room, Mahler thought of the look in Annie's eyes and wondered when she would learn of Greg Winter's administration of fentanyl to her husband and understand the role her own affair played in the death of her husband.

(ii)

(FRIDAY, 2:33 P.M.)

They leaned against Soto's BMW on South A Street behind Juilliard Park. Soto looked down the empty street in both directions. He pulled the package out from under his shirt, a paper bag rolled into a tube. He passed it to Jesse, who shoved it in the pocket of his hoodie.

"There's ten in there," Soto said.

"I know." Jesse handed Soto a pack of bills.

Soto took the money without looking at it. He pulled a cigarette from a pack and lit up.

Jesse watched the dealer blow out the smoke and saw a cut on his hand. "What happened to your hand?"

"Nothing to worry about." Soto turned his hand to examine the cut. "Someone sticking his nose where he didn't belong."

They watched a cyclist pedal in their direction. The cyclist smiled at them as he passed. Soto glared back and flicked ash into the street.

"Welcome to the business, *chico*." Soto showed a gold tooth in front when he smiled.

"That what you told Lopez?"

"Jorge was a dick. Keep your head down, you do okay."

Jesse saw how the other man acted his part of a dealer—raising his chin when he talked, jabbing his cigarette in the air like a weapon, strutting on his toes. An actor on a stage of his own, even here with only Jesse watching. What would his father have made of Soto? Compare him to someone in Shakespeare or Hardy? He wished he'd listened more to his father.

To the south, a dark SUV turned from Sebastopol Avenue onto South A and drove slowly toward them.

Soto watched the car and took another drag on his cigarette. "You have any problems, you come to me. Okay?"

"Yeah. Sure."

"You don't talk to anybody else. You don't worry about anybody else. Understand?"

"I know. Got it."

Suddenly the dark SUV accelerated rapidly, coming straight at the two men.

Seeing it, Soto pushed himself off his car and threw the cigarette in the street. He started to open the car door. Then, still watching the car, he let go of the handle and sprinted across the street toward the park.

From the north, two more cars sped down the street.

The dark SUV arrived first, driving over the curb and up onto the park grass to cut off Soto's path.

Officers jumped out of the cars, guns drawn.

"Santa Rosa Police," the officer in the lead yelled. "Get on the ground."

Soto raised his arms. He stared back at the officers defiantly. Then he slowly knelt on the grass and lay facedown.

An officer dressed in flannel shirt and jeans covered Soto, while a male officer and a female one knelt on either side of the man. The male cop pulled Soto's gun from his belt. The female officer reached across Soto's body and cuffed his hands behind him.

When the cars raced in, Jesse had stayed beside the BMW. One of the unmarked cars stopped beside him. Climbing out of the car, an older Hispanic officer held a gun on Jesse and directed him to lie in the street. The officer applied cuffs. Searching Jesse, he found the package of drugs and put it in an evidence bag. He helped Jesse to his feet.

It was Jesse's first time to feel cuffs on his wrists. Tighter than he expected, nearly cutting the skin. Was it part of the punishment? Was more to follow?

Two police patrol cars arrived with lights and sirens.

The cyclist who had ridden past earlier returned and talked into a radio.

Jesse watched Soto being led to one of the marked cars. Soto tried to shrug off the officer's hand on his shoulder, the part he was playing as a dealer already failing him.

The Hispanic officer guided Jesse into the back seat of another car. "This one's a minor," he called behind him. "I'll take him to Juvenile Hall."

Jesse sat uncomfortably against his cuffed hands. The back seat was made of hard plastic. He imagined others sitting in the same spot—dealers like him, DUIs, shoplifters, homeless street people. From the window, he recognized the familiar Sonoma Avenue of downtown Santa Rosa. He saw two teenagers on the sidewalk exchanging fist bumps. He felt far away, as if watching himself in a film.

The car drove into the police station driveway and parked behind the building. The officer appeared beside the car. He opened the back door, led Jesse out of the car, and removed the handcuffs.

"You okay?" the officer asked.

"Yeah," Jesse said. "Where's Frames?"

"He couldn't make it. He told us you called him. Asked us to handle it."

Jesse studied the officer. "Who're you?"

Hernandez rested his hands on his hips. "Noah Hernandez. Narcotics. Steve works for us. Sometimes."

The man was taller, older than Frames. So far, at least, less of a wiseass. "Why'd you bring me here?"

"We didn't want to do this in public where someone might see it."

Hernandez unwrapped the package taken from Jesse's hoodie and looked inside. "Soto just give you this?"

"Yeah. First one."

"Good thing you called us, Jesse."

Jesse watched the detective reroll the paper bag. "Where's Frames? Really."

"In the hospital. Concussion. Someone, probably Soto, hit him last night."

"He going to be all right?"

"Guy's an ex-Marine." Hernandez smiled. "So, probably."

On the street a car went by, out of its windows a loud, thumping bass.

"Soto's bad news," Hernandez said. "We're going to charge him in the murder of Jorge Lopez. Maybe in the assault on Frames."

"That's why I called," Jesse said.

"You saw where it was going?"

"Something like that. You think he'll come after me?"

"Soto?" Hernandez shook his head. "No. Soto's not coming after anybody. He'll be charged with first-degree murder. No bail. He'll do at least ten."

"What about the rest of the crew? They going to know I made the call?"

"I doubt it," Hernandez said. "Soto saw you arrested. That's all they'll know." He caught Jesse's attention. "You might lay off selling weed, for chrissakes. Keep a low profile."

"I figured."

"You're going to have to come inside and give us a statement. You understand?"

Jesse nodded. "Tell Frames I hope his head's okay."

"I'll tell him," Hernandez said.

"He's still an asshole. But I hope he's okay."

Hernandez smiled and guided Jesse inside the police building.

Chapter Thirty-Two

(i)

Eden sat in the VCI bullpen, rereading the draft of her report to the FBI on the Jory case.

At the start she'd written a bulleted list of the findings to give agents a brief summary. The bulk of the report focused on the work she and Bailey had done on the cotton sheets used to bind the victims. But she also added suggestions for revisiting the partial fingerprint on the console of Stanton's car, the discrepancies in the trucking company's software, and the misleading recantation from the Virginia Palmer witness statement. She made a few word changes to Bailey's report to conform to Bureau style and double-checked the accuracy of her own summary of the Brian Shaw conversation. To the last page, she appended the photos of the sheets and a word-for-word transcript of the Shaw interview.

In the email message, she reminded Senior Agent Chalmers

of his promise to investigate how Jory got hold of her name and address.

When she finished, she sent it all to Chalmers. She watched the green bar on the screen spread, left to right, telling her the email had been delivered. She closed her laptop.

Turning round, she discovered she was alone in an empty bullpen. The whiteboards were still filled with the Paul Behrens case. Behrens's doleful face stared back at her. She thought of his decision to meet John McFarland. *Had Behrens known how the meeting would turn out? What crazed desperation led him in the end to run into the ocean to escape McFarland? Did the water rushing toward him look in the dark like a refuge?*

Seeing Frames's empty station and remembering his admittance to the hospital, she texted: Hey, Detective! Up for a visitor?

His answer came quickly: Maybe tomorrow. Meds kicking in. Believe in goodness of man.

Eden smiled. See u tomorrow.

The other side of the room held a mountain of sixty FBI Bankers Boxes—ten stacks of six boxes. A forest of paper on one man's evil.

She reopened her laptop and clicked on the inventory list of the boxes. After a few minutes, she found what she was looking for. Lifting the lid from Box 4, she pulled out a worn paper map of the United States. She put the map in her purse and drove home.

In her apartment, Eden took a bottle of Glenlivet from a kitchen cabinet. She poured two fingers in a tumbler and went into the living room. She taped the map to the wall. From the sofa, she could sip the scotch and look at the map. The folds of the paper were worn from a thousand openings and closings. The colors of the states were faded. She let the scotch warm her throat and wondered if there would ever be a time when she could view a U.S. map without visualizing that one line across the country.

She stood and ran a finger over the path marked on the map, touching each pinhole. She drank the rest of the scotch in the glass. Then she took the map down from the wall, refolded it, and dropped it in the trash basket.

She took out her phone and found Chet Baker in her playlist. "Let's Get Lost." The rich, cool jazz trumpet filled her apartment.

In the kitchen, she boiled tagliatelle. While it cooked, she poured olive oil in a pan and sautéed onions and garlic. Noodles finished, she scooped the drained pasta into the pan and coated it in the mixture. Then she sliced fresh tomatoes and basil leaves on top. She opened a bottle of red wine and took her plate and drink to the living room.

She ate slowly. The food tasted wonderful. She couldn't remember the last time she'd eaten.

Chet Baker was now on to "But Not for Me." She closed her eyes and listened to the music. Baker—the "prince of cool," junkie trumpeter. She pictured the man's face thinned by heroin, front tooth missing from a fistfight. His voice was delicate, fragile. Love, he seemed to say, was for someone stronger than him.

After a few minutes, Eden opened her eyes and pulled herself up from the sofa. She took her dish to the kitchen and poured a second glass of wine. She sat on the sofa, drinking wine and reading her email. One entry from Chalmers acknowledged receipt of her report.

She stood and reached into the trash basket, took out the map, and laid it on her bookshelf.

She finally felt ready to give in to sleep. Or, at least a few hours of sleep before returning to help the team search the McFarlands' homes and cars, meet with the district attorney, and write reports.

But first, one more thing. She turned off the music and called her mother. Only after she dialed did she remember the time difference in Connecticut and the lateness of the hour. On the fourth ring, her mother picked up.

"Mother. It's Eden. I'm sorry. Did I wake you?"

"Yes, dear. Is anything wrong?" Her voice was heavy with sleep.

"No, Mother. I'm fine. I forgot how late it is there."

"That's all right, dear. What do you need?"

Eden smiled at her mother's New England pragmatism in which every call has a practical purpose. "I was thinking today of the camping trip you and Daddy took to Maine the summer after you married. Daddy used to tell me the story. Do you remember?"

"Of course I remember, Eden."

"Could you tell me again? I've forgotten."

It was a lie, of course. Eden remembered everything about that story. Her father always started the same way: "It was in the summer after a winter of heavy snow, and the nights were still cool." As a story, it wasn't much. An account of a few days of tent camping during her father's medical residency, back when her parents had little money. The night before, they had driven up the coast highway, through Massachusetts, into Maine, and turned west toward Bangor. Her mother claimed they were lost, but her father insisted he'd planned the route. They stopped for the night in a wooded park outside Exeter and set up their tent in the dark.

The story was nothing more than a description of the two of them waking in a sleeping bag with the morning light warming the canvas walls. Eden suspected they made love that morning, although her father never mentioned it. Instead he spoke of the patterns made by the sunlight on the sides of the tent, the sounds of the sparrows in the campground trees, and the smell of bacon cooking on a neighboring camp stove. For Eden, though, it was a story of the youth of her parents, who in her own lifetime always seemed old. It was a story from a time before her mother became so careful and before her father's unfaithfulness.

The phone was silent. For a minute, Eden thought her mother had hung up. Then she heard the chain pull on the bedside lamp and realized her mother was sitting up, putting on glasses.

Her mother cleared her throat. "Naturally your father told it better. But I think I can do it justice. Let's see. It was in the summer after a winter of heavy snow." She paused. "The nights were still cool."

Eden closed her eyes and held the phone close to her ear.

(ii)

(FRIDAY, 7:05 P.M.)

"Thank you for giving me a second chance," Mahler said. "I wasn't sure you would."

"I almost didn't." Franny smiled. "But my work with returning veterans is a world of second, third, and fourth chances. So what the heck." She raised her water glass and tapped it against Mahler's.

They sat at a quiet table near the back of Café Liguria in downtown Santa Rosa. The room was busier than two mornings earlier when Sharon Weyrich had stormed away from Mahler's booth in the front window. The air was now filled with the scents of baked bread, oregano, and garlic. Neapolitan ballads played softly on the sound system.

The owner, Carina, had greeted them at the door. "*Buonasera, Eduardo.*" She glanced at Franny and smiled. "*Due?* For two?"

After they were seated and Carina had left them, Franny leaned close. "Does the hostess know you? And what was that smile about?"

"She's the owner, and yes, I come here often enough she knows me." Mahler decided to dodge the smile question. The time wasn't right for an explanation of online dating. "The food's delicious. Northern Italian. I recommend the pansotti. It's a kind of ravioli in a wonderful walnut sauce. It's the house specialty."

"I'll take your word for it. Have you been to Italy?"

"One summer in college," Mahler said, "I stayed in a small town on the Ligurian coast called Santa Margherita. I remember two things. The Ligurians invented pesto, and the English poet Shelley drowned during a storm in the Gulf of La Spezia."

"Who says travel isn't educational?" Franny smiled. "So, Lieutenant Mahler, did you solve your missing person case?"

Had they solved it? "Solved" always seemed an odd word for the ending of a case, as if it was a puzzle or a question that had an answer. In his mind's eyes, Mahler saw himself guiding John McFarland out of the Behrenses' living room to the officers waiting outside. "As you know from Michael Behrens, we found Paul Behrens on the coast where he was killed. But we were able to identify and arrest his killer this afternoon. Which means there was resolution, although not a happy ending for the family."

"At least they have that knowledge. As far as I could tell, knowing what happened to his brother meant a lot to Michael. Paul's death was a terrible blow, but hearing the actual story took away the mystery. That's something. Isn't it?"

"I hope so. It turns out Paul was trying to do a good thing for one of his students. As time goes by, his family may take consolation in that." Mahler remembered looking back across the living room as he escorted McFarland and seeing Annie and

Claire on the sofa. Annie's arms were around Claire, but the girl had turned away from her mother. She looked at Mahler. Had she expected something different to happen or wished him to be someone else?

Franny watched Mahler's face. "It's never just the crime, is it?"

The question surprised him. *How did this woman know that?* He looked back at Franny. Thoughtful and smart, she wasn't easy to figure out. "No. No, it's not. Homicides like this reverberate through the victim's family and, frankly, the killer's. Speaking of which, once we finish dinner, I'll need to get back to the station to do all the work that comes at the end of these things."

With the arrival of the entrées, they focused on the food.

"This pasta is wonderful," Franny said. "I imagine this is the food we'll eat in heaven."

"Glad you like it."

"So about this second chance," Franny said. "What'd you want to talk about, *Eduardo*?"

"I wanted to tell you a story."

"A story is relevant, I assume, to why we're here?" Franny asked.

"I hope so. Last year an old Princeton classmate of mine was hired to do legal research in San Francisco. She ran across an audio recording of my father in a pretrial hearing and gave me a copy. It was interesting to hear his voice in a professional context, which I never actually got to witness."

"Was it an important case? Your father was involved in a couple landmark trials, wasn't he?"

"Yeah, but as far as I could tell, this was a routine matter. What struck me was the *way* my father approached it. He tore apart the opposing attorneys' cases with a devastating tactic. At the start he said very little. He asked questions and encouraged the opposing attorneys to elaborate on their points. But it was a trap. Once they committed themselves, he used their own words to undermine the positions. It was an Aristotelian textbook on argument."

"As I remember, James David Mahler had a reputation as a tough courtroom attorney."

"That toughness was definitely on display. But what I wanted to tell you is that something strange happened when I listened to the recording. In the beginning, I heard this disembodied voice coming out of my phone. Calm, unhurried, full of arcane legal expressions. I barely understood the points being made. Then, all of a sudden, something shifted. The voice became something else."

"What was it?"

"I'm not sure. But I had two immediate reactions to the sound. First, his voice was like a huge, unstoppable truck, barreling down the road, oblivious to anything in its path."

"Not surprising. I've known lawyers like that. Especially men. What was the second reaction?"

"It sounded like me. In fact, it wasn't *like* me. It *was* me. It was my voice."

Franny laughed. "What's that mean?"

"You've probably heard other people say this. We all imagine we're so different from our parents. Especially boys from their fathers. And then, no matter how hard we try, we grow into them."

"You're right. Common enough. How's it apply to you?"

"My father was an accomplished man. He changed city policy in San Francisco and modernized the way criminal law is practiced. He did more than I'll ever do. But he also lived a lonely life, without family or intimacy. And he died alone."

"Why'd that happen?"

"Because of who he was," Mahler explained. "Because of what he didn't know about himself."

"And you don't want to be like that? You want to know what he didn't?"

"I think so. I'm figuring it out." Mahler met Franny's eyes. "I'm seeing a therapist."

"Really? Wow. Okay, I'll be honest. I did not see that coming."

"To be clear, the department mandated psychological counseling after I shot a murderer last year. But—"

"But what?"

"I've continued the sessions after the mandated six weeks."

"Why is that?"

"It's interesting. I'm hearing answers to questions I didn't know I should ask. I think I've been in a reactive mode for a long time. Reacting to my father's abandonment, my sister's overdose, the victims of the crimes we investigate. Always reacting but not acknowledging my own feelings."

"To be fair, not many of us know how to do that."

"I've always been good at helping my team use their strengths—Daniel Rivas's memory, Eden Somers's analysis. I carried that over to my relationships. I let Kate handle the emotional part of our relationship. I thought it was enough for me to be there."

"Which is the concern I expressed last night. So where do things stand with you and Kate?"

"We're professional colleagues. Friends. We'll always be friends. I'm not in love with her. But I admit I may still have... What did you call it last night? A confused look in my eyes? And, as you said, I may not be sure where the ground is. But I'm trying to solve that confusion and find the ground. That's as much as I can tell you."

Franny looked at Mahler and smiled. "I appreciate that. It's not easy to talk about. Thank you for telling me."

Mahler felt shaken by what he'd told Franny. It was the first time he'd told anyone about his experience with therapy. He felt exposed and oddly visible, unsure of where the real boundaries of his privacy were—as if the table of four across the room knew his secrets, as if Carina over at the counter was now aware of his inner turmoil.

But he saw Franny's smile and felt reassured. Maybe it was better this way.

Franny straightened in her chair. "Since we're being honest, I think I owe you an explanation. When we were together last night, you were perceptive enough to see that my own area of reticence involves my admiration for my clients' commitment to discipline and order. You were right about that."

"We don't have to talk about it. Really. I wasn't expecting any kind of equivalence."

"No. But I thought about what I said last night. If I'm going to ask you to be responsible for your life, I need to do the same. So here's a story to match yours.

"My parents believed in letting my brother and me explore our freedom," Franny said. "We were allowed to do things most kids aren't allowed. Travel to Europe, Southeast Asia—alone. My dad helped Kenny buy a Ducati. They let us drink. They thought it was funny when I dated bad boys. I loved it all in my late teens and early twenties. Then it scared me."

"What changed?" Mahler asked.

"I grew up even if my parents didn't. I saw the dangerous side of things. Kenny's hitchhiking buddy in Thailand got busted for drug possession and died in prison. One of my bad boys—the last one—hit me."

Mahler winced and checked himself from reaching toward Franny. "You were seeing consequences," he said after a moment.

"Yes. And for me, part of facing those consequences was trying to find out who we are. Like I said last night, I got a couple of degrees in psychology and went to work. Applied psychology is the real, no-kidding world. It gave me all the limits I could handle. When I started working with returning service members, I found these men and women who grew up in a different universe from my own. Most of them lived with all kinds of limits long before they entered the service. Then the military codified the limits.

"For a while I envied their discipline. It seemed like a much saner way to go through the world. But after a few years, I saw that choice has its own challenges. Rigid boundaries leave people unprepared for life's ambiguities. Sometimes you can't rely on the guy next to you. Sometimes following orders gets you in trouble. And outside the service, order and discipline don't always exist. You have to learn to swim in the water you find yourself in."

"It sounds like you've got a perspective on it. So why's this such a sore point for you?"

"Because, as a psychologist for these returning service members, I face this issue every day—how the service gave them a life and a family, and how it failed them. And I'm still confronting the consequences of my own family's choices. Kenny's been incarcerated twice for drugs. Last night I told you my father passed away. Actually, my dad, the high priest of freedom, took his own life."

"That's a lot to deal with." Not the usual second-date conversation, Mahler thought. This terrible revelation of Franny's, an intimacy. It reminded him of Paul Behrens and the team's early consideration of that death as a suicide. "It must have been hard."

"It was awful. Not something I normally talk about with other people." Franny broke eye contact to look across the room. "So I'm doing a lot of work to understand my own life and to find out how I can make it better. This work—this psychological exploration into who we are and how we got this way—I've seen it do so much good for my clients. I believe in it. I know it's helping me. So I'm glad to hear you're open to it."

For a moment they were quiet. Across the room more diners arrived. On the sound system, a tenor was trying to break someone's heart with "Con Te Partirò."

Carina arrived at the table with two aperitif glasses. "*Un regalo per tranquillo, Tenente,*" she said. "A gift for the quiet." She smiled at Mahler.

Mahler smiled back, face reddening. "*Mille grazie, Signora.*"

When Carina had gone, Mahler pushed a glass toward Franny. "Limoncello. Lemon liquor. I believe Carina makes it herself." Mahler felt some relief in the lightening of the conversation.

Franny hesitated. "Okay. Wait a second. Again with her smile? And what's a gift for the quiet? Now you really do have to explain."

"Try the limoncello. I'm not drinking because I have to go back to work. But believe me, it's very good."

"Come on, *Tenente.* Cards on the table."

Mahler sighed. "All right. You should know. Telling you this is going to waste everything that happened so far tonight for you to have a good opinion of me: the food, this room's atmosphere, the secrets we've told each other."

"Tell me."

"It's pretty embarrassing."

"Tell me," Franny laughed. "I live for embarrassing."

"I've been doing online dating." Mahler waved a hand in defeat. "For months. And sometimes...I've met dates here."

"Here? In this restaurant? You're kidding." Franny laughed harder. "This is incredibly embarrassing. How many?"

"Five."

"Five? Oh my God. I'm number six?"

"I believe so, although I never thought of you like that."

"Really? Glad to hear it. And why is Carina grateful for the quiet? Did your other dates make noise?"

"I'll tell you another time. I think that's enough humiliation for one night."

"You're right. You can tell me on our next date." She raised her glass. "To Number Six."

Did she say "next date"? Mahler tapped his glass to hers. "To Number Six."

THE
SILENCED
WOMEN

Chapter One

(TUESDAY, 7:35 A.M.)

The dead woman possessed a rare beauty, Eddie Mahler thought as he looked at the thin, sculpted face and the soft down of her skin—the handsomeness spoiled now by an uneven line of dried blood falling loosely around the throat like a necklace come undone.

The victim lay on her side on a park bench, the body wrapped in a red woolen blanket from shoulders to feet. Mahler guessed her to be nearly six feet and in her mid-twenties. Streaks of red dye had been inexpertly applied through the bangs of brown hair. The eyes were closed, the lips slightly parted, as if she were about to speak. For an instant he imagined the sound of her voice, a word or two left behind, hanging in the air.

Then a car door slammed behind him, and Mahler's attention went back up the hill to the parking lot. The crime-scene techs had arrived, and two members of his Violent Crime Investigations, or VCI, team were waiting for him with a park ranger.

The bench sat on a hillside in Spring Lake Park, Santa Rosa's largest public park, beside a stand of oaks with a view of the water. Below the bench, the slope dropped sharply to an access road before falling all the way to the lake's edge. Valley fog diffused the early light and muted the sounds of the ghostly joggers and dog walkers traveling through the mist along the lakeshore.

An hour earlier, a call from Detective Martin Coyle had brought Mahler to the park. Now Coyle and a new investigator, Eden Somers, were "giving him his space" but checking every few minutes for his signal to join him. Beyond the crime-scene tape, a small group of spectators had gathered to peer down at the bench.

Mahler was short and powerfully built. He had close-cropped hair and wore a flannel shirt, jeans, and a golf jacket. A takeout coffee cup kept one hand warm, while his other hand was shoved in a pocket of his jeans.

He had awakened the night before with a migraine, the pain concentrated behind his eyes. For ten minutes he lay without moving, all his attention focused on the intense headache. Then he rose carefully on an elbow to get an Imitrex from the bed-side table. He slid the tiny pill onto his tongue and waited for its bitter taste to spread across the front of his mouth. When the pill was gone, he dropped three Advil in his palm and swallowed them with water. He eased back into bed and was nearly asleep when his cell went off with the call from Coyle. Now, here in the park, the migraine's intensity lessened, leaving him with a dull ache and sore neck muscles.

He turned again to the woman. Without touching the body, Mahler knew from the blood trail on her neck that a deep wound would be found on the back of her head. He could also tell from the absence of blood on the bench and ground, and the body's position, that the woman had been placed on the bench postmortem. He thought of the line at the end of the old film *Sunset Boulevard*, when William Holden says, "Funny how gentle people get with you once you're dead."

Closer up, he could see the top of her shoulders and the edge of a dark silk blouse. In the left earlobe, a pierced earring in the shape of a hollow star. The heavy fabric blanket covering her had traces of blond fibers. Animal hair. Maybe a dog.

Mahler had viewed the bodies of homicide victims for a dozen years but never got used to it. He felt how his presence invaded the victims' intimacy with their death. He had taught himself to see what he needed, to focus on the manner of interruption— the large-caliber bullet opening on the side of a gang member's head or the knife wound on a farmworker's chest that left no other trace than an uneven, pencil-thin line across his flesh. At the start, a veteran homicide cop named Tommy Woodhouse had told him, "When you feel like looking away, that's when you should look." Now Mahler bent close to the victim and studied the dried blood on her neck. Beside the blood, he saw the dark shadows of bruised skin.

The sight staggered him. As he rose, his legs weakened, and he held out an arm to balance himself. He looked as far from the body as he could, toward the distant lake, its quiet sur- face just visible in the fog. He thought of the other two times he had been called to this same park, to places across the lake, and stood beside the bodies of young women. The first in jeans and sweater, the second in running gear. Both facedown and so perfectly still among the native ryegrass and manzanita they seemed like something new and terrible growing there.

Mahler drank more coffee and felt his hand squeezing the cup. He waited to recover his balance. Then he looked up the hill and nodded. He wanted to be alone, not to have the conver- sation that was to come.

Coyle, Eden, and the park ranger worked their way down the hill. Coyle introduced the ranger as Officer Hadley. The ranger had a few inches on Mahler, with the chest and upper arms of someone who spent a lot of time in the gym. He wore a gray uniform, parks department baseball cap, and a pair of deep-black, rimless sunglasses that Mahler figured cost him half a paycheck. He stood stiffly with his hands folded in front of him.

"Dog walker found her about six." Hadley addressed himself to Mahler. "Older woman with a bunch of corgis. One of the regulars who come in every day before the park officially opens at seven. Entered at the Violetti Road gate at the top of the hill. She was making her way down to the lake when the dogs pulled her over to the bench. Made a call on her cell at six ten. We sent her home, but we have contact information if you want to talk to her."

Mahler could tell Hadley was speaking in a way he had heard on cop shows. The guard was probably also conflicted. On the one hand, he was in the middle of something important. On the other hand, he was already wondering how this was going to come back to bite him in the ass.

"Mind taking off your glasses, Officer?" Mahler saw Hadley's face color as the younger man removed his glasses. "How'd the dog walker get in before the park opened?"

"The gate here at Violetti Road is a steel-tube barrier. Closed from seven p.m. to seven a.m. It'll keep out a car, but people on foot have worn a little path around it. Not much we can do to stop them."

Mahler looked away. Eden was writing in a steno notebook; Coyle watched a spectator leaning over the caution tape to shoot photos with a cell phone.

"What's your routine after seven p.m.?" Mahler faced Hadley again.

"Two rangers on duty. We spend most of our time with the overnight campers on the other side of the lake. Every two hours one of us does a patrol in the pickup. We make a loop around the whole park on the paved road, over by the West Saddle Dam, in front of the swimming area, and back to the campground. There's a ranger hut in the campground where we can get out of the weather. The patrol takes about twenty-five minutes."

Mahler pointed to the road that passed the parking lot two hundred yards away. "So last night you or your partner drove down that paved road over there?"

"That's right. Every two hours after seven."

"You see or hear anything unusual?"

"No, sir."

"You shine a light over here when you go by?"

"No, sir."

"Ever vary the route?"

"No, sir." This last answer was slower than the two previous.

"Ever get out of the truck?"

Hadley looked confused. He turned to Coyle for help but was met with a blank stare. Hadley shook his head.

"You listen to music when you drive?"

Hadley hesitated. "Sometimes I take my phone. But, you know, just one ear."

Mahler hated everything about the young ranger now—his self-importance, his phony military bearing, and the carelessness with which he wasted their time. He knew the ranger wanted to move but was standing still as a show of strength. "What's the purpose of your patrol?"

"Sir?"

"The purpose. Why're you doing it?"

"It's part of the standing order."

"Part of the standing order," Mahler repeated.

"Someone—probably at least two people—carries a woman's body into the park and leaves it here, and you and your standing order don't see anything. Is that right?"

"Yes, sir. As I said, we run the patrol every two hours. So it could've happened between them."

"Or while you're driving past listening to Brad Paisley."

Hadley's fingers were pressed white around his sunglasses. He looked at his shoes.

"All right," Mahler said. "I'll send a couple uniformed officers over to the ranger hut. They'll get statements from you and your partner and talk to the campers. No one leaves until they've talked to an officer. Not even to go on patrol. Understand?"

"Yes, sir." Hadley replaced his sunglasses and walked up through the oaks toward the parking lot.

Coyle smiled as the ranger reached the top of the hill. "Well, that was fun."

Mahler finished his coffee. "He'll get over it. Right now he's thinking about what it would feel like to punch me in the mouth." He turned to Eden. "This your first?"

"Seeing a body?" She looked startled at being addressed. "I mean, a victim. No, I've seen . . . others."

Mahler saw fear trapped in her eyes before she retreated to the notepad. He realized they had spent little time together since he hired her two weeks earlier. She was smart, young for the team, but with a couple years' experience as an FBI analyst. "You okay? You don't have to be here."

"I'm fine." Eden straightened. "You should do . . . whatever you normally do."

"You think this is Partridge again, Eddie?" Coyle asked.

Mahler wondered if Coyle had noticed his unsteadiness a few minutes earlier. "Could be. Last I heard, he's still in town." He managed to get the words out but didn't trust himself to say more.

Coyle stepped close to Eden and gestured at the lake. "Two years ago, a young woman named Michelle Foss is killed in the park, over by the water tanks. Strangled, body left beside a footpath. Small town, public space like this, it's a huge deal. Chief puts on extra patrols, cars at the gates. We look at locals with a record of assaults on women, and right off the bat, we question a guy named Irwin Partridge. Matches a witness description of a man seen on a park trail the night Foss was killed. But the witness is shaky, and we've got nothing to connect Partridge to the killing."

Eden wrote in her notepad. "So you had to let him go."

"Yeah, he walks. Three days later, another body's found in the park. Susan Hart. Middle-distance runner at the junior college. This time down near the boat launch, but same type of victim, same strangulation pattern. It's as if the killer figures he won't get caught. The media start calling him the Seventy-Two-Hour Killer."

"Which scares people." Eden nodded as she continued to write.

"It's a circus. San Francisco TV stations have news vans at the park gates. A neighborhood watch is organized on the perimeter. One night our guys find a pickup by the dam—four heroes in the truck bed with deer rifles. Some knucklehead in a house above the park hears a noise outside and shoots his own dog."

Mahler stood apart. He disliked a lot of talking at a crime scene. The migraine pain now existed as an echo. He closed his eyes and pressed his fingertips on the lids. He remembered the crime-scene techs waiting in the parking lot. He waved at them. A dozen more spectators stood behind the yellow tape.

"What about Partridge?" Eden asked.

Coyle backed her away from the bench to give the crime-scene crew room to work. "With the Hart killing, we look at

Partridge again. Hold him on an old failure-to-appear warrant and take his life apart: house, car, job, family, past arrests, the works. All of which comes up with nothing. DA declines to indict."

"Then what?"

Coyle shrugged. "Then what? Nothing. We work a bunch of leads that go nowhere. But the murders stop, and the public and the media move on to the next tragedy."

"Unusual for a successful killer to stop. So the cases were never solved?"

"No." Coyle looked at Mahler. "No, they never were."

"So, if our victim here was murdered by the same killer," Eden said, "he could be starting again."

"Maybe, but this one seems different," Coyle said. "Someone bashed her head. The victims two years ago were killed by ligature strangulation."

"This one's strangled as well. There's bruising on her throat."

Coyle frowned. "You're kidding. You saw bruising under all that blood?"

"Yes. Just now. Want me to show you?"

"That's okay. Hear that, Eddie? Did you see it, too?"

Mahler looked back without speaking.

"But this bruising doesn't look like ligature strangulation," Eden said. "It's on the front of the throat, consistent with manual strangulation. Statistically, front-side strangulation is rare, usually committed by someone known to the victim."

Coyle snorted. "Statistically? Someone's studied it?"

Eden's face reddened. "Sorry. Was that the wrong thing to say?"

"Just not used to it, is all."

Mahler had had enough. He stepped between Eden and Coyle. "Detective Somers, tell the techs I want an initial crime-scene report by ten thirty." He heard his own voice, as if it were outside of him, talking too loudly. "And we need to find out who this woman is. Call Kathy Byers. Now. Tell her to put out a press release. No photos—physical description and clothing. Email it to the press, and put it on the public website. Have Kathy get tech support to set up an independent phone line for the public to call in."

He swung around to Coyle. "Where're Rivas and Frames?"

"With Gang Crimes, picking up Peña. They'll be back in a couple hours."

"Text them. Say they're on this. We're all on round-the-clock."

Coyle nodded. "You okay, Eddie?" When Mahler didn't reply, Coyle started typing on his phone. "The other thing is, the earlier victims weren't wrapped in a blanket like this one."

Mahler looked up the hill to the spectators behind the yellow caution tape, who were holding up phones. "You know what else is different from two years ago? We didn't have as much social media crap as we do now. By the time we get back to our cars, the photos from those phones are going to be on Instagram and Snapchat."

He turned back to the crime-scene crew, kneeling beside the body on the bench. "Once people see the pictures of this crime scene, all they'll care about is we found a dead woman in the park, and it could happen again in the next seventy-two hours."

ACKNOWLEDGMENTS

I'd like to thank the whole team at Poisoned Pen Press and Sourcebooks, especially my editor, Anna Michels, who read the book with care and insight. I'm also indebted to copy editors Diane Dannenfeldt and Jessica Thelander as well as Diane DiBiase, Shauneice Robinson, and Molly Waxman. Barbara Peters deserves special credit, too, for believing in the characters from the start and for getting the series launched.

My long-time critique group—Andy Gloege, Thonie Hevron, and Billie Settles—reviewed rough pages and chapters out of order and helped me to find new depth in characters and to keep the story moving.

Thanks also to early readers Chris Baker, Brian Fies, Carol and Robert Sanoff, and good friend and former VCI detective Tom Swearingen, who generously reviewed the whole book and gave me thoughtful, constructive notes.

I'm grateful for the kind words from Zoë Ferraris, Jeff Abbott, Joseph Schneider, Dana Stabenow, and J. P. Smith.

Finally, my wife, Meg McNees; my daughter, Chelsea Weisel; and my son-in-law, Steven Turner, shared the ups and downs of the writing process with unfailing encouragement.

ABOUT THE AUTHOR

Photo by Rob Martel

Frederick Weisel's debut novel, *The Silenced Women*, introduced the Violent Crime Investigations (VCI) Team series. *The Day He Left* is the second in the series. He graduated from Antioch College and has an MA in Victorian literature and history from the University of Leicester in England. He lives with his wife in Santa Rosa, California, and is at work on the third VCI novel. His articles have been published in *CrimeReads* and *Crimespree Magazine*. You can check out his website at frederickweisel.com.